ASHTON

LORD *of* TRUTH

GRACE BURROWES

Ashton Lord of Truth is Published by Grace Burrowes Publishing
21 Summit Avenue
Hagerstown, MD 21740
www.graceburrowes.com

To those who are disappointed in love.
Be of good cheer, for love is not disappointed in you.

CHAPTER ONE

"I am the bastard," Ashton Fenwick said. "I am the charming, firstborn bastard, and I'm good at it. Now you want to wreck everything. Is this your idea of fraternal loyalty?"

Ewan had the grace to look abashed. "As a matter of fact, it is. You will make a fine earl."

His rejoinder came in accents that were nearly Etonian—baby brother had attended public school—while the dialect of the Borders lurked beneath Ashton's every syllable.

Alyssa remained silent on the red velvet sofa, wearing her *don't make me cry* expression. The absolute unfair hell of it was, when Ashton's sister-in-law looked as she did now—eyes glistening, gaze resolute—he was nearly moved to tears himself.

"I will make no sort of earl at all," he said, pacing the length of the estate office. Because the estate belonged to the earl—not to Ashton—the chamber was spacious and the carpets thick enough to muffle his boot steps. "I stink of horses more often than not. I swear in at least four languages, I am ever so fond of a wee dram, and I am not the *perishing, sodding, bedamned earl.*"

Ashton had raised his voice, a Scotsman's prerogative when making a point to another hardheaded Scotsman.

"You have enumerated at least three characteristics of the typical lordling," Ewan said. "A titled man also, however, sires progeny on command, and that I have failed to do."

Ashton sent Alyssa an accusing glower. "I heard a sniffle. We'll hae none o' that snifflin' in this discussion. A countess doesna sniffle."

"I don't care if you're the bloody Duke of Argyll," Ewan retorted, marching up to Ashton. "You do not address my wife in such a fashion."

Ewan was an inch shorter than Ashton, probably the besetting disappointment of his lordship's handsome life. Though Ewan was the younger brother, he'd been raised to become the earl, and his skill with a verbal command was impressive.

"You even sound like an earl," Ashton said, patting his brother's lacy cravat. "You have earl hair, while I resemble a two-legged black bear."

One blond eyebrow lofted to an angle only a titled fellow could achieve. "Have you been drinking, Ash?"

"Of course, I've been drinking. A wee dram makes life rosier, so I'll just help myself to one now." Ewan hadn't offered him libation, because Ashton wasn't quite a guest at the family seat, and yet, he wasn't entirely family, despite being Ewan's full brother.

Alyssa exchanged a look with her husband that conveyed love, pleading, and more than a little pain. Ashton ignored that glance, filled two glasses with the best whisky the estate had to offer, downed both, then refilled them.

"To the earl." Ashton recited the toast he and his brother had been making for years.

"To the earl," Ewan echoed, his weary tone plucking at Ashton's last nerve.

"Why bring this up now?" Ashton asked. "You've sat on this information for months. Why do you choose now to ruin my future?"

"You call immense wealth, prestige, influence, a life of security and ease ruin?" Ewan asked.

The question was genuine, which made it that much more heartbreaking.

"Ewan, you were raised to value all of this," Ashton said, sweeping a hand in the direction of ornate pier glasses, intricate plasterwork, exquisite landscapes, and delicate gilt chairs each of which was worth more than Ashton's best horse.

"You were raised to value it as well," Ewan retorted, setting his barely touched drink on the sideboard. "Most people would have the sense to value beauty, comfort, and security."

"Why value what you know you can never have? I was warned over and over by every tutor and headmaster that I had to make something of myself, that nothing would be handed to me."

"And yet, Ashton, you were given an education, a roof over your head, love, a place to call home, skills, and above all, freedom to follow your own direction. As the only legitimate heir, I was wrapped in cotton wool, chaperoned, and lectured until I was nearly mad with it."

Ewan strolled to the window—no pacing about for him—as if mesmerized by a view of southern Scotland he'd had nearly thirty years to study. Thanks to a river that changed course every hundred years or so, a portion of the estate touched into England. The previous earl had considered diverting the river to rectify that disgrace.

"Tell him, Ewan." Alyssa's voice was husky, as if she'd already endured a bout of tears. "If you don't, I will."

The whisky curdled in Ashton's gut. "Is somebody ill?"

He loved these people as only a lonely Scotsman could love his two extant immediate family members. Ashton and Ewan had lost one sister to influenza and another to a lung fever within weeks. If Ewan or Alyssa were unwell—

"Not ill," Ewan said. "But in a delicate condition, nonetheless."

Ashton dropped onto the sofa beside Alyssa. "Now that's a fine thing. You had me worried when I should be rejoicing. I've never been an uncle before, but I'm sure I'll get the knack of it. Spoiling a wee niece or nephew is what uncles do best, and now that you've given me some warning—"

Alyssa put her head in her hands. "Ewan, make him understand."

Ashton shut his mouth, because when Alyssa Jean MacDermott Fenwick took to pleading, the end times were surely nigh.

"Alyssa has conceived before," Ewan said, back to the room. "We've lost the child in the early days all three times. This time seems to be going better."

Currents swirled about the elegant office, entirely human currents of anxiety, hope, and heartbreak. Some forms of wealth, not even a title could buy.

"Tell him the rest of it," Alyssa said.

"There has been talk," Ewan went on, fiddling with the red velvet tie holding the curtains in their precise, elegant folds. "Mama's old nurse has grown feeble-minded, and she wanders. Gunna found her way to the pub last summer and began reminiscing. Her sister, who is still quite sharp, didn't contradict her, and the talk hasn't gone away."

"We're in Scotland," Ashton said, patting Alyssa's hand. Her fingers were cool, and now that he was next her, she struck him as pale. "People will talk when they're not vying for a spot on the sinner's stool."

Alyssa winced at his reference to fornication, but without that particular vice, the stool at the front of the kirk would get a good deal less polishing by penitential backsides.

"The problem, brother, is that the talk is true. Alyssa was in the attics rummaging among the nursery trunks, and she found Mama's diary, from when Mama and Papa eloped."

"Diaries can be falsified."

Even as he spoke, Ashton felt the weight of doom closing in on him. A small Scots community thrived on gossip. In the nearby village of Auchterdingle, the elders still made mention of the mule that had given birth three years after the Forty-Five. The offspring had been named Jesus, and its arrival had been taken as a sign that Bonnie Prince Charlie's triumphant return was imminent.

That had been more than seventy years ago, and the miraculous mule was still frequently toasted. A potential scandal in the earl's family would never, ever cease being a topic of speculation.

"If I am legitimate," Ashton observed, "which I am not, then Mama and

Papa were married at the time I was born. Mama would have been sixteen, a mere girl by English standards, and Papa not much older."

"They were in love," Ewan said, taking a seat at the estate desk. "And in Scotland, unlike England, a sixteen-year-old woman need not have her parents' blessing to marry."

Ewan made a magnificent picture behind the oak monstrosity, all dapper and blond, but a troubled, magnificent picture.

"I've been in love a time or two," Ashton said. "Then I wake up with a sore head, and the affliction has passed." He'd been infatuated countless times, until the infatuations had run together, into an abiding fondness for all of the ladies.

Alyssa's lips twitched, an encouraging sign.

"Mama and Papa were passionately devoted," Ewan went on. "Prior to your arrival—and prior their setting up a household out on the isle of Rothsay—they managed a quiet little wedding. By the time Mama's family caught wind of her whereabouts, that household had three children. At that point, cousin Hugh and cousin Leith had gone to their rewards, and Papa had become the heir apparent. He went from being an unsuitable Scottish upstart to a Border lord's heir."

And that Border lord had become increasingly wealthy as the years had gone by, to the extent that Papa had apparently become *eligible* in the eyes of the English side of the family.

Alyssa rose and perched on the arm of Ewan's chair. They were a striking couple—both tall, well-favored, and fair, and their marriage had been a love match. Ashton hoped it still was, but this business of the succession had apparently put a strain on the relationship.

"Everybody was sure your papa would abandon his scandalous liaison with the Irish earl's wayward daughter, and marry a proper Scotswoman," Alyssa said, "one who'd bring wealth and standing to the union. Instead, after much argument with the old earl, your papa and your mama had public ceremony with her family in attendance. She was of age then even by English standards. Her family was relieved, for who else would marry a woman ruined by a Scottish rogue?"

Such a romance belonged among Sir Walter Scott's drivelings. "Why not reveal the earlier marriage before the public union began?" Ashton asked. Why deny Ashton and his sisters legitimacy when it might have made a difference?

"If you'd been the legitimate heir, your mama's English relations would have demanded to keep you in England," Alyssa said, "to be raised among the civilized English. They'd plucked her from Ireland at a tender age, and she well recalled the pain of leaving her home. She wasn't about to give you up or let you be separated from your sisters."

"Our father supported her decision," Ewan said, "If you'd been in line for the title, the old earl would have sent you south without a qualm."

The old earl had believed in currying favor with the English, a sensible, if unpopular, approach. A Scottish heir raised among the English would have had all the advantages of a medieval fostering, from a political perspective.

And might have received abominable treatment, even at the hands of his own relations.

"I came along a few years later," Ewan went on. "By that time, Papa was in command of his own household and could keep me here in Scotland. Nonetheless, Uncle took much too long to die, the earlier marriage had not been revealed, and you were being raised as a by-blow, though in our parents' household, not among English strangers."

"Ewan's legitimacy was unassailable," Alyssa said, "while yours was shrouded in secrecy and family squabbling. Had I not found your mother's diary, we would have pensioned Gunna off to the Midlands and dismissed her maunderings as fancy."

"Unfind the diary, then." Ashton loved his brother dearly, but a title sometimes deprived a man of common sense. Marriage records on Rothsay were likely to fall into the sea before anybody stumbled upon them.

"I'll not unfind the diary," Alyssa said, shoving away from her husband's side. "There's been enough dissembling and drama. I won't have my son's inheritance questioned when some meddling cousin unearths church records or finds an old diary from the English side of the family years from now."

The English were forever causing trouble, that was true enough.

"I thought you liked being the earl and countess." Ewan and Alyssa excelled at being titled. They were gracious, generous, handsome, Scottish when it mattered, and diplomatic when an Englishman was underfoot. "You've made the earldom look like no burden a'tall, though I know that's not so."

Being the earl was work, and Ashton suspected being the countess was no less effort. The estate was huge, covering woodlands, pasture, land in cultivation, crofts, sheep ranges, lochs, streams, three villages, and—thank the generosity of the Almighty—a distillery. The earldom also involved rights pertaining to fishing, forestry, quarrying, land use, Border regulations, local administration, church functions… the demands were endless.

The English tenants expected all the blessings and perquisites of English law, the Scottish tenants wanted only Scottish traditions and legalities.

And yet, Ewan was popular among all of the local folk and the neighboring titles.

"You'll make a fine earl," Ewan said again, though he sounded as if he were reciting a prayer rather than expressing confidence in his older brother.

"You don't know what you're asking." Ashton abandoned the sofa and spared a scowl for the portrait of their father over the mantel. "You are the earl, Ewan. You can foist the title off on me, but twenty years from now, when not a soul cares which of us is legitimate, you will still be his lordship, and I will still be 'the by-blow.'"

"Then you will be the by-blow earl," Ewan said, rising to slip an arm around Alyssa's waist. "My wife needs peace and quiet. She needs freedom from worry and to know that her children will not be tormented with old secrets. *I* need for my wife to be happy, and thus *you* need to be the earl."

Now there was some miserable logic.

"I need to get drunk, and this discussion is not over." Ashton strode from the room, intent on making a dramatic exit. The door had slammed behind him with gratifying finality, when he thought of the most sensible course of all. He'd destroy the diary. How hard could that be?

He turned on his heel, prepared to announce this brilliant solution to his dunderheaded brother, but immediately outside the door, a sound caught his ear.

Sobbing. Loud, upset, female sobbing, and a man's quieter, conciliatory tones. Alyssa wasn't given to dramatics or manipulation, and she was in a delicate condition.

She was also genuinely miserable and upset, because of him.

Ashton leaned his forehead against the solid oak door. "I don't want the bloody, fecking, miserable, sodding, bedamned, rubbishing, blighted title." He wanted to hike into the village, flirt the tavern maids and old women into good spirits, jest with the village lads, and enjoy an argument with the blacksmith over a few wee drams.

Alyssa's unhappiness crested higher, along with a few sharp words. Without warning, the door opened, and there she stood, her face tear-streaked. Ewan was at her side, his eyes full of pleading and worry.

A brother in trouble and a damsel in distress. Alyssa was also mad as hell, and at Ashton. His brother's ire, he might have withstood, but Alyssa's fury and disappointment were unendurable.

For an interminable moment, Ashton struggled against conscience and against the inevitable. When had being the bastard become so easy and comfortable? So integral to who he was?

Alyssa glowered at him, her lashes wet with tears.

"I'll be the earl," Ashton said, brushing his thumb over her damp cheek, "but I need one thing from the two of you."

"Anything." Ewan wrapped his arms about his wife. "We'll support you in every possible way. You've only to tell us, and we'll do it."

That was not an earl talking, that was a besotted husband and a very worried prospective papa.

"You,"—Ashton tapped Alyssa's nose—"will have sons. You will have nothing but sons, and they will be great, strapping bairnies whom I will spoil without limit, and one of those boys will be my heir. Understand?"

She nodded, a hint of a smile peeking through her tears.

"We'll do our best," Ewan said, cuddling his wife closer. "We'll do our very best for you, Ashton. My word on it."

"I'll hold you to that." Ashton closed the door, because the people he loved most in the whole world had presented such a picture of marital intimacy as to make a bachelor brother blush.

He took his walk to the village, all the while assuring himself that nothing needed to change. Ewan and Alyssa's children would inherit the whole mess, Ewan would manage the earldom, and Ashton would be free to flirt with tavern maids and old women.

A fine compromise all around.

Except that, after three years, Alyssa had three babies, twins followed by a single birth. The infants were indeed great, strapping specimens and the births as easy as births could be… and every one of the children was female.

* * *

A bump-and-jostle of the criminal variety introduced Ashton Fenwick to his temporary salvation.

Fortunately, she was neither the little thief who so deftly dipped a hand into his pocket, nor the buxom decoy who feigned awkwardly colliding with him immediately thereafter, while the real pickpocket quietly dodged off into the Haymarket crowd.

Or tried to.

Ashton was exhausted from traveling hundreds of miles on horseback, and had barely noticed the thief's touch amid the sights, noise, and stink of London's bustling streets. In the instant after the bump, and before the jostle part of the proceedings—a game girl, from the looks of her paint and pallor—Ashton realized how London had welcomed him.

"Stop the wee lad in the cap!" he bellowed. "He's nicked my purse!"

Five yards down the walkway, a woman darted into the path of the fleeing thief and faced off with him. A housewife from the looks of her. Plain brown cloak, simple straw hat, serviceable leather gloves rather than the cotton or lace variety.

Ashton had an abiding respect for the British housewife. If the nation had a backbone, she was it, not her yeoman or shopkeeping husband, whose primary purpose was keeping brewers in business and the wife in childbed.

The lady was diminutive, nimble and sharp-eyed. When the child dodged left, so did she, and she never took her gaze off the miscreant.

"Give it up, Helen. You chose the wrong mark." A hint of the north graced the woman's inflection, also a hint of the finishing school. A lovely combination.

The child gazed up, then small shoulders squared. "You needn't take on, Mrs. Bryce. I dint nick 'is purse."

"You didn't steal my purse," Ashton said, letting the thief's accomplice scurry away, "because I know better than to keep it where it can be stolen, but you got my lucky handkerchief."

"Hit's just a bleedin' 'ankerchief," the girl shot back. "Take it." She withdrew Ashton's bit of silk from inside her grubby coat, the white square a stark contrast to her dirty little fingers.

A crowd had gathered, because Londoners did not believe in allowing anybody privacy if a moment portended the smallest bit of drama. Some people looked affronted, but most appeared entertained by the thought of the authorities hauling the girl away.

"Helen, what have I told you about stealing?" Mrs. Bryce asked.

Helen's hands went to skinny hips clad in boy's trousers. "What 'ave I told you about starvin', Mrs. B? Me and Sissy don't care for it. 'E don't need 'is lucky piece as much as me and Sissy do."

Somebody in the crowd mentioned sending for a patroller from nearby Bow Street, and if one of those worthies arrived, the child's fate would be sealed.

"We won't settle this here," Ashton said, taking the girl by one slender wrist. "Let's repair to the Goose and have a civilized discussion."

Her eyes filled not with fear, but with utter terror. Ashton was big, male, and he was proposing to take the child away from the safety of public scrutiny. Well, she should be terrified.

"Mrs. Bryce," Ashton went on, "if you'd accompany us, I'd appreciate it. Ashton Fenwick, at your service."

"Matilda Bryce." She sketched a curtsey. "Come peacefully, Helen. Unless you want to find yourself being examined by the magistrate tomorrow morning."

The child was obviously inventorying options, looking for a moment to wrench free of Ashton's grasp. As many spectators as had gathered, somebody would snabble her, and she'd be in Newgate by this time tomorrow.

"If you'd join us for a pint and plate, Mrs. Bryce," Ashton said, "I'd be obliged. I realize a lady doesn't dine with strangers, but the circumstances are—"

"She's a landlady," Helen said, stuffing Ashton's treasure back inside her jacket. "Down around the corner, on Pastry Lane. Was once a bakery there. I could use a bite to eat."

The child could use a year of good meals, for starters. Ashton hoped the thought of hot food would tempt the girl from more reckless choices, but he kept a snug hold of her wrist nonetheless.

"Helen offered to return your goods, sir," Mrs. Bryce said. "Can't you let it go at that?"

"Perhaps," Ashton said. "But the longer we stand here debating, the more likely the authorities are to come along and take the child off to the halls of justice."

"Move, Helen." Mrs. Bryce seized the girl by the other wrist and started off in the direction of the nearest pub. "If the law gets hold of you, it's transportation or worse. Heaven knows what will become of your Sissy then."

Mention of the sister wilted the last of the child's resistance, and Ashton was soon crossing the street while more or less holding hands with a small, grubby female.

Who still had his lucky handkerchief.

The Goose was a respectable establishment, and because the theater custom was in general a cut above London's meanest denizens, the food might be better than passable. Ashton bought steak, potatoes, and a small pint for each of the ladies.

For himself, brandy. He was in London, prepared to take up residence at no less establishment than the Albany apartments. Titled lords ready to embark on the joys of the social Season drank brandy, or so Ewan claimed.

Besides, Ashton was hoarding his whisky for emergencies and celebrations, which this was not.

"Now," he said, when the child had shoveled down an adult portion of food in mere minutes. "You, Miss Helen, need to work on your technique if you're intent on a life of crime. Would you like some cobbler?"

Her eyes grew round while Mrs. Bryce wiped the child's chin with a linen serviette. "Don't encourage her. She'll end up on the gallows at the rate she's going. Do you want her death on your conscience?"

"Do you want her starvation on yours?"

Over the empty plate, the child's gaze bounced between the adults on either side of the table. "About that cobbler?"

Ashton reached into the girl's coat and withdrew his handkerchief, then passed it to Mrs. Bryce. "Wait here, child, if you want your cobbler."

He went to the bar, placed an order for three cobblers, and kept his back to the tables while the kitchen fetched the food.

When they'd chosen their table, Mrs. Bryce had taken off her hat and gloves. Her hair was an unusual color, as if she'd used henna to put a reddish tint in blond hair, which made no sense. Few women would choose red hair over blond, but then, Ashton was in the south. Everything from the sunshine to the scent of the streets was different.

"Your cobbler, sir," said the publican, putting a sack before Ashton. "We expect return of the plates in a day, if you please. Mrs. Bryce is always very good about that."

The barkeeper was short, graying, and solid—not fat. His blue apron was clean and free of mending.

"Mrs. Bryce patronizes your establishment often?"

"We're neighbors, across the alley and down a street, and her tenants frequently send out for their meals. She always sees to it we get our wares back. Haven't seen her in a bit, or had an order from her lately. Please give her my regards."

"She runs a good establishment?" Ashton asked.

"We hear nothing but compliments from her tenants. The place is very clean, very quiet, if you know what I mean. A widow can't be too careful. She keeps out the rabble, which isn't always a matter of who has coin, is it?"

Ashton had a very particular fondness for widows of discernment.

"True enough," he said, putting a few coins on the bar and gathering up the cobblers. "My thanks for a good meal."

A hearty meal. Not the refined delicacies Ashton had been expected to subsist on from the earldom's fussy Italian chef.

Mrs. Bryce was dissuading Helen from licking an empty plate when Ashton rejoined the ladies.

"I have here three cobblers," he said, setting the sack in the middle of the table. "I'm too full to enjoy my portion. Perhaps Helen's sister would like it?"

Fine gray eyes studied him from across the table. Mrs. Bryce's gaze was both direct and guarded, which made sense if she'd lost her husband. Widows were as vulnerable as the next woman, and yet, they had more freedom than any other class of female in Britain.

"Sissy loves her sweets," Helen said, kicking her legs against the bench. "I'm right fond of a treat myself."

Ashton slid onto the bench. "I'm fond of young ladies who take responsibility for their actions."

Helen shot Mrs. Bryce a puzzled glance.

"He means, you stole his handkerchief, and now we must decide what's to be done." Mrs. Bryce folded up Ashton's handkerchief and passed it to him.

Ashton set the cloth beside the cobblers. "What would you do, Helen, if somebody had stolen your lucky piece?"

"Ain't got a lucky piece. If I had a lucky piece, maybe I wouldn't be stealin' for me supper."

Ashton snatched off the girl's cap, and ratty blond braids tumbled down.

The child ducked her head as if braids were a mark of shame. "Gimme back me 'at, you!"

"How do you feel right now?"

"I'm that mad at you," Helen shot back. "You 'ad no right, and now everybody will know I'm a girl."

Ashton passed over the hat. Helen jammed it back on her head and stuffed both braids into her cap before folding her arms across her skinny chest.

"I gave you back your hat. All better?"

"You know it ain't. Damned Treacher saw me without me cap. Now I'll have to cut me hair again and stay out of his middens for weeks."

Mrs. Bryce watched this exchange, looking as if she was suppressing a smile. She had a full mouth, good bones, and a sunrise-on-summer-clouds complexion worthy of any countess. She was that puzzling creature, the woman who didn't know she was attractive.

Or perhaps—more puzzling still—she didn't care that she was attractive.

"So, wee Helen," Ashton said, setting the empty plates out of the girl's reach. "You've returned my handkerchief, and I've returned your cap. You still disrupted my day, gave me a bad start as I arrived in your fair city, and have inconvenienced Mrs. Bryce, who I gather is something of a friend. How will you make it right?"

The child scrunched up her nose and ceased kicking the bench. "I don't have anything to give you. You could thrash me."

From her perspective, that was preferable to being turned over to the authorities. Mrs. Bryce was no longer smiling, though.

"Then I'd have a smarting hand," Ashton said, "and more delay from my appointed rounds, because you would require a good deal of thrashing. Fortunately for us both, you are a lady, and a gentleman never raises his voice or his hand to a lady."

Now the looks Helen aimed at Mrs. Bryce were worried, as if Ashton had started babbling in tongues or speaking treason.

"Your papa wasn't a gentleman," Mrs. Bryce said gently. "We mustn't speak ill of the dead, but Mr. Fenwick is telling you the truth. Gentlemen are to protect ladies, not beat them. In theory."

"I don't know what a theory is, ma'am. Can I 'ave my cobbler yet?"

"May I," Mrs. Bryce replied. "I think Mr. Fenwick expects an apology, Helen, and you owe him one."

"I'm sorry I nicked your lucky piece. If I'd known it was a lucky piece, and not just fancy linen, I might not 'ave nicked it. Next time, keep your purse in your right-hand pocket, and nobody will be stealin' your lucky piece."

Helen clearly didn't realize this earnest advice was in no way helpful.

The comforts of the Albany awaited, and those comforts had been sufficient for ducal heirs, nabobs, and Byron himself. Once Ashton stepped over the threshold of that establishment, he declared himself the Earl of Kilkenney in new and irrevocable ways.

He'd rather be enjoying a plain meal at the Goose, and getting lessons in street sense from a half-pint thief.

"As it happens, I'm glad you didn't get my purse, because I'm newly arrived to Town this very day, and to be penniless in London, as you know, is a precarious existence."

"Perilous," Mrs. Bryce translated. "Dangerous."

"Not if you know who your mates are and are quick on your feet," Helen said—more misguided instruction. She was a female without protection or means. Odds were, sooner or later, the London streets would be the death of her.

"You have nonetheless taken up a good deal of my time when my day was already too busy," Ashton said. "I need to establish myself at suitable lodgings. I need to hire a tiger for my conveyance. I need to get my bearings in anticipation of taking up responsibilities for the social Season."

Not only a busy day, but also a damned depressing one.

"You need a home," Mrs. Bryce said, and she wasn't translating for Helen. "Or a temporary address to serve as your home."

Her gaze turned appraising, though not in any intimate sense. The tilt of her head said she was evaluating Ashton as a lodger, not a lover. A novel experience for him, and a bit unnerving.

His attire was that of the steward he'd been for years before he'd become afflicted with a title. Decent, if plain, riding jacket. Good quality, though his sleeve had been mended at the elbow. His linen was unstarched but clean enough for a man who'd been traveling, and a gold watch chain winked across his middle.

"What is your business in London, Mr. Fenwick?" Mrs. Bryce asked.

He was here for one purpose—to find a woman willing to be his countess. She'd have to comport herself like a faithful wife until at least two healthy male children had appeared. Not a complicated assignment, and the lady's compensation would be a lifetime of ease and a title.

Ashton had had three years to reconcile himself to such an arrangement, three years during which he'd tried to find the compromise—the woman he could adore *and* marry, who might adore him a little bit too—but she hadn't presented herself.

Though three wee nieces had arrived.

"My excursion to the capital is primarily social," Ashton said. "I'm renewing acquaintances with a few friends and tending to business while the weather is fair. I'll return north in the summer."

And be damned glad to do so. According to Ewan, house parties followed the social Season, and rather than hunting grouse, Ashton could pass his summer with further rounds of countess hunting.

He could take up that apartment at the Albany some other day. Next week would do.

Or the week after.

A voice in Ashton's head said he was putting off the inevitable, retreating when he ought to be marching forward. Another voice said Mrs. Bryce would not consider offering a strange man lodgings unless she needed a lodger desperately.

"As it happens," Mrs. Bryce said, "I have an apartment available. A sitting room and bedroom, with antechamber, and kitchen privileges. Breakfast, tea, and candles are included, and your rooms will be cleaned twice weekly, Tuesday and Friday. Bad behavior or excessive noise is grounds for eviction, and if you sing or play a musical instrument, you will do so only at decent hours. Coal is extra, payable by the week."

"Mrs. Bryce makes the best porridge," Helen added. "She puts cream on it if it's too hot."

Don't put off what must be done. Don't shirk your duty.

"What is your direction?" Ashton asked.

"Pastry Lane is around the corner and halfway down the street," Mrs. Bryce said. "The rooms are quiet, clean, and unpretentious, but suitable for entertaining such callers as a gentleman might properly have."

No game girls, in other words.

"There's a garden," Helen offered. "Big enough for Mrs. Bryce's herbs, but not big enough for a dog. She has a cat."

Mrs. Bryce also, apparently, had something of a champion in Helen.

The child was skinny, but not starving. When truly deprived of food for a long period, the body lost the ability to handle a meal of steak and potatoes washed down by a small pint of ale. Helen's diet might be spare and irregular, but Mrs. Bryce's porridge figured on the menu often enough to keep body and soul together.

"I like cats," Ashton said. "What about a mews?"

"No mews, I'm afraid," Mrs. Bryce said, brushing a hand over the handkerchief on the table. "If you need a mews, I can suggest Mrs. Grimbly, off of Bow Street, though you must provide your own groom."

The fingers stroking over Ashton's handkerchief were slightly red, the back of Mrs. Bryce's hand freckled. No rings, and a pale scar ran from wrist to thumb.

Not the hands of a countess, though, to Ashton, beautiful in their way.

"I can stable my horses elsewhere," Ashton said. "My brother is more familiar with London than I am and recommended an establishment he and his friends use. What do you charge?"

She named a figure, neither cheap nor exorbitant, though her focus on the handkerchief had become fixed. The cuff of her cloak was fraying, her straw hat was the lowliest millinery short of Helen's battered cap.

Mrs. Bryce was in need of coin, while Ashton was in need of peace and quiet. The social Season hadn't yet begun, and a week or two of reconnaissance was simply the act of a prudent man—or a reluctant earl.

"Mrs. Bryce bakes her own bread," Helen said. "And she serves it with *butter and jam.*"

"May we start with a two-week lease?" Ashton asked. "I am new to London, and a trial period makes sense for all parties."

"That will be acceptable, though I'll want the rent for both weeks in advance with an allowance for coal."

Ashton extended his hand across the table. "Mrs. Bryce, we have a bargain."

CHAPTER TWO

The angel of bad fortune had plagued Matilda Bryce for the past nine years, but since January the wretch had been perched on her very doorstep. Her last tenant had fled to the Continent with three months' rent and coal fees owing, and he'd kept his apartment roasting.

No suitable replacement had appeared even as London's ranks of single gentlemen had swelled with spring's approach. Ashton Fenwick wasn't suitable either, but needs must when the devil taxed every window and bar of soap a woman owned.

Mr. Fenwick's nails were clean, not that clean nails signified anything. He was handsome, too, and that was the problem. Not in a pretty, Bond Street way, but in the robust, muscular manner of the countryman. Dark hair and dark eyes suggested Celtic ancestry, and for all his brawn, his manners were fine.

In fancy ballroom attire, he'd turn every head, which was the last reaction Matilda wanted her lodgers to inspire.

"About the cobbler?" Helen asked as Matilda withdrew her fingers from Mr. Fenwick's callused grip.

"Mrs. Bryce and I are having a wee business negotiation, child. We'll get to your cobbler."

Helen sighed gustily, despite having had a brush with disaster. The girl had no idea how lucky she'd been to pick Mr. Fenwick's pocket, rather than that of a less tolerant citizen.

"If I'm to rent from you," Mr. Fenwick said, "I'll need a servant of sorts, somebody to let my groom know when I need my horse, to fetch my evening meal from the chophouse, to polish my boots. Have you a boot boy or underfootman who can serve in that capacity?"

Well, drat and perdition. If it wasn't a gentleman's horses Matilda couldn't accommodate, it was his boots.

"I have only a maid of all work, though your quarters provide room for a servant in the attics, should you wish to hire one."

Mr. Fenwick's gaze roamed the interior of the Goose, a typical London public house. The ceiling was low and the beams exposed. The plank floor was uneven and centuries of smoke had turned the rafters black.

The patrons at the Goose came from many walks of life: the swells and dandies dangling after the actresses, the working folk happy to end their day with a pint, and the actresses and shopgirls who needed a safe place to take an occasional meal.

The highest and mightiest of polite society, however, did not frequent the Goose, and thus Matilda could tarry with Mr. Fenwick and try to haggle him back under her roof.

"I'm sure we can send your boots out," she said, "or my maid can have a go at them." To do a proper job on a gentleman's boots was time-consuming. Matilda did not flatter herself that she had the skill, or she'd gladly take it on.

"I can be your boot boy," Helen said. "Me da taught me how to shine boots, and I'm ever so fast if you want a note delivered or a meat pie brought 'round."

"Helen, you're not a boot boy," Matilda said. "You're not a boy at all."

"But you are a thief," Mr. Fenwick said, his tone appraising. "If an incompetent one."

"I told you," Helen retorted. "If you'd carried your purse where a purse ought to go, I'd have nicked it clean and proper. If I wasn't a damned good cutpurse, me da would have beat me lights out. He told me so himself."

At the bar, Mr. Treacher's rag stopped its rhythmic polishing. One of the tavern maids slanted a glance in Helen's direction, and Matilda had all she could do not to slap her hand over the child's mouth.

"If you think I'll put a serving of cobbler in front of you to prevent you from crying your own doom," Mr. Fenwick said, "think again, my girl. English law lists more than two hundred hanging offenses, theft among them. A little thing like you would take a very long time to die on the end of a rope."

For once, Helen looked daunted.

Thank God.

Mr. Fenwick was tall, broad-shouldered, and exactly the sort of man Matilda ought not to be giving a key to her house. She had a separate lock on her own rooms, but the hardware was old, and Mr. Fenwick was in his prime. She'd put him not much past thirty, with a history of manual labor such as a steward or wealthy yeoman might undertake.

Gentlemanly manual labor, which ought to be a contradiction in terms.

His speech was educated, but accented—Borders, or perhaps Cumberland— and his attire suggested he knew better than to advertise his means on the open road. That he wanted only two weeks' lodging was a shame. He was from out of town, which was good, and he had dealt kindly with Helen so far—which was very good.

"Have you ever ridden a horse?" Mr. Fenwick asked Helen. "The truth, or no cobbler."

"How will you know if I'm lying?"

"You'll be dead," he replied, opening the sack of cobbler so the scent of apples and cinnamon wafted about the table. "My horse is an enormous specimen named Destrier. If you don't know what you're about, he'll toss you to the ground like so much dirty linen."

"I could lead him."

"You're considering hiring Helen as your lackey?" Matilda interjected. The Goose made a very fine cobbler. She'd forgotten that.

"For two weeks," Mr. Fenwick said. "My needs are modest, Helen knows the neighborhood, and she can use the wage."

"You'd *pay* me?"

Helen's consternation tore at Matilda's heart and woke up her distrust. "I cannot condone an arrangement which puts a little girl into the direct employ of a man about whom I know next to nothing." Terrible things happened to children loose on London's streets. Things Matilda could not have comprehended at Helen's age, things Helen had probably witnessed firsthand.

Mr. Fenwick put a serving of cobbler down before Matilda. "We are strangers, true. What would you like to know about me, Mrs. Bryce?"

The second serving he set before Helen, who at least recalled to put her linen back on her lap before she picked up her fork. Matilda tried to impart some manners on the rare occasions when Helen came by for a meal, but etiquette stood no chance against a ravenous belly.

Matilda took a bite of spicy, fruity delight while she considered Mr. Fenwick's question. The cobbler needed to be a bit warmer and slathered in cream to be truly exquisite, but it was very good nonetheless.

"I want to know that you are honorable," Matilda said. "You appear without character references, so I don't see how we're to establish your trustworthiness. I can demand your coin before you set foot in my house, but Helen's safety is less easily guarded."

"I love cobbler," Helen said. "He doesn't have to pay me. Just let me eat cobbler every day."

"Wee Helen, if I feed you cobbler, how will you buy a new cap when somebody snatches that fine bit of millinery from your head?"

"I'll snatch it back."

Mr. Fenwick plucked the cap from the girl's head again, and this time she smiled. "You're very quick, sir. I could show you how to pick pockets, if you like."

He plopped the hat down on her head. "Wages, my child. Cash in hand, coin of the realm. That's how you want to be paid. All else is dross, and be mindful of Mrs. Bryce's example. I'm to pay her first, and when she's seen my coin, then and only then will I have what I need in return."

Helen was perilously pretty when she smiled. Better for her if she were homely and pockmarked. In a very few years, her beauty would become a liability, unless Matilda could make a parlor maid, or a—

Inspiration struck. "What if I raised your rent to cover Helen's services?" Matilda asked. "She'd be answerable to me, but available to fetch your horse, tend your boots, and buy your meals?"

"You'd give her a bed in the attics?" Mr. Fenwick asked as Helen slurped up her cobbler. "Breakfast, laundry services?"

"Mrs. B can't do my laundry 'cause these are my only clothes. I stole 'em off a clothesline, and they still fit me."

"She's determined to get herself hanged," Matilda muttered. "I try, but her older sister undermines my efforts."

Helen's head came up. "Don't you say nuffink bad about my Sissy."

"If today is any example," Mr. Fenwick said, "Sissy is no better at crime than you are, and that is a compliment. How much to hire Helen as my general factotum?"

The arrangement was unusual. Little girls didn't sport about in trousers and work for gentleman lodgers. And yet, those trousers had probably yielded Helen more security and well-being than Matilda's occasional bowl of porridge had.

Matilda named a sum—a fortune by Helen's standards, a pittance compared to what many earned in service to a great house.

"Done," Mr. Fenwick said, rising. "Helen, you'll need a name I can call you in public. Hector, I think. It suits you. You will take this cobbler to your sister, explain where she can find you for the next two weeks and that you'll be biding in Mrs. Bryce's house. You will report to my quarters two hours from now, and I'll show you where I'm stabling my cattle."

"How will I know it's two hours?"

"You listen to the bells," Matilda said, for she'd had to figure that out when she'd sold her last watch. "The cathedral bells just chimed a quarter past the hour, so you listen for seven more chimes. By the eighth tolling of the bells, you'd best be at my house."

Helen counted off on her fingers. "Eight times. Can I take Sissy her cobbler now?"

May I. Matilda saved the grammar instruction for another day.

"Off with you," Mr. Fenwick said, gently tucking the girl's braids back up under her cap. "Two hours, or you'll be sacked before you begin."

Helen—miraculous to relate—stood still while Mr. Fenwick fussed with her hair. She then snatched the sack holding the last cobbler and darted off.

"She is quick," he said. "You were quicker. Why did you stop her?"

By preventing Helen's flight, Matilda had left the child open to the risk of incarceration, or worse.

"Instinct, I suppose. If somebody doesn't intervene with her, she won't last much longer. I met her when she tried to break into my house last year. A lame, drowned rat would have been less pathetic, and her sister means her no good."

Mr. Fenwick rose. "Will we see her again?"

He was big and fit. Helen must have been desperate to think she could steal from this man with impunity.

"I honestly don't know. I hope so. Shall I show you to your lodging?"

"I'd like that." He offered his hand, as if Matilda hadn't been getting up off her own backside unassisted for years. "I'm mostly in need of a bath and a nap. If you'll offer me those, I'll be your devoted slave for the next two weeks."

He wrapped Matilda's hand around a very muscular arm, as if she were a proper lady. He had a mama, then, or sisters. Possibly a wife.

The thought shouldn't bother her.

"We haven't far to go," she said as they emerged from the Goose. "I assume you have baggage?"

"Aye, and once I have your direction, I'll see to having a trunk delivered. Can you recommend a decent chophouse in the area?"

He made pleasant small talk with her for the short walk to Pastry Lane, and Matilda had the first inkling that Ashton Fenwick might be trouble. He was a considerate escort, matching his steps to hers, always taking the outside lest some passing coach splash her skirts.

He tipped his hat to the women who took notice of him.

He bore a faint fragrance of bayberry shaving soap, and he tossed a coin to the crossing sweeper.

Any one of these observations would not have alarmed Matilda, but the longer she walked at Mr. Fenwick's side, the more convinced she became that he was a gentleman in truth. Probably a wealthy gentleman, given how circumspect the Scots were when it came to displaying their riches.

"If I needed to stay on a bit longer than two weeks, could that be arranged?" he asked as Matilda led him up the front steps to her house.

The last person she ought to accept as a lodger was a wealthy gentleman about whom she knew little and from whom she had no references.

"Why don't we see how you like the accommodations?" she replied. "They might not be to your taste."

"The accommodations will be entirely acceptable," he said, pushing the door open and waiting for Matilda to precede him through.

The manners were a subtle reminder of all she'd run from, all she'd left behind, and yet to him, they were the most casual exercise of consideration.

She showed him the rooms—clean, as she'd said, comfortable, unpretentious. The bed was huge, being an antique from when the house had been a grander establishment. The windows overlooked her tiny garden rather than the noisy street.

"I'll be more than happy here," he said, tossing his hat onto the hook above the sideboard. "If you don't mind, I'll have that nap while I wait for my general factotum to report for duty. I'm very glad we met, Mrs. Bryce. You're the answer to my prayers."

He took her hand and bowed over it, which would have been a fine, if somewhat theatrical, gesture.

The damned man smiled, though, not extravagantly, mostly with a pair of dark brown eyes. He gazed down at Matilda as if they shared some delightful secret, and that was ludicrous.

"I'll get the maid started on your bathwater," she said. "By the time you've had your nap, we should have enough heated in the laundry to accommodate you."

She withdrew quickly and took her secrets—not a one of which was delightful—with her.

* * *

"I'm not sure I understand, my lord." Cherbourne's brows were knit in puzzlement, though Ashton's valet was a bright man. He was conversant in six languages that Ashton knew of, as well as the deferential-servant dialect of the King's English. His attire was the pattern card of a proper gentleman's gentleman, and his graying fringe of hair was precisely trimmed every seven days.

Ashton had inherited him from Ewan, and in some ways, Cherbourne was a worse curse than the title.

"The idea is simple," Ashton said. "I'll not be staying here for at least two weeks. Set up the rooms with my needs in mind, get to know the neighboring households, find us the best chophouses and coffee shops. I'll come by periodically when I need the horses or to collect my mail."

"But, my lord, who will starch your cravats? Who will polish your boots? Who will *shave* you?"

Helen, braids tucked under her cap, sat on one of the many trunks stacked in the middle of the airy parlor and watched this exchange as if it were a panto down at the market.

"Cherbourne, I value your services, but please recall that for most of my adult life nobody starched my cravats, I polished my boots, and I even managed to shave myself occasionally. You are to have a holiday."

And so am I.

The valet looked around as if Ashton were about to abandon him to the stink of Newgate jail rather than to twenty-foot plaster ceilings, enormous sparkling windows, and imported furnishings.

Ashton well knew that Cherbourne's distress was not with a two-week holiday, but rather, over the more pressing question: *What shall I tell your brother?*

"I'll send Hector around at least once a day to see if you have messages for me," Ashton said, for the girl needed to be kept out of trouble somehow. "I need time to reconnoiter before polite society starts gawking at me."

Cherbourne took out a handkerchief and mopped his brow. "I must in all honesty tell you, my lord, this is very irregular. You'll have no one to brush off your coats, lay out your clothes, oversee the laundresses, trim your hair. I cannot like this idea at all."

Ashton loved the idea. Wished he'd thought of it three years ago when Ewan had dragged him south to make the acquaintance of Fat George and the sartorial thieves on Bond Street.

"I'll manage, but I'd appreciate it if you'd not inform my family of my decision."

Cherbourne took inordinate care refolding the handkerchief. "My lord, I would not presume to correspond with persons so far above my station."

Helen's snort was worthy of a dowager duchess.

"You would presume to correspond with my butler," Ashton said, "who would have a word with the housekeeper, who might let something slip to the nursery maid, who'd mention to Lady Alyssa that you'd sent word up from London that the earl was acting peculiar again. Every time I took you with me to see friends in Cumberland, you sent off more dispatches than Wellington on the eve of battle."

Cherbourne straightened his shoulders, though nothing would make him an impressive figure. He was a small, dapper, balding little mole of a man, right down to the squinty expression and buck teeth.

"A gentleman's gentleman is allowed proper concern for his employer," Cherbourne replied. "I consider it part of my role to describe my experiences of the wider world to the staff not fortunate enough to travel. They share my concern for you, my lord."

"I'm an ungrateful wretch, is that it?" This discussion was overdue, and it should have been uncomfortable.

Starched cravats were uncomfortable.

"Your lordship is tired from the journey," Cherbourne said. "London can be overwhelming, I know. Your brother took some while to adjust to the demands made upon a titled gentleman here in the capital, but I'm sure, in time, you too will move effortlessly among your peers."

For three years, Ashton had been Cherbourne's work in progress, his Galatea, a block of stone to be fashioned into a titled paragon.

Helen shot Ashton a look, as if he'd missed his lines.

"Cherbourne, I will write you a glowing character, if that's what you want. In London, you should have no trouble finding employment worthy of your skills. Here's what I want: No more subtle laments, sermons, or scolds. I pay your salary, you give me your loyalty and your service. Me, not Ewan, not Lady Alyssa, not your cronies among the staff. You don't tattle on me as if I'm a naughty underfootman. You don't presume to criticize my need for a little privacy. You are the valet, I am the earl. Keep to your place or find another position."

Three years ago, Ashton could not have carried out the threats he was making.

"I... but..."

"Or I can write you a modest character, confirming dates of employment and competence only."

"My lord, you cannot... that is... This is most irreg—"

Helen drummed her heels against the side of the trunk.

"No character at all," Ashton said. "Out on your ear. I'll save some coin and get shut of that most disgusting exponent of dishonor, a spy under my own roof. I can shave myself. Did it for years."

"You should apologize, Mr. Chairbug," Helen said. "Turns 'em up sweet, and you might get a cobbler."

"Do we understand each other?" Ashton asked.

"Say yes," Helen chirped. "I don't think you'll get a cobbler, though."

"We understand each other, sir."

"Delightful. That took only half an hour I shouldn't have had to waste. Hector, let's be off. Cherbourne has much to do, even if he isn't sending hourly missives to people who have no business meddling in my life."

Helen hopped off the trunk and darted to the door. She'd shown up at Mrs. Bryce's exactly on time and peppered Ashton with questions the whole way to the Albany. Her opinions were marked, original, and incessant.

And, bless the child, not a one of those opinions came with a "my lord" attached.

"So you're a nob?" she asked as they made their way down the steps.

"I'm Mr. Ashton Fenwick."

She gazed up at him. "Mrs. Bryce don't hold with lying. I'm fair warning you, because I'm your general tote 'em, though you haven't given me nuffink to tote yet. If I take your coin—and your cobbler—then I should look out for you."

"You will carry my confidences. My name is Ashton Fenwick. Whatever else I might be is of no moment, and you won't mention it."

Helen hopped down the stairs. "Right, guv, and I'm the Queen of the Fairies. Mention that all you please, especially to old Sissy when she gets in a taking about one of her flats."

Flats were the men who hired prostitutes. That Helen knew of such goings-on wasn't wrong, because what she grasped she could take steps to protect herself from.

That she *needed* to protect herself from her sister's customers was very wrong, indeed.

"Time to introduce you to my horse," Ashton said. "Then you're to show me where we can find some supper."

"I've never met a horse before. Met plenty of horses' arses."

"So have I."

"Mrs. Bryce doesn't like bad language."

"I do, when it's done properly. Don't tell her I said that."

Helen stopped at the foot of the steps. "Cost you a cobbler."

Ashton continued out into the early evening sunshine. "No deal. Mrs. Bryce will hear my bad language herself if the situation arises where I'm inspired to express myself colorfully. You will not comment on my behavior before others lest I turn you off without a character."

"What's a character?"

"A reference. A written testament to your competence and ability."

Helen skipped along at his side as he made his way back to the mews, and damned if the child hadn't the knack of skipping like a boy.

"Can't use no written character if nobody can read it. Only nobs and reformers can read. Parsons too, but they're all reformers. Mrs. Bryce can read."

"Get Mrs. Bryce to teach you to read, Helen. It's not that difficult once you learn the letters."

"I know my name. H-E-L-E-N. How many letters are there?"

"Twenty-six."

"Twenty-two to go. That's a lot. If you teach me one a day for a fortnight, I'll still have eight left."

"You can do sums, but you don't know your letters?"

"Sums is money, guv. I know all about sums."

The introduction to Dusty—Destrier in formal company—went well. The horse was a good soul, patient, happy to please, and tolerant of barn cats, reluctant earls, and stable boys who whistled off-key.

"He's big," Helen said, brushing a hand down the gelding's long nose. "He's big as an elephant."

"Not quite. I was encouraged to find a more refined mount, but he suits me." Ewan all but groaned every time Ashton climbed into Dusty's saddle, but the horse was proof that Ashton hadn't always been the earl, and thus as precious as a holy relic.

Helen proposed dinner at the Unicorn, based on her scientific comparison of its middens and clientele with those of its competition. Her judgment was vindicated by the fare. Hot, hearty, plentiful, and plain—Ashton's favorite kind of meal.

He used the dinner hour to acquaint her with the letters *d*, for Destrier, and *b*, for Mrs. Bryce, by drawing with his fork in her gravy.

The girl could eat like a horse, but had some manners, probably as a result of Mrs. Bryce's ceaseless efforts.

"I should take this last bit to Sissy," Helen said. "She'll be out and about now. She starts by the theaters in case any of the gents want a go before the performances. They usually do, but there's more business later."

Helen's blasé recitation made Ashton's dinner sit uneasily in his belly.

"If any of those gents ever make you feel awkward, you tear off. Don't be nice, don't smile, don't ignore the look they're giving you. Don't give them any warning you're getting ready to bolt, Helen. You run like hell and scream bloody murder. Up a drainpipe, down a coal chute, but run."

Helen licked the last of the butter from her knife. "Sissy says the same thing. I've pulled a bunk a time or two. They can't catch me."

Not yet, they couldn't. When Helen was hampered by skirts, they might.

"Here," Ashton said, holding out a few coins to Helen. "Buy your Sissy some food, and then it's back to Mrs. Bryce's with you. A general factotum who's not at her post isn't worth her hire."

Helen looked at the coins in Ashton's hand, then up at his face, a question in her eyes.

"I'm not looking to become one of your sister's flats. This is a vale, a little extra coin for starting off your job on the right foot. Keep up the good work, and you might earn a bit more."

The money was gone, and Ashton hadn't felt Helen's fingers touch his palm.

"Good evenin' to you, guv. I'll tell Sissy I found the blunt in the street."

The child apparently never walked. She skipped, ran, strutted, scampered, and fidgeted, much as Ashton had at her age.

He'd been the bastard firstborn, perhaps subject to sterner discipline than the heir, but he'd never had to worry about his safety, not as Helen had to.

He was still pondering that injustice as he neared his temporary lodgings. Pastry Lane was what an Edinburger would call a wynd, more of a courtyard at the end of a covered passage than a proper lane. The houses on either side hung out over the passage, though they didn't quite meet. No conveyance would fit down Pastry Lane, and little sunshine leaked onto the worn cobbles.

Keeping intruders out would be easy, as would keeping an eye on the neighbors. Mrs. Bryce's abode opened onto the small courtyard where the lane ended, a space shared with four neighboring houses.

Ashton was across the main thoroughfare one street up from Pastry Lane when he saw a familiar brown cloak and straw hat bobbing along the walkway twenty yards ahead of him.

Mrs. Bryce, apparently returning from the last shopping errand of the day. She carried a parcel under her arm and made her way briskly in the direction of home.

Ashton watched for a moment, appreciating the energy in her stride and the good fortune that had put them in each other's path. Two weeks of hot porridge, simple meals, and freedom from servants, sycophants, and meddling family would be heaven.

He was about to cross the street and offer the lady his escort when he became aware of another man trailing Mrs. Bryce about thirty feet back. Close enough to keep her in sight, far enough away to avoid detection.

He wore the uniform of the man of business. Plain brown breeches and jacket, slightly worn, no walking stick or other distinguishing accoutrements, not even a hat. When Mrs. Bryce stopped to chat with an older woman leading a child by the hand, the man following examined the wares on display at a potter's shop.

Mrs. Bryce bid the other woman farewell and went on her way, and the man behind resumed walking as well.

Ashton was across the street in long strides and kept on moving until, as if in an effort to overtake Mrs. Bryce, he bumped the package from her grasp.

He stopped, tipped his hat, and picked up the parcel. "You're being followed," he said, beaming to all appearances sheepishly. "Let me carry your package, and please accept my escort."

Those fine gray eyes took a casual inventory of the surroundings. "Thank you, sir. I'm sure there's no damage."

Ashton winged his arm, and bless the woman for her common sense, she took it and let him lead her away from Pastry Lane.

CHAPTER THREE

If Matilda believed in one eternal verity, one immutable law of nature that would hold true down through the millennia, it was that Men Were Dreadful. Not all men, not all the time, which meant a woman had to be that much more vigilant to dodge the worst transgressors.

But most men, most of the time, were dreadful. They displayed petty dreadfulness, such as the tenant who was too lazy to carry his dirty dishes downstairs even on his way out for a morning stroll. He made more work for Pippa, the maid, and wasted her time. Was any disrespect quite as purely rotten as wasting a busy person's time?

A tenant who nipped off to France without paying three months' rent was more dreadful still and left Matilda to wonder if that tenant would have treated a landlord with the same disregard as a landlady.

No, he would not.

In a league of their own were men who arranged a daughter's future so she was bound to an ungrateful tyrant, one who held her accountable for matters even the Church agreed were the exclusive province of the Almighty.

Worse yet were the men whose ungovernable urges meant their wives died in childbed, or suffered regular violence for no reason.

Dreadful, dreadful-er, and dreadful-est, as Helen would have said.

Matilda could have fashioned her own version of the circles of hell based on the transgressions which the male gender considered its casual right, simply because that gender had more muscles and less sophisticated procreative apparatus.

She was at a complete loss when Mr. Fenwick appeared at her side, her parcel in his hands, and a warning on his lips. She took his arm, very much against her inclinations. A woman who could work eighteen hours every day and still stay awake through Sunday services most weeks was capable of walking down the street unassisted.

And yet, if Matilda *was* being followed, she was in Ashton Fenwick's debt. "Can you describe the person following me?" she asked quietly.

"He's dressed to blend in," Mr. Fenwick replied while, to all appearances, wandering along on a pleasant spring evening. "Plain brown clothes, no hat, no gloves. Medium height, medium age, medium everything. The perfect invisible man. Let's have a cup of coffee, shall we?"

"I don't care for it."

"Neither do I."

Mr. Fenwick was adept at eluding pursuit. One moment, Matilda was walking down the street beside him, the next, she was inside a coffee and pastry shop more genteel than most around Haymarket proper.

"I'll order for us," Mr. Fenwick said. "Chocolate for you?"

Matilda loved chocolate, but seldom took the time or spent the coin to indulge. The shop wasn't crowded, the dinner hour having arrived, but neither was it deserted. Clerks and shopgirls, housewives and older men occupied scattered tables. A young waiter in a bib apron moved about, cleaning up dirty dishes and scrubbing tables.

"Chocolate would be delightful." The scent of the place was heavenly, full of baking spices, with the aromas of coffee, chocolate, and black tea blending as well.

"That table," Mr. Fenwick said, passing Matilda her parcel. "The one in the corner, so we can both sit with our backs to a wall."

Matilda did as he suggested, because his reasoning made sense. She kept an eye on the street beyond the windows and saw, bobbing among the crowd, a bare-headed man of middle years and middle height saunter past, his attire a plain brown.

Mr. Fenwick came to the table and took the seat facing the street, while Matilda faced across the dining area. He set a plate bearing three scones in the middle of the table.

"You bought scones? Cinnamon scones? Fresh cinnamon scones?"

"I'm from the north. We appreciate a fresh scone at any hour."

Men bearing cinnamon scones were worth tolerating, at least temporarily. Matilda set her hat on the bench beside her and removed her gloves. The waiter brought over butter and jam, and before Matilda had properly buttered her scone, the chocolate arrived.

"If you're trying to bribe your way into my good graces, it won't work," she said. "The attempt is delightful, nonetheless."

"I'm trying to prevent somebody from following you home," Mr. Fenwick said, holding his cup of chocolate beneath his nose.

That nose was in proportion to the rest of him and had been broken at least once.

"You needn't trouble yourself further, Mr. Fenwick. I saw your medium-height, brown-garbed man go by when you placed our order. That was Aloysius Aberfeldy. He's a man in love, and he frequently follows me."

Mr. Fenwick set his chocolate down untasted. "Do you enjoy his attentions?"

"Aloysius isn't in love with me. He's in love with my house. These scones are marvelous." Fresh, warm, light as a wish, and dusted with sugar. Matilda promised herself she'd bake a batch on the next rainy day.

"I am quite fond of my horse," Mr. Fenwick said, sipping his chocolate, "but in love? Surely you indulge in hyperbole."

Mr. Fenwick's manners weren't so much dainty as Continental. He savored his food, tore off one bite of scone at a time, and enjoyed it.

He'd probably be a good kisser, which signified exactly nothing.

"I am indulging in euphemism," Matilda said, dipping a corner of her scone into her chocolate. "Mr. Aberfeldy covets my house. If he married me, my house would become his house, absent convoluted trusts and vigilant trustees. Even with those in place, my dear husband could have me committed at his whim to one of those very quiet estates with very high walls tucked very far in the country. Then he could do with the house as he saw fit."

Mr. Fenwick eschewed butter on his scone, for which Helen would have castigated him at length.

"You have a flare for the dramatic, Mrs. Bryce."

Matilda paused in the middle of what constituted a small orgy, for Mr. Fenwick was *humoring* her, and that transgression required immediate correction.

"Doesn't it strike you as odd, sir, that the Almighty, in His perfect wisdom, has given us no commandment against coveting our neighbor's husband?"

Mr. Fenwick sat straighter. "There's the one about adultery."

"Irrelevant," Matilda replied. "Adultery contemplates a man's bad behavior again, with a wife not his own, as if the Deity wanted to emphasize a point through repetition of the obvious, perhaps. None of the commandments address the possibility of a woman straying onto some other lady's preserves. Why do you suppose that is?"

"I'm sure you will enlighten me."

"I will offer you my theory. Your chocolate is getting cold."

"While you are warming to your topic. You should have chocolate more often."

"Perhaps I should. In any case, I think the Creator knew that after a woman has had a glimpse of the wonders of holy matrimony, she will have no inclination to cavort with anybody else's husband."

Mr. Fenwick chewed his scone contemplatively. "People remarry."

"Men remarry so their children have a mother, or their household has an unpaid drudge who's also required by the church and the law to grant her husband other favors. Women remarry lest they starve or worse."

Matilda was being honest, but she was also presenting herself as a female about whom no sane male would develop wayward notions. She'd been dewy-eyed and sweet once upon a time.

Fat lot of good that had done her.

Mr. Fenwick's gaze remained on the foot traffic beyond the windows. He'd eaten one scone, finished off his chocolate, and was apparently waiting for Matilda to finish hers.

She'd love to fault his manners, except she couldn't. "Say something, Mr. Fenwick."

"We have something in common," he said. "The status of wife is much desired in certain circles. Among young ladies, to marry well is considered the accomplishment of a lifetime, though marrying well and marrying happily are not synonymous. You attained the status of wife, though apparently at the cost of your regard for the institution of marriage. So too, with my situation. I have means and influence many long for, and I don't want them. There he is again."

Matilda wanted to ask Mr. Fenwick what the devil he meant by those Delphic observations, but she instead focused on the passersby. A bareheaded man in a brown suit strolled past, though he studied the surroundings as if inspecting the marvels of Pompeii rather than a typical London street.

"You're sure that's the fellow who was following me?"

"I'm sure. You stopped, he stopped. You moved on, he moved on. He's passed by here twice while we've been eating, as if he can't figure out where you got off to."

The luscious scone, the rich chocolate, the pleasure of airing opinions all turned to so much bile in Matilda's belly.

"That's not Mr. Aberfeldy. I've never seen that man before in my life."

* * *

Mrs. Bryce of the misanthropic theological theories had become a subdued creature who followed Ashton out the back of the coffee shop and accompanied him through gloomy alleys and side streets into a tiny back garden.

"We have a problem," she said, surveying her own back door. "This door locks from the inside rather than with a key. Pippa has likely sought her bed, and my key fits only the front door."

Ashton could go around to the front and let himself in, but whoever was following Mrs. Bryce had seen her accept his escort. The sun had set, a single cricket was trying to ignore the spring chill, and Ashton was not about to leave a woman alone in the gathering darkness if he could help it.

"We'll improvise." He extracted his folding knife from his boot and examined the ground-floor windows. The house was old, glazing cost money, and he was determined.

"That is a nasty bit of weaponry, Mr. Fenwick."

"Success in life is largely a matter of having the right tools." If you were a bastard. If you were not, then coin and social connections would suffice.

The first window had been tightly latched, but the second, which opened into a sitting room, proved accommodating. Ashton used the slim blade to lift the latch from the outside and soon had the window open.

"Don't let Helen see you do that," Mrs. Bryce said. "She'll get ideas."

"She needs an entire team of instructors and tutors," Ashton said, tossing the package into the sitting room and hoisting himself through the window. "For that child, a single governess wouldn't stand a chance." He leaned out the window, scooped up the lady, and hauled her in after him. Mrs. Bryce was a curvaceous armful of female, agreeably scented with lemon verbena, and he'd caught her by surprise.

A pleasure that.

She yelped, and the instant her feet touched the carpet, she jerked away from him. "You might have simply unlocked the door for me, Mr. Fenwick."

He picked up her package and passed it to her. "You're welcome. Why was that man following you? Does he covet your house as well?"

If Mrs. Bryce thought the lovestruck Mr. Aberfeldy was solely interested in her real estate, she was daft.

"I'd never seen him before. I told you that."

The parlor was all but dark. Lighting candles or starting a fire in the hearth would mean a trip to the kitchen. If Ashton left the room, though, he suspected Mrs. Bryce would disappear to her own quarters.

Possibly for the next two weeks.

"You should replace the latch on this window." He closed the shutters, then the window itself, and secured the latch.

Shutters kept out wind and sun, true, but their first purpose was to prevent an intruder from bashing through the glass and gaining access to the house. Shutters couldn't serve that purpose unless they were closed and latched from the inside.

"Thank you for that very obvious reminder, Mr. Fenwick. You neglected to mention that I should chide my maid for not securing the shutters before retiring. That job, however, is mine, and I was detained by no less person than yourself."

The parlor was chilly, Mrs. Bryce's tone was arctic.

"He frightened you."

Mrs. Bryce's fear reassured Ashton, because a woman living with only a young maid on the premises and limited security was easily preyed upon. Weapons might increase her danger, because they could be turned upon her.

"You frightened me," she shot back, rubbing her arms. "He merely trailed behind me on the walkway, along with a substantial portion of the neighborhood's working population. You're the one who claims that man's attentions were cause for alarm."

She was very frightened, indeed. Ashton took off his coat and draped it around her shoulders.

"Have you another hypothesis to explain his casual patrol of the street where he last saw you?"

Mrs. Bryce clutched Ashton's coat close when he'd expected her to toss it back at him. "Maybe he was looking for you, and he saw you escorting me from the Goose earlier in the day. It's been years since I've been pursued by any save Mr. Aberfeldy and his ilk. Then you show up, and I supposedly become quarry of a different sort."

She'd been pursued by somebody at some time. Ashton saved that admission for exploration when he had enough light to assess her demeanor.

"I'll need a candle for my rooms," he said. "Shall we take this discussion to the kitchen?"

Mrs. Bryce led the way through a house grown dark, her steps sure, even on the stairs leading down to the lower floor.

"Is there a cellar below the kitchen?"

"Yes," she said as they reached a large, cozy kitchen. "For storage and coal deliveries."

"You'll want to make sure your coal chute is securely locked."

In most households, the fire in the kitchen hearth never went out. It could burn down to ashes and coals, which would be carefully banked for the night. The coals in Mrs. Bryce's kitchen cast some illumination, enough for Ashton to see that his landlady was pale and angry.

"I know you mean well, Mr. Fenwick, and it's possible you have spared me a problem with your escort tonight, but I have owned this house for more than five years without being inconvenienced by criminals. My lodgers, by contrast, are a good deal of bother. Please stop presuming I'm stupid."

"I'm trying to be helpful."

"And failing. I am very mindful of my safety, and Pippa's. The coal chute is locked."

He retreated into silence while she scooped fresh coal onto the hearth and worked a bellows that mostly sent ashes up the flue.

This woman did not give up, nor did she let up. Ashton admired her tenacity as much as he disliked her bitterness.

"I'm sorry," she said, putting the bellows aside and dropping onto the raised hearth. "I ought by rights to dwell in a one-room cottage in the West Riding, where my shrewish temperament need be endured by only my cat. The income from renting out the rooms upstairs exceeds what I could make in the cent per cents. Then too, this house is worth more now than when I bought it, and I expect that trend to continue as long as I'm here to maintain the premises."

She spouted economics, an improvement over her scolding. Ashton decided to meet her halfway, though he was tempted to snatch a candle and leave her to her ire.

"I'm more comfortable in the country myself."

"What brings you to London?" she asked as the fire caught. "Besides the usual platitudes."

"Duty. I became responsible for properties and the people on them a few years ago. I am obligated to perform certain functions here in London as a result. I don't anticipate being in Town past the end of June."

"You cannot perform these functions through third parties?"

"I tried that. No luck." Alyssa had set him up with all manner of blushing young maidens, each more tongue-tied and well dowered than the last.

"You can sit, Mr. Fenwick. I'm not some duchess that all must stand on their manners before me."

Even her graciousness had a bite. Ashton took the other side of the hearth, so the fire crackled between them. Shadows danced on the kitchen walls, and an old house settled in for another night.

"I'm tired," Mrs. Bryce said. "I thought being a widow would be the great prize for which I endured years of marriage. I know that makes me sound like a monster. My husband was unkind, and those who arranged the match knew it. Now I live the smallest possible life, bothering the fewest number of people. Why would anybody want to follow me?" she asked more softly. "I've devoted the last five years of my life to being nobody."

Ashton understood her lament, for he'd enjoyed very much being the next thing to a nobody.

"I might have overreacted to what I saw," Ashton conceded. "If you're fatigued, I should leave you in peace."

He knew Mrs. Bryce hadn't referred to a simple lack of sleep, though. She was weary of contending with a world that refused to accommodate her terms. Most people gave up that struggle for the lesser effort of merely coping.

She rose and took a twisted taper from a jar on the mantel and used it to light a carrying candle. The light revealed both her beauty and a bewilderment Ashton suspected she'd die rather than knowingly let him see.

"Good night," he said, taking the candle from her. "Thank you for sharing your accommodations with me."

She said nothing, as if sincere thanks were a forgotten element of her English vocabulary. As the fire leaped higher and gave off both light and heat, Ashton realized she needed him to leave her alone in her own kitchen.

He kissed her forehead and took himself up the stairs, though he'd rather have stayed and at least offered the woman a shoulder to lean on while she cried.

* * *

Ashton Fenwick, eighth Earl of Kilkenney, Viscount Kinkenney, Baron

Mulder, paced about in Benjamin Portmaine's library as if he were a stall-bound horse, his enormous energy confined in much too small a space.

"The stink alone should repel any who approach the metropolis," Fenwick groused. "Then there's the racket. Does London ever stop making noise? Does it ever grow less crowded?"

"In the parks, first thing of the day," Benjamin began, "there's peace and—"

"There's no peace a'tall," Fenwick shot back. "Behind every bush, at every bend in the bridle path, there's some damned baroness or duke cluttering up my morning with 'good day' and 'what a handsome horse you have.' Auld Dusty is the next thing to plow stock. Do they think I'm simple?"

Three years of being a Scottish earl had deepened Fenwick's burr. Bush became *boosh*, t's were sharpened to elocutionary quill points, and vowels acquired a growled quality their English cousins lacked.

For Benjamin, who held an earldom in Cumberland, Fenwick's accent was nearly the sound of home. Fenwick had spent years as the steward at Blessings, the Hazelton earldom's seat, and had kept a close eye on Benjamin's sister when Benjamin had dwelled in London.

Three years away from the stables had not improved Fenwick's disposition, which had been almost as inclined to temper as flirtation—almost.

"They think you're new to Town," Benjamin said, taking a corner of the sofa that afforded him a view of the entire room, "and deserving of a friendly welcome."

"While they count my teeth and how many acres I own." Fenwick settled into an armchair, Benjamin's favorite because it was the least elegant in the house. Maggie, his countess, threatened to replace it periodically, and then Benjamin would remind her how comfortably two could occupy that chair when a countess cuddled in her earl's lap.

"You're here to find a bride," Benjamin said. "The morning hack can save you time. If I'd known you were in Town, I would happily have joined you and begun the introductions."

Fenwick ran a finger around the collar of his cravat. "You knew I was in Town. You know everything."

Once upon an impecunious time, Benjamin had earned coin as an investigator for the wealthiest families of the realm. A wastrel son who disappeared into the stews, an errant daughter attempting to elope, a necklace pawned by a dotty aunt… He'd discreetly handled all manner of delicate situations, though now most of that business was in the hands of an enterprising relative.

"I don't know everything," Benjamin replied. "Knowing even a few secrets is a greater burden than you'd think. I do know your trunks arrived at the Albany two days ago, your horses arrived the day before that, along with your town coach and your phaeton. The entire entourage appeared on schedule, but no Earl of Kilkenney showed up with them. As far as I can tell, you're still not in residence at your assigned direction."

Fenwick was back on his feet, wearing a path before the pink marble fireplace. "I'll thank you not to be assigning me directions, Hazelton. I've found other quarters for the moment."

This would not do. Fenwick was canny, capable, and big enough to look after himself in most situations. London in springtime for a single earl of means was not most situations.

"Fenwick, you're new here. Now is not the time for frolic and detour. In parts of London the rats are the closest you'll come to good society. If you think Mayfair is crowded now, wait another month. You won't be able to walk down the street without a parasol poking you in the eye."

Fenwick came to a halt beneath the portrait Benjamin had commissioned of his countess. Maggie was tall, red-haired, and the very definition of formidable—until her husband tickled her feet.

"How's your family?" Fenwick asked. "Apologies for not inquiring after them sooner."

"That you launched your invective against Old Londontowne before observing the civilities is proof of how rattled you are. You've always had excellent manners."

Fenwick's smile was devilish and bashful. "For a bastard, ye mean?"

"For a scamp," Benjamin said. "Maggie is already making lists—note the plural—of young ladies who might suit you. She has five sisters, Fenwick, and her mama's a duchess. Your bachelorhood might as well be the last grouse on the moor on the final day of the shooting season."

Fenwick collapsed into the chair, its joints squeaking. "Sweet Jesus ascending. Ye canna put a stop to it? I'm not here forty-eight hours, and you've set the matchmakers on me. If that's your definition of loyalty, we need to have a wee chat."

"One doesn't tell my countess what to do. You must steel yourself to be charming, agreeable, even friendly. To dance until all hours, then go without sleep to pretend a cold saddle at dawn is your definition of manly delight."

"Marriage has addled you, if a cold saddle fulfills that job."

"Marriage has pleased me enormously," Benjamin shot back. "If you'd stop whining, you might consider that marriage offers pleasures no other circumstance can equal."

Fenwick stretched out his legs and stared at his boots. "I can see the contentment on you. Ewan has the same air, when he's not wearing his cravat too tight. Please recall, you chose your lady with no pressure from family, friends, or list-making strangers. I still expect to wake up to a barn full of horses impatient for their hay, but no, I'm here, in bloody London, the last place I ever wanted to be."

Fenwick was desperately homesick for that horse barn. Maggie corresponded with Benjamin's sister Avis, who corresponded with Fenwick's sister-in-law, Lady Alyssa. Year by year, niece by niece, Fenwick grew grimmer, more serious, and less the devil-may-care flirt who'd kept Benjamin's estate running for years.

"You will soon be a Scottish curmudgeon," Benjamin said. "Is that what you want? No children, your title going to some fourth cousin, or worse, back to the crown?"

"Of course not, but neither do I want you setting your dogs upon me before I've even washed the dust of the road from my boots."

His boots gleamed. Somebody had done a proper job on them, possibly Fenwick himself.

"I didn't set my dogs on you, but I am acquainted with several gentlemen who bide at the Albany. I came across two of them in the park this morning."

Before he'd seen Fenwick having a mad dash on his warhorse at an hour when polite talk and a sedate canter were the done thing. Benjamin had waited until Fenwick's gelding had cooled out to accost the errant earl and invite him to pay a call.

"Right," Fenwick said. "My whereabouts were the subject of innocent gentlemanly gossip. Like I believe that. Then explain why last evening, somebody was following either me, or the person who's renting me temporary lodgings. I realize pickpockets abound in this temple of civilization, along with housebreakers, members of Parliament, drunks, and other fine company, but this fellow knew what he was about."

To anybody else complaining of having been followed, Benjamin would have offered mindless reassurances—all in your head, lack of rest, new surroundings, overset nerves, nothing to bother about. He had too much respect for Fenwick's instincts, and his fists, to attempt such platitudes.

"Describe the fellow."

"Attired to blend in. No hat, walking stick, watch fob, mustache, nothing to distinguish him. Attired in brown, not too flashy, not too plain. He'd fit in at any tavern and not quite offend when paying a call. Parson-ish, but no collar, if you know what I mean."

"A journalist," Benjamin said, relief coursing through him. "They haunt Piccadilly, Bond Street, the Strand, St. James's. All the neighborhoods where fashionable society can be spotted out of the preserves they exclusively control."

"This grows bizarre." Fenwick rose, a prime specimen in his riding attire. "I'm just a man who doesn't want to spend the rest of my life without a lady of my own. A little on the rough side, but good-hearted, according to most—most of the time. I don't want to be a public spectacle, Hazelton. If you have hired somebody to watch me, call him off, or I'll have to protect my privacy as I see fit."

"That is exactly the kind of talk that will get you gossiped about if you make such threats among your peers. You've a title now, and while you may not—"

Fenwick brushed a gloved finger along the bottom of Maggie's portrait. "Benjamin, your word, please. No surveillance, no hiring the urchins and game girls to note my comings and goings. Violate my privacy again at your peril. My valet is on probation for the same offense, so don't approach him to do your spying."

The threat was insulting—spies were universally vilified, no matter how indispensable they were—and yet, Fenwick was serious. He dreaded this bride hunt, a challenge most men looked forward to, reluctant though they were to admit it. Taking a wife marked the last division between boyhood and manhood, and most adult males were eager to make that transition as soon as they could afford to.

Then too, companionship, an ally in life, an intimate partner with whom one could be oneself, children, a true home rather than bachelor quarters… Marriage done right would suit Ashton Fenwick to his big, Scottish toes.

Benjamin rose and extended a hand. "You have my word, no surveillance."

Fenwick shook. "That goes for your countess too. The ladies excel at gathering information."

"That they do, so why not simply tell me where you're staying?"

"You can get word to me at the Albany for now. I'll move there soon, but first I'm getting my bearings in less conspicuous surroundings."

Brilliant strategy. "Be careful, Fenwick. This isn't the Borders or Cumberland, where you can spot a man riding toward you from halfway up the valley."

Fenwick muttered something as he scowled at his white glove.

"I beg your pardon?"

"I'm not stupid, Hazelton. I'll thank you to recall that. Next you'll be reminding me to keep my coal chute locked. You're sure that was a journalist following me?"

"Almost certain. I can promise you, whoever it was doesn't answer to me. My people would never be that obvious. Have dinner with me at my club the day after tomorrow. Maggie and her sisters get together for cards—or so they claim—and I'm orphaned for the evening."

"You're not orphaned, you're bachelored. Dinner at the club will do for an opening move. My regards to your countess."

Benjamin saw his guest to the door and discarded the notion of following Fenwick to his lodgings. Fenwick would likely notice in the first place, and kill him in the second.

A small boy in a grimy cap walked Fen's horse up and down before the house. After Fenwick had donned riding gloves and climbed into the saddle, he stuck out his boot and hauled the child up behind him.

Not the done thing. Doubtless, the talk had already started in the clubs as a result of Fenwick's dawn charge through the park, and now he'd trot the length of Mayfair with an urchin riding pillion.

The Season was off to an interesting start, and Benjamin couldn't wait to compare notes with his countess.

* * *

Fifteen years ago, Ashton would have raced the length of the realm and arrived in London ready to drink, dance, and chase skirts for a week straight.

Five years ago, he would have managed at least a night or two of high spirits.

Three years into being an earl, and a day in London left him craving yet another nap. The fatigue was not entirely of the body. Melancholia threatened to get its foul hooks into him, hence the dawn gallop in the park. No matter how fast he rode, once he took a countess from among the glittering crop on offer in Mayfair, his title would have him by the throat.

A soft warmth insinuated itself against Ashton's side as he drowsed in the afternoon sunshine, followed by gentle pressure tiptoeing across his chest.

Maybe London wasn't all bad.

On the heels of that hazy thought, rough dampness scraped across Fenwick's chin.

"What the devil?"

He opened his eyes to behold a pink nose, whiskers, and two green eyes, belonging to an enormous black and white cat.

"You must be Solomon. Your fame has preceded you." Helen had much to say about the cat and his mighty exploits in the pantry as well as in the alley.

Solomon began to knead Ashton's chest and rumble with contentment.

"I can't sleep if you're making that much noise, and I'm sure Mrs. Bryce would rather you minded your post in the kitchen."

The damned animal had claws, and rotten breath, and yet, Ashton lay for a moment, savoring the pleasure of sharing his bed with even a cat, something no earl was permitted to do.

"Come along," Ashton said, sitting up, much to the cat's disgruntlement. "You're absent without leave from the kitchen, and I have matters to attend to."

He'd come straight back from his morning call on Hazelton, not wanting to deal with Cherbourne's longsuffering sighs, or the correspondence doubtless waiting at the Albany. Sleep in the less genteel parts of London was elusive, for even in the dark of night, coaches passed, the night-soil men trod the alleys, and milkmaids plied their trade.

Without bothering to put on his coat—why get cat hair on that too?— Ashton made his way down the stairs, past the closed door to Mrs. Bryce's private chambers, and on to the kitchen. The maid, Pippa, was nowhere to be seen, and Mrs. Bryce stood at the counter, chopping apples.

Her movements had a beauty to them, regular, rhythmic, economical. Ashton stood for a moment in the doorway, holding the cat and watching a woman at home in her own kitchen. Slices went into a bowl, and another apple went under the knife.

A sense of homesickness swamped him, for a kitchen of his own and a wife who made him apple pies. As earl, he could have had apple pies four times a day, but they'd be the creation of a chef, the recipe calling for nutmeg and God knew what else besides good old cinnamon and love.

The best apples he'd ever eaten had been the ones he'd plucked off a tree to share with his horse on a crisp autumn day.

The cat commenced purring again, a pathetic comfort to a man who owned thousands of acres.

Ashton walked up behind Mrs. Bryce. "My bed was visited by a fugitive."

She whirled, knife in hand, eyes glittering. "Get away from me."

Ashton released the cat, relieved the lady of the knife, and set it a safe distance away on the counter.

"Mrs. Bryce?" Ashton had a hand around her wrist, her pulse galloping beneath his grip. Her gaze was indignant, and her posture—tense despite the ridiculousness of the moment—radiated both defiance and fear.

"What in seven heavens do you think you're doing in my kitchen, Mr. Fenwick? Were you trying to get yourself stabbed?"

"I was trying to return your cat to his place of work. He got into my apartment and insinuated himself into my bed." The same cat was now stropping himself across Ashton's boots. "I thought you'd want him where he belongs."

She looked down as if noticing her own feline for the first time. "Solomon was in your rooms?"

"He might have followed Helen in, or Pippa. I also leave my windows open, and an enterprising tom has ways of going where he pleases. Are you all right?"

"You gave me a fright. I'm not in the habit of being accosted by strange men in my kitchen."

He'd given her a terror, which inspired him to step back and leave the lady some room. "You were focused on your cooking. Do I smell a pie already baking?"

Ashton took up the knife—which might have done him considerable damage had Mrs. Bryce known how to use it—and began chopping the apple she'd abandoned.

"Tarts. I start with the tarts, which call for smaller pieces of apple, then graduate to the pies. If you've no objection, I'll make a pot of tea."

"This is your kitchen," Ashton said, popping a bite of apple into his mouth. "I have no authority to object. If King George himself were to appear and command you to chop your apples rather than slice them, in your own kitchen, as a self-respecting English housewife, you'd ignore him with impunity. What or who are you so afraid of, Matilda?"

She swung the tea kettle over the coals in the fireplace and subsided onto the raised hearth. "I haven't given you leave to use my name."

Ashton set some apple slices on a plate and passed them to her. "I'm Ashton, and you were ready to carve your initials on my chest for bringing you that cat. I'd say that puts us on a first-name basis."

She looked up at him, the wariness in her expression all wrong. This was *her kitchen*, the one place a woman ought to reign supreme, and she was cautious about accepting a bite of apple from him.

She took the plate and set it beside her on the hearth. "Thank you... Ashton."

CHAPTER FOUR

Ashton went back to chopping apples, though with another woman, he might have turned the moment to teasing.

Not with Matilda Bryce.

"A widow is a target for the unscrupulous," she said, taking a bite of apple. "All women are, but especially widows. I should have realized that."

"Anybody can get his pocket picked," Ashton pointed out. "I'm trying to teach Helen her letters, by the way. At each meal, we'll tackle two or three, and when she has the alphabet in hand, we'll start finding simple words."

"You can get her to attend you when she's eating? I would have thought that impossible."

The kettle began to steam as Ashton filled the ceramic bowl with chopped apples. "I try to use relevant objects. *S* will be for Solomon, *t* for tart. She's frighteningly quick."

"She's frightening, period." Matilda finished a second slice of apple. "You startled me earlier. I was thinking of my father-in-law. I did not get along well with my husband's family, and to this day, I don't trust them."

That was probably the queen of all understatements. "Would they try to accost you in your own kitchen?"

The cat hopped up on the hearth and sat, licking a front paw. Matilda watched him, her gaze desolate.

"They might. I don't know. It's been years since my husband died—six years—but they have nothing better to do than plague the unwary and torment the undeserving. You're very good at chopping apples."

"I have been a bachelor my whole adult life. One develops skills or starves. The water's hot."

"It has to boil for a minute, else the tea won't be right." The last of the apples disappeared, and she brought the plate to the sink, adding it to a pail half full of water. "I should not have reacted as I did. I apologize if I gave you a bad moment."

She might have given him a serious wound, but her aloneness cut at Ashton too. He didn't know Matilda Bryce well, but she was a woman alone, and she'd trusted him enough to give him a temporary place in her household.

He owed her more than she knew.

"I'm not your in-laws," he said. "I'm a wealthy man, half-Scot, half-English, and all unhappy to be biding in London. I'm very appreciative to have a fortnight of peace and quiet before I tend to less enjoyable pursuits, but if you've enemies, Matilda, you'd better tell me."

The kettle began to squeal in earnest. She wrapped her apron under the handle to take the kettle off the hearth and set it on the hob. While Ashton finished with the apples, Matilda measured tea from the caddy into a strainer and filled a plain brown teapot from the steaming kettle.

"I don't know if I have enemies," she said, setting the kettle back on the hob. "But when in doubt, it's best to assume one does. Will you stay for tea?"

Ashton wanted to resume his nap on the big, soft bed upstairs, but he also wanted a bite of warm apple tart, consumed fresh from the oven and cooled with a dash of cream.

The way to a man's heart was surely through his belly. Why was there no handy aphorism for the way to a woman's heart?

"One cup," he said. "Though you must make me a promise."

She put the lid on the teapot and regarded him sidelong. "I don't make promises lightly."

She wasn't a countess burdened by a title, and yet, he hadn't seen her do *anything* lightly.

Which was a damned shame. "In my case, please assume I'm your friend. You needn't brandish a knife at me to defend your tarts. Agreed?"

She used a folded towel to remove a steaming dish from the oven, heat and cinnamon wafting across the kitchen as the unbaked pie took the place of the tarts.

"Don't sneak up on me, don't lie to me, and we have an agreement." She set the pan on the wooden counter. "We have an agreement, *Ashton.*"

They shared an apple tart, complete with cream and washed down with hot, strong tea. It was the best damned apple tart the eighth Earl of Kilkenney had ever eaten.

* * *

For so long, Matilda had sustained herself with anger. Anger didn't leave room for self-pity, regret, or defeat. Anger was a forward-moving emotion. Without anger, Matilda doubted armies could bear to engage in the atrocities of the battlefield, much less find pride in victory.

Without anger, Matilda could never have endured her marriage.

And yet, like most sturdy armor, anger was heavy and made the combatant clumsy.

She'd been mentally counting the days when Mr. Fenwick had brought Solomon back to the kitchen. Counting the days, slice by slice, until the seven-year anniversary of her husband's death, and finally, finally, that number was below 365.

Then she'd heard a man's voice, caught the word "fugitive," and sensed size and strength at her back. The rest had been instinct and awkwardness.

The least she owed a lodger she'd nearly stabbed was half an apple tart. Solomon was enjoying a teaspoon of cream as a peace offering as well.

"Did you make these tarts for Helen?" Mr. Fenwick asked.

"Yes, though I like them too. Helen is trying to be good. It won't last, but one should reward effort."

"What do you know of her sister?"

His manners were impeccable, and yet, Mr. Fenwick enjoyed his food. No other lodger had presumed to eat with Matilda in her kitchen, and she enjoyed the sight of a fellow who relished his sustenance.

In bed, Ashton Fenwick would be lusty. He'd revel in pleasures of the flesh, not undertake them with a combination of dread and resentment. He'd be affectionate *and* amorous, a combination Matilda had never encountered firsthand.

"I know next to nothing of Sissy," she said, "except that she'll introduce Helen to the wrong sort of man all too soon. Helen seems resigned, and I hate that."

Mr. Fenwick's spoon clattered to the bowl. "The girl can't be but eight years old."

"She's probably close to ten. Children raised in chronic poverty are scrawny. Helen has some time before maturation costs her the last of her safety, but not enough time. Would you like another cup of tea?"

Mr. Fenwick sat across from Matilda at the worktable, making the kitchen feel smaller, but also—Matilda was honest with herself—*safer.* He'd plucked the knife from her hand faster than she could blink, and he kept a knife in his boot too.

He held up his cup for Matilda to pour him more tea. "What I'd like is for wee Helen to grow up in safety. Do you think she'd return to Scotland with me?"

"If there's cobbler involved, she might." But would Matilda permit the girl to leave with Mr. Fenwick when the time came? Part of her said no, that Mr. Fenwick was quite the unknown quantity, but another part of her wanted to thrust Helen into his arms and tell him to depart at dawn.

She poured her own tea and, because her nerves had been given a start, allowed herself a dash of cream and sugar.

"But you would not want Helen to go off in the company of a strange man," Mr. Fenwick said. "I don't blame you. I have friends here in London, though. Good friends, well placed, and even titled. One of them might make a place for Helen as a scullery maid."

Matilda knew people in London too, well placed and even titled. That was a risk she took, but also part of her defense. Nobody would think to look for her among the working classes, wearing plain cloaks and tired straw hats.

"Helen wouldn't last a day as a scullery maid," Matilda said. "I've kept the girl's attention for an afternoon here and there, shown her a few things, but she's feral, only half tame, and that's kept her safe. You'd have your hands full convincing her to accept another lifestyle."

Mr. Fenwick scraped his spoon through the combination of cream, apple juice, and cinnamon at the bottom of his bowl.

"She doesn't want the title," he said, which made no sense. "She's better off in the wild, by her lights. Perhaps she and I can compromise. She might enjoy working in a dairy, for example, or as a goose girl or shepherd. Plenty of fresh air, nobody much to bother her, and the good company of the beasts."

That recitation convinced Matilda that Mr. Fenwick had land and lots of it. He wasn't merely rich, he was landed wealth, the kind British society most respected.

So far, Matilda respected him too, which was something of a revelation, and also a relief.

"You will please not make promises to Helen that you cannot keep," Matilda said. "Rebuilding a child's broken trust in her elders is a delicate undertaking, and Helen's trust is in tiny pieces scattered all over the slums of London."

Mr. Fenwick took Matilda's bowl and scraped the dregs from it as well. "Is that what happened with your in-laws? You joined their family expecting a decent match and found yourself surrounded by enemies, your trust in pieces?"

More or less. "I joined my husband's family hoping for a decent match and was sorely disappointed, as my father knew I would be."

"So your father broke faith with you," Mr. Fenwick said, setting the second bowl down. "That had to hurt. My parents weren't entirely honest with me either, though they had their reasons."

He took the dishes to the wash bucket, then returned for the tea cups. The experience of a man other than a footman cleaning up after her was novel and gratifying, despite the impulse to shoo him back to his seat. Matilda had certainly cleaned up after an endless procession of men.

"Thank you," she said. "For your company and for your concern for Helen. I haven't known what to do for the girl, other than put some manners on her when I could tempt her to sit still for a bowl of porridge."

"She's an apt pupil, which encourages me, and she's decided to trust you, which should encourage you."

"I'm encouraged," Helen said, swinging in through the window above the sideboard. "I smelled the apples cooking from halfway up the alley."

"Helen, what have I told you about coming in the windows?" Matilda retorted. "Use the doors, or stay out of my house."

Helen picked up the cat and took a seat at the end of the table. "Mr. Fenwick said you were followed last night. I was being careful."

"She climbs in the laundry room window too," Matilda said. "Pippa leaves it open for fresh air and then forgets to close it."

"Getting to be a snug fit." Helen scratched Solomon's chin and touched noses with him. "Too much good food. Right, old Sol?"

The cat shamelessly craned his neck in pursuit of more affection.

"We needn't be concerned about last night," Mr. Fenwick said. "I've been assured the pursuer was a journalist, probably trailing me rather than Mrs. Bryce."

"'Cause you're a bloody, wealthy—?"

Mr. Fenwick put a gentle hand over Helen's mouth. "Because I'm a wealthy provincial who has declined to take on the expensive lodgings I'd arranged for on the date agreed. The newsmen apparently hang about the Albany like flies hover over a dung heap, and one of them must have seen me on the premises there."

"What a delightful analogy," Matilda said.

And what a towering relief. A stupid, nosy journalist—what an enormous, huge, wonderful relief.

"Alas for me," Mr. Fenwick said, "I must return to the Albany. I'll need some proper clothes to meet a friend for dinner tomorrow night, so Helen, if you're intent on begging a tart from Mrs. Bryce, do it now."

"She'll spoil her supper," Matilda said.

"You and Mr. Fenwick just spoiled yours," Helen retorted, "and Sol spoiled his too."

Mr. Fenwick plucked the cat from Helen's arms. "If that's your best attempt at importuning, you've some work to do, Helen. With what letter does the name Bryce begin?"

"B."

"Name me three other words beginning with *b*."

"Bugger, bloody, bedamned."

"Three words that begin with *d*."

"Damned, deuced, dratted."

"Dear me," Matilda interjected. "I suppose I'd better stuff some apple tart in your mouth before you turn the air blue with your vocabulary. Tart begins with *t*, by the way."

She rose to cut Helen a quarter of a tart.

"Try a vowel," Mr. Fenwick said. "Three words that begin with *e*."

Helen looked thoughtful. "Enormous, equipped, earl."

Oh dear, indeed. Equipped was slang for rich.

"What?" Helen said, her gaze uncertain. "That's three."

"So it is," Matilda replied. "Three very unusual words to call to mind at once. When you've washed your hands, you may eat your tart."

Helen was off the chair and down the corridor to the washroom as Mr. Fenwick set the cat on the floor.

"I'll work with her," he said. "Provided she doesn't reduce me to tears in the middle of the street. Thank you for the tart and the company."

The thanks ought to go the other way, though Matilda couldn't admit that, not yet. Maybe in two weeks, when she knew Mr. Fenwick had one boot out the door. He'd probably take Helen with him, and that thought gave Matilda a pang.

"I'm off to retrieve my jacket," he said. "Make her say grace before she eats next time."

"Ambitious, but a good plan. Good day, Mr. Fenwick."

He leaned closer. "Ashton. The child's off pretending to get her hands wet, Matilda."

Matilda put a hand on his shoulder and kissed his cheek. "Ashton. Good day."

His expression went from puzzled to pleased, and then he was sauntering up the steps, off to retrieve finery from one of the finest lodgings in the whole of London.

Surely Helen would be safe in his care, even if she accompanied him when he left London? Safer than she'd be popping in and out of Matilda's laundry room window.

On that thought, Matilda sat with Helen while the child devoured her apple tart and cast about for words that began with *f*.

Fenwick, faraway, flirtation.

"Tell Mr. Fenwick you're ready to leave," Matilda said, stuffing Helen's braids more neatly under the girl's cap.

And don't tell him that I wish, when he leaves London, he'd take me along too.

* * *

"If you wait much longer, it will be too late, Uncle."

Stephen's knee bounced, for all his warning came out in a languid drawl. The boy couldn't sit still, couldn't be patient, couldn't allow his uncle's common sense to prevail over high-handed impetuosity.

"My good fellow," Charles, Earl of Drexel, replied, "we still have nearly a year to locate your step-mama. During that year, the funds you're so anxious to inherit are in good hands and the warrant for her arrest remains valid."

Drexel had had this discussion with Stephen in this same library at least six times a year for the past six years. Drexel's hands were the ones holding Stephen's fortune, and Drexel had no intention of letting go until the last possible instant.

"Hang the damned warrant," Stephen said, popping to his feet. "Locating Step-mama has proved a fruitless endeavor."

Unlike his late father, Stephen was damnably good-looking. Tall, blond, pleasant-featured with an athletic build. Drexel suspected his nephew had been a cuckoo, for poor Althorpe had been distinguished by a foul temper rather than a fair appearance.

"Besides," Stephen went on, "I'd rather locate proof of Step-mama's demise. That would save us the trouble of a trial. Damned Bow Street probably took Papa's coin to help her hide."

The longer Matilda hid, the longer Drexel could manage his late brother's estate. Once she was declared dead, Stephen would become the sole heir, and his squandering of the family wealth would begin in earnest, while the earldom's resources were already dwindling by the year.

"Why don't you stop around Bow Street and have a word with the runners?" Drexel suggested. "The Season hasn't truly started, and you surely have an hour or two to spare?"

Stephen paused before the window, sunlight turning his hair into a golden halo—an effect he had been exploiting since childhood.

"Uncle, you jest. Between my boot-maker, my haberdasher, my glove-maker, my tailor… my time is hardly my own. Besides, Bow Street is full of criminals."

How could one young man be so greedy and so lazy? At twenty-four, Stephen knew everything and everybody and had a frivolous use for every groat. The wrong sort of woman fell all over herself to attract his notice, and he enthusiastically yielded it, along with half his quarterly allowance. Stephen already had two bastard daughters, of which he took scandalously little notice.

"I'll send a note to the runners," Drexel replied, "but with polite society thronging to London, now is hardly the time to revive old scandals. Chasing Matilda to ground—if she's still alive—can wait until summer."

Stephen took out a gold snuffbox with an odalisque painted on the lid, flipped it open with his fourth finger, and helped himself to a pinch. Filthy habit, no matter how elegantly the boy sniffed and postured.

"Justice delayed is justice denied, Uncle. Step-mama ought to have been hanged by the neck until dead six years ago. A murderess is a murderess."

"And a scandal is a scandal. If you've any thought to taking a bride this year, you'll let Matilda kick up her heels for another few months."

Stephen snapped the snuffbox closed. "If Step-mama reached France, there's no telling where she may be now. I want her found, and you will cease pressuring me to marry. I'm far too young to consider taking a wife."

No, he wasn't, though God pity the woman who had Stephen for a husband.

"I've had the ports watched closely for years," Drexel said. "A woman traveling alone, much less a gently bred young woman with a very attractive figure, does not take ship without a number of men remarking it."

"Step-mama wasn't that pretty." Stephen snorted a second pinch of snuff.

Matilda had been exquisite, poised between girlhood and womanhood, her youth and vivaciousness enough to warm any man's blood—almost any man's blood.

"You mustn't let me keep you from your appointments," Drexel said, rising from his desk. "I was young once and recall well the pleasures a bachelor enjoys in spring. Try not to overspend your allowance."

Stephen's signature charming smile appeared, as Drexel had known it would. "As to that, Uncle, I've had a few extraordinary expenses, played a bit too deep last week. Would a small advance be possible?"

"Stop around at Basingstoke's tomorrow afternoon," Drexel said. "He's been warned." *Again.* Drexel's solicitors were nothing if not responsive.

"You are the best of uncles," Stephen said, bowing with a flourish. "My thanks. Let me know if you hear anything from Bow Street."

Drexel was not the best of uncles, but he was a competent accountant. Every penny of Stephen's "small advances" came out of funds the boy stood to inherit. That would come as something of a shock, but Stephen was overdue for any shock that might result in a sense of financial responsibility.

"If there's any news to report regarding Matilda, I'll alert you on the instant."

Stephen was on his handsome way not two minutes later, ready to do his part for the trades and the game girls. To Drexel, the most puzzling aspect of Stephen's behavior was why the same pleasures—if drunkenness, stupid wagers, and whores qualified as pleasures—year after year hadn't bored the boy silly.

His father had certainly had no taste for diversion, though poor Althorpe had chosen a lovely second wife. Lovely, and more clever than anybody had realized, damn the luck.

Though Drexel had spoken the truth: Matilda was too pretty to take ship without some randy sailor noticing. She was also too lovely to hide in the shabbier neighborhoods of London without occasionally being spotted.

* * *

"I'm to give you this." Hazelton passed a folded piece of foolscap across the dinner table. "My countess has been busy."

Ashton did not want to take the piece of paper, but they were at Hazelton's club at an hour when the dining room was full. Viscounts, earls, sons of dukes, and the like were consuming steak, port, and gossip on all sides.

"A busy woman should always hold a man's notice," Ashton said, unfolding the paper. A list of names marched down the page in an elegant, legible script, not a blot to be seen. "These are all females."

"Maggie started with the ones to avoid," Hazelton said. "The young ladies who claimed to have spent a year in Paris directly after their come outs, though nobody saw them there. The ones whose mamas play too deep, the ones whose sisters are on a perpetual visit to an aunt in Wales."

The list had at least two dozen names on it. "My thanks. I'll make it a point to seek these ladies out."

Hazelton looked up sharply, then glanced about the room. "I did not give you that list so you might set one of them up as a mistress. That lot is to be left alone, Fenwick."

Ashton's companion was a shrewd man, and he'd doubtless omitted use of the Kilkenney title in these privileged preserves on purpose.

"You regard them as too decent to become mistresses," Ashton said, "but not decent enough to be wives?"

"Exactly."

Hazelton placed their order with the waiter, who was more punctiliously attired than if Cherbourne had dressed him.

"You make no sense, Hazelton," Ashton said. "I'm not a paragon, that I should be inflicting myself on some maidenly innocent, and yet, I'm not exactly wicked, despite my dubious antecedents. Your list is the perfect place to start."

"Don't you dare, or my countess will disown me."

The waiter reappeared, presenting a bottle of wine as if he were about to perform some sleight of hand involving the contents. Hazelton nodded, then sampled the contents and nodded again, after which the waiter poured precisely the same amount into each of two glasses, bowed, and withdrew.

"Tell your countess that you are not my nanny," Ashton said. "And remind her that I am not some empty-headed debutante who needs my mama and papa choosing my spouse for me."

Matilda, who was by no means empty-headed, had endured a rotten marriage thanks to the one person who ought to have been safeguarding her happiness. How many of the debutantes on offer were doomed to the same fate?

"Your situation is complicated," Hazelton said. "Though you are wealthy. That doesn't hurt."

"Don't delude yourself. Wealth matters inordinately."

"A tasteful display of wealth matters," Hazelton countered. "If you're interested in setting up a mistress, I can make some recommendations."

Good God, was nothing private in this bastion of masculine gentility? "Now you're procuring for me? I assure you, in this regard, I'm capable of fending for myself."

Though Ashton hadn't done any fending in far too long. When a steward offered a lady a turn about the dance floor, so to speak, she knew exactly who and what she was getting, without any confusion on either side. When an earl made the same offer, all manner of aspirations developed on the lady's part, none of them having to do with a mutually agreeable, temporary sharing of pleasure.

Once again the waiter intruded, this time bearing plates of thick steak and two bowls, each holding a baked potato from which the skin had been removed.

"I'd prefer my meat cooked," Ashton said.

The waiter's brows shot up, and he looked to Hazelton, as if Ashton might have accidently used a word that didn't mean at all what Ashton thought it meant.

"You heard the man." Hazelton twirled a languid hand. "Tell the chef to give that steak another turn."

"A chef is involved," Ashton said as the waiter strutted away, nose in the air. "That explains it. They can criticize plain English fare, intimidate, and pontificate, but I've yet to find one who can cook a satisfying meal. Where's the butter?"

"One uses the gravy and a dash of salt."

"One uses butter." Helen knew that, for God's sake, and teaching her the letter p—pointless, perishing, polite society—would have been a more engaging discussion than the topic Hazelton had raised.

"Butter is for bread, Fenwick."

"None of which graces this table. I'll not be taking a mistress."

The Lord of Culinary Disapproval came back to the table, and Hazelton asked for both bread and butter, which request was met with yet another bow.

"A mistress might be a good idea," Hazelton said. "The right woman could be a strategic ally, keeping you apprised of developments you'd otherwise learn of too late. Then too, if you chose somebody of, say, Mrs. Bellingham's caliber, you might elevate your status in the eyes of your rivals."

Ashton hadn't taken so much as a bite of potato, and already his belly was sour. "You are telling me that if I pay the right woman for her favors, her cachet will improve my own, though she's disgraced and I'm titled? And what sort of loyalty goes only to the highest bidder, Hazelton? What of friendship, or giving a fellow a chance on his own merits?"

"That's all well and good on the cricket pitch," Hazelton said, "but matchmaking in Mayfair is the biggest high-stakes gamble in the realm. Finding the right spouse is deadly serious business, and if you sentimentalize it, you're sure to end up with the wrong wife."

Before Ashton could retort, the waiter reappeared, a sizzling piece of charred meat on a platter before him. He deposited the meat on Ashton's plate, bowed, and withdrew without comment.

Hazelton was trying not to smirk, while Ashton's irritation was genuine.

"Somebody raised this animal from a calf, investing at least two years of pasture, fodder, and shelter, and then sent it off to market hoping for a fair price. The meat is wasted, along with the fodder and the two years, because

I've offended the tyrant in the kitchen who calls himself a chef. Tell me why I should search for a wife in a place such as this, Hazelton. Why shouldn't I choose a name at random from this list?"

Hazelton was saved from replying by the reappearance of the waiter, who put a dish of butter pats on the table, each imprinted with the shape of St. Edward's crown.

"You forgot the bread," Ashton said.

The waiter bowed. "My apologies."

The damned cipher was making excuses to disrupt the meal, the better to collect gossip. Ashton knew this, the way he knew when his horse was about to pitch a fit out of sheer boredom.

"Shall you eat that?" Hazelton asked, gesturing with his fork at the ruined steak.

"I'll take it home for my landlady's cat," Ashton said. "He's fierce and none too particular about his sustenance."

"While you survive on what?"

"Apple tarts," Ashton said, "fresh from the oven and slathered in cream." Matilda Bryce also set her table with honesty. If she didn't approve of a man, she brandished a knife at him. She wouldn't gossip about him behind his back or play games with steak and bread.

"You look dyspeptic," Hazelton said around a bite of rare steak. "Not like a man contemplating apple tarts."

Ashton waited until the bread had been brought to the table before replying.

"I'm contemplating lists, Hazelton. Your countess, without much thought, came up with two dozen names of young ladies I'm to avoid. My name is doubtless appearing on lists all over Mayfair, or my title is, and without having met me, I'll be deemed worth a look. I'm not a man with whom some young lady will have to rub along, or make children, I'm a title and a bank account. That is no way to find lasting happiness."

Hazelton paused, knife in one hand, fork in the other. "You are a romantic. My sister suspected as much."

"I'm *human*," Ashton retorted, "and you are a hypocrite. You didn't find your countess by making lists and eliminating the dubious contestants. You fell in love and snatched her up, and now you counsel me against letting my heart guide me similarly. Not well done of you."

Hazelton moved his potato to his plate and swam a bite about in the meat juices. "Maggie has cousins as yet unmarried. I'll introduce you to them, and Windhams generally marry for love. It's not unheard of."

As the rest of Hazelton's steak disappeared, Ashton figured out what the master of discretion wasn't saying.

A wealthy duke's offspring married for love. An earl from the Borders whose pedigree was checkered probably wouldn't have that luxury. Ashton needed an heir if his brother's progeny weren't to be deprived of much of the family wealth upon Ashton's demise.

And to produce a legitimate heir, Ashton needed not merely a wife, but a countess.

He parted from Hazelton without further mention of difficult topics, and yet, on the walk back to Pastry Lane, when Ashton should have been thinking about prospective countesses, lists, and settlements, he was preoccupied with a soft kiss to his cheek, offered by a woman who trusted nobody, had no fortune, and kept many secrets.

He wanted more of her kisses, and not just to his cheek.

A problem, that, or a challenge, and Ashton Fenwick relished a challenge.

CHAPTER FIVE

"You seen Mr. Fenwick when he went off to dinner," Helen said, settling to the carpet cross-legged. "You could do worse, Mrs. B. He's a gent, the genuine article."

"As long as he pays his rent on time," Matilda replied, "he can be a crossing sweeper, for all I care. You're not to get ideas, Helen."

Though Matilda had had a few ideas at the sight of Ashton Fenwick in evening finery. His entire demeanor had changed, from gentry new to town, to a man about town, complete with gold and amber cravat pin and cuff links.

Gold, not pewter or silver, and his walking stick had been topped and ferruled with gold. He'd worn a signet ring too and a grassy scent that had tempted Matilda to steal another kiss from him.

Helen watched Matilda's embroidery needle in the flickering light of the parlor sconces. "I don't dare tell Sissy what I'm about with Mr. Fenwick. Sissy will take him away from me."

Matilda put down her hoop. "I beg your pardon?"

"I saw him first," Helen said, plucking at the carpet fringe. "He's mine. Sissy can have all the other gents in London, but Mr. Fenwick should be mine. I'm learning how to look after his horse, I look after his boots, he teaches me letters. I think we should keep him."

We? This went far beyond getting ideas. "Helen, people aren't books to be hoarded up on a shelf. Mr. Fenwick is leaving in less than two weeks."

"He likes it here. You can ask him to stay. Sissy says gents are easy to persuade if you give them what they want."

Mr. Fenwick had made no advances whatsoever, which was probably why Matilda could entertain odd notions about him.

She really ought not to have kissed his cheek. "Sissy will have diseases to show for taking that approach, Helen."

"Don't say bad things about my Sissy. She gives me food sometimes." Lately, Helen had been doing more to look out for her sister than the other way around, which might explain why her defense of Sissy had a perfunctory quality.

"Mr. Fenwick is an impressive gentleman," Matilda said, "but he's a lodger. Lodgers move on, and my job is to provide them comfortable accommodations for a price while they're under my roof. It's time you moved on to bed, Helen."

Helen grinned. "Oh, right. Bedtime. Will you tuck me in and read me a story, Mrs. B? Listen to my prayers?"

Helen might disdain that ritual aloud, but some part of her doubtless longed for it.

"I'll swat your backside if you don't take yourself off. If Mr. Fenwick wants to go for another gallop in the morning, you'd best have his riding boots ready."

"I already did 'em," Helen said, rising from the floor in one move. "Being a general tote 'em is hard work, and I like sleeping in a bed."

Matilda wanted to hug the child good-night, give her a kiss, a pat on the shoulder, something. "You're earning your wages, but if Mr. Fenwick is asking too much of you, let me know."

Helen paused at the door to the parlor. "Will you make him pay me more?"

"I'll make him give you a half day, the same as Pippa gets, and time off for Sunday services."

Helen shuddered. "No preachers, please. All they talk about is lakes of fire and eternal damnation. London winters are damnation enough for me."

"Get to bed, Helen, and don't forget to clean your teeth and wash."

The child darted away, her footfalls suggesting she took the steps two at a time.

"And tell your Maker you're grateful for your many blessings," a masculine voice called up the steps. Mr. Fenwick appeared in the door to Matilda's parlor. "I locked the front door, in case you were concerned."

"I would have locked it before I went to bed."

Mercy, but he was a striking figure. Many gentlemen padded their shoulders, even their calves, to look more impressive in their evening attire. Ashton Fenwick needed no padding. His adornments were understated by London standards, and yet, he dazzled.

"May I sit?"

Matilda didn't usually allow her lodgers into her private rooms, but then, her lodgers didn't usually ask admittance.

"You may. If you'd close the door, we're less likely to be overheard by a certain general factotum."

"Helen, go to bed," he bellowed up the stairs, "or you'll get no cream for your porridge in the morning."

A door closed on the third floor.

Mr. Fenwick also closed the parlor door and took the only other chair. "She needn't have waited up for me. It's not like I'd allow her to be my valet."

"Have you a valet?"

"My valet has me," Mr. Fenwick said, staring at his tasseled Hessian boots. "He's a fussy little martinet who makes much out of nothing and spies for my family. I don't like him. Did you have a come out, Matilda?"

Working-class women did not have come outs. "If you dislike your valet, why keep him on?"

"Because to discharge him would cause upheaval, and that I have been unwilling to do. My sister-in-law was carrying, or had a new baby in the nursery, or somebody was teething. I always had a reason to keep the peace, and Cherbourne grew complacent. Then too, I was supposed to take a wife and I had hoped she might replace my valet."

Only very lofty gentlemen kept a valet when they had a wife. Perhaps Mr. Fenwick was newly wealthy, or not so terribly wealthy after all.

"Did you fancy a particular lady?" This was none of Matilda's business, but in eleven days, Mr. Fenwick would be gone, and confidences exchanged with his former landlady late at night would matter little.

"I fancy a rare and particular woman," he said, removing his cravat pin. "She is a commonsensical creature, good-natured, though she doesn't suffer fools. She's attractive without being vain, also warm-hearted at least where family and friends are concerned. She fancies me for myself, not for my family wealth or connections, and she's not afraid to laugh or cry, or dress me down should I need it. She has my undying loyalty, and my only wish in life is to keep her safe and make her happy."

"Ouch!" Matilda dropped her hoop and stuck her finger in her mouth. The taste of blood was metallic and unpleasant.

Mr. Fenwick took out a handkerchief, pried Matilda's hand free, and wrapped the white linen around her finger.

"My lady also swears," he said, "when the moment calls for it."

He withdrew his hand, and Matilda was left holding his handkerchief around her finger. "You speak very highly of this woman, and yet, she must have refused you."

The idiot. Even drunk, Ashton Fenwick would never raise his voice at a woman in anger, never embarrass her before others, or blame her for problems she hadn't caused.

"I haven't met her," he said, smiling wistfully. "She'll find me soon, I hope. I've grown lonely waiting for her. You never did answer my question. Did you have a come out?"

Matilda was preoccupied with Mr. Fenwick's admission that he hadn't met his ideal woman, and yet, his list of attributes wasn't that ambitious. He sought a good woman, kind, pleasant, and affectionate. Not a paragon or a great beauty or an heiress. Why couldn't Althorpe have sought such reasonable qualities in a wife? Why had he needed silent, pretty perfection?

"I had a come out," she said, "of a sort. My father's wealth was tied up in investments and properties, and I had only an aunt to introduce me about."

Why bother introducing a niece to polite society when that niece was all but spoken for? Though Aunt Huberta had tried. But for her efforts, Matilda would not have been presented at court, or had any Season at all.

"What was it like?" Mr. Fenwick asked. "Being a debutante during the London Season?"

Matilda might have expected that question from Pippa, if the girl left off mooning over the neighbor's eldest son long enough.

"My come out was anxious," she said, thinking back to the time before marriage had blighted her life. "And disappointing. I kept waiting for some sense of radiance to come over me, some wonder, but week by week, I was more bewildered, tired, and disappointed. My gowns were the same simple, pale creations worn by every other young lady, my dance partners the same spotty boys or gouty barons. I began to suspect that women sought marriage as an alternative to sore feet and boredom."

She fell silent as unexpected compassion for that unhappy, helpless young woman rose. Why had that girl's expectations differed so greatly from reality? She'd had no chance to defend her self-respect, to guard her heart, or develop allies.

"Has the bleeding stopped?" Mr. Fenwick asked.

"I beg—oh." Matilda peered at her injured finger. "Yes, thank you. I haven't stabbed myself for ages. I've got blood on your handkerchief. I'll soak it in cold water overnight, and it should wash out."

"You must keep it," Mr. Fenwick said. "What would have made your Season happy?"

He was an odd man, admitting loneliness and finding no awkwardness in a late-evening chat with a mere widowed landlady.

"A different marriage would have made me happy," Matilda said. "No one can know how a union will progress, but my husband was a cold man, and even in my innocence, I had misgivings. I should have heeded them, not that it would have done any good. My father's mind was made up."

"I'm sorry, Matilda. Sorry your heart was broken. We're tender-hearted when we're young."

The wistfulness was back, and Matilda let it pull at her. "You are so very old, I take it?"

"I am old enough. So are you. Why did you kiss me?"

She had no idea. "You are in a mood tonight, Mr. Fenwick."

"Ashton. Humor me, please. I had a disagreeable dinner with a man who professes to be my friend, and the upcoming weeks will be worse yet."

Matilda spread his handkerchief on her lap in anticipation of folding it. One corner bore a family crest—a unicorn couchant with roses vining its horn. The opposite corner was spotted with her blood, redder than the roses.

"I like you," she said. "I don't like much of anybody, and very few men, but so far, I like you. This is an interesting seal."

"Our land lies astride the Border, such as the Border is these days, hence the Tudor rose entangling a Scottish unicorn. I like you too, Matilda."

His admission was so simple, and yet, no man had ever told her that before. She'd been desired, coveted, flattered, and physically admired as a man might admire a healthy heifer, but not *liked*.

"Even when I wave a knife at you?"

"Especially then. I like your spirit, your quiet ferocity, your kindness to Helen, and your apple tarts."

Warmth bloomed in Matilda's heart. Stupid, silly, and precious. "Helen is growing attached to you."

"You're shy," Mr. Fenwick said, "or maybe you're out of practice. When somebody pays you a compliment, you thank them. As for Helen, I'm growing attached to her too. My horse, who is an excellent judge of character, approves of her."

"If you encourage her attachment, she'll be devastated when you leave."

Dark eyes regarded Matilda levelly. "Will she?"

"Helen isn't as tough as she wants the world to think she is."

Mr. Fenwick stood, and he was so very tall in his boots. "I will consider Helen's situation, between now and when I remove to the Albany, but for now, she's safe upstairs in bed, her hands nominally clean for a change and her belly full."

"You're off to bed?" Matilda said, folding up his handkerchief and setting it aside.

"I'm away to my slumbers, though there's something I'd like to do first."

Matilda's heart beat faster, and an old memory came to her of standing on the edge of a ballroom, the orchestra tuning up, the sets beginning to form. Would she be asked to dance, or would she sit out, or best of all—stroll the terrace on the arm of a witty, charming gentleman?

She'd forgotten that old vulnerability, or maybe it was a strength—the courage to hope—and now here it was, back at the most unlikely time.

"What will your last task for the day be, Mr. Fenwick?"

He drew her to her feet. "Not a task, but rather, an expression of gratitude. I'd like to kiss you good night."

* * *

Ashton had wandered the streets of London after his dinner with Hazelton, thinking over the coming weeks. The countess's list was tucked in a pocket for later study, and homesickness had kept him company along every street.

London stank, outside of Mayfair proper. The stars weren't in evidence, because even in spring, coal smoke obscured the night sky. Noise was unceasing, and game girls flirted from doorways while elegant coaches tooled past mere yards away.

Ewan had no use for London, which was some consolation. The Scottish peerage didn't travel south en masse when Parliament sat, but rather, sent a small delegation, whom Ewan referred to as the hostage party or the forlorn hope.

When Ashton had turned his steps to Pastry Lane, he'd felt as if he were arriving at a sanctuary, a small island of sanity and peace in a heaving sea of loud, noisome, striving humanity. Matilda's stoop was adorned with potted heartsease, and he'd sat on her front steps in his lordly finery eavesdropping on the quiet exchange of the ladies in the parlor.

Lodgers move on.

Ashton wanted to go home, not move on, and yet, he wanted Matilda Bryce too. When he drew her to her feet, he saw acknowledgment of mutual attraction in her gaze.

Acknowledgment was not the same as assent. "As much as I'd like to kiss you," Ashton said, "I'd rather we kissed each other."

The curtains were drawn, fluttering in the mild evening breeze. Nobody would see Ashton and Matilda standing so close in the candlelit parlor.

"What is the difference if you kiss me, or we kiss each other?" Matilda asked.

Her husband must have been stupid in addition to cold-hearted. "This is me kissing you," Ashton replied, brushing his mouth over hers. "Not quite a mutual endeavor."

"This dinner with your friend upset you," she said, stroking his hair back from his brow.

Ashton wanted to move into her caress as a cat pushed against a friendly hand. "The conversation tonight saddened me. Difficult negotiations lie ahead, and I've put them off for too long."

"And I'm to kiss it better?"

As a younger man, Ashton would have taken himself upstairs and indulged in solitary pleasures rather than endure this exchange. Matilda was entitled to her caution, though. All ladies were, and he'd had to learn caution as well.

"When was the last time anybody kissed your hurts better, Matilda?" He captured her hand in his and kissed the finger she'd pricked earlier. "I'm not proposing a marital alliance to end twenty years of war. All I'm asking for is a kiss."

He sought to share a moment of sanctuary and pleasure amid a season of posturing and foolishness.

Her hand slid around to Ashton's nape, her touch cool and confident.

Matilda wasn't anchoring herself so much as learning his contours. She brushed her fingers over hair growing too long for fashion, then braced her other hand on his chest.

She glossed her mouth over his lips, repeating his overture more slowly. Ashton held still, letting her decide whether to venture on or retreat. A breeze licked at the curtains, and one of the sconces guttered.

Maybe that was a sign to her, for she embarked on a kiss that fit with shadows and quiet. Her explorations were tentative to the point that Ashton wondered if she'd done much kissing even during her marriage.

He brought her closer, and she yielded, becoming a sweet, soft weight against his chest. When Ashton ran his tongue over her lips, she reciprocated, but didn't seem to understand that he wanted *in*. Wanted into her mouth, into her mind.

Into her heart, to the extent a temporary liaison could involve the heart.

He went slowly, enjoying all the curves he'd missed for so long. Feminine shoulders both elegant and sturdy, the taper of a female back, the swell of a woman's hips, the fullness of her derriere. The Creator had surely improved on the initial model when he'd fashioned woman, and Ashton reveled in all the wonders of having Matilda Bryce in his arms.

She warmed to the kiss, pressing close, clutching at the back of Ashton's head and pulling his hair. Arousal tugged at him as well, a friend who'd been away for too long.

"Does that qualify as kissing each other?" she asked, subsiding against Ashton's chest.

"We did, indeed, share a kiss. Thank you, Matilda." For a few moments, polite society, burned steak, and stupid lists had faded from Ashton's awareness. He owed her for that, if nothing else.

"Now what?" she asked.

Now, Ashton could embark on negotiations of a sort he'd been conducting since he'd turned fifteen. More kisses, bolder caresses, whispered promises to use a sheath and withdraw, because Ashton put little stock in an apothecary's tricks.

Secret touches between a woman's legs that tempted her past propriety, attention paid to her breasts that bespoke pleasures yet to come.

He knew the entire dance, and all of its variations, but he was also coming to know Matilda Bryce.

"Now, my dear, I hope you dream of me."

She relaxed, which meant Ashton had guessed correctly. Matilda was not a merry widow, ready to pounce on the next randy swain who yodeled beneath her window.

"I'll likely dream of you long after you've gone," she said, patting his chest. "They will be pleasant dreams."

She was both complimenting him and reminding him that his lease was very short-term indeed. He ought to be relieved that she sought nothing from him but timely rent and pleasant dreams.

Ashton wasn't relieved at all.

He stepped back, keeping his arms about her shoulders. "I will go up to bed. I left a parcel on the stairs that I should take down to the kitchen first, some meat for the cat from Lord Hazelton's club. The chef ruined it, as chefs often do, but it needn't go entirely to waste."

Matilda slipped away and busied herself putting embroidery paraphernalia into a workbasket. "You dined with a lord?"

"The earl is a neighbor at a distance up north, and a friend of sorts. He's one of few people I know in London, and I didn't want to offend him, though I'd rather not dine at his club again."

Matilda's mood had shifted in the last few moments, from drowsy and kissable, back to the landlady with much to do. When her workbasket was tidy, she closed and locked both windows.

"I'll wish you good night, Mr. Fenwick."

"I'll wish you sweet dreams, Matilda."

He was halfway out the door, the scent of overcooked steak perfuming the stairway, when he turned.

"I will go to my fate in less than two weeks, Matilda. You needn't worry that I'll tarry here and make a nuisance of myself. Any fool can see you treasure your independence and suffered greatly to arrive at it. I have no designs on your freedom. I well know how precious that freedom is."

She blew out that last candle, plunging the parlor into darkness, save for what light leaked down from the sconce on the floor above.

"I will never surrender that freedom, Ashton. Not for all the kisses in the kingdom, not for gold sovereigns raining down from the sky, not for a palace or a crown. I'm glad you grasp that."

Ashton bowed and made his way down the steps. In the dark, he delivered the ruined meat to the kitchen, then returned to his apartment, Matilda's final words ringing in his head.

She'd told him much in those few sentences.

First, she wasn't interested in marriage to *anybody*, which was a consolation. Her objection wasn't to him, it was to an institution in which she was bitterly disappointed.

Second, she and Ashton had in common a taste for self-reliance and independence. He respected that about her, even as it made him wonder about her past.

Third, she had no family worth the name. Ashton wasn't contemplating marriage for money, prestige, or power. He was marrying because his family needed him to, and for them, he'd do anything. Family had betrayed Matilda

Bryce, and what a bleak, unfathomable loneliness she must carry as a result.

Finally, Matilda Bryce wasn't interested in surrendering her freedom, but she'd not rejected the possibility of a brief, pleasurable indulgence with somebody who had no aspirations toward a greater commitment.

Ashton hadn't rejected that possibility either.

* * *

Matilda woke early the next day, an odd lightness in her heart. Then she recalled that it was the third Tuesday of the month. The weather was fair, and thus she'd make the walk to Hyde Park.

And yet, she didn't pop out of bed, head for the kitchen, and start the day's first pot of tea.

She was also aware of a lightness in her body, an *aliveness* as foreign as it was pleasurable. Ashton Fenwick had kissed her. Not a chaste peck on the cheek or the forehead, not a presumption visited upon her hand, but a kiss.

Her first real kiss, truth be known, and it had been *lovely*. Mr. Fenwick was respectful. The more intimate his touch, the more it approached reverence. Matilda had never felt so cherished or so flustered, because she did not know how to cherish him in return.

Somebody should be cherishing Ashton Fenwick. Why hadn't his bachelor status ended years ago?

Solomon hopped onto the bed, doubtless exhausted from a night of debauchery in the mews.

"Good morning."

He sat and wrapped his tail about his front paws, looking sagacious and inscrutable.

"I am contemplating foolishness, my friend."

The cat slitted his eyes.

"Mr. Fenwick is making a positive impression, and he has no designs on my future." Matilda could not see past the seventh anniversary of Althorpe's death, which would pass in less than a year. After that date, she could breathe, she could plan, she could think.

More than Mr. Fenwick's kiss, his embrace had opened in Matilda a vast awareness she'd struggled to ignore. She wasn't merely lonely, she was in the last, exhausted throes of self-reliance, without anyone to trust, without a source of affection, without anywhere safe to truly rest.

In Ashton Fenwick's arms, she could rest. When he kissed her, the 347 days remaining to her sentence disappeared along with the constant fear of discovery and the anger.

Ashton Fenwick made the fear and anger subside, and the magic of that was beguiling.

"But I must away to the park today," Matilda informed the cat, who'd begun circling at her hip. "I leave the warmth of the covers to you. Behave yourself, or you'll be living in the mews."

The threat was meaningless. Matilda could no more turn away a cat seeking shelter than she could have locked her windows against Helen's visits.

By the standards with which Matilda had been raised, she was on the poor end of respectable, but the freedom she enjoyed was an unexpected delight. If she wanted a cup of tea, she went to the kitchen and got it. If she wanted to braid her hair rather than arrange it in a bun, she braided it. She had only six dresses, one for heavy cleaning, one for Sunday services, and four that offered shapeless, drab ease of movement.

On her feet she wore house slippers, half boots, or nothing at all.

Life was simple and every choice her own, and today was a day to walk in the park. When Matilda joined Pippa in the kitchen and found a pot of hot tea waiting for her, her satisfaction was complete.

"Did you make this for me?" she asked, pouring a cup.

"That tray was for Mr. Fenwick, ma'am, but he's off to see his solicitors. Helen pinched an apple tart for her breakfast. Mr. Fenwick said he'd fend for himself when his meeting was over."

A fraction of the morning's joy dimmed, because Mr. Fenwick had mentioned dining with *an earl* last night, at his club. Titled lords figured in Matilda's worst nightmares. She didn't need them ruining her breakfast too.

"I believe I'll have an apple tart for breakfast too," she said. "You're welcome to join me, Pippa."

Pippa was the maid of all work, a refugee from a Magdalene house, where, according to Pippa, the women did laundry six and a half days a week for virtually no pay. They were not permitted to leave the facility, and even conversation among the residents was frowned on.

This life was supposed to be an improvement over streetwalking, or the endless toil Pippa had known in Jamaica. Matilda suspected medieval convents had been run with more genuine compassion than the Magdalene houses showed for the women they housed—and those convents had had a more positive impact on the ladies' eternal souls.

"I had my porridge," Pippa said. "I do like that Mr. Fenwick. He's tidy." Her words, and her approach to life, bore a hint of the island sunshine into which she'd been born. She'd been a slave amidst all that sunshine and tropical beauty, while on England's colder shores, she was free, albeit free to starve.

Also free to admire any man who caught her fancy.

Matilda hadn't been in Mr. Fenwick's rooms since he'd moved in. "Tidiness is a virtue in a lodger. You'll give his rooms a cleaning today?"

"Aye, ma'am," Pippa said, pouring water over a bowl of eggs Matilda had purchased the previous day. "Won't take me but a moment. He doesn't track in the mud, hoard his dishes, or put his boots on the furniture. You're off on your errands?"

"I beg your pardon?"

"Third Tuesday of the month," Pippa said, setting the pitcher on the counter. "If the weather's fair, you put on that awful brown walking dress and disappear for the morning. The only time you miss is when it's pouring rain. Whoever he is, I hope he appreciates you."

Matilda left off fussing with the tea things. "Mind your tongue, Pippa. I don't meet a man. I go to the park."

Pippa set an apple tart before Matilda on a plate. "Oh, that's lovely. I used to spend many an afternoon in the park. So many fine carriages and handsome gents."

What Pippa had likely done in those carriages with the handsome gents made Matilda's cheeks warm.

"Do you miss your afternoons in the park, Pippa? If I'm to replace you, some warning would be appreciated." Matilda couldn't hire just anybody. She needed competence, discretion, and common sense in a domestic who'd attract no notice.

Pippa took the place across from Matilda, something no servant would have done with the Earl of Kittridge's daughter. But then, that daughter had never ventured into a kitchen until the day she'd married and the housekeeper had given her a tour of Althorpe's domicile.

"I don't miss the flats," Pippa said. "I miss the other girls. You never met a better lot, Mrs. Bryce. We looked out for each other, but then, we had to. I was lucky—I didn't start too young, and I kept my health—but sooner or later, you get into the wrong coach, or into the wrong alley. There's some as like to beat women, some like worse than that. You can never tell the devils from the charmers, because they all have coin, and they think that means they own you. From tailors and boot-makers, the gents buy a service and a skill. When it comes to women, that coin is supposed to be worth everything she is."

Matilda's heart broke for Pippa, who spoke with a chilling detachment, and she saw in Pippa's circumstance an echo of her own situation.

"If you ever think that life is preferable to what you have here, I want to know, Pippa. Don't leave me wondering what's become of you."

Pippa rose. "I have to set an example for Helen now, don't I? She's earning a proper wage, sleeping safe at night. If I do a bunk, Helen's bound to follow me, and she's going to be a stunner with her golden hair and blue eyes. That Sissy knows it too."

The apple tart wasn't as good cold, but it was still an improvement over plain porridge. "You don't care for Sissy?"

"She puts on airs," Pippa said, gently washing a dirty egg to smooth, white perfection. "Can't abide a game girl puttin' on airs. Sooner or later, we're all put to bed with a shovel, no matter how grand we think we are."

As theologies went, Pippa's had the advantage of simplicity, but Matilda couldn't match the girl's pragmatism.

Ashton Fenwick was different. He didn't seek a woman who'd increase his fortune or his consequence. He wanted a companion, a lover, a heart mate. Or so he'd implied. Pippa's point was worth noting too, though. The charmers and the devils could look vexingly alike. Althorpe had been a plain man, though his manners had been punctiliously correct before Matilda had married him.

"I won't be back before noon," Matilda said, "so please tell Helen that one apple tart a day is her limit. She can have porridge for lunch, or whatever you fix for yourself, but she's not to subsist on purloined sweets."

"Aye, ma'am," Pippa said, washing a second egg, "but my guess is Mr. Fenwick will fetch something from a chophouse and see to Helen's meal. Looks like a man fond of his victuals."

And of his horse, and of Helen, and of luscious, late-night kisses.

"Lock the front door if you go out, Pippa, and I should be back this afternoon." Matilda ate the last few bites of tart in solitude, while Pippa finished washing the eggs, then went up to clean Mr. Fenwick's rooms.

Matilda put on her awful blue dress, for a change, and arrived to the park by way of detours through Knightsbridge. The precaution was likely pointless, but it gave her time to fortify herself against the morning's challenges. She'd brought a book too, though that was a prop.

She needn't have bothered with the book. Before she reached the bench where she typically lurked, she spotted a small child playing catch with her governess. The governess was youngish and had first appeared in the park the previous month. The young ones—the ones who laughed, played catch, and flew kites—never lasted.

Matilda adjusted her straw hat lower across her brow, got out her sketchbook, and prepared to have her heart broken all over again.

CHAPTER SIX

"Your finances prosper, my lord," Rupert Harpster said, positioning a silver standish precisely above the center of a tooled leather blotter. "Your brother was a good manager, but I must say, the earldom has seen some handsome returns in the past few years."

Harpster was a spare, natty, older fellow whose blue eyes held shrewdness even when he smiled. Ashton was not for one moment fooled by the solicitor's flattery, nor was he willing to sit before his lawyer's handsome desk like a supplicant importuning a bishop.

"If the earldom prospers," Ashton said, on his hundredth circuit of the office, "then projects Ewan and his predecessors put in train long before the title befell me are the cause. Is it possible to sell off the English portion of the land?"

The previous hour had been spent reviewing yet more grievances from the English tenants. Ashton went out of his way to accommodate them. Their cottages were not merely snug, they were handsomely commodious. Any tenant could have free use of the earldom's draft teams if new sod had to be broken in spring. The home farm kept them supplied with out-crosses for their sheep and goats, and if rents were late, Ashton seldom took action.

The more he gave, the more they took advantage.

"Sell the tenancies in England?" Harpster murmured. "I cannot recommend such a course, my lord, even if it could be construed as permissible."

"So you don't know if I could sell that land. It's one-eighth of my property and eight-tenths of my headaches. The tenants have grown lax, expecting special consideration and forgiveness when their incompetence results in a bad harvest. Look at their yields, Harpster. Everything from wool to hay to barley falls below what the Scottish tenants can produce on smaller acreages."

This problem could be laid at Ewan's feet, to some extent. Unwilling to provoke a vocal minority, he'd yielded to the advice of his fellow landlords on the English side of the river, and Ashton had inherited the resulting mess.

"The initial grant of land that went with the Mulder barony was quite small, my lord," Harpster said, gaze fixed above the sideboard, where a full-length portrait of King John signing the Magna Carta hung. "The earls of Kilkenney added to it mostly by purchase and marriage. Where the English tenancies fall, I could not precisely say. Some might be saleable, some might be entailed."

"I want a map," Ashton said, "and I want it soon. Show me which farms I can sell, which I'm stuck with, and any that fall somewhere in between. Once the harvest is in and the rents paid, I'll be making some changes." A lot of changes, actually.

Ashton would never do as some landlords had done and burn out tenants on Christmas Day for his convenience, but neither would he tolerate more years of idleness while good land went to waste.

Harpster folded his hands on his blotter and bowed his head as if an unjust sentence had been pronounced. "Very well, my lord. Would a month from now suit?"

"One week. You have copies of the letters patent, and all the land not described therein should be saleable unless an entail was subsequently added. I'll see you next week."

Ashton headed for the door, ready to leave behind the silk-covered walls, thick carpets, and idealized landscapes in their gilt frames. The pen tray on Harpster's desk was chased silver, as were the ink bottles sitting on the standish. This wasn't workmanship displayed for the sake of beauty, this was a subtle means of impressing clients, or perhaps intimidating them.

Helen would have nicked the lot of it, and Harpster would have had no clue where his vanities had gone.

"There was one other topic I thought we should discuss, my lord," Harpster said, remaining at his desk. "I'm told you're in London with matrimony in mind, and that can be a complicated legal undertaking."

"Who told you that?"

Harpster's smile was smug. "I have my sources, the better to serve the clients whose trust reposes in my office."

Harpster had Ashton's coin. He did not have Ashton's trust. "That's something I've never understood."

"My lord?"

"If my earldom is Scottish and my lands are mostly Scottish, why is my solicitor English? It's not as if the legal profession has no Scottish exponents and not as if English law is controlling in Scotland."

Now Harpster got to his feet. "Your much-respected forbearers saw fit to give this office their custom, my lord. We have served your family for generations, without apparent complaint. As it happens, you do own land in England, and London is the cultural and political capital of the empire if not the world. Surely you would not rely on lesser resources when you already have the best at hand?"

Oh, that was as subtle as a peacock's mating call.

"I'll see you next week," Ashton said, one hand on the door latch, "and you'll have a map for me."

Harpster came around his desk. "About your matrimonial aspirations, my lord. I've taken it upon myself to prepare a list, based on information gathered over the years regarding various families whose good fortune includes a marriageable daughter making her curtsey this year. In a few cases, I've included ladies who made their come out last year, in the interests of giving you the widest possible—"

"Next week," Ashton said, swinging the door open. "And I'll take a copy of the map with me."

He shut the door in Harpster's face and gestured to Helen, who was waiting in a chair by the door of the clerk's room.

"Let's be off," he said, not stopping. "I'm in the mood for a gallop."

Clear back to Scotland.

Helen fell in step without asking questions, suggesting Ashton's foul mood was apparent at ten paces. Another list, for God's sake. As if young women were so many vegetables at market. No wonder Matilda Bryce had no use for marriage, if this was how her family had approached it.

"You're for home," Ashton said, flipping Helen a coin as a hostler led Dusty from the livery. "Get something to eat and stop by the Albany for my mail. I'm off to the park."

"I could come with you."

"I'm after a hard gallop, or the pale imitation available to me in this cesspit of greed. Tell me three words that begin with *w*."

They'd worked on this on the way to the solicitor's office.

"Wedding, want, wife."

Why those three? "Three that begin with *l*."

"Lord, lying, lodger."

"Be gone," Ashton said, swinging into the saddle. "And the next letter we're working on is *r*. Rotten, rascal, reprimand."

"What's a reprimand?"

"A scolding." Ashton sent Dusty off at a trot rather than respond to further taunts from Helen. *Lord, lying, lodger.* Matilda Bryce wouldn't care if Ashton were a duke or a dustman. Either way, she'd send him packing and be about her business.

That thought blended with the lingering frustration of the meeting with Harpster and sent Ashton at a brisk canter down the first unoccupied bridle path he found in Hyde Park. Though the greenery covered hundreds of acres, it was crisscrossed with lanes, carriageways, paths, and walkways, and a truly mad gallop was unlikely so late in the morning.

Ashton let Dusty have his head, and the horse accelerated from canter to gallop. Maybe Dusty was unhappy in London too, or maybe he was reacting to Ashton's mood.

All too soon, a sedate group of riders clogged the path, and Ashton had to rein in his horse. He pulled Dusty around and gave him a loose rein rather than overtake the group. Introductions would have followed, and Ashton was in no mood for that ordeal.

He allowed his gelding to idle along until the horse's sides were no longer heaving and a sense of calm descended. The day was lovely, and the Season hadn't started yet. Life yet held a few apple tarts, and—

Dusty broke from a hedgerow into a quiet corner of the park. If Ashton had had to guess, he'd have said they were closer to the Knightsbridge side, south and west of Mayfair proper.

And there sat Matilda Bryce on a secluded bench, alone and clearly upset.

* * *

The governess and child were leaving already, after playing catch for less than thirty minutes, most of which Kitty had spent poking about the hedges nominally looking for her ball. The governess, whom the child had called Miss Reynolds, had been patient with that exercise.

Any young woman employed by the Derrick family would need great quantities of patience.

Kitty looked to be in good health, and when Miss Reynolds said it was time to go, the child acquiesced without making a fuss. The girl's robust energy was encouraging, but her docility gave Matilda a pang.

Docile little girls turned into docile young women.

The governess and her charge toddled down the path hand in hand. The sight broke Matilda's heart, as it did every month she was lucky enough to see it.

Kitty should be holding my hand. In 346 days, Matilda would start planning how to bring that about. Nothing could happen quickly or in a manner Drexel might notice, but the past six years had given Matilda vast stores of determination and not a little cunning.

Someday, some fine day much like this one—

"You look like you're watching the funeral of your dearest friend." Ashton Fenwick came down on the bench beside her.

Matilda nearly shot into the air, she was so surprised. "Where did you come from?"

"The angels delivered me to my mother's doorstep, to hear my old nurse tell it. My father's version differed in the details. Mama maintained diplomatic silence on the matter. Who is the girl, Matilda?"

The girl was the reason Matilda had fled six years ago, the reason she'd managed to stay alive since.

"None of your business, Mr. Fenwick."

He stretched an arm along the back of the bench, a handsome man enjoying a pretty day. Part of Matilda wanted to turn her face into his shoulder and weep. The rest of her wished he'd take himself back to Scotland by post.

"I have nieces," he said. "Three wee, chubby darlings for whom I'd lay down my life and my freedom. The youngest one is named Jeannie, and she's afraid of me—or pretends to be—but I'll charm her around. She's making me work for her favor, and that's as it should be."

Oh, to be charmed by Ashton Fenwick. "Spare me your clumsy metaphors. You're my lodger, for now, and my life is none of your business."

"The girl looks like you," Mr. Fenwick said. "About the chin and when she smiles, as best I recall the rare occurrence of your smile."

Kitty had Matilda's tendency to cock her head when she was thinking too. "Shut your mouth. You know nothing about it."

He crossed his booted ankles, not a care in the world to all appearances. "Matilda, you've aptly described me as your lodger, but would it be so awful to consider me a friend? I have means, for one thing. Never hurts to have a wealthy friend or two. I wasn't always so well-to-do and know of what I speak."

He knew how to kiss a woman so her insides turned to warm, honey-drizzled apple tarts too. "Means can't fix every problem." Though they counted for a lot. Kisses had to count for nothing, though.

Had to.

"Nothing can fix every problem, but sharing a burden can lighten the load. I'm alone here in London, without many allies, and dreading what lies ahead. I might be more sympathetic to your situation than you think, but you're so busy judging yourself, you can't imagine others won't be just as critical. I know how that feels too."

He passed her another embroidered handkerchief, and for a moment, Matilda considered confiding in him. Had he not had dinner with a lord, one he considered a friend, she might have yielded to the temptation.

The Earl of Drexel was a lord, and he'd been full of avuncular concern, a font of understanding and commiseration—until he'd called for the magistrate.

"I appreciate your solicitude," Matilda said, "and apologize for being cross, but my problems are my own."

"Stubborn," Mr. Fenwick said. "I like that. I'm stubborn too, which is all that has allowed me to hold up my head sometimes. I'll bid you good day. My horse has been as patient as I can trust him to be."

He bowed, tipped his hat, and sauntered off, while Matilda clutched his handkerchief so tightly even her heaviest iron would have to be nearly scorching hot to smooth out the wrinkles.

* * *

Tattersalls was crowded on sale days. The auction house catered to blood stock, selling the equine variety to its human counterparts. The establishment was situated at a corner of Hyde Park, and as Ashton rode past, he spotted Benjamin, Earl of Hazelton, chatting with a tall, blond, well-dressed fellow. Hazelton introduced the man as Sir Archer Portmaine, a cousin.

Sir Archer had the sense to take himself off shortly thereafter, saving Ashton the trouble of snatching Hazelton by the arm and dragging him behind a hedge.

"I need a list," Ashton said. The sight and scent of so much horseflesh should have comforted him, but the dandies and lordlings idling about ruined the pleasure of a stable environment.

"You've come to your senses," Hazelton replied. "Do we sort the prospective countesses by height, hair color, temperament, or fortune?"

"Don't be obnoxious. Women are not broodmares, and bachelors are not stud colts. I need a list of scandals."

Hazelton pretended to study a lanky bay gelding, probably rising four. The youngster's muscling suggested he'd been started under saddle, though he was by no means a finished prospect.

"If you take all the trouble to come to London," Hazelton said, "why would you then wreck your chances of finding a bride by causing a scandal?"

"As if I'd need a list for that. I need a list of the scandals that were the talk of London six or seven years ago. If you're considering the bay for jumping, his shoulder angles are somewhat wanting."

Hazelton sauntered along, one of many gentlemen talking, inspecting sale prospects, and enjoying the spring day.

"Scandals are a daily occurrence here, Fenwick. Town thrives on scandal. You need to be more specific."

"Scandal involving a woman, probably a married woman."

The earl came to a halt before a golden filly with a cream mane and tail. The coloring was unusual, suggesting Iberian bloodlines.

"Most scandals involve women," Hazelton said. "If you can give me the name of a specific woman, I can read over my journals from the years in question and consult with a few sources."

The filly stuck her nose in the air and curled back her teeth.

"No consulting with sources."

Hazelton ran a hand down the mare's neck, over her shoulder, and along a foreleg. She flinched, but didn't shy.

"The list could be quite long. You won't give me any other specifics?"

"I don't have any more specifics, but I suspect this wasn't a minor tempest. The lady would be at least twenty-five now, possibly closer to thirty. Well-born, English, and gently raised."

Hazelton walked around the filly and repeated his inspection on the second side. She flinched again and whisked her tail.

"Was money involved?" Hazelton asked. "Violence? A lover? A duel? Can you give me anything to go on, Fenwick?"

Ashton cast back over his dealings with Matilda Bryce—if that was her name. "The woman involved is still very much afraid the past will haunt her and those she cares about. You shouldn't buy this mare, by the way. She's back sore, suggesting poor care and overwork. That wears on a lady's spirits."

That little girl in the park was wearing on Matilda's spirits. Ashton put the child's age at about six or seven. The woman with her had been a governess, not a mother or auntie, and the child's schedule was regular enough that at an appointed time on an appointed day, Matilda could see the girl.

From a distance.

"Does this scandal involve a by-blow? All manner of well-born women stray once the heir and spare are in the nursery. I wouldn't say it's expected, but it's certainly tolerated."

The next stall appeared empty until Ashton got close enough to peer over the boards.

Hazelton came up on his shoulder. "What's that doing here?"

That was a small, gray donkey, burrs in its mane and tail, a gash across its quarters. The animal remained motionless, head down, as if trying to avoid detection.

"Excuse me, gentlemen," a groom said, shoving the stall door back. "I'll just be finding somewhere else for this eyesore to bide until the knacker comes around."

He fastened a headstall on the donkey, who docilely followed the groom from the stall.

"A moment," Ashton said.

The groom glanced around, as if even being seen holding the wretched little animal's lead rope was an imposition.

"Fenwick, don't do it." Hazelton spoke softly.

"The beast is sound," Ashton said, running a hand down each sturdy, hairy leg. "Is it fit to ride and drive?"

"Aye," the groom said. "Poor mite is willing enough, but too small to be of any use. Gent sent it along with a group of hunters. The manager didn't want to offend a customer, so we took the ass along with the hunters, and I'm to hand it off to the knacker quiet-like."

"Fenwick, you asked me earlier about scandal. Men of consequence don't buy donkeys, much less sorry specimens such as this. If you're seen leading that beast through Mayfair, I won't answer for the consequences."

"I'm not asking ye to." Ashton found the donkey's sweet spot, which happened to be under the animal's chin. When Ashton scratched there, the donkey relaxed, despite the activity all around and the presence of much larger equines.

He looked at the creature's teeth and in its ears, picked up each foot, tugged on its tail this way and that. Pressed on its spine, listened to its belly.

"You are drawing notice," Hazelton said. "This is a donkey, not a candidate for pulling the coronation coach."

"Such as this," Ashton said, petting the donkey, "bore the Holy Child's mother into Bethlehem, Hazelton. Don't be insulting your betters."

The groom smirked, Hazelton walked off a good six yards, and Ashton bought the donkey.

"Don't expect me to leave the premises with you and that, that malodorous embarrassment to the equine race," Hazelton said when the transaction had been completed.

"All I need from you is the list I've requested. I'm not interested in scandals less than five years old, nor more than seven years old."

"I'll have to talk to Sir Archer about it. He's in charge of the investigations now, and he'll take my confidences with him to the grave."

The donkey was going to sleep against Ashton's thigh, as if it knew how close to a bad end it had come.

"Portmaine is an investigator?" Ashton asked, scratching at the base of long, gray ears.

"And a cousin. He was my partner in the investigation business before holy matrimony gave me more pleasant duties to fill my days."

"And your nights. Speak to your cousin then, and time is of the essence."

"Oh, of course, always. Whatever your lordship needs," Hazelton muttered. "You're invited to join my club, by the way. Some have waited years for such an invitation."

"I will decline that signal honor," Ashton said, leading the donkey along. "Any place that can't cook a decent steak doesn't deserve my custom, meaning no insult to present company. I'm sure your steak was done to a turn. Odd how that works."

Hazelton fell in step on the other side of the donkey, though he ignored the creature sniffing at his glove. "I'll tell them you're thinking about it."

"Tell them 'no, thank you,'" Ashton said. "When the chef ruined a fine cut of meat, he insulted me, you, and the poor cow. Insults to you and me I might tolerate, but the cow did nothing wrong."

"Fenwick, do you *want* a reputation for eccentricity?"

"You make it sound as if eccentricity is one of the seven deadly sins. I'm not the one who wrecked a dinner out of pique. What should I name this fine beast?"

Hazelton stopped and glanced down at the donkey. "It's appealing, in a hideous, pathetic, noxious sort of way."

"Another deadly sin?"

The earl's lips twitched. "Name him anything you please. I'll have your list in a week or so."

"I'll name him Marmaduke," Ashton said. "Duke, for short. The stable lads will appreciate the humor and treat the beast well as a result. My felicitations to your countess. Send word around to the Albany if you need me."

Ashton collected his horse and led the donkey to the Albany by way of Piccadilly. He was tempted to detour down through St. James's—let all the dandies in their clubs have a look at the Earl of Kilkenney's first purchase at Tatts—but the donkey was probably hungry and weary.

Ashton was too.

* * *

"I would like to tell you a story," Mr. Fenwick said.

He stood on the threshold of Matilda's parlor, looking magnificent in his riding attire. His boots were dusty, and he'd been gone most of the day. Matilda had listened for his footsteps on the stairs, both hoping and dreading to hear him returning to his apartments.

He'd seen Kitty, and he'd sensed a connection between her and Matilda. That wasn't a disaster.

The worse problem was that he'd offered to help, and Matilda had been tempted. She couldn't accept his help, lest he be named an accessory after the crime, but she had wanted to unburden herself, to talk through the whole problem with somebody who hadn't been terrified for six straight years and angry for longer than that.

"Have you had your supper?" Matilda asked.

"I'm not telling you my story over supper, Matilda Bryce, unless we're taking a plate out to the wee garden where none will disturb us."

Matilda occasionally took her mending outside, because sunlight made close work easier on the eyes. She'd been mending half the day, making tight, even stitches in the plain fabric that characterized her wardrobe now. Never again would she take for granted the beautiful creations fashioned at the expense of a poor woman's eyesight.

"We can enjoy the evening air," she said. "For a short time."

"Oh, aye, a short time. My story isn't complicated, and it has a happy ending."

"You don't sound happy."

He bowed her through the back door, a ridiculous courtesy. "I'm not, but my troubles are minor and easily resolved. The matter wants determination, is all."

Matilda took the only seat, a worn bench along the wall of the house. Her herbs sat in pots and raised beds, and a small plane maple straggled up toward the evening sky. Mr. Fenwick came down beside her, the bench being too small to allow for any distance between them.

For a moment, they sat in silence, though Matilda liked too well the solidness of him beside her.

She liked *him* too well, and that was a problem.

"Once upon a time," he began, "there was a young man, a fine, braw, bonnie lad, sent off to university."

"That is not a very original story."

He took her hand. "Haud yer wheesht. It gets more interesting. This lad was handsome, from a good family, but from the wrong side of the blanket. Have you noticed that many of the handsomest lads are illegitimate?"

"I have not." His levity was telling, though. A by-blow would have all the airs and graces of a legitimate son, but less of the arrogance, for polite society would never let a by-blow forget his antecedents.

"Well, they are. Fine lot of specimens, but this particular lad had two problems. The first was a miserable temper. He was a good-sized fellow, and when he was vexed, he'd let fly with his fists."

Matilda withdrew her hand. "I have no patience with foul-tempered men."

"He was little more than a boy, and years of minding the horses kicked that temper right out of him. He's the soul of patience now."

Ashton Fenwick was very patient. Matilda couldn't deny that. "What was the other problem?"

Apparently, illegitimacy was not a problem, suggesting the lad's family had been very well-to-do indeed.

"This young man was lonely. He had only the one brother, several years younger, and they were not raised to be as close as most brothers. Though the family was loving, and nobody dared ostracize the young man overtly, there was talk."

Was there any creature more tender-hearted than a small boy? And if that small boy had been Ashton Fenwick, he would have sensed the talk and the unkindness behind it.

"There's always talk, Ashton. You can't mind it."

"You can't ignore it if you're a very young man at university, where scholarship comes a distant second to bothering tavern maids and learning to hold one's liquor. I fell in with a bad lot. I knew better. I didn't even like them. They were spoiled, mean, not too bright, and headed for trouble, but they allowed me to drink with them and invited me to their houses during the holidays."

Matilda allowed Ashton to take her hand again. "You promised me a happy ending, Ashton." To the story, at least. Not too much to ask.

"That I did. One of the party, a rotten little devil who'd been sent down from one school after another, took it into his head to anticipate the wedding vows with his fiancée, an earl's daughter who lived on a neighboring estate. A kidnapping of sorts followed, and it became very clear to me that the lady was not receptive to her intended's advances. I rode off to seek help, but my efforts were in vain. The young lady was grievously wronged, her sister badly injured.

She broke off the engagement."

An earl's daughter? "As well she should have. I hope her family pressed charges."

"You know they did not. She withdrew from society, her sister left the area, and public opinion was divided. Most engaged couples anticipate their vows, after all, and she and her sister ought not to have been out riding on their own land without a groom, according to some. That was utter tripe, according to our young man."

The temper Ashton claimed to have mastered simmered below his words.

"One takes a groom for safety. Any horse can come up lame, or toss a rider in a bad moment."

"So she rode with her sister, over familiar terrain, on her family's land. The group that abetted this crime was a half-dozen drunken lordlings. A groom would not have prevented what happened and might have lost his life trying to. I blame myself for not realizing sooner that the outing would turn malicious. My need to be accepted by those young jackanapeses blinded me to common sense, and two young women paid a very high price."

"What happened?" Because Matilda could not envision any happily ever afters following such a scandal, except for the violent, dishonorable, pig of a young man, of course. He'd probably found another fiancée with a larger dowry.

"When the young lady withdrew from society, I attached myself to her household and made sure her safety was never at risk again. She and her sister both met good men and have started families of their own."

That was two happily ever afters—if the men were truly good. "And the rotten little devil?"

Ashton patted her hand. "A lovely, fatal accident befell him. Divine providence at its finest."

Matilda sat in the lengthening shadows holding hands with a man and simply enjoying the contact. She ought not. She ought to pretend she'd never kissed Ashton Fenwick, hadn't listened for his footsteps all day, and hadn't tucked his laundered handkerchief into her clothes press, between her spare chemise and her only pair of silk stockings.

"Why are you telling me this, Mr. Fenwick?"

"Ashton. Because I want you to understand that I know how men can be. I know that a woman can find herself entangled in problems not of her own making. The law is a fine concept, but its enforcement is an unreliable undertaking, particularly when your neighbors, the Bow Street runners, are paid rewards for convictions rather than for thorough investigations."

"And they have been known to manufacture evidence, intimidate witnesses, and mistreat the accused." Every time Matilda saw a runner, the fear nearly choked her.

"Your hands are cold," Ashton said. "Shall we go inside?"

Darkness was falling. Matilda stayed where she was. "I was not wronged by a fiancé, Ashton. I was married in a church, my family in attendance, and when I spoke my vows, I meant them."

"That was the unkindest cut of all, I'm guessing. You meant them, your husband meant something else entirely. Is he truly dead?"

"Yes."

"And is that wee lass in the park your daughter?"

Well, of course he'd think that. "She is not. If she were my daughter, I don't know how I'd bear the separation, but she is not my daughter."

He enveloped Matilda's hand in both of his, his grip warm. He'd let her go if she withdrew her hand, though. Of that, Matilda was certain.

"You would die for that child, Matilda. If she's not your daughter, who is she?"

CHAPTER SEVEN

"I prided myself on a modest competence solving mysteries and puzzles," Hazelton said. "Fenwick bought a damned donkey, Maggie mine. What am I to make of that? A belted earl, and he sashays into Tatts, passes up the finest blood stock in the land, and buys an odoriferous little wretch he can have no possible use for."

The Countess of Hazelton prowled around the billiards table and took Benjamin's cue stick from him.

"You are too easy for me to best in this mood, my love. I suspect the greater puzzle is that Fenwick turned down membership in your club. Are you concerned or annoyed?"

In the few short years of their marriage, Benjamin had come to rely on Maggie's judgment, though he was still surprised when her discernment made short work of his own moods.

"Both, I suppose. I belong to only the best clubs."

Maggie kissed him. She was a voluptuous armful of redhead, and her kisses were the surest remedy for Benjamin's foul humor.

"You belong to only the most expensive clubs. Fenwick is a Scot anticipating all the bother of a social Season. If he already belongs to a few clubs, why take on another?"

Maggie's explanation was simple, and it fit the facts, but it did not fit Ashton Fenwick.

"Fenwick is not tight-fisted," Benjamin said. "But he's proud as hell. Are we finished for the evening?"

The hour was early by the standards of the upcoming Season. Some families would have just sat down to their evening meal. Benjamin's household included two sons, the younger less than a year old. Maggie kept the schedule to country hours, though that would probably change once the social whirl began.

"Let's go upstairs," she said. "Fenwick has aroused your curiosity to the point that you're pacing my carpets. You haven't been this overset since your second-born had the audacity to waste six hours in the birth process."

Benjamin settled his arms around his wife. Nothing in all of creation brought him as much pleasure as simply holding the woman he loved—well, almost nothing.

"Perhaps Fenwick has aroused my temper. A donkey, Maggie? What could he have been thinking? Every gentleman, horse, and groom at Tatts watched him leading that beast from the premises. And then there's this business of avoiding the Albany until the last possible moment. Fenwick is putting up at some lodging house, while one of the finest apartments in London sits empty, and at a price that would buy many donkeys their freedom. He's forbidden me to attempt any sort of surveillance."

"Spying is ungentlemanly," Maggie said in ironically prim tones.

"Also unladylike. What do you know that I don't?"

Prior to his marriage, Benjamin had dealt with various delicate problems for the realm's better families, and done so discreetly. He'd used logic, dogged persistence, audacity, and common sense to stop the occasional elopement, retrieve a purloined journal, or find missing valuables.

Maggie's intuition eclipsed Benjamin's pedestrian deductions by leaps and flights.

"Fenwick's tiger is a young girl," Maggie said. "When he first called upon you, I saw her walking his horse up and down the street. At one point, a braid came loose from beneath her cap. Boys can certainly have long hair, but the way she stuffed the braid back out of sight was feminine, a very young lady vexed by her coiffure."

"This grows alarming," Benjamin muttered, turning Maggie under his arm and escorting her to the door. "Fenwick asked me to research scandals that occurred between five and seven years ago. He was precise about the time and not about anything else."

"Perhaps he's already chosen somebody to wed, and she has a shadowed past."

"Chosen somebody to wed in less than a week? Even Fenwick doesn't work that quickly. I was hoping you'd review my journals with me."

Maggie had been firmly on the shelf when Benjamin had married her. As the daughter of a duke, she'd seen many Seasons from a vantage Benjamin had not. A minor scandal might have escaped his notice. It would not have escaped hers.

"We were still at war then," Maggie said as they wandered toward the stairs. "And the military has its share of scandals. Poor old Mad George was still nominally the sovereign, while Prinny engaged in unbridled foolishness."

With Mad George's death, the Regent—also named George—was on the throne, though he got little credit for what sense and wisdom he had.

"Fenwick said this scandal likely involved a woman, possibly a married woman."

"He's selected a bride, then, or the next thing to it. Better still, she's from an appropriate strata of society."

At the foot of the stairs, Benjamin stopped to regard his lady by the light of the sconces. "How can you know such a thing? Fenwick might be indulging idle curiosity, chasing down a rumor at his family's request, or gathering intelligence on a business associate."

Maggie started up the steps, counting off on her fingers. "First, he came to London to find a bride and only to find a bride. He's not looking for investments, and his family doesn't move in polite circles as their English counterparts might. Second, the scandal involves a lady, and Fenwick has a protective streak that rivals the North Sea for width and depth. Third, only ladies—proper, genteel, sheltered ladies—get involved in scandals. Laundresses, alewives, and fishmongers can do as they please. Fenwick might not even realize the extent to which his affections are engaged."

"Some of us resist engaging our affections," Benjamin said, opening the door to their apartment, "because we're stubborn and foolish."

"I wasn't stubborn or foolish," Maggie retorted, preceding him through the door. "I was cautious and slow to trust. We are married now, are we not?"

"The signal blessing of my otherwise dull and unremarkable existence," Benjamin said. "You've given me an idea."

"I do so love when you get ideas, Benjamin."

"With you for an inspiration, my love, ideas are inevitable. This idea concerns Fenwick."

"We ought to call him Kilkenney," Maggie said, locking the sitting room door. "He should use the title when referring to himself."

"I'll take him with me to the next court levee. Once he's been through that ordeal, he'll forget all about burned steak, neglected donkeys, and old scandal. Even the Duke of Moreland's ballroom will be no challenge for him after he's been inspected by the king himself."

Maggie's papa might own one of the finest ballrooms in the land, but the Duchess of Moreland ruled over that ballroom. Sooner or later, Fenwick would have to make his bow to Benjamin's in-laws, and then the matchmaking would begin in earnest.

When Maggie cuddled close, something else began in earnest behind Benjamin's falls, and the problem of Ashton Fenwick, his unusual tiger, and his interest in old gossip was forgotten until long after the moon had risen.

* * *

Bad luck had allowed Ashton Fenwick to catch a glimpse of Kitty, and worse luck yet had apparently informed him that Matilda would do anything to preserve the child's happiness.

"That little girl," Matilda said, "is nobody you need to be concerned about. She's thriving, content, and safe, for now."

Ashton looped an arm around Matilda's shoulders. "She's your strength and your vulnerability. That's how it is when you love somebody. My sister-in-law has quite a temper. She'll tear a strip off me most days of the week for singing in the library, wearing boots to dinner, ruining my nieces' supper. I love her scolds, because they mean she's not truly upset."

Ashton loved this sister-in-law, and he wasn't ashamed of that sentiment. Didn't mince past it as if sneaking an extra apple tart from the larder.

"You love her for finding fault with you?"

"She's no' finding fault. She's taking me in hand, for, as she says, somebody must. When Alyssa is quiet, when she won't even look at me, I can't stand it. I'll do anything to earn her forgiveness. The same malady in a more severe version plagues my brother, for Ewan and Alyssa were and are a love match. She's a grand woman and always a lady. She amazes me."

This panegyric for a woman Matilda would never meet caused both heartache and wonder. She'd never heard a man wax so openly affectionate about a female relation, and certainly nobody had ever spoken about Matilda with such affection.

"Are you in love with her?"

"In love—with Alyssa? She'd geld me for even speculating in that direction. Ewan would kill me straight out. If you saw them together, you'd know that their union is inviolable, though they never dote or fawn on each other in public. Their disagreements are high drama, and then they disappear into their apartment for twelve straight hours while I reassure my wee nieces they haven't been orphaned."

His nieces would believe him, when they'd have no such faith in their nurses and nannies.

"I can't imagine that type of warmth between family members. Can't grasp that it might exist."

At one time, Matilda had hoped, if not for affection, then for at least cordial regard from her husband. That hope had lasted mere days after her wedding. She'd conveniently forgotten it had ever plagued her.

Ashton kissed her temple. "Such familial bonds exist, and they're the only thing that makes life bearable sometimes. A bastard learns that lesson. The rules, the proprieties, the legalities, they matter naught compared to the love."

The sky held only the last vestiges of light. Even if somebody were spying over the garden wall, they'd not see Matilda stealing these moments with her lodger.

She kissed Ashton's cheek, and he regarded her in the shadows. "Much more of that, and we'll be discussing a different kind of warmth, Matilda Bryce."

How Matilda hated that name. She kissed Ashton again, at the corner of his mouth.

With him, the two kinds of love, familial and intimate, could exist in harmony. He would love his wife as he'd love a dear friend, and he'd desire her as he yearned for a lover. Ashton Fenwick, whether because of his bastard upbringing, his maturity, or his inherent nature, had the courage to love all at once, not in stingy pieces and reluctant morsels.

"I want—" Matilda managed before finding his mouth again.

He smiled against her lips. "You want me?"

She wanted so much. She wanted the sanctuary of his arms, the pleasure of his kisses, the joy of his passion.

"I shouldn't," Matilda said, her mouth a half inch from his. She could feel his heat, smell the combination of soap and horse that characterized him at the end of a day.

"Why not?" he replied, kneading the muscles at the nape of her neck. "Why not have some pleasure, Matilda? I'll be careful, and in the morning nothing will have changed. The terms of my lease remain in full force and effect. Your ownership of the house isn't jeopardized."

Her heart would be jeopardized. "If I do this with you, I'll regret it."

This. A euphemism for the biggest risk she'd taken in six years and the most mundane of human pleasures, shared by couples dwelling in shepherd's huts and palaces.

Ashton sat back, keeping his arm around her. "Will you regret it more if you don't?"

His question landed in the middle of whirling thoughts, like a bucket of water tossed on a Catherine wheel. Whatever else was true, Matilda was a widow and free to share her favors as she pleased. Even polite society accorded a discreet woman that much latitude.

"My hesitation has to do with hope," Matilda said, closing her eyes and leaning her head back against Ashton's arm. Hope that she could not afford to nurture, though she didn't examine too closely what that hope might entail.

A passing pleasure with Ashton Fenwick couldn't amount to anything. If the past six years had taught Matilda anything, it was that hoping was a waste of courage.

Ashton scooped her into his lap as easily as Matilda might have picked up Solomon when he was in a willing mood.

"Your hesitation, for which I esteem you, has to do with fear. If you find a space between duty and propriety to take a little pleasure for yourself, will your self-respect remain intact? One doesn't want to part with self-respect lightly. If it matters, I very much respect you, regardless of your choice. I daresay Pippa and Helen share my opinion."

But did Matilda have the courage to seize what she wanted without feeling ashamed and hesitant? For six years, she'd been vigilant, self-reliant, and unceasingly careful.

And lonely. So lonely, she'd begun to wonder what all her caution and tenacity was for. The voice of despair whispered that Kitty was well cared for, and even if Matilda lasted the next 346 days, what could a woman in hiding do for a young girl dwelling in the household of an earl?

A relatively impoverished woman whose best hope was a life of quiet disgrace.

Ashton apparently didn't expect Matilda to reply. He instead recommended kissing her, on the mouth, the brow, the jaw. His kisses were sweet and gentle, but Matilda was sitting in his lap, and she'd been married for three interminable years.

He was growing aroused.

As was Matilda. She at first didn't recognize what the restlessness and agitation were, but when Ashton settled a hand on her breast, her discontent eased.

So this is desire. Madness and pleasure in a perfect balance, blended with longing, joy, and a hint of anxiety.

"Relax, Matilda. You own this house." Ashton spoke metaphorically, but the warmth of his breath on her neck was very real.

Matilda did own the house, and her body, and her future, at least until Drexel found her. She did not own Ashton Fenwick and would see the last of him in mere days.

She scooted around until she was comfortable in his arms and kissed him back as if his departure were in the next hour, not the next week. He growled a happy, soft growl and gathered her close, and for the first time in six years—for the first time *ever*—Matilda said yes to her own pleasure.

* * *

"Uncle thinks I'm a fool," Stephen said, tracing a fingernail around the inlay on a chased silver bottle of sand. By the candlelight in Basingstoke's office, the pattern in the metal appeared to shimmer and dance. "I want you to find the missing heiress, the sooner the better. Step-mama would never go far from the girl, and Uncle ought to know that."

Damon Basingstoke wasn't like most other solicitors Stephen had come across. No prosperous paunch, no ostentatious side-whiskers, and what clerks he had were kept mostly out of sight in a back room, not arrayed about in a front room for clients to count or send out for coffee.

Basingstoke was the youngest exponent of a firm that had served the Derrick family for generations, and in Stephen's opinion, he was very much a modern man, willing to meet even after hours if necessary to accommodate a client's needs.

Stephen did his best thinking after hours. Always had. Any who doubted that could ask his mistresses.

"What is the urgency of this search?" Basingstoke replied, steepling his fingers. "While your step-mother—possibly your late step-mother—remains unaccounted for, you have the benefit of her portion of the inheritance as managed by your uncle. He's not afraid to look after his own funds, which too many of his ilk think beneath them, and you stand to come by a significant sum in less than a year."

Basingstoke was a bit rough around the edges, and his sense of fashion missed elegant by a few details. He had the gold watch—a man who billed clients for his time would need a reliable watch, after all. Nonetheless, his cuff links were onyx rather than gold, and he didn't bother with a cravat pin.

A mistake, that. A cravat pin could make a man's ensemble. Brummel had declared it so years ago, and nobody had dared contradict him just because his fashion sense had nearly landed him in debtors' prison.

Basingstoke also lacked Stephen's aristocratic Saxon coloring. The solicitor's hair was dark, as were his eyes. He was on the tall side, an inch or two taller than Stephen. A bit too tall, in other words.

"What is the urgency?" Stephen snapped. "There's the girl, for one thing. She's costing me money. Uncle claims he's using his own funds to look after her, but that's a lie. He's using Step-mama's portion of the estate, and using it lavishly, which means he's using money I stand to inherit. I suspect that governess is simply an overworked mistress. No governess should be that pretty or that happy."

Basingstoke studied the chandelier above, which flickered in some stray night breeze.

"I am a family solicitor, Mr. Derrick," he said. "My role is to advance the best interests of the family within the guidelines established by my father as owner of this firm. That means the earldom's concerns take precedence over your own. Lord Drexel has instructed me to remain alert for any sign of your step-mother and professes concern for her. I can be particularly vigilant in that regard without a conflict of interest. If the family's financial arrangements are not to your liking, you will have to take that up with your uncle."

Stephen set the bottle of sand on the solicitor's blotter and took a seat. The chairs lacked padding, another oversight a more genteel businessman would have noticed.

"I'm not asking you to set yourself against my uncle." That was exactly Stephen's agenda. "I'm asking you to find a well-born, wrongly accused, sheltered young lady who has been fending for herself for far too long. If she will accept the protection of her late husband's family, we can clear up all that nonsense about Papa's death, divide his estate, and get on with our lives."

Get on with spending all that lovely money.

"I will continue to look diligently for your missing relation, Mr. Derrick. You do know that the law prohibits you from marrying your step-mother?"

Step-mama had been pretty six years ago. Stephen had considered marrying her, but there would be settlements, and settlements often resulted in trusts, and trustees. Uncle would circle like a vulture over a fresh carcass, and Stephen had had enough of Uncle's interference.

"I'm aware of the law, Mr. Basingstoke." He was *now*, not that it mattered. "I've wondered if my uncle isn't set upon marrying the woman."

"The law would prohibit that union as well, else younger brothers would be motivated to conspire with unhappy wives to kill a wealthy, titled elder sibling, wouldn't they?"

Basingstoke was making a point. Stephen couldn't be bothered to decipher it. The hour was growing late enough that gentlemen all over Mayfair would be sitting down to cards, opening a second bottle of port, or climbing into their mistress's bed.

"Having no older siblings, I can't speak to that rather vulgar speculation, Mr. Basingstoke. Uncle said you had a bank draft for me?"

"I can write you a draft," Basingstoke said. "Will ten pounds do?"

The question provoked in Stephen a rage so cold, so deep, so violent, he almost understood why his step-mother had committed murder.

"Fifty, Mr. Basingstoke."

Basingstoke opened a drawer and drew forth the requisite form. He took his sweet, damned time filling it out, all tidy and legible. With a languid hand, he sprinkled sand over the ink and set the bank draft aside.

"You and your uncle would do well to have a thorough discussion of family finances," Mr. Basingstoke said. "You refer to these disbursements as small advances, but your subsequent quarterly allowances are never reduced to reflect the sum already spent. Has your uncle told you how he's accounting for them?"

Well, no, he hadn't, and Stephen hadn't asked. "That is none of your affair, sir." Stephen stood and shook the sand from the bank draft onto the blotter. Some of it cascaded onto Mr. Basingstoke's lap. "Do forgive my clumsiness."

The solicitor rose, ignoring the mess Stephen had made. "Will there be anything more, Mr. Derrick? The hour grows late, and this draft could have been written in the morning."

When all the world would have seen Stephen trotting around to the solicitor's office two weeks shy of the quarterly disbursement?

"This evening was more convenient for me," Stephen said. "Until next we meet, Mr. Basingstoke."

Marceline would want to see the bank draft before she opened her door to Stephen. She was the most mercenary female Stephen had ever met, and who knew that greed in a woman could be an arousing quality? But then, everything about Marceline was arousing—her hands, her mouth, her vulgar words, her inventiveness.

Stephen let himself out of the offices of Basingstoke and Basingstoke and climbed into the carriage waiting for him at the corner.

The last question the solicitor had asked—where did Stephen's advances come from?—had been insightful, despite its impertinence. Uncle was doubtless taking the coins from Stephen's own pockets, and that just meant finding Stepmama had become all the more urgent.

Decent of Mr. Best Interests of The Earl Basingstoke to provide the reminder, though, or as decent as a solicitor could be.

* * *

Ashton had a theory, developed over many a tankard of ale and between many a pair of sheets. A woman responded to intimacies the same way she responded to life. A lady given to dramatics and impetuosity was easily set off into ecstasy. A female inclined to caution and shyness took more coaxing and patience, but then committed to her pleasures with an intensity that stole a man's breath.

Women did not leave their personalities at the bedroom door, no matter what the hellfire preachers spouted about Eve, temptation, and the weakness of the female mind.

Matilda Bryce had a slow fuse, but her fire burned hot and bright.

As Ashton added caresses to his kisses, the lady came alive in his arms, returning kiss for kiss and exploration for exploration.

She shaped his jaw, his ears, his neck and shoulders, as if she were blind and had never encountered the adult male before. Her touch was careful but curious, with an unhurried thoroughness that delighted Ashton.

Young men were idiots, all dash and fire, missing the best parts in their haste to find satisfaction. Ashton had taken much too long to grow up, but Matilda Bryce made him glad he was no longer a stripling.

By degrees, she relaxed, until only Ashton's embrace supported her in his lap. They needed a damned bed, but if Ashton so much as spoke, she'd probably scamper off to her kitchen, and the opportunity would be forever lost.

That would be a regret. For him and also, he hoped, for her.

Ashton let Matilda take the lead with the kissing, and though her forays into his mouth were delicate, her plundering took a toll on his self-restraint. Back in Scotland, opportunities for sexual congress had become fraught and few.

Opportunities for true intimacy rarer still.

Matilda sighed, signaling an intermission in the festivities. "You make me wish, Ashton Fenwick. I'd thought myself beyond wishing."

"Nobody should be beyond wishing." At the moment, Ashton wished they had more commodious accommodations than a hard bench upon which to further their acquaintance.

He grasped her ankle and, when she took no exception, lazily stroked her calf. She wore no stockings, no pantalets, nothing to deter skin-to-skin contact—or coitus.

"Your hands are warm," she said, as if even that mundane fact were a revelation to her.

"Your legs are strong," Ashton replied, hoping someday he could see the knees, calves, and thighs he was touching. "But if you could spread them just a little... another inch..."

Matilda accommodated him, one of her feet sliding to the paving stones.

Ashton had made love in gardens, haylofts, meadows, elegant boudoirs, and everywhere in between. This tiny crowded space behind Matilda Bryce's home had to be the most humble location to date. It had privacy, by virtue of the darkness.

But that was all it had, and even that privacy wasn't adequate for what Matilda deserved.

Ashton resigned himself to a compromise. Pleasure for the lady, frustration for himself—this time. He adjusted his hold and stroked up over the muscles of Matilda's thighs.

"You're certainly indirect about this," she muttered.

Indirect? If he were any more headlong, Matilda's skirts would be about her ears, and the bench would go up in flames.

"Matilda, has nobody ever pleasured you?"

Her harrumph became a sigh when Ashton trailed his fingers higher. He petted her, he teased, he was ready to curse her damned skirts when she scooted and gave him more leverage.

"That's better," he whispered. "Close your eyes and tell me what you like."

"Not that," she muttered. "It's too... It's vexing."

Ashton eased the pressure of his thumb on a place other women had very much encouraged him to touch.

"It's worse when you stop," Matilda said. "I can't hold still."

"Then, for the love God, woman, *move.*" He was contemplating using his mouth, or carrying her up to bed, when she met his next caress with a small shift of her hips.

"Like that?" she asked.

Clearly, her husband had died of stupidity. "Move however you please, Matilda. Relax and see where it goes. We're in no hurry."

Ashton's back had begun to ache, which was fortunate, because the pain distracted him from the pleasure stealing over Matilda as gradually as the rising sun spread over night-dark land. She became both more pliant and more restless, clinging to Ashton as he kept up a steady, relentless stroking.

She came apart in a silent, thrashing paroxysm of satisfaction that sent the bench scraping against the paving stones. The lady was possessed of more vigorous animal spirits than her prim demeanor would have suggested.

By the time she went still in Ashton's embrace, his arms ached in addition to his back, and his breeding organs were paining him as well.

He'd never enjoyed bringing pleasure to a woman half so much. The experience reminded him that before he'd been an earl, and even now, when he was Kilkenney, he was Ashton Fenwick, a bachelor, and a man in his prime.

"Mr. Fenwick." Offered in a breathless, bewildered whisper.

"Aye?"

Matilda hugged him, her arms snug about his neck. "Oh, Mr. Fenwick. Ashton. You…"

She was happy, possibly even delighted. Ashton felt the joy in her embrace, which was rife with enthusiastic affection, where previously she'd been shackled by caution. He heard the satisfaction in her voice and sensed it in her utter relaxation.

She was happy, and to his surprise, that was enough for him to be happy too. Despite the upcoming social Season, the damned English tenants, the looming ordeal of residence at the Albany, and the utter hell of wearing a title around his neck, Ashton Fenwick was happy.

* * *

"Mr. Fenwick, you are attending a court levee, not an execution," Matilda said. "Most people would be overjoyed to make the acquaintance of the sovereign."

Matilda had not been among their number, though she saw no need to tell Ashton that. She'd met the present George before he'd ascended to the throne, and he'd struck her as a sad, exceedingly well-fed man.

"I'm no' attending the damned levee," Ashton shot back as a pair of dancing slippers the size of small canoes went sailing into the wardrobe. "Hazelton can take his buggering idiot invitation and shove it—"

Helen snorted, and Ashton left off rummaging in his trunk, a pair of satin knee breeches in his hand. He'd been hurling items of apparel about his bedroom for the past twenty minutes, ever since Helen had brought the morning post from the Albany.

A roaring spate of Gaelic had ensued, so loud that Matilda had heard Ashton in the kitchen. Helen had summoned Matilda just as two porters had set down a large trunk in the middle of the bedroom.

Matilda's lover from the night before, a knowing, subtle, toweringly competent man, had been replaced with a large Scot in a larger temper. The previous night, Ashton had held her as she'd drowsed in his arms, the rhythm of his heart lulling her to sleep. She'd wakened when he'd carried her into the house and deposited her on the sofa in the unlit parlor, then settled an afghan about her.

He'd not taken her to her bedroom, much less joined her there, and she was grateful. She'd had enough trouble meeting his gaze over apple tarts at breakfast, though all he'd done was wink and pronounce the morning the loveliest he'd seen in London.

Ashton Fenwick had good aim with a compliment and with a rolled-up pair of stockings, which he used to send Solomon scampering from the room.

"Hazelton has no business dragooning me into this outing," Ashton said as the cat went yowling on his way. "I've made His Royal Majesty's acquaintance, and I'm confident one encounter was enough for both of us. Somewhere in this trunk is a lap desk, and I'll be penning his lordship a note declining his generous meddling."

"I could go meet the king," Helen said, hopping down from the windowsill and making an elaborate bow. "Tell the Earl of Hazelnuts you're sending your general tote 'em."

"Hazelnuts." Ashton tossed the breeches into the open trunk. "I like that. One can't send a minion to a court levee, though. I will kill Hazelton for this."

"How?" Helen asked, tossing Matilda the ball of stockings. "Will you run him through with a sword? Blow out his feeble English brains? Strangle him with his own cravat?"

"Child," Ashton said, "you will give me nightmares, more than you already do."

Matilda took the satin breeches from the disarray of the trunk and folded them, her hands lingering on the texture of the fabric. The stitches at the seams were exquisitely small and even, the gold embroidery at the knees a work of patient genius.

I miss this. Missed clothing that was beautiful to the touch and to the eye and made the wearer feel beautiful too. As a girl, she'd reveled in all things feminine. A new bonnet had occasioned joy. A reticule and shoes to match were cause for much strolling about in public.

What a fool she'd been, though she'd been a fool with lovely taste, which was part of the reason Althorpe had chosen her.

Matilda tucked the breeches into the clothes press and accepted another pair from Helen—cream rather than white. Ashton had a half-dozen pairs of formal knee breeches, each one more elegant than the last. His waistcoats were similarly breathtaking, though none approached ostentation.

Matilda wanted to press her face to the soft wool of his jackets and coats, wanted to gather up the lot and hug the heather and lavender scents close.

She blamed this yearning for long-lost luxuries on Ashton Fenwick. Her dreams the previous night had been marvelously sensual, and her awareness of her body was forever changed. By allowing Ashton to pleasure her—his deceptively tame term—she'd let loose a view of herself that was neither convenient nor familiar.

"Why don't you want to go?" Helen asked him. "It's only a morning in your good clothes. There won't be preaching, will there?"

Ashton dragged the trunk over to the clothes press and passed Matilda a lawn shirt. The fabric was cool and light, so fine she might have seen through it but for all the minute tucks and billowing folds.

"There will be preaching," Ashton said. "In ways subtle and overt, I'll be pressured to contribute to this or that project, to perform favors for His Majesty, to support a business venture with no more chance of success than you, wee Helen, have of becoming queen."

"Queens are old and fat," Helen said. "They don't get to wear breeches."

"What is the real problem?" Matilda asked. A fortune in fine tailoring had been folded into the trunk, and putting it away was a waste of time. Even a dedicated dandy couldn't wear this many outfits in little more than a week's time.

Matilda went on with her task anyway, because each item of clothing was another small insight into Ashton Fenwick. He favored brown and gray over blue or green, elegance over fussiness. His jewelry box was small, his lap desk solidly made and unadorned, though the family crest had been carved onto the lid.

"Did you make that yourself?" Matilda asked, tracing the unicorn's horn.

"Aye. How did you guess?"

"It reminds me of you." Sturdy, serviceable, unpretentious, and yet, the man who owned all this clothing was not merely wealthy gentry. He commanded formidable resources. Helen had said there were five more trunks at the Albany just as large as the one Matilda was emptying. The mews housed a team of chestnut geldings matched right down to their star, strip, and stockings.

"What's this?" Helen asked, holding up a length of folded plaid.

"A sash for the fancy dress kilt my sister-in-law insisted I bring along. Might have to attend some Scottish lord's wedding, she said. Very subtle, is our Alyssa. Easier to pack the outfit than argue with her."

Ashton had avoided Matilda's previous question, and that bothered her. A man who owned this much finery would have no trouble blending in with the Tuesday-morning levee crowd. The king would spare him a passing word or two, other gentlemen would be politely bored, and that would be that.

Drexel might attend. He was a proper Tory toady, and he would not know what to make of Ashton Fenwick.

The thought pleased her.

"Wear the kilt," she said. "The whole kit with the sporran, sash, and bonnet."

"How do you know of the accoutrements?" Ashton asked, taking the plaid from Helen. He handled the wool respectfully, unlike the silk and satin.

"Because it's your national dress," Matilda said. "And others of appreciable rank and status have worn it before you. You won't offend George by cutting a dash, and you will make a statement."

"Statement begins with *s*," Helen informed them, "like smart, saucy, and swive."

Ye gods, the girl was growing worse. "Shame begins with *s* too, young lady."

"I have a few days to make up my mind," Ashton muttered, fishing a tasseled sporran out of the trunk. "I'd be noticed."

"You'd be noticed on your own terms," Matilda said, taking the sporran from him. "And to blazes with anyone who doesn't like those terms."

He'd laid the folded plaid across his shoulders. The pattern was a subdued brown and gray with hints of red, suggestive of the hunting plaids designed to blend in with foliage and bracken.

"I'd like to see you in your kilt," Matilda added. *Just once.*

Ashton took the plaid from his own shoulders and looped the length of it around Matilda's back, pulling her a step closer.

"Then that settles it. I'll greet the king in my plaid, or not at all. The lady of the house has spoken."

His smile was relieved, suggesting he'd needed somebody to remind him that he had a choice, that he wasn't a bondsman indentured to the whims of his titled friend.

And Matilda had needed somebody to remind her that she was *alive.* Not quite an even trade, but she was glad to have been a friend to Ashton in even a small way. Maybe when the sun went down, she'd become his lover in truth, and not simply the woman he'd pleasured once upon a time in the back garden.

CHAPTER EIGHT

"Duke has a *u* in it," Helen said, running her hand over the donkey's shaggy neck.

"What else do you hear in that word?" Ashton heard pomposity, wealth, arrogance, and politics. Yesterday's decision to wear his kilt to the levee would probably raise a few ducal eyebrows, and that gratified Ashton more than it should.

"Duke also has a *d* and a *k*," Helen replied. "D-u-k."

"Very good. Can you think of a word that rhymes with it?"

Spelling was something of a performance art for even the well-educated, and Helen was suspicious of vowels. Her original definition of a vowel referred to a note of hand to secure a debt of honor, an I Owe You, not some peculiar letter that changed its sound on a whim.

Ashton had taken several days to get to the bottom of her confusion, though with Helen, confusion manifested as indignation and profanity. Always.

"A word that rhymes with duke would be..." She moved her lips in a silent canvassing of the alphabet.

Ashton breathed a sigh of relief when she'd passed *f*—Helen delighted in mocking his burr—but realized where she was heading when she grinned at him over Marmaduke's back.

"Puke," she said. "P-u-k."

"You might have said fluke. It's an odd kind of fish. Marmaduke likes to have his chin scratched."

Helen delighted in the donkey, and the donkey, being no fool, delighted in her. Buying the beast had been an impulse, but worth it for the consternation he caused at Tatts and in the fancy stables attached to the Albany.

The unexpected benefit had been Helen's reaction. Never had a lowly ass been regarded with such reverent amazement.

As Ashton showed Helen the basics of equine grooming and further parsed the mysteries of long vowels, he also considered Matilda's reaction to their evening in the garden. Yesterday, she'd taken charge of his wardrobe, such as one trunk constituted a wardrobe.

Ashton had liked the sight of her handling his clothing. Her hands on his satin breeches had provoked stirrings of the private sort, but then, so did her admission that she'd enjoy seeing him in his kilt. For her, he'd wear the plaid anywhere.

Or take it off. She hadn't given him any indication that she wanted it off of him, so Ashton waited, and let his bath water cool thoroughly before he washed.

"Where are we going today?" Helen asked as Ashton adjusted a pony bridle to fit Marmaduke's ungainly head.

"To pay a call on a solicitor. You'll stay with Dusty."

"Mr. Harder," Helen said. "I don't like him."

"You don't like much of anybody, and his name is Harpster. What has he done to offend you?"

Helen used an overturned bucket to scramble onto Duke's back and accepted the reins when Ashton looped them over the donkey's head.

"Mr. Harpster looks hungry, when he gets plenty to eat," Helen said. "His clerks aren't getting enough to eat, though. They had scared eyes. Some of the game girls have eyes like that. The young ones."

Ashton accepted Dusty's reins from a groom—the Albany's stable help was excellent—and led the horse out to the mounting block.

"You will never ply that trade," Ashton said. "Put it from your mind. You will be better situated than your sister if you apply yourself to your letters and learn the manners Mrs. Bryce is trying to teach you."

Helen made a show of petting the donkey, but Ashton could see the questions in her eyes. A very few courtesans were well provided for, and even fewer married a besotted protector. Fairy tales came true just often enough to let a game girl keep plying her trade, despite disease, violence, penury, and disgrace. A country maid might walk the streets for a few years and retreat to her village before her health suffered irreparable harm, but whispers would follow her for the rest of her life.

Rather like being a bastard earl.

"How long will we be at Mr. Harpster's?" Helen asked as Ashton turned his horse into the street.

The girl could out-eat a yeoman in haying season. "Not past your midday meal."

"You want to get back to Mrs. Bryce's."

Ashton hadn't wanted to leave the quiet, tidy house with the tiny garden and the passionate landlady. "You should ride behind me a few yards, keep a respectful distance, and watch for any who'd do me harm."

For all her insouciance, Helen took her job with touching seriousness. She dropped back a few horse lengths, and anybody watching would not have associated the lad on the shaggy donkey with the fine gent on the dark gelding.

Harpster was all genial welcome, though Ashton couldn't help confirming Helen's assessment. The solicitor's gaze was avaricious, even when he smiled and welcomed Ashton into his office.

"My lord, good day. Shall I ring for tea?"

"I'm here to do business, Harpster, not socialize. Have you prepared the map I requested?"

"As to that, I invite you to have a seat. We will discuss the status of your tenancies in as great detail as you please. The day promises to be splendid, does it not? Spring always gladdens the heart after the dreary months of winter."

And unnecessarily long meetings with wealthy clients doubtless gladdened Harpster's heart. Ashton took a seat and maintained his silence, while Harpster bustled around to the other side of the desk and prattled on about the events of the upcoming Season and the benefits of having the Earl of Hazelton as a sponsor.

As if Ashton were a debutante?

"About my map?"

"You shall have it!" Harpster went to the door, stepped into the other room, and conferred with a clerk, or made a pretense of doing so. On the desk were stacked five thick ledgers, all green, all embossed with the Kilkenney crest.

Ashton took the account book on the bottom of the pile and leafed through it. The record was from five years ago, when Ewan had still held the title. Farm by farm, month by month, expenses and revenues were tallied in a tidy hand. Comparable records were kept in Scotland, but as far as Ashton knew, nobody had ever set the two side by side.

"My lord," Harpster said, striding back into the room and closing the door. "I am very sorry to say that the requested map is not yet complete. My staff has failed me, and thus I must disappoint you. The work was ongoing when a matter pressing toward litigation seized my head clerk's notice, and our progress on your assignment has fallen short of the goal. I see you have taken notice of the estate ledgers. I hope all is in order?"

The avarice in Harpster's gaze was laced with something else. Anxiety, ire, resentment. Ashton couldn't tell exactly, though Helen might have been able to parse it.

What did it say about the firm of Harpster and Sons that Ashton trusted a juvenile pickpocket's judgment more than he trusted his own firm of solicitors?

"I have much to do today, Harpster."

"As well you should, with the Season nigh upon us. The tailor's fittings alone can take half your time, and then there are social calls that must be attended to, the early entertainments, the blandishments found only in the capital. I do understand, my lord, and we are ready to assist in any and every regard. Perhaps we might use this morning's appointment to discuss your views on marriage settlements?"

For the past three years, Ashton had tolerated Harpster's fawning and smiling on those occasions when travel to London had been unavoidable. Ewan had inherited the firm along with the title, but had never particularly sung Harpster's praises.

"Our appointment is over," Ashton said, rising, "as is our association. If you can't prepare a simple map in a timely fashion, then you should at least have the decency not to waste my morning with a meeting for which you are unprepared. I understand that the press of business can be compelling. I do not understand rudeness. A note rescheduling would have been sufficient, provided you apologized for the delay."

Harpster remained by the door, as if one pale, paunchy solicitor would stop a Highlander intent on charging to freedom.

"You are being very hasty, my lord. Travel has doubtless left you fatigued, and the capital can be overwhelming to those more comfortable in the shires. I'm willing to overlook this outburst, though in future, given your unfortunate past, you would be well advised to—"

"I'll wish you a good day now," Ashton said, scooping up the ledgers, "lest I kill you and ruin what remains of your morning and mine. If you complete the map by close of business, you may send it 'round to the Albany with a final bill for services rendered."

Ashton took a moment to savor the consternation on Harpster's face, then bowed and stalked out.

"You!" Ashton called to the largest of the clerks. "You will please run these over to the Albany for me and stop by the chophouse on your way back. The lot of you can use a decent meal." He set the ledgers on the boy's desk and slapped a pile of coins atop the books. "Bring that one with you," he said, pointing to the next-sturdiest boy, "to help carry the food and the ledgers."

"Yes, milord," the clerk said, scrambling off his stool and dropping the coins into his pocket. "At once, milord. C'mon, Smith. The man wants his ledgers delivered."

The boys were out the door as if the excise men were galloping up the High Street. Ashton followed at a slower pace.

"Short meeting," Helen said as Ashton tightened Dusty's girth.

"I sacked him."

"Good."

"Not good. Now I must find another firm to handle my business." Which meant a call on Hazelton, damn the luck.

"Too bad for you, London hasn't but one or two solicitors, and none of them will want to do business with a wealthy earl."

Ashton climbed into the saddle. "You're to follow a few *respectful* paces behind."

Helen scrambled onto Duke's back. "At once, my lord. I live to serve your worship. Serve begins with an *s.*"

"So do swat, spank, and sermon."

Helen resumed her vigilance on the ride to Mayfair, and Dusty was sufficiently blasé about town traffic that Ashton had a moment to consider his decision to sack Harpster.

Harpster was arrogant, self-interested, greedy, lazy, and untrustworthy. A solicitor could be all those things and still be competent, as could an earl. Ashton had sacked Harpster because such a man couldn't be allowed to have anything to do with fashioning marriage settlements.

Not when Ashton himself could barely fathom such an undertaking.

He set that thought aside and made his way to the Earl of Hazelton's abode, though the hour still early for a social call. Hazelton was in his library, correspondence in piles around him, a tortoiseshell cat who rivaled Solomon for size and self-possession lounging amid the chaos.

"I don't have your list of scandals yet," Hazelton said, coming around the desk. "And if you're here to beg off regarding Tuesday's levee, spare me your pleading."

Ashton wandered the shelves of books, wondering how many had actually been read. Most, he'd guess. His lordship had a mind that did not tolerate boredom.

"For your information, Hazelton, I've met the sovereign twice. On both occasions, he harangued me about the presumptuousness of a certain Northumbrian coal nabob whose importuning for a spot on the honors list annoys the royal person. Though I've not been to Newcastle since I was fifteen, George expects me to know this worthy—I'm from 'the north,' after all—and to inspire him to leave off lusting for a barony."

"You've been introduced to the king *twice*?" Hazelton was surprised, which was some satisfaction in itself.

"The Duke of Atholl and I get on well, and Ewan dragged me to meet George nearly three years ago. Your neighbor, Viscount Landover, sent a letter of introduction, and some of his friends were good enough to speak on my behalf."

Hazelton used his quill pen to tease the cat's nose. "So my patronage isn't required?"

Ashton liked Hazelton, but the time had come to make a few things clear.

"Your good intentions are appreciated, but if you ever again commit my time without my permission, I will show you how a bastard Scotsman expresses his displeasure with another's rudeness."

Hazelton sat back, his dark features shuttering. "Rudeness? I arrange for you to spend time in the presence of your king, and you thank me with that insult?"

Ashton leaned over the desk. "Do I commit your time without consulting you? Does your countess even take that liberty? Does your father-in-law-the-bloody-duke speak for your time or constrain your freedom with stupid social obligations?"

The cat played with the quill, mangling one end, then batting the whole feather over the side of the desk. Ashton maintained a glower that had convinced three-quarter-ton draft stallions to turn up as biddable as lambs.

"I apologize, Fenwick. It won't happen again."

"When you're trying to be humble—and failing badly—you might consider using the title," Ashton said, picking up the white feather. "How is your countess?"

Hazelton rose with the cat in his arms. "She also reminds me to use your title, but I thought you were avoiding it."

"I am, for now, but my days as just another breathtakingly handsome face are numbered, thanks in part to you. I need the name of a trustworthy solicitor."

The cat took up a perch on Hazelton's shoulder, which gave the earl the air of a sorcerer—or an eccentric.

"I thought you used Harpster. He's reputed to be competent."

"I let him go. Got airs above his station and wasted my time. Harpster took to corresponding directly with my English tenants, and they with him. I never gave him leave to speak for me in that fashion. The correspondence grew unnecessarily heated and costly. That sort of assistance would soon land me in the poorhouse."

"I see."

The cat tried to lick Hazelton's ear, which moved the picture they made squarely into the eccentric camp.

"Harpster could not contain his enthusiasm for negotiating marriage settlements," Ashton said. "I gather a canny solicitor can ensure those negotiations are more time-consuming than the courtship itself. I don't care for that approach to marriage, and I don't care for being told my situation is so delicate that even a lazy London solicitor knows more about how I should go on than I do."

Ashton plucked the cat from the earl's shoulder. The beast must have weighed nearly twenty pounds.

"Fenwick, you can't—"

"Kilkenney. I need the practice."

"Kilkenney, you can't toss aside everybody who tries to help you step into the earldom's shoes."

Ashton's patience hit the end of its tether. "How long ago did I assume the title?"

"Several years."

"How long ago were you married?"

"About the same."

"Do you expect other men to tell you how to manage with your countess?"

"One doesn't manage with Maggie. One worships from a respectful distance, or an even more respectful proximity."

"I've been the earl for as long as you've been her husband. Bugger off, Hazelton, and don't defend those trying to take advantage of my generous nature. I don't want the most expensive, respected, well-established firm of solicitors. I want somebody hungrier and less impressed with their grandfathers' portraits."

What Ashton longed for were the days when he'd had no use for solicitors of any kind.

"I know of a firm that might suit you. The youngest member is a bastard, in every sense of the word. He uses the family name and was raised in his father's household, but the talk never seems to entirely die down. He's surly, does not suffer fools, and has too good an opinion of himself."

"Sounds eminently qualified."

Hazelton used the mangled pen to scratch a direction on a slip of foolscap. "Will you come to the levee?"

Ashton set the cat on the desk, careful not to disturb his lordship's piles of letters. "Wouldn't miss it. We'll take my carriage, and then you'll join me for lunch at my club."

Hazelton held up both hands. "I've apologized. You needn't belabor the point. I'll be happy to join you for lunch, though I'd rather be invited than commanded to appear."

Ashton scratched the cat's ears in parting. "Your sister always claimed you were a smart lad. What's this solicitor's name?"

"Damon Basingstoke. You'll get on with him famously."

* * *

Helen was off to groom Marmaduke, or so she'd claimed, and Pippa had gone across the alley to visit with other domestics during the late-afternoon lull before supper preparations. Solomon had left the house at midday and probably wouldn't be seen again until morning.

Everybody had somewhere to be and somebody to be with, except Matilda. She considered doing some baking, because the last apple tarts had met their fate at breakfast, but baking created a mess and meant she'd have to remain in the kitchen for the next two hours.

She could read, though she'd read her six-book library many times. Other than skimming the morning paper to watch for news of Drexel and Stephen, she avoided the inflammatory drivel that passed for London journalism.

Ashton had brought a few books with him. He'd probably not mind lending her one or two, provided she returned them prior to his remove to the Albany. Matilda started for the stairs, then paused at the sitting-room door.

Was any pretext more transparent than borrowing a book?

A door opened above, and Ashton stepped out of his rooms. "Matilda. I was wondering if I might borrow needle and thread?"

He wore a subdued version of morning attire, though his ensemble was a bit rumpled, as if he had caught a nap on the sofa in the past hour.

"I'm happy to do a spot of mending for you," Matilda said.

He pulled the door closed and came down the steps, his deliberate tread an echo of Matilda's heartbeat.

How did one embark on a liaison so temporary, it needed another name? She'd seen Ashton Fenwick's exquisite finery, heard Helen describe his matched team and his grand rooms at the Albany. Biding at that august address, he'd rub shoulders with the sons and cousins of all the best families.

Which meant that when he left Matilda's household, he'd be well and truly lost to her.

He stopped on the step above. Close enough that Matilda caught the scent of heather and had to link her hands behind her back lest she grab his cravat and haul him close for a kiss.

"I lied," he said. "I have my own sewing kit, and I'm as handy with a needle as the next bachelor. I wanted an excuse to seek you out."

Matilda moved up a step, and then one more, so she was eye to eye with him. "I was about to ask you for the loan of a book."

"I have several. Do you read French?"

"Yes, but that's not the point."

He cocked a hip against the bannister. "I see."

"I'm glad somebody does. I have no idea what I'm about. You make me feel things in the dark that sunder my reason. Then at breakfast, it's 'pass the salt' and 'lovely weather we're having.' Do I sit in my parlor and hope you'll come by with mending, take you fresh biscuits, or slip into your bed in the dark of night?"

"Matilda?"

"I'm babbling. This is a novel experience. Even when I was a debutante, anticipating my first waltz, even on my rubbishing wedding night—"

Soft lips pressed against her mouth. "A gentleman doesn't presume, my dear. The next move belongs to the lady."

She rested her forehead on Ashton's shoulder and kept her hands and her kisses to herself.

"You are in error, Mr. Fenwick. Ladies do not make *moves*. They smile, they favor a fellow with a dance, they tat lace, and go barmy, but they do not march into a gentleman's quarters and announce a desire to have their way with him."

Though Matilda would, before that gentleman left for the most commodious quarters in the metropolis and forgot she existed.

"Let's do an experiment," Ashton said, taking Matilda by the hand and leading her up the stairs. "I assume the house is empty but for the two of us?"

"It is."

Ashton opened his door and escorted Matilda straight into his bedroom. "If you would please state a desire for my person now, the experiment will be complete."

"One hears the Scots are prone to eccentricity."

"We're prone to genius, also modesty. Ask me, Matilda."

The bed sat two yards away, a venerable monstrosity that seemed to be everywhere Matilda looked.

"I'll feel pathetic," she said. "Begging you for... for that."

"Never beg. Simply tell me you want me to be your lover."

The words made her shiver. "In broad daylight?"

"I want you to be my lover."

At first, Matilda thought Ashton was instructing her, but as he unknotted his cravat and shrugged out of his coat, she realized he was stating a fact. *He wanted her to be his lover.*

The shiver took on an edge of pleasurable anticipation. She'd dared elude the law, dared to seek safety in her enemy's backyard. Surely she could dare to indulge in an hour of passion?

"I know nothing of being a lover, and I was no kind of wife, to hear my late husband tell it."

"Then he was a blundering disgrace." Ashton draped his coat over the back of a chair and started unbuttoning his waistcoat.

"What are you about?"

"I'm showing you what's on offer," he replied, hanging the waistcoat over the jacket, "in broad daylight. I revel in a daylight loving, myself. A lady at her pleasures is a beautiful creature."

Matilda had never been a beautiful creature. "Don't you dare throw that shirt to the floor."

He pulled his shirttails from his waistband. "I was about to toss it over the chair." The shirt came off over his head, and Matilda forgot all about daylight and Scottish modesty. Ashton was naked above the waist, and all at once, regret stole over her.

"I never saw my husband unclothed, but he wouldn't have looked as you do." The difference would have started with Ashton's defined musculature and a sprinkling of dark chest hair. Althorpe had been tall, but pale and running to fat. The more significant difference would have been that Ashton Fenwick was entirely at ease without clothing.

Althorpe's expression when anticipating marital privileges had been impatient, imperious, and disdainful. Matilda was to accommodate him, ask no questions, and make no demands.

If she offered Ashton Fenwick mere accommodation, he'd toss it straight out the window.

"Your expression is more disgruntled than eager," he said, standing directly before her. "Am I taking too long?"

Matilda had no conscious thought to put her hand on his chest. Her hand simply ended up there, over warm flesh, smooth muscle, and odd, crinkly hair. The rhythm of Ashton's heart beat beneath her palm in a steady tattoo.

"My marriage was miserable."

She'd thought those words a time or two, but compared to the upheaval following Althorpe's death, the prison her marriage had become was a detail.

Except, it wasn't. Saying the words aloud reminded Matilda of months spent immured in the countryside, where she was to read improving tracts, await her husband's brief visits, and pray to conceive a son. The time spent in Town was worse, ignoring pitying looks on the few occasions Althorpe bothered to escort her.

"I'm sorry," Ashton said, enfolding Matilda against his naked chest. "Shall I be your revenge on the old boy's sainted memory?"

"It's not that simple," she replied, letting him have some of her weight. "Althorpe was a miserly martinet twenty years my senior. His only son could do no wrong. I was to provide a spare, which I failed to do. The boy took a fancy to me. I wouldn't know how to entice Solomon over the back stoop with a fresh haddock, but according to my husband, I was Lilith, the temptress."

Ashton stroked a hand over her hair. "It's no' supposed to be like that. Shame on them both, father and son. They're a discredit to the male gender."

He spoke softly, but his words were also a sentiment Matilda hadn't heard from another soul. For Ashton to pronounce sentence so easily, so confidently, relieved a niggle of self-doubt Matilda had carried for years.

"I was glad when Althorpe died. I didn't wish him dead, but I was glad to be free of him." The words might once have made her ashamed, but in Ashton's arms, she merely spoke a pathetic truth.

"I'm glad he's gone too and will further admit I wish you'd never married him."

The ultimate regret, and Ashton had had to say it for her.

This exchange was extraordinary in so many ways. Matilda was pressed against a half-naked man and wanted nothing but to press closer. She was being honest about her past. She was exchanging intimacies she'd never thought to share with another, and all of this was transpiring while the sunshine poured through the window.

Revenge wasn't the right word for what Matilda was about to do, but neither was it entirely wrong. She would finally learn what it meant to be a lady about her pleasures, to have a lover who was also a friend, however temporarily.

"Ashton Fenwick, will you be my lover?"

CHAPTER NINE

Ashton had made love with angry women, jubilant women, sad women, lonely women, lusty women, bored women, and everything in between. He'd been happy to share an interlude of pleasure and comfort with each of them and hoped they recalled him fondly.

He did not want to be a mere fond recollection for Matilda Bryce. He wanted to be the man who showed her how lovely life could be when shared with a true partner, and he wanted her to show him the same marvel. This was doubtless a form of dementia brought on by the London air, for Matilda wanted nothing to do with partnership of the permanent variety.

"I will be your lover, Matilda, with joy and with pride. I will also be your lady's maid."

For a woman who'd been married, Matilda knew nothing about flirtation or bedroom protocol. Her idiot husband had much to answer for, but so did the nonsense that passed for a genteel woman's education.

"You can't just get in bed, take off your breeches, and close your eyes?" she asked.

"Take off my—under the covers, you mean?"

A blush crept up her neck. "Or I could turn my back."

"For God's sake, woman. I long to bare all my treasures to you, and you want to turn your back?"

Matilda's face was pink, and the sight of her discomfiture was anything but humorous.

"Turn around, then," Ashton said, taking her gently by the shoulders.

She jumped when he began undoing the hooks down the back of her dress. The fit was loose enough that she might have contorted herself into the garment unassisted, or maybe Pippa aided her. After the hooks came her laces, and then Ashton gave her a gentle push in the direction of the privacy screen.

"I'll be under the covers, with my breeches *off.*"

She rustled away, and Ashton took a moment to lock the door to the stairway, secure the windows against any housebreaking ventures Helen might attempt, and close the door to the bedroom.

When Matilda emerged from the privacy screen in a worn, wrinkled shift, Ashton was sitting with his back to the headboard, the covers drawn over an erection that wanted the merest hint of encouragement to come to full attention.

She took his breeches from where he'd draped them across the desk and folded them tidily. Next she folded his shirt, sleeves precisely matching, collar tucked just so, cuffs smoothed flat. His waistcoat would doubtless divert her for another quarter hour.

"The sunlight coming in the window reveals more to me than you intend, Matilda."

She scampered over to the bed with the speed of a startled cat. "I'm trying to figure out a way to explain something to you."

"I know where babies come from."

"That is not funny to a woman whose sole excuse for taking up space under her husband's roof was her ability to reproduce."

Well, hell. "Matilda, have you any reason to believe the problem lay with you? Couldn't the issue have been on your husband's part?"

She sat on the bed, her back to Ashton. Why didn't women grasp that every part of the female anatomy was delightful to behold? The nape of a woman's neck could inspire ballads, the curve of her spine could make a man ache.

"I suspect he was the problem. Althorpe was not enthusiastic about... That is to say, he put forth great effort..."

Ashton studied the angle of Matilda's jaw, the set of her shoulders. She wasn't embarrassed, but she was grasping for vocabulary.

"He couldn't finish," Ashton said. "He'd fuss about, heave and groan, flail away, curse, and probably leave you sore, but he couldn't finish."

She snatched up a brocade pillow and hugged it to her chest. "Not often, and that was my fault too. I didn't know what to do, so I asked somebody more knowledgeable than I."

The goose girl probably knew more about intentionally arousing a man's interest than Matilda did.

"Who was this expert?"

"She maintained a common nuisance across the square from Althorpe's town house. They do that, you know. Set up the bawdy houses in the decent neighborhoods. The woman told me her employees were safer that way, made better money, and were more easily available to the men who could pay well for their frolics."

"I can continue admiring the lovely view of your back, Matilda, or I can put my arms around you while we hold this discussion. The choice is yours."

More than ever, Ashton understood that the choices must remain hers.

Matilda slanted a glance at him over her shoulder, then cast the pillow away and tucked herself against his side.

Ashton wrapped an arm around her shoulder, lest she wander off into the sunbeams. "What did the madam tell you?"

"That I was the bravest fool she'd ever met. I had often been called a fool, but never brave before. We talked for a long time, and when I was…" She paused to pull the covers up over her legs. "When I was newly widowed, she was very kind to me."

"She assured you the lack of a son was not your fault?" Whoever she was, Ashton silently thanked the woman.

"She assured me that despite what any physician or midwife might say, it was nearly impossible to tell for certain why conception hadn't occurred, but that my husband was likely to blame. I asked her what I could do about it."

"And she suggested an affair?"

Matilda shifted about some more, until her head was resting on Ashton's thigh. "Everybody knows more about this business than I do. Yes, she suggested an affair, even going so far as to remind me that my husband's close family members presented the best hope of siring a child who'd look like him. She also suggested a few intimate…"

"Tricks," Ashton supplied, searching for the pins in Matilda's hair.

"For want of a better word. The first time I acted upon one of those suggestions, my husband scolded me for being a slut. What are you doing?"

"Taking down your hair."

She was silent for a moment, while Ashton freed her braid from a dozen hairpins. When he sank his fingers into her hair and massaged her scalp, she sighed.

"That feels sinfully good."

"Matilda, if this is your idea of sinfully good, then your notions of sin are woefully unimaginative."

Through the thin sheet, she bit Ashton's thigh, not hard. "You inspire me, Ashton Fenwick. I wish I'd met you a year from now."

He had no idea what she meant, but then, her mouth was inches from his cock, and his store of ideas was growing predictably focused.

"Are you fond of that chemise?" Ashton asked.

"I'm not fond of it, but it's one of only two that I own. Why?"

"Because I'm not fond of it either. What must I do to persuade you to take it off?"

She rolled to her back and braced herself on her elbows. "One removes every stitch?"

Her question told him volumes, all of it sad. "Your husband came to you after all the servants were abed, probably wearing a nightshirt large enough to double as a sail for the royal yacht, but no larger than the nightgown he never asked you to remove. He climbed under the covers, wedged himself between your legs, and without so much as kissing you, started poking and thrashing about. If and when he achieved satisfaction, he heaved himself off of you without a word and took himself back to his own bed."

Matilda regarded the expanse of coverlet, which was white with embroidered sprigs of lavender. "Sometimes he said good night before he left."

Ashton wanted to howl, but Matilda had spoken quietly. No howling, no beating the pillows, no roaring and cursing in Gaelic, French, Latin, or Greek.

The bed shivered minutely. Matilda's chin hitched, and Ashton braced himself for her tears. Her chin hitched again, then dipped and a snort escaped her.

"He said... good night," she repeated. "He made a complete, bleating, humping cake of himself, and then..."

She chuckled, she chortled, and then she was whooping against Ashton's side. "He was ridiculous, pathetic, and sad. I ought to be angry at him, but you're right. Althorpe's nightshirt could have been the tent over a Venetian breakfast, and he never brought so much as a single candle into my bedroom. He was ashamed, I suppose. The poor man. If he'd once acknowledged the situation, if he'd set aside his posturing for an instant...."

"But he didn't," Ashton said, getting comfortable on his back. "Any offer you made to help would have acknowledged that at least part of the problem was his. No wonder he married an innocent right out of the schoolroom. A woman with experience would not have stood for his bullying."

Matilda curled up against his side, her head on his shoulder. "Bullying. That's what it was. I was beginning to see the truth of that. Althorpe never laid a hand on me in anger, else I might have seen his true nature sooner. Let's talk of something else now."

Excellent notion. "Your chemise?" She had only two, and the one she wore looked too worn even for mending. No manly displays of disrespect for her apparel, then.

Matilda dove under the covers, like a duck in search of food, then came up holding a wad of soft linen. Her expression was disgruntled, wary, and determined.

I love her. The thought emerged into Ashton's mind whole, certain, and true. He loved Matilda's courage, her resilience, her ability to laugh—he adored hearing her laugh—and he loved that she wanted him. Not his title, not his wealth, not his lordly consequence.

Just him. This was not the infatuation of a young man for all the ladies, or even adult male approval for a woman of spirit and substance. Ashton loved Matilda with a conviction no less permanent for being irrational and inconvenient.

He plucked the linen from her hand, strolled over to the privacy screen, and took his sweet damned time about hanging the nightgown over the top. His return to the bed was just as leisurely, and thank the lusty cherubs, Matilda watched his every step.

"Turn around again," she said, sitting up with the sheet tucked under her arms. "Slowly."

Ashton obliged, arousal and joy roaring through him. "Look as much as you please, Matilda mine."

She motioned toward the carpet beside the bed. "Come closer."

An inspection followed and an interrogation.

"How did you get the scar on your foot?"

"Horse stepped on me."

"Who broke your nose?"

"Same horse, neither injury on purpose. He's retired, gentle as a lamb, but still clumsy."

"Where is your favorite place to be touched?"

"My heart."

Matilda patted the pillow. "You are awful. Come back to bed."

Ashton was awfully aroused. She hadn't asked about that. Maybe the evidence spoke for itself.

"Have you more questions, Matilda?"

"I've dithered enough. Do you have questions?"

Ashton hadn't been expecting that offer. "I can ask them without words."

He climbed under the covers and wrestled Matilda over him. She looked him up and down, then curled close, her hair tickling his chest.

"You are warm. I like that you're warm."

That bastard Althorpe had come to his wife with cold hands and cold feet. "Kiss me, and I'll grow even warmer."

Matilda obliged, and by degrees, she grew more enthusiastic about straddling an aroused man. Ashton kissed her in return, learned the contours of her naked back, and began a gentle exploration of how she enjoyed having her breasts touched.

And all the while, she hovered above him, denying him her weight and even a brush of her sex.

"I like that you have callused hands," she whispered. "And hair on your chest, and scars on your foot, and a broken nose."

"Such flattery. Give me your weight, Matilda. I'm aching for you." Her breasts filled his hands, and that felt lovely, and tasted lovely, but it wasn't enough.

"I'm not sure—"

Ashton took her by the hips and showed her. "Like that. Say hello and stay for a wee friendly chat."

"You want me to—?" She tried a slow glide, barely touching him.

A lightning strike would have been less of a shock to Ashton's senses. "That's a start. More would be nice too."

Nice was a monumental understatement. Matilda got into the spirit of the undertaking, sliding and wiggling, teasing and—she had a diabolical streak—pausing.

And thank the everlasting powers, she grew damp, then slick, though she didn't seem to notice.

"This daylight loving has much to recommend it," she said, rubbing the side of her breast against Ashton's cheek. He hadn't shaved since rising, and the infernal woman apparently liked that too.

"Aye, though with you, I think any hour would be an adventure. Are you happy where you are, or should we indulge in some variety?"

"I am not happy," she said, sitting up and drawing circles around Ashton's nipples with her fingernails. "I am discontent, inside, and—you're looking at me."

"I'm staring, love. Growing visually inebriated, and maybe a bit cross-eyed. You are a fiend, Matilda, and that feels... I could spend just from what you're doing with your fingers."

She stopped. "Please don't. Once you spend, it's good night, isn't it?"

God love her. "More like, we ring for a fresh pot while contemplating further shared pleasures. I'd need about two cuddles and a kiss before being ready to oblige you again. I'm happy to prove I'm not boasting if you'd be so good as to take me inside you."

Please, please, please.

"Like this? I don't have to lie beneath you?"

"Exactly like this, or lying beneath me, on your side, against the wall, on all fours, sitting in the middle of the bed with your legs wrapped around—"

She kissed him before he'd got through a quarter of his list of fantasies. When it became apparent Matilda either didn't know how to start their joining, or couldn't bring herself to touch his cock, Ashton took himself in hand and found her heat.

"You have to do this part," he said. "You have to decide how deep, how fast, how hard and how—St. Robert the Bruce in a tree."

Matilda sank onto him in one slow, relentless slide. Ashton had to bring to mind swimming in a loch in April to prevent himself from spending in one great, thrashing shudder.

"Did I do that right? It feels right. You feel right. You feel... satisfying. Abundant. I don't know how to describe it."

"I get the general notion. How does this feel?" Ashton thrust lazily, and Matilda soon had the knack of counterpointing his efforts.

The rest of the conversation was silent and ranged from Ashton's hands whispering across Matilda's back, to her mouth teasing at his ear, to his thanks sent quietly heavenward as Matilda began to move more urgently.

Ashton grabbed for self-restraint with both hands, even as he sent his lady flying free. When Matilda went soaring in his arms, he wanted to laugh as she had—joyously, heartily, gratefully.

This was how loving was supposed to be. Trust and tenderness, intimacy and freedom, all wrapped up with gladness and pleasure. Ashton held on to those sentiments as Matilda subsided against him, panting and pliant.

She was his, he was hers. He'd found his countess before the Season had even started, and all because he'd taken a little time to be himself before strutting about as the blighted earl.

"Time to order a fresh pot?" Matilda murmured.

Ashton hadn't spent, nor would he until he'd offered the woman a proper proposal. "This pot's still plenty hot. Perhaps you'd like another cup?"

She struggled up, bracing herself above him. "What on earth are you talking about? If you think I can make *moves* now, as you put it, when you've obliterated my ability to think, then I can assure you—"

Ashton had to close his eyes, lest the rosy flush over her chest stir him past all control. "I'll show you. You don't even have to move. Just hold me."

Matilda held him, and he showed her that the right teapot offered as many servings as she wanted, served exactly as she pleased.

* * *

"You have a very pretty singing voice, ma'am," Pippa said. "Don't believe I've heard you sing before."

Matilda had forgotten how, but yesterday afternoon in Ashton Fenwick's bed, she'd started to recall.

"Singing is supposed to be one of a young lady's accomplishments, though my gift was more at the pianoforte. I like to sing. I'm not as keen on folding laundry."

She and Pippa were in the laundry, the end of the week being when all the wash that had spent the past several days drying could be taken down, folded, and put away. Rainy weeks were the worst, because only the kitchen could effectively dry anything. Racks and clotheslines cluttered the entire space, and large items such as sheets never felt entirely dry.

Ironing them dry was one of Matilda's least-favorite chores, but damp sheets were a recipe for sickness and poor sleep.

"I don't mind laundry here," Pippa said, taking up a pillowcase. "Nobody bellowing at me to turn from the life of Jezebel and repent of my sins. I never did repent of 'em, but I got bloody sick of having an empty belly. If I were a man, I'd be ashamed to think a woman put up with me only because she was starving. Doesn't seem to bother most of the gents, though."

Matilda folded her good chemise, the one she saved for Sundays and special occasions, not that she'd had special occasions in the past six years.

"Not all men are like that, Pippa. Some are decent, honorable, and kind."

And glory of glories, some of the decent, honorable, kind ones were fiendishly talented in bed. In the space of a few hours the previous afternoon, Ashton Fenwick had not merely educated Matilda, he'd enlightened her— illuminated entire parts of her life, much less her body, that had been shrouded in ignorance.

"I fancy that Nathan," Pippa said, folding the pillowcase into a precise square. "He's a good sort, and he doesn't judge me for making do as best I could."

Nathan was the neighbor's oldest boy, and from what Matilda could tell, he was a fine young man. Nathan was not quick, but he thought for himself, and when he did come to a conclusion, he based his opinion on facts and reason, rather than the loudest gossip in the marketplace.

"You could ask Nathan to walk you home from services," Matilda said. "He might be waiting for you to make that move."

Ladies did make moves, take the initiative, and even give orders. She knew that now.

"I go to services because you make me," Pippa said, taking up another pillowcase, "and to set an example for Helen. Where's she off to, by the way?"

"She and Mr. Fenwick are preparing for his eventual remove to the Albany, and he said he wanted to pay a call on some Scottish duke who's new to town."

"So that's why he wore that kilt get-up. You're a good influence on him, ma'am. Him too."

In his kilt, Ashton was a different man. More free, more imposing, more devilish. He'd made sure to tell Matilda that beneath his kilt, he wore nothing save the treasure God had stowed there.

Matilda set aside her good chemise and started on the endless, everlasting, bottomless pile of towels.

"I will be sorry to see Mr. Fenwick leave us, and not simply because he's a good lodger."

Pippa's grin was in the tradition of a happy Jezebel. "Fancy him, do ya? I expect he'll pay you the occasional call even once he moves to that fancy apartment."

Matilda hoped so, which was foolish and risky—also entirely understandable. Maybe by this time next year…

She snatched another towel from the pile. "Mr. Fenwick has to go home eventually, Pippa. Scotland is very far away."

Scotland also had its own legal system. That realization had Matilda creasing the edges of the towel precisely. Would an English warrant be enforceable in Scotland? If so, why did criminals flee over the Border?

"Scotland is right next door, Mrs. B. Right up the Great North Road. I'm told it's pretty too."

As the pile of clean laundry gradually became stacks of folded wash, Matilda dreamed. She shouldn't. If the past six years had taught her anything, it was that dreams were for the lucky or the unwise.

And yet... Scotland wasn't England. As the mistress or even the wife of Scottish gentry, Matilda would be safe from Drexel's investigators and Stephen's greed. Kitty was well provided for, and maybe in a few years, when the girl was old enough to understand—

Helen swung through the window. "I love the smell of clean laundry here. Has his lordship come back yet?"

"Helen, the least you can do is use the back door," Matilda said. "You track in the garden mud on rainy days and let every urchin in the alley know exactly how to gain entrance to the domicile."

One of Helen's braids had slipped from her cap. She shoved it back out of sight, but it immediately drooped free again.

"Ain't any urchins in the alley. I run 'em all off before Christmas. That's my alley until I say somebody else can have it. What's for lunch?"

Pippa tossed a clean flannel at Helen. "Hard work. If you've been loving on that jackass, at least wash your hands before you finish folding this wash."

"Marmaduke is a donkey," Helen said, crossing to the washtub, "not an ass. His lordship says we must take care not to insult our betters."

Matilda's haze of cheerful speculations—not dreams—floated a little closer to earth. Something Helen had said...

"Helen, you referred to Mr. Fenwick as his lordship. Were you speaking metaphorically?"

Helen was absorbed with washing her hands and making some noise at it. She might not touch a single piece of laundry, but neither would Matilda allow the girl to eat with filthy hands.

Not anymore.

"Beg pardon, Mrs. Bryce?"

"Never mind. There's bread, cheese, and ham in the kitchen. You may help yourself."

"Thanks." Helen went skipping on her way, stuffing the errant braid under her cap yet again. "Ham begins with a haitch," she called from halfway down the corridor.

"Helen should cut her hair," Pippa said as the girl's footsteps faded. "Never met a boy who wore braids. Some have longish hair, but not braids."

"I'll offer to do the honors, though I'm hesitant to deprive Helen of any manifestation of her femininity."

Pippa took a set of folded towels to the cabinet along the wall. "You mean, you don't want her to forget she's a girl? Soon enough, her body will remind her.

She's safer as a boy. I know what I'm speaking of, Mrs. B."

Matilda knew as well, but then, she'd thought she'd known about being a wife, about being a debutante, about *teapots*...

Now she was dreaming of traveling to Scotland and telling herself that 344 days was nothing, if she was safely over the Border. Two clouds shadowed her sunny musings, three, counting the thought of being so far away from Kitty.

The second problem was that Ashton Fenwick was a good man, and Matilda had not yet shared her past with him. Deception was a sure way to earn his disgust, and yet, Matilda's problems were not his to solve. Time could solve them, to some extent, and meddling in her affairs could get Ashton in significant trouble.

The third problem had to do with Helen referring to Ashton as his lordship. Ashton was not a lord—what lord took up lodging on Pastry Lane for two minutes, much less two weeks, or purchased a donkey for his temporary tiger?—but he was well connected, witness today's call upon some Scottish duke.

The polite world was tiny, with everybody living in everybody else's pockets. Ashton knew at least one English earl and one duke. By the end of the Season, he'd know everybody, and many of those people would recall the scandal that had befallen the Derrick family six years ago.

The prudent course would be to send Ashton on to the Albany with a fond kiss farewell.

Matilda wasn't sure she could do that. Not now. Maybe not ever.

* * *

"You should sack Basingstoke," Stephen announced, "or at least have the youngest one kept away from our affairs."

Drexel made it a point to finish reading the newspaper's latest tally of who'd arrived in Town before acknowledging his nephew. The hour approached noon, which was early for Stephen to rouse from his slumbers.

"Good morning, Stephen. If you'd like to start the day with a bit of hair of the dog, help yourself to the brandy."

The sideboard sported so many varieties of libation, it resembled a pipe organ of spirits. Very little of what was on display was good quality, but then, Stephen's tastes weren't refined. His dear step-mama might have brought a bit of polish to the boy's outlook, had circumstances been different.

Stephen helped himself to enough hair of the dog to stuff a sofa cushion, then—in broad daylight, in the very library—wiped his mouth with his sleeve.

"Better," he said, leaving his dirty glass on the reading table. "Damon Basingstoke was impertinent to me. I asked him for a report regarding his efforts to locate the family murderess, and he balked."

Well, no, he hadn't. Basingstoke had sent a note around confirming disbursement of fifty pounds to Stephen and relating Stephen's insistence that the search for his missing step-mama be intensified.

"The last course one follows with an impertinent solicitor is let him go, Stephen. Do please have a seat. Your perambulations will make me bilious."

Stephen cast himself into a chair opposite Drexel's. Both were positioned by a window, the drapes pulled back to let in sunshine and reveal a view of a tidy back garden. The morning light showed the resemblance between Stephen and his late father that would emerge as the years passed. For now, Stephen was robust, golden-haired, and outgoing, but in another ten years, he'd have his father's receding hair to go with the already evident receding chin.

Also his father's devotion to the bottle, alas. That took a toll on a man in many ways.

"One doesn't tolerate disrespect," Stephen retorted. "Basingstoke doesn't know his place."

"He's the youngest son, probably the only one doing any real work at his papa's firm, and his antecedents are irregular. What do you think will happen if I let him go or complain to his elders about him?"

Stephen slouched against the cushions and stared at the ceiling. "We'll hire somebody who will find the damned woman and put her on a convict ship for the Antipodes. She's an earl's daughter and will never survive the voyage. Then I can have my money, you can have Kitty's money, and we can get the meddling fools from the Chancery court out of our hair."

Althorpe had despaired of his only son, and Drexel understood why. Stephen was both stupid and arrogant, a dangerous combination, and the very reason much of the rabble had cause to resent the aristocracy. An intelligent man, even if arrogant, would exercise a certain prudence where his self-interest was involved, and a stupid man could be coaxed to follow the guidance of more shrewd mentors if the fellow had a shred of humility.

Stephen would charge forth in the worst possible direction, convinced of his own infallibility.

And yet, Stephen was the earldom's heir, so Drexel possessed himself of patience.

"Say we set aside the firm of Basingstoke and Basingstoke and hire another solicitor. What then, Nephew?"

Stephen burped and thumped his sternum with his fist. "They find Stepmama, and I get my money."

"Before that. How do they know where to look, Stephen?"

He rubbed a hand across his forehead. "We explain what happened, they nose about, somebody recalls seeing Matilda milking cows in Chelsea, or flat on her back in some bawdy house, and then we have her arrested."

"That nosing about, what do you suppose it entails?"

"Chatting with the help, for starts."

"And what happens when somebody chats with the help?"

"The help gossip among themselves, but what do we care how a lot of laundresses and link-boys spend their idle time?"

Maybe drink was robbing the boy of what few brains he'd been born with. "Stephen, the help gossip, and so word of a renewed investigation comes to some lady's maid, and she passes it along to her employer. A valet mentions it to one of my peers. Whispers start in the clubs. If your step-mother is anywhere in London, she'll be listening for those whispers. And what will Basingstoke and his papa make of our taking our business elsewhere?"

"They'll learn a lesson they won't soon forget."

"And the loss of our business will go entirely unremarked in the legal community, after generations of patronizing the same firm and relying utterly on their discretion? We simply choose another firm that knows nothing about our history, our properties, our occasional peccadilloes? With no additional effort on our part, all proceeds smoothly and at no greater expense?"

A light finally, finally dawned in Stephen's bloodshot eyes. "The wretched vermin will charge us a fortune to take on our affairs. Basingstoke will go crying in his ale, and half the Middle Temple will hear of it by sundown. God, I hate lawyers."

The family solicitors were the sole reason Stephen hadn't been sued for breach of promise where his older daughter was concerned. He'd not even reached his majority when the child had been conceived, and her mother had been from decent, if humble, family.

"Solicitors, physicians, clergy,"—*heirs*—"they are a necessary blight upon civilized society. I won't be changing firms, Stephen, and you will acquire some patience. The Season should present you with diversions aplenty, and then we'll deal with your dear step-mama. I do wonder if she was carrying when she hared away in the middle of the night."

Stephen tugged the curtain half closed, so the sun no longer struck him in the face. "Carrying? With child, you mean? Papa said she couldn't."

Which might explain why Stephen had made such a plague of himself to his own step-mother.

"My dear boy, your papa said many things." Few of them complimentary toward the man's only son. "That brings us to another topic. I can understand why you are reluctant to choose a bride, but the fate of an earldom now rests on your shoulders. If you're not inclined to marry, I might have to reconsider my own widower status."

The threat was empty. Drexel had been married for fifteen long years and had been unable to sire a child. The French flu was said to have that effect sometimes.

"*You're* thinking of marrying?" Stephen pushed out of the chair, wove slightly, then headed back to the sideboard. "Aren't you a bit mature to be taking a bride? Nothing more pathetic than some doddering title rutting on a schoolgirl in hopes of reclaiming his manly humors."

Melancholia threatened Drexel's normal calm. This sneering, vapid, vain young man would inherit the consequence and resources of the Drexel earldom, and all of Drexel's efforts to conserve those resources, to husband them efficiently, would come to nothing. Stephen would gallop through the family fortune in less than ten years, and a once proud heritage would become so much grist for the gossip mill.

"Stephen, you are too much your father's son sometimes. I am not yet fifty. The companionship of a kind and merry woman, her management of my household, her children in my nursery, would be a fitting reward for my years of stewardship where the earldom is concerned."

Stephen poured another portion of truly terrible brandy and tossed it back. "You're lonely? Why not get a mistress?"

Anything to prevent a son from coming between Stephen and the title, of course. "You know how a mistress can be, and her role is different from that of a wife. You could break your neck in your next curricle race, Stephen, and where would the earldom be?"

Stephen fancied himself quite the whip.

Also quite the ladies' man.

Quite the card player.

Quite the dandy.

Stephen was a tiresome boy, and Althorpe had been the template from which he'd sprung. No wonder the magistrate had believed that Althorpe's wife had sent the tiresome fellow to his final reward.

Drexel well knew the shy, mannerly Mrs. Althorpe Derrick—Lady Matilda, more properly—hadn't bashed her husband's brains out, but that version of events had left Drexel managing a sizeable fortune for years. The girl, Kitty, was no trouble and allowed Drexel to keep a toothsome young woman in his employ without causing talk.

"I'm to look for a bride, then?" Stephen asked, pouring yet another portion of spirits. "That's the threat? I'm to marry some giggling twit with good hips, or you will disinherit me?"

Drexel hoped he could tie up some of the family wealth in trusts once the seven years had run to locate missing heirs.

"Don't be obtuse, Stephen. I can't disinherit you from the title or the assets that attach to it, not unless I produce a legitimate son. Even if I do have children, I will always provide for you."

And for Stephen's daughters, and their mothers. Both women could be difficult if regular sums weren't dispatched for the maintenance of their offspring.

"Very well," Stephen said. "Have Basingstoke père prepare a list, and I'll choose a bride. If there's one endeavor about which I can muster enthusiasm, it's swiving. Find me a pretty one, I'll get some sons on her, and you can settle fortunes on them all."

He sauntered on his way, the drink evidently restoring his spirits. Drexel pitied the young lady who became Stephen's bride, but she would, indeed, be well provided for. Of course, the same consolation had been offered to the Earl of Kittridge when he'd betrothed his daughter to Althorpe.

Drexel wrote down the names of half a dozen prospective brides for Stephen, all pretty, all in at least their third Season. The right woman would enter the union with her eyes open and her hand stuffed deep into Stephen's purse, if not his breeches.

A thought intruded, one of those unpleasant, sticky thoughts that could upset the digestion and ruin good sleep.

Solicitors truly motivated to find Althorpe's missing wife would hire investigators, and those investigators would indeed start by interviewing the help. Stephen was just idiot enough, and just greedy enough, to attempt that same task himself.

Drexel's conscience twinged, for the only provision Drexel had made for the late Earl of Kittridge's daughter in the past six years had been to see a murder warrant issued for her arrest. Drexel wished Matilda no particular harm, but if Stephen found her, she could well hang.

A pity, that.

CHAPTER TEN

"That is a damned kilt, Fenwick," Hazelton snapped. "Don't tell me you've been prancing around Mayfair doing your impersonation of William Wallace."

Ashton smoothed a bare hand over the wool draped across his knee. The Hazelton conservatory was cool and shady, also private, and this conversation required discretion.

"You bloody English put Wallace to death as a traitor. His is the last example I'd follow. I'm the Earl of Kilkenney, and if I choose to dress in a manner appropriate to my station, you will contain your envy. When I paid a call on the Duke of Murdoch, I turned quite a few heads, most of them female."

Hazelton left off trimming the stems of a bunch of daffodils. "Murdoch is the new Scottish duke?"

"Aye, and a fine man. Thought I'd show a fellow Scot some moral support. He was wearing a kilt as well, and I have it on the best authority that a duke's fashion sense is above reproach."

Murdoch's whisky had been so far above reproach, Ashton had nearly begged for a second wee dram. His Grace had offered to send a bottle around to the Albany—the duke's younger brother owned the family distillery—and Ashton had reciprocated with an invitation to attend an impromptu card party.

All very friendly, and also—mirabile dictu!—likely to be an enjoyable evening. Matilda would doubtless approve of such gentlemanly hospitality.

"Murdoch has a pair of unmarried sisters," Hazelton said, dumping the flowers in a clear glass vase. "I'm told they're comely."

"Edana and Rhona MacHugh. My sister-in-law refers to them as independent spirits, which translates south of Hadrian's Wall as right hellions. That vase is too small. You should trim up the stems to create a pleasing arrangement."

"You do it," Hazelton said, gesturing with his shears. "You're the expert on turning women's heads—now. Last week, you were determined to hide in the hedgerows for the duration of the Season. What's changed?"

Everything had changed. "I put on my kilt. Daffodils don't last well once cut. Who are these for?" They were for Hazelton's countess, of course, else some footman would be messing about with damp stems and sharp shears.

"Yellow daffodils stand for chivalry. You're cutting them too short."

Ashton picked up another stem and trimmed two inches from it. "You gave me the shears, now be a good earl and let me work my magic. Don't suppose you'd care to join Murdoch and me for a few hands of cards Monday night?"

"I'm telling you, you're ruining those flowers."

"Fetch me a stem or two of fern, about eight inches long, please. Make it three stems. Ferns symbolize fascination."

Hazelton disappeared between an orange tree and a lemon tree. "You're hosting a card party?"

"At the Albany. My first social gathering. Murdoch's brother will likely attend, but we could add another foursome if you'd like to increase the guest list."

Hazelton emerged from the greenery, fern fronds in his hand, one of them with dirt clinging to its roots.

"Hazelton, one cuts the ferns, one doesn't yank them out like weeds. You seldom bring your lady flowers, I take it?"

He shook the hapless ferns, sending dirt everywhere. "One of my endless supply of brothers-in-law mentioned that at some point every week, he brings his lady flowers. The other fellows acted as if that was simply a required gesture. Another prides himself on fixing his lady her morning chocolate exactly as she prefers it. Another reads to his wife at the end of the day. Yet another has learned how to knead bread, simply because his wife—a countess, mind you— enjoys puttering in the kitchen."

Hazelton looked both bewildered and annoyed as he clutched his bedraggled fern. "Maggie likes flowers."

Ashton appropriated the ferns and trimmed off the roots. "She likes you. No accounting for taste."

The earl took a seat on the bench Ashton had vacated. "I think Maggie prefers our sons to her husband. She's a devoted mother."

"For which you adore her. I might need another pair of ferns. You should tell her you miss her."

"I don't—" Hazelton stretched an arm along the back of the bench and crossed his legs. He'd shed his jacket, and he presented the picture of a wealthy gentleman at his informal leisure. "One can't miss the woman beside whom one sleeps."

Ashton had been missing Matilda his entire adult life and hadn't realized it. "The hell one can't. What other blooms do you have?"

"That pink thing," Hazelton said, waving toward a bush growing beside the glass wall.

"Quince. Signifies temptation. She'll like that."

Ashton added three small sprigs of pink, positioned the ferns among the flowers, and surveyed his work.

Not quite right. He took a thirteenth daffodil from a bucket sitting beside the workbench, cut an inch off the stem, and stuck it dead center in the arrangement.

"Perfect. Present the lady with your bouquet and tell her you miss her. Kidnap her for a picnic out at Richmond and take your traveling coach so the journey might include a few marital intimacies."

Hazelton considered the little pot of flowers. "The last time I saw you, you were glum, resentful, and eccentric. Clearly, you enjoyed a sample from the duke's liquor cabinet."

"You will too," Ashton said. "Murdoch's brother, a former army captain, owns a distillery or two, and the man knows what he's about. Has an excellent head for business, does Colin MacHugh. Will this do?"

Hazelton sniffed the daffodils and got pollen on his lordly nose. "How do you know how to arrange flowers? I understand that you can shoe a horse or train one, that you're accomplished at manual labor, and have other skills as a result of your tenure at Blessings, but arranging flowers?"

"When a man is a lowly steward, he's not entirely a gentleman. He works for his wage, even though others work for him too, and the work is hardly genteel. When he approaches a woman, he knows his paltry wealth, standing, and consequence mean nothing to her. He must acquire the courage to be desired for himself and for what courtesies and considerations he can bring along. Failing that, a bouquet of flowers never hurts."

"You're lecturing me. You, the confirmed bachelor, the reluctant earl, the noble bumpkin in a kilt no less, and yet, I must admit you have a point."

"Your lordship has pollen on his nose."

Hazelton produced spotless linen and erased the evidence of his proximity to the flowers. He went to the door and summoned a footman next, proving that rank was no guarantee of brains.

"You don't have the footman deliver the flowers, Hazelton. You seek out your lady and present them yourself. She will be pleased, and you will be on hand to enjoy her reaction. How did you ever solve mysteries, if this is an example of your deductive abilities?"

"I solved them by dogged persistence and grim determination. I will, of course, bring her ladyship the flowers in person, but the footman will know where she is."

Oh, right. Ashton swept the trimmed stems into his hand and tossed them among the greenery. "How is my list of scandals coming?"

Hazelton resumed his place on the sofa, his posture more relaxed. "I've unearthed a good half-dozen juicy scandals, two of which never appeared in the papers. I can send you a written summary, though it will be unsigned. I don't investigate anymore."

"You should. You enjoyed it, and you helped solve difficult problems."

Such wistfulness crossed Hazelton's saturnine features, Ashton would have thought the countess was biding up in the north, hundreds of miles away.

"I meet with my cousin from time to time to discuss cases."

"Tell Sir Archer you want an assignment or two, especially if they involve the court set, or polite society. Not everybody has that sort of entrée."

"Few do. Speaking of court entrée, do you know a man named Hannibal Shearing?"

They had been speaking about curing Hazelton of a case of the blue devils. "Shearing is a coal nabob in Northumberland. Wants a spot on the honors list so badly he's probably funding half the renovations at Brighton to get it."

Ashton pushed away from the workbench, gave a sprig of quince a half-inch nudge to the right, and considered the bouquet complete.

"He asked me to accompany him to a levee," Hazelton said, "of all the presumptions. You will be there on Tuesday?"

"We've been over this. You will show up for cards on Monday. Tuesday morning, I will pick you up in my coach. Bring Murdoch and your-cousin-the-investigator to the card party, and I will fill them in on all the Scottish gossip. Did any of the scandals you researched mention somebody named Althorpe?"

Hazelton rose and picked up the bouquet. "No. Is that a first name or a family name?"

"First name, I'm guessing, but it could be a family name." Matilda might have resorted to use of her maiden name, or she might be traveling under an alias.

"Doesn't ring a bell. My thanks for the flowers."

"My thanks for the scandals. Keep looking, will you? Focus on gossip surrounding somebody named Althorpe who's no longer among the living. I have a hunch it's important."

Hazelton assayed another whiff of the daffodils and bowed with the flowers in hand.

Ashton took his leave without informing his lordship that a streak of fern-dirt now graced the earl's cravat. Hazelton's countess would find that detail adorable, as she very likely found the rest of her earl adorable, did the poor fellow but know it.

* * *

"Please be sure the words 'She Should Have Known Better' are prominently etched on my tombstone," Matilda said, "assuming I'm interred in hallowed ground."

Pippa hung her bonnet on a hook near the back door. "If you say so, ma'am, but are we to be coming and going through the garden now?"

"Yes," Matilda said. "And Pippa, if you have other prospects for employment, you should pursue them."

Pippa was savvy, and she'd made the transition from streetwalker back to respectability, or its shabby near-relation. Helen's situation was more difficult. Ashton would see to the girl, if Matilda asked it of him, which she would.

Then there was the house. Matilda could probably rent the entire premises to a gentleman in town for the Season, but after that, it should be sold, though a documented legal transaction was always risky.

"I don't have other *prospects for employment*," Pippa said, "not unless you want me chasing Sissy off her street corner to flaunt me wares again, which I don't fancy. The French ailment is everywhere these days, and it will put you in the grave, they say, after it drives you mad."

Matilda was going mad, though with that peculiar manifestation of insanity that allowed her to think clearly with part of her mind, while collapsing into a howling fit with the other.

"I'm back!" Helen called from the laundry room. "What's for lunch?"

"Pippa, please find Helen something to eat, and don't forget your own meal. I have a few matters to sort out."

One option was to grab the bundle Matilda kept under her bed and disappear. Mrs. Bellingham had taught her to do that. All the women in a bawdy house learned to keep a bundle close at hand for when the authorities raided the premises.

"Do a bunk," Matilda muttered. Street talk for disappearing into the night, not a trace to be seen.

Another option was to stay right where she was and let the damned law find her. She'd considered that option many times.

Or she could take a short time to plan and then leap in the most sensible direction.

The front door closed, and a distinctive tread sounded in the front hall. Abruptly, the thinking side of Matilda's mind stumbled to a halt as Ashton Fenwick came down the stairs.

Booted feet, bare knees, soft wool pleats and a plain leather sporran, trim waist, dark jacket with a lacy cravat, and then the part she'd miss the most—his smile.

"Mrs. Bryce, good day. These are for you." He held out a bunch of daffodils, their bright color more cheering than a simple bouquet should be. "Miss Pippa, good day to you as well."

"My thanks," Matilda said, ignoring Pippa's smirk. "My vase is in the sitting room, and there's a pitcher of water there as well." She had only the one vase, a cheap vessel that had been pressed into service far too seldom.

He offered the flowers with a flourishy bow. "They need water. I've carried them from Mayfair, and I learned a thing or two on the way."

How would Matilda learn to leave him, much less without a word? "Tell me." She took the daffodils and led him up the steps to the parlor.

"A man in a kilt turns heads, but a man in a kilt who's carrying flowers makes conquests. Your suggestion that I wear the dress of my homeland was sheer genius."

Utter folly, more like. Any suggestions that made the members of Matilda's household distinctive had been stupid in the extreme. A woman trying to live her life beyond the notice of the law knew better, though self-recrimination was pointless.

A woman raised for nothing more than genteel family life couldn't be expected to turn herself into a very successful fugitive.

"Matilda, is something wrong?"

Everything was wrong. "Market was crowded this morning, and Pippa is in a mood." She fetched her humble vase from beneath the sideboard. The vessel was cylindrical, periwinkle blue, with a slightly uneven lip. No chips or cracks, but no art to it either.

Ashton stood behind her while she arranged the daffodils in the container. Her hands shook, then she nearly spilled the water trying to pour it from the pitcher.

"I left you after breakfast," Ashton said, "and your smiles could have lit up the Outer Hebrides on a January night. I come home, and you're as pale as a lost soul and as tense as a fiddle string. Did you see Mr. Aberfeldy's ghost again?"

This was not his home. Soon it wouldn't be Matilda's either.

Ashton topped off the vase with the water, but the stems were too long for the container, and the whole business looked pathetic. He used his handkerchief to wipe up the drops of water Matilda had spilled on the sideboard.

Such a competent man. Matilda took the sorry bouquet from the sideboard thinking to set it in the windowsill. The flowers were doomed to fade and die, but they might as well have the comfort of sunshine in their final days.

Ashton stood in the middle of her parlor, making the scarred sideboard, faded carpet, and plain vase that much more humble by comparison. His expression said he was concerned for her, and all Matilda could think of was how to leave him with most of his ignorance intact.

She'd been moving too swiftly, or too thoughtlessly, and misjudged the distance to the windowsill. The bottom of the vase smashed against the woodwork, and water, glass, and flowers went everywhere.

"Blast it to Hades. That was my only vase."

And the only bouquet any man had ever brought her.

Ashton's arms came around her. "Did you see our journalist again?"

Oh, the comfort, the safety, the rightness of his embrace. "How did you know?"

"Because you're furious, and frightened. A mere journalist would not have put you in this state."

"Ashton, he's not a journalist. He's a thief-taker, and he's after me."

* * *

Matilda was shaking with upset, while water dripped from the windowsill to the carpet in a steady stream. Ashton got out his flask and tipped it to her lips.

She drank, she coughed, she waved a hand in front of her face, and some of her color came back.

"Tell me what's afoot, Matilda, or I will march out your door, find this thief-taker, and give him a drubbing he won't soon recover from. If you nicked a purse in a weak moment, I'll make it right. I have the funds, and you wouldn't steal unless somebody you loved were starving."

Matilda stood in the circle of his embrace, but she wasn't there. She wasn't his vibrant, articulate, easily annoyed Matilda.

"I don't know how to nick a purse, and I nearly did starve. If I tell you any more, you'll become an accomplice after the fact of my crime. I couldn't bear that."

He led her to the sofa, sat her down, and put his flask in her hand.

"The flowers…" she said, looking as if she'd pop right up and tend to the housekeeping rather than discuss the danger she was in.

"I can clean up a wee mess," Ashton said. "If you think to protect me by remaining silent, you're daft. I've already set a man to unearthing the scandal in your past, and—"

"*You didn't.*" She'd closed her eyes and clenched her hands around Ashton's flask so tightly she might well crumple it.

"A very discreet man, who's doing nothing more than reading his journals and consulting his lady wife at present. He's not the reason a thief-taker has been after you since nearly the day I met you."

Water dripped in a slow trickle from the windowsill, and Matilda offered Ashton no contradiction.

Well, damn. "Stay right there," he said. "I mean that. No climbing out the window with the clothes on your back, Matilda. I'm off to find a dustpan and broom, and you will compose your story from the start."

She eyed the window Ashton had hauled her through days ago. "I'll stay."

For now. The words silently echoed about the room along with the fragrance of daffodils.

By the time Ashton brought a broom, dustpan, and rags to the parlor, Matilda had moved from the sofa to the house's only rocking chair. Ashton tended to the destroyed vase, put the flowers in a drinking glass, and left the wet rags, broom, and dustpan outside the door.

"Talk to me," he said, taking a place cross-legged on the worn carpet beside Matilda's rocking chair. "Tell me the truth, Matilda. Lies at this point will only waste time and put me in a temper."

"Lies might save your life. An accomplice to murder can swing beside the murderess."

"You're a murderess now?"

"I'm stating a fact of English law."

Ashton didn't care if she'd taken a life, because Matilda Bryce would have done so only in self-defense or in defense of a loved one. Even that blighted convolution of common sense known as English law forgave a life ended under those circumstances.

Though Matilda might not forgive herself.

"Don't tell me facts, then, tell me a story, a fanciful tale of a young woman, gently raised, whose marriage was a disappointment."

"She was a good girl," Matilda said, rocking slowly, "but ignorant, as good girls are meant to be. She married an earl's heir, and she'd become a countess in time. This was supposed to matter."

"Earldoms are forever causing problems," Ashton said. "Go on."

"Her husband was not the worst man ever to take a bride. He was unkind, his weapons of choice harsh words, disparaging glances, public insults. He was a trial, and his sole purpose in taking this young woman to wife was to get a spare on her, for the man's older son was also a trial."

"Tends to work like that, acorns and oaks being what they are." Sitting cross-legged in a kilt on a worn carpet was uncomfortable, though Ashton would not have left Matilda's side if the 95th Rifles had aimed every gun at the parlor window.

"Just so," Matilda said, "and all might have eventually settled into tame, domestic animosity, but the young lady did not conceive."

"Or her husband didn't get her with child."

Matilda stroked a hand over Ashton's hair, just the once. "Thank you. A child did not bless the union, much less a healthy male child. Tensions rose, and to make matters worse, the son tried to assume liberties with his step-mother. He was little more than a boy, just gone up to university, but he was a persistent boy, with one thing on his mind."

Ashton had missed a piece of glass glinting among the fringe of the worn carpet. The jagged edge would cut an unsuspecting foot badly on some dark night, so he crawled over and retrieved it, then set it on the windowsill.

"Most boys have the same thing on their minds," he said, "as do many men. They have enough couth not to act on their urges, though."

Or some obliging father, uncle, or older brother would beat the manners into them and, by example, educate the young cretin regarding the pleasures of having one's bodily privacy disrespected. Ashton had provided that education to two of the stable lads who'd worked for him at Blessings, and the housemaids had nearly gathered around to applaud.

"Couth was in short supply among my in-laws," Matilda said. "I mean, the young lady's in-laws. An older brother, the title holder, was the worst of the lot. He appeared full of genial understanding and occasionally attempted to diffuse tensions, but all the while, he was making plans of his own."

"If he succeeded where the son did not—"

"His lust was for the young lady's money, which he does indeed have control over and has for the past six years. The marriage settlements were generous, for the young lady was one of only two daughters, and the other child was a mere infant."

The cut glass caught the sun at an odd angle and reflected a bright beam right onto Matilda's hands. She did not have the pale, idle hands of a lady. Her nails were short, her fingers red, and in the bright sunshine, the scar near her wrist was in high relief.

Ashton wanted those hands on his body every night for the rest of his life, so he summoned patience and a question.

"How did your husband die?"

"An accident. He accused me of betraying him with his son, shouted at me, and for the first time, I feared he'd raise a hand to me. I shouted back—I'd had enough by then—and this only enraged him further. He'd been drinking, of course.

"If Althorpe had shown me a tenth of the affection he had for the bottle, ours would have been a pleasant union. The row went on until I couldn't tell if I was being castigated for cheating with Stephen, or for refusing Stephen's overtures. The boy had been sent down for getting some girl pregnant, proving his ability to sire children, and this upset his father terribly."

"Not the life you'd envisioned for yourself," Ashton said, weathering a wave of shame. He'd pouted for three years because a title had been thrust upon him in place of a muck fork. Matilda had got a house full of spoiled, greedy imbeciles in place of her domestic dream, and she'd yet to complain.

"My ambitions have become modest, Ashton. I'd like to remain alive and at liberty."

Ashton's vision of the future had changed as well. He'd like Matilda to remain alive and at liberty and to have a title as she'd been promised long ago— his title.

"So you and Althorpe were arguing. Then what?"

"I stood near the fire, which a footman had just supplied with fresh coal. Althorpe railed at me from across the parlor, near the sideboard on which a plethora of decanters stood. When I told him I was going up to bed, he rushed at me with a drink in his hand. I thought he meant to cast the spirits at me, which was the outside of stupid with the fire roaring at my back. I stepped aside, he pitched his drink, and then he stumbled and fell."

"As drunks are wont to do."

That earned Ashton another caress. "Althorpe fell face first onto the hearth, then rolled to his back. The hearth stand toppled, scattering the implements and making a great racket. I expected Althorpe to struggle to his feet, and I knelt to set the stand back up. When Stephen charged through the door, I had the poker in my hand, and Althorpe still hadn't moved."

"But," Ashton said, "he had a great gash on his forehead or temple, or some bloody where, and you stood over him with the poker in your hand."

"He had a welt, but I think he broke his neck. His head was at an odd angle to his shoulders. I've been assured a jury would convict me of murder, regardless of the facts. I was an embittered young wife, unable to conceive a child, shackled to a nasty drunk twenty years my senior. What jury would have allowed me to flounce on my way with handsome settlements in my pocket?"

Fair question. "So you fled?"

"Not at first. At first I was too upset, too bewildered, and too trusting. Althorpe had been annoying, but I'd learned to tolerate him, and even have some pity for him, because he was unhappy. The spirits he consumed to deal with the unhappiness only worsened most of his problems, but he couldn't see that."

"Bugger your compassion, Matilda. The man was a disgrace."

Matilda slid from her chair and sat next to Ashton on the floor, her head on his shoulder. "If only I'd met you years ago."

"I was far to the north and smelled often of the stable. When did you realize you were in jeopardy?"

"My brother-in-law was summoned to the scene, and his lordship was concerned for me. He ordered Stephen to await him in the library, poured me a stout drink, and told me to get straight up to bed. I took the drink but didn't sip it. Brandy had made my marriage miserable and likely cost my husband his life. Then too, I assumed the authorities would interview me, and evidence of strong drink even under the circumstances wouldn't be ladylike."

Ashton looped an arm around her shoulders when he wanted to pace and shout and hit things—Matilda's in-laws, for example—hard.

"You made the shrewd choice, Matilda. If you'd been drinking when the magistrate questioned you, your credibility would have been ruined. Stephen could have drained three bottles while conversing with the king's man, and his word would have been taken as gospel."

"His word *was* taken as gospel. I couldn't sleep and I wanted to retrieve my journal from the library before the magistrate and Bow Street runners were loose in the house. Outside the library door, I heard Stephen explaining to the magistrate that I'd always had a spoiled girl's temper. Stephen went on to claim he'd seen me beating his father with the poker and heard me shout at his father that I hated him and wished he were dead."

"And Stephen was doubtless in tears at the recollection?" Ashton was nearly in tears.

"Oh, of course. For a hale man badly beaten by his much smaller wife, Althorpe had had only the one welt when I'd seen him. I expected my brother-in-law to speak on my behalf, to counter Stephen's allegations, because I'd told his lordship Stephen was making a pest of himself."

"And the earl remained silent?"

"Not quite. He cleared his throat and hemmed and hawed and left no doubt that I'd been very much of a problem from the day I'd joined the family—my fits of pique and ungovernable temper had become apparent only after the wedding. A warrant was issued for my arrest, the charge murder. My money—including a generous inheritance from my father—has been in his lordship's hands ever since. Because I haven't been convicted of anything, even the portion of Althorpe's estate that was left to me in his will has been languishing in the earl's hands. My disappearance was very profitable for the earl, who is managing all of Althorpe's estate until my fate is settled."

Which meant Stephen had more reason than ever to wish his step-mother ill. "The whole estate is tied up in chancery proceedings?"

"The whole estate is in a temporary trust, thanks to friendly chancery judges, and that trust is managed by the earl, along with my settlements. I left with little more than the clothes on my back and a few of the jewels my husband had given me as a part of my dower portion. Those, at least, I could not be regarded as stealing."

For a young woman who'd been traumatized by the loss of her husband, and by the betrayal from his family, Matilda's clear thinking was remarkable.

Ashton hauled her over his leg so she sat on the floor between his knees, cradled against his chest.

"What was your plan, Matilda? You have a plan. I can feel it in you." Right along with the anger, bewilderment, and despair.

"My plan was to die, and that is still my plan."

CHAPTER ELEVEN

Matilda hadn't told Ashton the whole of it, but she hadn't *intended* to tell him any of her past, so she waited for his next question.

He kissed the top of her head. "That plan will not do, not if it involves hastening the Creator's original schedule for you. I've grown fond of your apple tarts." His tone was gently chiding, his hold was utterly secure.

He'd grown fond of her apple tarts? Matilda wasn't fond of Ashton, she was enthralled with him. Entranced by his patience, his humor, his stubborn brand of honor, his disdain for the world that had delighted in a scandal that might yet cost her her life.

He'd grown fond of her apple tarts.

An old, familiar ache started in Matilda's chest, then got a tight hold on her throat. This time, she could not think, move, or flee past it. The tears ambushed her, coming even more unexpectedly than Lord Drexel's betrayal, more unexpectedly than Althorpe's unkindness.

"I never cry. It does n-no good."

"Where's the harm in admitting you have much to cry about?"

Six years and twenty-odd days' worth of tears was a lot of tears, and they left Matilda weak, hot, and spent. She remained in Ashton's arms, not only because his embrace was an ineffable comfort, but also because without the anchor he provided, without the tears to weigh her down, she might have dissolved on the next spring breeze.

"How did you survive, Matilda? How did you, a gently bred countess-in-training, avoid the law and make a new life?"

"It's not a pretty tale," she replied, "but the long and short of it is, I grew up. I was in the habit of saving back from my pin money, because I liked to buy my husband an occasional gift or surprise. A pair of cuff links, a book I thought he'd enjoy. I eventually gave up on the gifts—nothing ever pleased him—but I kept the habit of living within my means."

Ashton rose with Matilda in his arms. The sensation was like a ship casting away from the dock. Calm one minute, in the grip of a powerful tide the next.

"This calls for a sofa, at least," he said, depositing her on the cushions. "Would you like a glass of water?"

"Yes, please."

Matilda hoarded up the sight of Ashton pouring her drink—doing for her, as Pippa would have put it—right down to the grip of his hand on the plain glass. He settled beside her, stretched an arm along the back of the sofa, and passed her the drink.

She took a sip, the cool liquid sliding down her throat like balm.

"So you took your money, crept down the back stairs, and disappeared?"

"I'd read enough Gothic novels to know I needed to mound the pillows on the bed first, and I instructed my maid that I wasn't to be disturbed, for any reason, until the earl summoned me in the morning. I knew the magistrate would have to examine me before I could be bound over, and he was hardly likely to haul me off to Bow Street to spend the night with habitual drunks and abbesses."

"There is worse company."

"I know that now."

Matilda fell silent, reveling in the sense that Ashton would sit right beside her, no matter how long her recitation took, no matter what misdeeds she'd done in the name of survival. Tomorrow, she'd likely be on her way to France, all the lonelier for having trusted him.

For the moment, she was sitting beside a man who was a true friend, the first true friend she'd ever had.

"You collected your money, your wits, possibly a small bundle, and away you went, into the London streets in the dark of night."

"Not quite the streets. I had socialized among our Mayfair neighbors enough to know where a ducal mews was, and I took shelter there until morning. I hid for days, venturing out at dawn before the grooms stirred, and traveling not into the parks or squares familiar to me, but east, into the part of London that works for a living. I took great comfort in sharing the leavings of my chophouse meals with the alley cats."

"For me, it was the horses," Ashton said. "I was never entirely alone as long as I could confide my troubles in a friendly equine. I gather your money ran out."

"My money was stolen. I had purposely let my cloak get dirty, but it was finely made. My reticule was stolen the second week. By then, I carried only money in it. My comb, jewels, and other bits and bobs remained hidden in whatever stable I was sheltering in, thank God."

"I gather the tale grows darker."

Matilda gave in to temptation and curled down to rest her head on his thigh. "I nearly starved. I wasn't any good at rooting through garbage to find sustenance, and the best garbage heaps are fiercely guarded by those tough enough to make use of them. I knew I couldn't pawn my jewels for two reasons. First, I would be cheated, being a woman clearly in desperate straits, and second, word of the transaction would get back to my brother-in-law. He's shrewd; he'd know that pawning jewels was one option open to me."

Ashton began pulling pins from Matilda's hair, his touch already familiar and dear. "I'm afraid to ask what happened next."

"I grew desperate and might have taken up sharing a street corner with Sissy and Pippa, but I recalled Mrs. Bellingham, the madam from whom I'd sought answers once before."

"The fallen woman," Ashton said. "Of course."

"She'd been gracious to me, a stranger from among those who disdained her, and had told me she was available for further discussion if I ever had the need. I slipped into her kitchen, a bedraggled, dirty, wretched version of the woman she'd known. She took one look at me, ordered me a bath and a pot of tea, and asked what man was responsible for my misery."

"Almighty, ascending angels. You do realize she might have locked you in a room upstairs and auctioned off your favors?"

"*Now*, I realize that. At the time, an assurance of food, clothing, and shelter might have been adequate compensation for my virtue. I was beginning to think myself the murderess my in-laws had painted me. The newspapers got wind of the scandal, and I saw handbills advertising a reward for my arrest and conviction."

Because that was how justice worked in Merry Olde England. The citizenry was expected to aid in the enforcement of the king's laws, but the victim was the only person motivated to bring the criminal to justice. Bow Street's men were paid their reward when a conviction was earned, no matter if the true culprit had been apprehended, or some unfortunate fool who merely looked guilty to a jury.

"Mrs. Bellingham had to have seen those handbills," Ashton said. "She could have turned you in for the reward, stolen your jewels, or tossed you in the river."

"You describe my titled in-laws, not the woman who explained to me that I must travel to Amsterdam as a French widow, sell the jewels there, and then learn to live as quietly as I could among a much lower strata of society. She also told me that I must never cover the same ground twice. I wasn't to return to her, or to Amsterdam, or to my in-laws' properties. 'Run forward and run alone,' she said, as if she knew exactly what was needed based on personal experience."

Ashton had removed every last pin, and he was massaging Matilda's nape with a slow, deep pressure. Her eyes grew heavy, though she dared not fall asleep lest he be gone when she awoke.

"A good hunter will watch his quarry's back trail," Ashton said. "But you went to Amsterdam and did as suggested. Then you bought this house?"

"I waited nearly a year, living at lodging houses and taking in mending or doing piecework. A young lady is taught how to embroider and tat lace. I couldn't support myself on those proceeds, but I could supplement my funds and learn to be just another poor widow."

She did close her eyes, lulled by caresses and fatigue. "When the scandal had faded," she went on, "and this house came up for sale, I bought it. I'd been lodging here on the third floor and knew the building was sound. The owner was Dutch and wanted the transaction handled from Amsterdam, which suited me perfectly."

"You survived on luck, cunning, and the kindness of strangers. Your family should be pilloried."

Ashton's words were all the more ferocious for being quiet.

"My parents are gone," Matilda said. "My father died thinking his older daughter a murderess, and for that, I will never forgive my in-laws."

Ashton's hand paused as he traced the curve of Matilda's jaw. "What of your inheritance from your parents? Your brother-in-law kindly manages that?"

"Yes. He's welcome to the whole of it too, as long as he leaves me in peace. I suspect he's been happy to have my fate twisting in the wind, because as soon as I die, he loses control of much of the money. I won't be exonerated—my in-laws have seen to that—which brings us to your original question. My plan was to die."

"You'll not be dying any time soon if I can help it," Ashton said. "I can have you on the way to Scotland at first light."

He spoke so casually, his words took a moment to penetrate the lassitude pulling at Matilda. She needed to pack up and run, but she also needed to rest and say her farewells.

"You'd send me to Scotland?" she asked, struggling to a sitting position. Her hair was loose about her shoulders, which made the undertaking more complicated.

"You are innocent of wrongdoing and were either betrayed or abandoned by the people who should have protected you." Ashton was off the couch, pacing the small parlor, his kilt flapping about his knees. "Your brother-in-law, the earl, should have told the magistrate Althorpe had fallen after another night of over-imbibing—the simple truth—and that Stephen was a greedy, randy boy. The matter would have been dealt with quietly."

"You're very sure of this."

"Your brother-in-law is titled. If he lies to an officer of the law, his perjury is tried in the House of Lords. They don't convict their own, so there's no point bringing charges against them except in extreme cases. Althorpe was a commoner, disagreeable, and likely a known drunk. The whole business would have been a nine days' wonder, and that would have been that."

Matilda wanted to believe him, wanted to know that Drexel's betrayal had been deliberate, not a product of rattled nerves.

"How do you know what consequence an earl can or cannot command?" she asked. "Drexel is subject to the law, as is Stephen, even if they are from an influential family."

Ashton stalked over and leaned close, bracing himself on one arm of the sofa. "Don't be daft. An earl is a law unto himself, guided only by the limitations of his coin and his conscience. I ought to know, because I am one."

"*You are an earl?*"

He smiled, the most startling, diabolical, handsome, frightening smile. "I'm *your* earl, and that will make all the difference."

* * *

"Don't you be piking off now when Mrs. Bryce needs us," Pippa said, sweeping the crumbs from the kitchen table. "I know that look in your eye, Helen, and unless you want to end up like Sissy, you stay put."

Pippa had been nobody to cross when she'd been on the stroll, according to Sissy. If a flat got too rough with one of Pippa's friends, Pippa would climb into the gent's coach the next time he came around, and she'd be all flirtation and simpering as the footman handed her in.

She'd be just as sweet and pretty when she got out of his coach, but the gent wouldn't come around after that.

"If Mrs. B and Mr. Fenwick are having an argument," Helen said around a mouthful of bread and butter, "then I'll be looking to myself, won't I? Mrs. B pays my wage, but Mr. Fenwick gives me the work."

"They're not arguing," Pippa said. "That Jonas Samuels was hanging about the market, and I told Mrs. B he's a thief-taker. She pulled me behind the booth that sells eel pies, and we traded cloaks and bonnets. I led Samuels a merry chase while Mrs. B slipped away. When I was sure Samuels wasn't on my tail, I met up with Mrs. B and we came home. That bloody bugger rattled her, though."

"He's a damned toad. Has his nose up the runners' arses, thinks he's better than everybody else."

"And we know Mrs. B ain't no thief," Pippa said, wrapping the day's loaf in a clean towel. "I purely despise a man who preys on women. I suspect Mr. Fenwick does too."

"He's a right proper gent," Helen said around another mouthful, "and he's Mrs. B's gent."

Pippa took the seat across the table. "What have I told you about eavesdropping, Helen? You'll hear no good of yourself, and folk don't like girls who sneak about."

"I wasn't sneaking. I heard 'em on the stair, plain as day. They fancy each other. There's no harm in it."

There probably wasn't any future in it either. Mr. Fenwick would leave, as Mrs. B had predicted he would. Didn't do to get attached, especially not to a man who paid as well as Mr. Fenwick.

"Mr. Fenwick is a match for Samuels," Pippa said, brushing crumbs to the floor. "He'll send Samuels away with some blunt, and Mrs. B can get on about her life."

"That won't serve," Helen replied, licking a dab of butter from the butter knife. Nothing in the whole world like fresh butter. "Samuels might go away, but a hundred other thief-takers will stand in his place. Doesn't matter if Mrs. B is innocent. She'll look guilty."

Pippa snatched the butter knife away. "She will. I can't figure her. She's a lady, but she doesn't want anybody to know it. Not my business and not yours."

"Not Mr. Fenwick's, then, either, is it?" Helen asked. "He's supposed to be finding a wife, not courting scandal and ruin. A man can swing for stupidity, Sissy always says."

Pippa rose and cuffed Helen on the side of the head. "Sissy this and Sissy that. If Sissy's so smart, why's she on the game? You're letting your hair get much too long. Shall I give it a trim, or are you ready to be a girl for a change?"

Helen hadn't known how to ask, but now that the opportunity to part with her braids had come, she couldn't bear to do it.

"Thanks, but Mr. Fenwick might need me this afternoon. I'd look like an idiot, one braid chopped, the other still on my head. Maybe tomorrow."

Assuming Helen still bided with Pippa tomorrow. Thief-takers caused serious trouble, and it might not be Mrs. B old Samuels was after.

* * *

"You are an *earl?*" Matilda repeated. "You have a title? An estate, a seat in the Lords?" She was dismayed at this disclosure, just as Ashton had been when the title had befallen him.

"No seat in the Lords. I'm a Scottish earl and not inclined to join the delegation. For most of my life I thought I was an illegitimate firstborn, but it turns out, there was a wedding ceremony before I made my appearance."

Matilda shot to her feet. "You are an *earl.* I have taken under my roof the worst lodger imaginable. Why am I always so gullible? So stupid? Why didn't you tell me you have a title? This is a disaster, Ashton Fenwick."

Her reaction reassured Ashton, in a perverse way. He'd felt exactly the same when Ewan and Alyssa had foisted the title on him, and he still wasn't entirely happy to be the Earl of Kilkenney.

Though he was less unhappy now than he had been when he'd left Scotland. "If I'd told you I'm an earl, would you have rented a room to me?"

"Of course not! Not if you were the last lodger in London. I cannot do anything to draw notice to my household, and you, my lord, will have to leave.

The sooner the better. I'll refund you the pro rata portion of your rent and wish you well, but I cannot accept the risk your august personage brings to my doorstep."

Oh, that was a fine speech to cast at a smitten swain. "Haud yer wheesht, Matilda Bryce, if that's your name. I know an earl authored your downfall, but an earl can resolve your situation as well."

She whirled on him, her hair flying about her shoulders. "How? Can you make arrest warrants disappear? Can you make the price disappear from my head? I'm worth fifty pounds to the man who's managing my entire fortune. He's an English earl, much liked, and well respected. Even I liked and respected him, and he doubtless has magistrates and runners in his pocket."

Ashton loved Matilda's fire, but loathed her fearfulness. "I can make you disappear, because that's what you meant when you said you planned to die, isn't it?"

She subsided onto the couch with an unceremonious thump. "If I can remain at liberty for another year, then I can be declared legally dead. I've made it this far. I'll not give up now, Ashton. I'll spend that year in Italy or France if I have to."

He took the place beside her. "You don't mention Scotland."

"It's not far enough away."

Scotland was at a much greater distance than the French coast. "You don't need to travel by sea to get to Scotland. Don't you think your brother-in-law has agents watching for you at most of the ports?"

An earl could just as easily have eyes watching the Great North Road and every other turnpike in the realm. Ashton spared Matilda that observation.

Matilda looked away, at the single piece of jagged glass on the windowsill. "They didn't see me last time."

"Think, Matilda. We're no longer at war, such that widow's weeds would get the same respect they did six years ago. The coastal traders who doubtless smuggled you to and from some rural shore are all but out of business, and in the time you've been in hiding, your step-son has grown up. If your brother-in-law isn't watching the ports, your step-son will be."

Ashton could not afford to indulge Matilda's stubbornness, not when her life hung in the balance.

"I have to go somewhere," she retorted. "The thief-taker has seen me twice just a few streets over. He'll ask enough questions, give pennies to enough crossing sweepers, and sooner or later, one of them will point him here."

"I don't intend that you stay here waiting for the warrant to be served on you. I intend that you be provided sanctuary until we can sort the whole mess out and see your in-laws held accountable."

She put her face in her hands, reminding Ashton of Alyssa three years ago. "I don't want or need anybody held accountable. I want to be left in peace.

That's all I've ever wanted, to be left in peace."

"You're lying to yourself," Ashton said, sweeping her hair back from her shoulders. "You want to be left in peace, but you also want to live long enough to see your younger sister grow up, safe and happy, and without the scandal of a murderess in the family blighting her life." The child had to be her younger sister. That explained the resemblance and the attachment.

Matilda glowered over at him. "I hate you."

She was so fierce and so alone. "Understandable, but will you move to the Albany with me anyway?"

"I cannot move to—the *Albany*? Gentlemen bide there. Of course I can't move to the Albany. I can't go to the Low Countries, because I've already been there, and France is the next logical place, so I shouldn't go there either."

She rose and plucked the lone shard of glass from the windowsill. "Lisbon is supposed to be lovely and not too expensive. The difficulty will be getting to Portsmouth to take ship, but Pippa can remain here for a few days, wearing my cloak and bonnet, attending to my usual errands. I assume you will look after Helen for me, and I can write a character for Pippa if you'll sign it."

Matilda had indulged her bout of sentiment and thrown Ashton a crumb of trust. The instinct to flee was rising in her before his eyes, and if he didn't intervene, she'd be gone before sunset.

"Matilda."

She set the shard of blue glass before the daffodils sitting all askew in their makeshift vase. "My real name is Maitland, but everybody has always called me Matilda. Not even my husband knew that, or he forgot it if he did know it."

Ashton withdrew his knife from his boot and joined her at the sideboard. "You're telling me your real name because you're preparing to run and your guilty conscience wants to leave a token behind."

"You'll cut yourself."

He trimmed up the flower stems, one after another, and pitched the leavings out the window. "Your flowers," he said, lifting the bouquet beneath her nose. "Was your maiden name Bryce?"

"Even I know better than that. My maiden name was…"

While Ashton watched, her eyes filled with tears. "Matilda? Or do I call you Maitland?"

"I haven't spoken my own true name for years," she said, taking the bouquet from him. "I was born Lady Maitland Marie Bronson Bellamy and am the oldest daughter of the late Earl of Kittridge. My sister is Lady Catherine Marie Kitts Bellamy. She's called Kitty, and Drexel manages her inheritance too."

What a cruel irony that Matilda had been born a lady and had left her honorific on Drexel's back stairs, while Ashton had been reared as a bastard and now wore the title like an ill-fitting coat.

"Matilda, you cannot flee to Portsmouth. Not now."

"And you cannot tell me what to do, Ashton Fenwick. I don't care how wealthy you are, or how respected your title. To stay here is to court death for a crime I did not commit."

"I didn't mention it earlier, because I hadn't made the connection, but on my way back from Mayfair, as I came through Piccadilly, I saw handbills advertising a reward for the capture and conviction of a suspected murderess. The likeness was poor, and no name was mentioned, but somebody is clearly still looking for you."

She set the flowers down hard on the sideboard. "Perishing, rubbishing, dashed, deuced perdition."

Ashton took her in his arms, and she came to him. He recalled telling her that the lady of his dreams cursed when the occasion called for it, and took encouragement from Matilda's foul language.

Because the situation definitely called for it.

* * *

"You're wearing breeches now," Helen said. "You can't walk like a girl. You have to walk like you got the world's greatest treasure tucked up your arse."

"Or tucked behind your falls," Pippa added earnestly. "You want to walk smug and randy, as if everybody ought to look at you for the sheer pleasure of it and the world is lucky you strut about."

"The world is lucky to have me," Matilda replied. "How's this?" She sashayed across Ashton's sitting room, trying to put arrogance where for more than two decades only modesty had dwelled.

"No," Helen said, popping off the windowsill. "This is you." She flounced across the carpet, nose in the air, skinny hips swishing. "Don't be a streetwalker on the stroll, be a flat who knows for a bit of coin he can do as he pleases with dozens of women."

"What an ugly source of pride."

"That ugly source of pride keeps many a bird from starving," Pippa said. "Try again."

"Think with this," Helen said, patting her crotch. "You're the king of the world, and that's your golden scepter."

Helen's determination to help broke Matilda's heart, but the child got the point across. With Stephen Derrick in mind, Matilda paced the room again. No hurry, no concern about somebody looking at her wrong, no fear for her bodily safety, no apology for moving too quickly or too slowly, no smile handy for any gentleman to whom she'd been introduced.

"Better," Pippa said. "In those clothes, you'll pass well enough if you don't say much."

"The longer you do it, the easier it gets," Helen said. "Once you learn to smoke, drink, scratch, and spit, you're a bloke and nobody looks at you twice. I don't care for spitting, but that's men for you."

"Swear under your breath a lot," Pippa suggested. "God's cods, St. George's hairy arse, that sort of thing. Burping helps and the occasional cheeser. Then act like it's hilarious no matter how bad the stink."

Cheeser being...?

"A right, ripe fart," Helen offered. "Begins with *f.* I like to leave God and the saints out of it. Bloody sodding shite, miserable damned blighter. If I can learn my letters, you can learn to swear."

"A fine attitude," Ashton said, coming through the sitting-room doorway. "And I'm happy to help you. Cherbourne's attire is a bit loose on you, which is good. Your wig."

He closed the door to the stairway and passed Matilda a box. The wig within was auburn, which suited her coloring, and longish for a man.

"This is well made," she said, "not simply a theater costume."

"Only the best for my manservant, Matthew," Ashton said, taking the wig from her. "We'll need to braid up your hair. Ladies, if you'll excuse us, Matthew and I have a few details to discuss."

"Maddie might do," Matilda said, as Pippa herded Helen out the door. "My father allowed my mother to put Maitland on the baptismal lines, because it was a family name, but I've been Matilda all my life—or Maddie."

Ashton led her by the wrist into his bedroom. "Are you thinking to cut and run on me, Maddie?"

The old nickname sounded wonderful, coming from him.

"Why would you think that?" Matilda had been thinking that. Had been planning on how to get her emergency bundle from her house to his apartments unnoticed.

"I can see it in your eyes." He patted the back of the vanity stool. "Have a seat and explain to me why you'll leave just as you've found an ally with some influence."

Sitting in breeches was different—easier. Everything was easier without skirts to maneuver, and Matilda felt safer in breeches, despite having the contours of her legs more or less on display.

Easier for her to run, harder for anybody to trifle with her. Was that why men were horrified by the thought of women wearing breeches?

"You are forever taking pins out of my hair," Matilda said. "Perhaps I ought to cut it."

"Perhaps you ought to trust me," Ashton said, getting to work. "It will take you much longer to grow your hair back than it will for me to confront your in-laws and hold them accountable."

He was a competent lady's maid, damn him. Matilda hadn't had anybody tend her like this for years.

"You asked for my plan," she said. "I will hide until the law pronounces me dead. Hiding with a man who mingles among the very people my in-laws consider friends might work for a few days, but by this time next week..."

He drew his fingers through her unbound hair. "You'll leave me? You're giving me one week to slay dragons who've been besieging your castle for years?"

Maybe not even a week. "I want to live, Ashton. You can slay dragons while I'm taking the air in Sicily."

Though Sicily was so very far from London, and Kitty, and everything Matilda knew.

"Do you speak Italian?"

"No."

"Then Italy will not do for a woman alone without significant means. America makes more sense, but because it's the logical place to go other than France, you shouldn't consider it. You could marry me."

Matilda bent forward, resting her forehead on her folded hands. "A marriage is a documented, public undertaking, particularly if you're having banns cried. Whether by special license or not, I'd have to use my legal last name, which at this point is Derrick. If you did find a way to make me your countess, I'd still be a commoner, and commoners hang."

But oh, to be *his* countess. To have this fierce, wily, kind man for her husband. Italy wouldn't be nearly far enough away to preserve Matilda from the temptation Ashton offered.

When her hair was in disarray about her shoulders, Ashton knelt beside her so they were almost eye to eye.

"You have been afraid for so long, and on your own for so long, that nothing I say or do will have any merit in your eyes when it comes to putting your situation to rights. It's not fair that I should have more influence and credibility than you, it's not just. I'm sorry for that, but all I can do about it is put my resources at your disposal."

He brushed out her hair in silence, while Matilda wrestled with the instincts clamoring to send her pelting for the docks in her newly acquired men's attire. Beneath the compulsion to run, though, was a weariness she hadn't been able to admit and a loneliness so vast she could drown in it.

"Two braids will be easier to put a wig over," she said. "Like Helen's cap."

"She's another one who needs some dealing with," Ashton muttered, starting on the right braid. "If you leave, what will become of her?"

"She'll be better off for having learned a few letters and some manners, and you will look after her."

He tied a brown ribbon around the first braid, then started on the second. "You trust me to look after a street thief who will likely steal from me before the week's end, and yet, I'm not to have seven days to do my best for the woman I love?"

The wretched, awful, shameless... A man would have better curse words, but those were the best Matilda could do over the thumping of her heart.

"Keep your flirtations to yourself, my lord. Hanging is a terrible, undignified way to go. It's not your neck that will be in the noose."

"Nor will it be yours. I promise you that."

He dispatched the second braid as quickly as the first, and Matilda cast around for any way to put some distance between herself and the man trying to prevent her flight to safety.

"Are you adept at braiding hair because you've loved many women, my lord?"

"My lord, my lord, my lord. You are as relentless as the Hebridean wind. I'm good at braiding because I'm a horseman. A braided mane and tail are less likely to get caught in the brambles and burrs. Have you consulted a solicitor regarding your situation?"

Ashton was the relentless one, like a warrant that never expired, and yet, Matilda was inordinately relieved to know his expertise had been gained in a stable.

"How could I meet with a man of law? Do I explain that I'm wanted for murder, but please keep my little problems just between us?"

"If he were a barrister, he'd have to keep your confidences, like a priest. I can ask hypothetical questions, changing a few details to obscure the truth. Might do just that."

"Please don't. Asking questions, poking your lordly nose into scandals, and threatening the hold Drexel has on my fortune will only create curiosity, which is the last thing I want or need."

Ashton had the knack of pinning her hair without gouging her scalp, which skill the horses might also have taught him.

"You are the bravest woman I've ever met," he said, settling the wig over the braids. "That includes my sister-in-law, who had the courage to marry into the Fenwick family. But you can't see straight, Matilda. You've been ridden hard for too long. Your wind is broken."

"Now you insult me," she said, shooting to her feet. "For God's sake, don't hold my chair. I've managed on my own for six years, and one more year isn't that long. Less than a year, in fact. I will accept your aid so that my next journey is well planned and discreet, but don't expect me to hand you control of my life. Abdicating responsibility for myself to the nearest man hasn't gone well, ever."

From Papa, to Althorpe, to Drexel, each one had put his self-interest ahead of Matilda's well-being. Admitting it aloud solved nothing, but with nobody to contradict her, it felt *good*.

"So be responsible for yourself," Ashton said, "and listen to me. You can be declared dead next year and your funds disbursed to your in-laws, never to be returned to you. Your troubles will have become only more complicated if you allow that to happen."

"Not if the warrant for my arrest is withdrawn." Why couldn't he see that?

"Do you know what a statute of limitations is?"

Matilda moved away, lest she smooth Ashton's lapel or fluff his cravat—any excuse to touch him.

"Something legal and therefore onerous."

"Actually, no," Ashton said, sitting on the bed. "The idea behind a statute of limitations is, if a long enough span of years goes by and a criminal isn't brought to justice, then clearly, he or she has learned not to get caught committing any more crimes. The law turns its attention to more recent wrongdoing."

"Where there's a hope of collecting a reward."

"Perhaps, but the result is that after a time, the law essentially forgets, even if it doesn't forgive. At common law, for many serious offenses, that period is twenty-one years."

"And you know this, how?" He knew too many things—how to braid a woman's hair, how to teach a child her letters. How to steal a heart that ought to be un-stealable.

"Because I had a fine education, and many a younger son or by-blow has found a career in the law. I didn't, but not for lack of exposure to its concepts. The problem, Matilda, is that after you're declared dead, if somebody finds you—you, who think you are safe at last—then you've perpetrated a fraud on the crown. The warrant is reinstated, and you're tried not only for murder and fleeing the king's justice, but also for fraud. That's your idea of a solution."

Matilda sank to the bed beside him, her knees simply refusing to bear her weight. Ashton would not lie to her. He probably wouldn't lie to anybody, for any reason.

"The warrant can be reinstated? *Even after I'm dead?*"

"Your in-laws might be planning on that very course."

Drexel was that devious, and Stephen that tenacious. The gnawing terror that had gripped Matilda immediately after Althorpe's death threatened to claim her. Fear once again became a physical misery, destroying her ability to concentrate, making her weak and queasy.

She wanted to run, but honestly could not think of where or how. "I'll go to the Albany with you and give you time to do what you can without making the situation worse, but you must promise me one thing."

"Name it."

"No matter what happens to me, you must promise me that you'll look after Kitty. God knows what Drexel has planned for her when she comes of age, and if anything happens to Drexel, then her care falls to Stephen. Girls can be legally betrothed long before they reach their majority. Stephen is greedy enough to marry her for the fortune she might inherit from me."

Matilda waited to hear Ashton's assurances that Kitty would be well provided for, that Kitty should be the least of her worries.

He put an arm around Matilda's shoulders. "I'll do my best, but your safety comes first. I can't marry a dead woman."

CHAPTER TWELVE

"I was told you're the best, Samuels." Stephen had been assured Samuels wasn't too particular about how he caught a fugitive.

"I am the best," Samuels replied, blowing the foam off a tankard of ale and making an urchin at the end of the bar hop away. "For six years, nobody has seen hide nor hatpin of your fine lady. Now you want me to find her overnight on the basis of old gossip and an older miniature. If she was so precious to her family, why hasn't she turned to them for help?"

Samuels belonged in the Goose, an establishment that exploited its proximity to the theaters in one direction and thriving shops in the other. Sometime in the last two hundred years, the Goose had acquired venerability, which to most of the populace counted for more than respectability. Not all of the women who patronized the place were for sale, for example, and the ale was decent.

Stephen considered himself a connoisseur of ale, as every good Englishman ought to be.

"I'm offering you considerable coin to locate this woman," Stephen said. "Matilda is in London. She'd not go far from the girl."

Samuels took a considering sip of his ale. "That narrows it down considerably, doesn't it? All I need to do is line up a hundred thousand blond women and ask them if they killed somebody six years ago. Who did you say her victim was?"

"Her husband."

"Not very original, guv."

The publican took a few coins from the urchin and disappeared into the kitchen. Stephen had agreed to meet Samuels at the Goose because the activity at a commercial venue allowed a certain privacy that a club or park bench did not—and some safety.

"She killed him," Stephen said quietly. "Saw it with my own eyes. Bashed my poor father repeatedly about the head when the dear man was in his cups and unable to defend himself. A woman with a temper like that will kill again."

Samuels studied his ale as if a fine summer brew was more interesting than Stephen's eyewitness account of a killing.

The magistrate had believed Stephen, and that was what mattered. Why would Matilda have run off if she hadn't been guilty?

"You ever been bashed with a poker?" Samuels asked.

"Certainly not."

"Takes a prodigious lot of bashing to even put out a man's lights. Makes me wonder what you were about to let her have at him that way while you stood by and did nothing."

Samuels apparently spoke from experience when it came to delivering fatal bludgeonings, and this conversation had gone on too long.

"I'm paying you ten pounds to find the woman, Samuels, and that's in addition to the fifty my uncle has promised upon conviction. I'm not paying you to make a Gothic novel out of a family tragedy."

Samuels wasn't overly large, and he dressed respectably, but he had a stillness Stephen distrusted. In the clubs, men talked, laughed, played cards, ate, and drank. If a fellow sat unmoving, he was dozing off over his last glass of port.

Or he was dead. Old Baron Shanahan had expired in his club's reading room, the day's paper clutched in his hand. The staff had considerately folded a lap robe over his knees, and nobody had realized he'd stuck his spoon in the wall until morning.

"You are paying me ten pounds to kill your wealthy step-mother," Samuels said, as if discussing whether to put two bob on Exeter's Folly in the third race. "Or do I misapprehend your intentions?"

Stephen had read a minimum of law at university, but he knew conspiring to commit murder was frowned upon by the authorities. The idea rather unsettled the ale in his belly too.

"I'm increasing the reward my uncle has already offered. We seek to ensure my step-mother's safe return to the bosom of the family who've been frantic with worry for her for too long."

That bit about a single blow not being enough to kill a man was speculation on Samuel's part. That Matilda had profited by Papa's death was fact, and she'd not only run, she'd hidden long and thoroughly.

What innocent, penniless female could manage that?

The publican emerged from the kitchen and passed a sack to the dirty child shifting from foot to foot at the end of the bar. The child darted for the door, pausing long enough to pass food from the parcel to a skinny blond woman who'd apparently been waiting for a meal.

The blonde began eating a meat pie even as she departed the premises after the child.

"The fare here is good," Samuels said, gaze on the blonde's retreating figure. "You should try it."

"I'll leave the streetwalkers to those who can't afford better," Stephen said. "Find my step-mother, Samuels, or I'll set a more skilled man on her trail."

Samuels lifted his tankard of ale. "Go right ahead, guv. Offer a hundred pounds while you're at it, and you'll doubtless see a parade of guilty step-mothers apprehended by sundown. A violent lot, step-mothers."

Stephen rose, resisted the urge to dust off his backside, and pulled on his gloves. "Mind your attitude, Samuels. This is serious business, and you can easily be replaced."

When reprimanding the lower orders, having the last word mattered. Stephen made a dignified, if purposeful, exit and wondered how much a pawnbroker might give him for his second-best gold snuff box. Matilda Derrick needed finding, the sooner the better.

* * *

Matilda made a credible secretary, to Ashton's relief.

She stood about his apartment at the Albany, looking like a pale, academic young man who spent too much time hunched over a ledger and not enough time on a cricket pitch.

"I ought to find something secretarial for you to do." Ashton scooped up a pile of unopened correspondence from the escritoire by the window.

Matilda snatched them from his hand. "Give me those. A personal secretary opens your mail and sorts it by urgency and type."

They were alone, Ashton having sent Helen off to fetch them a midday meal from the Goose, and Cherbourne to retrieve the latest batch of finery from Bond Street.

Pippa had remained at Pastry Lane. She'd periodically scurry about the market in Matilda's cloak and hat and otherwise support the fiction that Matilda yet bided several streets away.

"You've had a personal secretary?" Ashton asked.

"Of course. You haven't?"

Matilda was more qualified to be a countess than Ashton was to be an earl. She communicated easily with the French chef who cooked for the duke's heir lodging across the corridor. She'd directed Ashton's footmen to rearrange the parlor furnishings to take better advantage of the warmth of the hearth and the light from the windows.

And damned if Ashton didn't adore watching her take charge of his domicile, striding about in trousers, to all appearances a fussy young fellow with airs above his station.

"I had a secretary," Ashton said, moving a bud vase from the escritoire to the window. No daffodils for a lordly abode. Only a forced rose would do. "Like many of the trappings of the title, I inherited my secretary from my brother,

Ewan, and he'd inherited old MacFarland from our papa, who'd inherited him from the previous earl."

"You retired him," Matilda said, taking up a nacre-handled letter opener and slitting the first seal. "Or perhaps he expired?"

Ashton had hoped that men's attire would mute Matilda's attractiveness, but no. Trousers made her more alluring, even with a proper swallowtail coat hanging to the backs of her knees. The blade in her hand made her more alluring. The auburn wig that exposed the nape of her neck and the curve of her jaw made her more alluring.

"I pensioned MacFarland off." Ashton took a chair before the hearth, lest he perch himself on the desk, within sniffing distance of his secretary. She still smelled of lemons, and the competence in her hands struck Ashton as unfairly attractive.

Matilda studied a single sheet of paper covered with Alyssa's handwriting. "Why not replace him?"

"I had much to learn," Ashton said. "How better to become acquainted with my own business than to read my correspondence firsthand and reply in my own words? Ewan told me I was daft, but he's my brother. He's been telling me I'm daft since he was in dresses."

Matilda set the letter aside and slit open the next seal. "Write to your sister-in-law and tell her you're keeping well, but you miss her and your brother."

With a staggering ache, now that Matilda had said the words. "I *appreciate* Ewan, more than I could have five years ago. I miss the children, I miss my sister-in-law." And Scotland. Sweet Jesus at the wedding feast, did Ashton miss Scotland.

"This is from a tenant," Matilda said. "Don't you have a land steward?"

"I have three land stewards. One for the tenancies, one for the estate holdings, one for the villages and commercial undertakings." The recitation made Ashton tired. The sight of Matilda attired as a man but still every inch a female made him randy.

"So why does this…"—she turned the letter over—"Mr. Breckenridge write to you?"

"Because he's one of my English tenants, and they are the whiniest damned lot of sluggards you ever met. They are eternally annoyed to have a Scottish landlord when their holdings lie in England. I understand now why my uncle considered diverting the river, despite the expense and the—"

Helen popped around the door from the antechamber. "A proper nob coming up the steps. Drives a coach and four complete with liveried footmen and grooms."

"Thank you, Helen," Matilda said, rising from the escritoire. "I'll admit him. You can't, my lord. You're the earl, and the footmen are on half day."

"If it's Hazelton, I'm no' home," Ashton said.

"Don't be a coward," Matilda shot back, but she was smiling the same smile Helen wore when holding forth about the letter *b*—bum, backside, bosom.

"What should I do with the meat pies?" Helen asked, holding up an aromatic sack.

"Take yours upstairs," Matilda said. "His lordship will eat when his guest has departed."

Helen helped herself to a pastry and nipped up the back steps while a knock sounded at the front door.

"His lordship," Ashton said, brushing a kiss to Matilda's cheek, "will eat with his secretary while we plow through that lot of drudgery."

He patted her backside as she bustled off to the door and braced himself for a recitation from Hazelton about every scandal to plague London in years past.

Except that the guest Matilda admitted was one Hannibal Shearing, late of Northumberland. Shearing was as rich as he was plainspoken, though his clothes were the finest money could buy.

"Mr. Shearing," Ashton said, bowing with a sense of futility. "You will please excuse the household's disarray. I am only newly come to London."

"Been keeping an eye out for you," Shearing said, passing Matilda his walking stick and hat. "Birds of a feather and all, you being from the north. Hear you're going to the levee on Tuesday."

Matilda silently left the room and would probably wait in the porter's nook while Ashton expired from the demands of lordly hospitality.

"A friend has asked me to accompany him. I can have tea brought up from the kitchen if you're so inclined?"

"Cat lap—bah. The missus makes a great to-do over her tea service. I prefer more gentlemanly libation." Shearing produced a flask, held it aloft as if Ashton was supposed to admire the sunlight winking on the silver, then downed a portion.

"Shall we have a seat?" Ashton asked.

Shearing had the brawn of a yeoman—broad shoulders, barrel chest, and oddly trim legs and waist. He stood with that chest thrust forward, a caricature of military posture, and his white hair bristled in all directions, despite obvious use of pomade.

"I won't take up much of your time, Kilkenney. All I mean to say is this: If I return to the north without a barony to my name, the missus will bar me from my own premises. Both of her sisters married baronial heirs, and she settled for me."

Ashton had heard some of this recitation before. "Clearly, your wife is a woman of discernment."

Shearing ran a gloved hand through his hair, further disarranging his locks. "She's a woman of a certain age, if you know what I mean. Poor lady has more hysterics than a biddy hen when the fox is digging under the fence. I mean for her to be a baroness, my lord, and I'm enlisting your aid to make it so."

Ashton liked Shearing, liked his bluntness, his determination, and his devotion to his would-be baroness. If anybody deserved a barony, it was such as he.

"Shearing, I don't even sit in the Lords. I'll be lucky to have five minutes of George's attention." Lucky being a relative term.

"He'll dodge me entirely," Shearing said. "George ain't as stupid as folk want to believe. He'll have his hand in your pocket one moment and pretend he's never met you the next. Fair warning, in case he hasn't got up to his tricks with you yet."

"I've been spared so far, but I appreciate the admonition. How long will you be in London?"

"Too damned long," Shearing said. "Place stinks worse than a muck pit in July, and every shopkeeper and footman thinks he's next in line to the throne compared to a Yorkshireman's son. Where's that young man got off to with my walking stick? It's my favorite. My oldest girl gave it to me on my fortieth birthday. Just wanted to ask you to put in a word with George, if the opportunity arises."

"I'll see you out," Ashton said, "and I expect I'll see you again on Tuesday. Good to know there will be at least one friendly face amid all the lords and princes."

"Do I still sound like a dalesman?" Shearing asked as Ashton herded him toward the door. "Been taking lessons, you know. Silliest damned thing, teaching a grown man how to talk, how to dress. I'm supposed to read books about taking tea and paying calls. This barony will be the death of me, Kilkenney. I probably shouldn't have said that."

Ashton passed Shearing his hat and a simple carved walking stick that would do fine service as a cudgel.

"What clubs do you belong to, Shearing?"

"Clubs? The Engineers and Surveyors, though they mostly survey the brandy and engineer the whist and piquet. Useless damned lot."

"If you were invited to join a more prestigious organization, one frequented by some of the titles, would you care to accept?"

Shrewd blue eyes assessed Ashton from beneath bristling white brows. "I'd be a damned fool not to, though I'd rarely set foot on the premises. I'm not a complete bumpkin. They take my money, and someday, my grandsons might play cards with theirs, provided my family continues to prosper and theirs persists in trying to live exclusively off the land rents."

Ashton's great-uncle had seen the folly of that snobbery decades ago—thank God. "The Lords needs more men like you, Shearing. I wish you the best of luck with George."

"The Lords needs a swift boot in the arse," Shearing said, tapping his hat onto his head. "Pity you ain't taking a seat."

"Perhaps in a few years, when my household is better established."

Shearing smiled, a jocular, charming expression that would have suited a blacksmith or a publican.

"You need a missus. We all do. Makes all the difference, and even Fat George can't help with that dilemma, young man. Pity my girls are all married off, eh?"

"My loss, I'm sure," Ashton said, and a few weeks ago, he'd probably have meant that. "Good day, Shearing."

"Until Tuesday, Kilkenney. Remember, George is after our groats, and there's nothing wrong with that, provided he dispenses a bit of favor in return."

Shearing went jaunting on his way, the soul of England's future and, doubtless, the apple of Mrs. Shearing's eye.

"What an interesting man," Matilda said, emerging from the porter's nook. "I liked him."

"So do I. I also like that we're alone, and nobody will disturb us for at least the next two hours."

* * *

Damon Basingstoke's office was more modestly kitted out than Harpster's. No age-darkened portraits on the walls, but rather, a single painting of St. Paul's dome as viewed from the countryside south of the Thames hung over the mantel. Writing implements littered the desk blotter, along with a sanded sheet of vellum covered with precise, slanting script.

Ashton had to approve of a man who actually worked at his profession.

"My lord," Basingstoke said, with a short—not quite rude—bow. "And...?"

Matilda hung back, secretary-fashion, a leather satchel in her hand, but she made a credible bow to the attorney.

"Mr. Matthew MacFarland," Ashton said. "My personal amanuensis. Mr. MacFarland is entirely in my confidence."

Ashton had been two kisses away from getting Mr. MacFarland into bed when a messenger had arrived with a note saying Basingstoke was free to meet with his lordship on the hour. Matilda had insisted Ashton keep the appointment; Ashton had insisted she accompany him.

She needed to become comfortable in her disguise, an objective she couldn't achieve in Ashton's bed—damn the luck.

"How may I be of assistance to you?" Basingstoke asked, gesturing Ashton to a chair facing the desk.

No tea and crumpets, no blethering about the weather—better and better.

"I've sacked Harpster," Ashton said, taking a seat while Matilda did likewise. "He wasted my time."

Basingstoke settled into the chair behind the desk. "So that I might avoid the same blunder, I will ask you to be more specific about the services you seek, my lord."

If Ashton had to sum up Basingstoke in a single word, he would have been hard-pressed to choose between self-contained and seething. Basingstoke set the pen in the standish, capped the ink bottle, and poured the sand off into a dustbin. His movements were economical to the point of parsimony, as were his words.

He gave the appearance of tidying up his desk while casually listening, but Ashton suspected he had Basingstoke's whole attention. The document in progress left on display had likely been intentional too.

Shrewd, then. And good-looking, in a broody, Gothic-novel way. Basingstoke's dark hair even needed a trim.

"I asked Harpster for a list of the properties I am free to sell," Ashton said. "He couldn't produce one, despite having copies of all the letters patent, deeds, and land transactions attached to the earldom and the family's private holdings."

Basingstoke folded his correspondence into thirds and set it aside. "Is the earldom in difficulties?"

Harpster would have taken two hours to get to that question. "The earldom thrives. My brother was a conscientious and discerning manager, but land rents alone are no longer a sensible means of safeguarding a family fortune. If I sell off some property, I'll have more cash to invest in non-agricultural projects."

Basingstoke's gaze flicked from Ashton to Matilda, who'd produced pencil, paper, and a small lap desk from her satchel. She sat on the edge of her seat, pencil poised, head down.

"I've looked over your records," Basingstoke said. "The original land grant passed down with the Mulder barony is attached to the earldom's title and cannot be sold. Most of the estate added by purchase since then, however, can be liquidated with no encumbrance on the title. The entail can be broken on other portions, because any transaction your brother made as the earl—such as renewing a voluntary entail—is arguably invalid."

Good news—and bad news. "I've been the earl for three years," Ashton said. "Why wouldn't Harpster bring up the need to ratify some of my brother's decisions?"

Basingstoke rose and fetched a lit taper from the mantel behind his desk. He used the flame to light a stick of red sealing wax and dripped a portion onto the folded vellum.

"I can think of two explanations," Basingstoke said as one red drop followed another onto the paper. "Harpster might not have realized that decisions made by your brother could be repudiated by the rightful earl. Your situation is unusual to the point of…" He blew out the wax candle, smoke rising from the extinguished wick. "Your legal posture is fascinating, my lord. A hundred years from now, law professors and judges will cite your case in their lectures, as they do the Duke of Atholl's, whose title at one point went to a second son when the first was declared a traitor while biding in France."

Basingstoke had dripped a perfect circle of wet, red wax onto his missive. He used not a ring to press the seal into the wax, but a seal produced from a desk drawer. Perhaps a bastard son eschewed wearing the family signet, or hadn't been given one.

"The second explanation for Harpster's silence?" Ashton asked.

"Harpster doesn't want anybody examining the transactions completed on your brother's behalf too closely."

Sweet Jesus in a boat. Ashton thought back over land purchases, investments, contracts for goods and livestock, dowries negotiated for cousins, and pensions established for retired servants. An earldom was a vast enterprise, and abruptly, his stood on uncertain ground.

"*You* examine those transactions closely, Basingstoke. Examine them with a quizzing glass, and when you get that itchy feeling in your lawyer's mind, examine the transactions more closely still."

The wax Basingstoke had used was apparently scented, for a frisson of lavender wafted about the office—lavender symbolized distrust, probably Basingstoke's notion of a joke.

"You are retaining me, then?" Him, not his firm, and yet the question was the embodiment of diffidence.

"I'm retaining you to research the period from Ewan's assumption of the title to the present. I'd also like to talk to my English tenants about selling them their parcels. I'll happily hold the mortgages, but I'm tired of holding the hands of men whose families have been farming since the great flood."

"Any other assignments?"

On the street below, shod hooves clattered against the cobbles, and somebody shouted to make way. Ashton rose and went to the window, because nobody with any sense should have been driving a coach down such a narrow lane.

"That crest looks familiar," Ashton said. Not merely a coach, but a coach with bright red wheels, four spanking grays in the traces, and red livery on the coachman and grooms.

"The Earl of Drexel has arrived to meet with my father," Basingstoke said, joining Ashton at the window. "His lordship lives half a mile distant, if that."

Matilda's pencil went clattering to the floor.

"He's not here to meet with you?" Ashton asked as Matilda scurried to retrieve her pencil.

"My lot is usually to deal with impecunious nephews and younger sons," Basingstoke said. "That you requested my services specifically caused a gratifying amount of consternation among my older brothers."

"Happy to oblige," Ashton said, resuming his seat. Also happy to know Basingstoke was prey to a normal complement of sibling rivalry. "Is there any reason an earldom's concerns would exceed your expertise?"

"None, my lord. Drexel manages a great deal of family money, as you do yourself. My father is intimately familiar with the earl's situation, and my tendency to interpret the law narrowly would not be a good match with Drexel's style."

So Basingstoke was a legal stickler, while Drexel was high-handed at best.

Matilda was bent over her paper, scribbling furiously. Ashton glanced over her shoulder.

Drexel steals from Kitty's trusts?

"Under what circumstances can a marriage be rendered void?" Ashton asked.

Basingstoke let the curtain fall and resumed his seat. "Are you asking for yourself, my lord?"

"I'm asking a hypothetical question, and I'm paying you to answer it."

Basingstoke put away the gold seal, in no hurry at all. "Before I *accept* tuppence from you, my lord, please understand that my integrity is not for sale. If you married some village girl before you came into the title, I'll not subvert the law to allow you a better match now. If your brother's wife wants to dissolve her union with him in order to marry you, then another solicitor will have to—"

"Basingstoke, cut line. I've never found a woman willing to have me for the rest of her life, and I couldn't pry Alyssa and Ewan apart with a gold-plated crowbar. I hope to marry soon, and the question is general."

Unless your name happened to be Maitland rather than Matilda.

"Three grounds, generally, give rise to suits for annulment." Basingstoke folded his hands on the blotter, like a scholar called upon to recite.

"Annulments are heard by the bishop of the see where the couple dwelled," he went on. "Incompetence is the first ground, such as one party being underage and lacking parental consent. Insanity is another form of incompetence. Fraud, of identity or assets, constitutes the second ground, and the third is inability of the husband to perform the marital act. For the third ground to be actionable, the wife must be demonstrably untouched."

"What is fraud of identity?"

"Using the wrong name on the marriage lines, leaving off a title, neglecting to add all the middle names for a man of your station," Basingstoke said. "The bishops can deny the request if it's a matter of a lifelong nickname for some squire's son, but they can also grant annulments on the merest pretext when a man whose union has failed to produce an heir is moved to donate to some cathedral's maintenance fund. Any other questions?"

Matilda's pencil was poised over her paper, her posture that of a raptor over a fresh kill.

"If, in my tenure as earl, I've mismanaged the assets of a minor of whom I hold guardianship, what are the consequences?"

"I trust this is another hypothetical?"

Hardly. "One you will keep in confidence."

"The guardian owes to the minor ward a duty of utmost care and concern," Basingstoke said, "a fiduciary duty, which requires best efforts to safeguard the ward's well-being. All manner of legal repercussions will result if you've mishandled some child's funds, my lord. As much as I loathe relinquishing responsibility for any aspect of your affairs, my father would be in a better position to advise you further on a matter such as this."

Because he'd doubtless advised Drexel on the same topic. "Could I be tried in the Lords for mishandling funds?"

Matilda had left off pretending to take notes and positively glowered at Basingstoke.

"Of course, if the charges are for felony wrongdoing, though the evidentiary standard for criminal convictions is high. You can forget finding a wife if you're courting that degree of scandal, my lord, and I must warn you, the Lords occasionally like to make an example of one of their own."

Drexel, who'd exploited not one but two daughters of an earl, would make a fine example. "You will be relieved to know that I have no wards, Basingstoke."

"Meaning no disrespect, I am indeed relieved."

Basingstoke knew the law the way Ashton knew horses and whisky, not by dint of rote memorization or dogged effort, but by heart.

"When can you have a report for me on my English tenancies?"

Basingstoke consulted a silver pocket watch. "One week, my lord. You will be billed at the end of the month, and my time will cost you dearly."

"As it should," Ashton said, rising and extending a hand.

He'd surprised the canny and blunt Mr. Basingstoke and got a firm handshake and a startlingly warm smile in response.

"Good day, my lord, Mr. MacFarland."

Matilda bowed—a prudent choice, when her hands were bare—and followed Ashton from the office. She kept her silence all the way to the street, which was a quiet side lane near the Inns of Court. The coach and four remained outside the solicitor's establishment, blocking wheeled traffic in both directions.

"Why did you ask about annulling my marriage?"

"I wanted to see if Basingstoke knew the answer." Not every solicitor would have.

"My marriage to Althorpe might never have been valid?"

"In the absence of an annulment while Althorpe lived, your marriage will be presumed valid, which means your inheritance from Althorpe remains truly yours."

"Mine in name, you mean. Drexel has possession of my fortune and Kitty's."

They approached an intersection and had to wait for a curricle and a phaeton to pass a coal wagon. A flyer offering a reward for information leading to the arrest and conviction of "Lady Matilda Derrick, Murderess at Large!!!", had been affixed to the nearest lamppost.

Ashton tore down the flyer and stuffed it in a pocket.

"The marriage might have been subject to annulment," Matilda said, "but the murder warrant is all too real. If Drexel is stealing from Kitty—and I'm sure he is—then he has all the more reason to see me hanged."

She marched off across the street, looking for all the world like an angry young man.

CHAPTER THIRTEEN

The flyers were everywhere, and hour by hour, Matilda's hard-won peace slipped away. Mortar fire could bring down walls that had stood for centuries if the pummeling and noise went on long enough.

From the apartment below, she heard the rumble of men enjoying an evening of cards. Ashton's guests included a Scottish duke, a ducal spare, an earl, a knight, the duke's heir who kept the apartment across the corridor, another earl from the north, and Mr. Shearing, probably the wealthiest of the lot.

"You look sad," Helen said, smacking her pillow.

Matilda put aside the adventures of Robinson Crusoe—a slow top, in Helen's opinion, who hadn't the sense to avoid obvious scrapes—and settled on the end of Helen's cot. The room was little more than a dressing closet, but to Helen, it was a pleasure dome. The child delighted in owning a nightgown, in having her hair brushed and rebraided, in wearing slippers at the end of the day.

Such simple, profound pleasures.

"I'd forgotten that men can be good," Matilda said.

"I miss my pa," Helen replied, tucking her nightgown over her updrawn knees. "I don't miss his fists. He's the one who sent Sissy on the stroll, though I don't think he wanted to. If you don't work, you don't eat, for such as us."

"Not all men think of themselves first, Helen." The evening was mild, and through the open window, Matilda caught a hint of cigar smoke tinged with vanilla. The scent was expensive and reminded her of her own father.

Helen scooted under the covers with a gusty sigh. "All men think of themselves first, except his nibs. He thinks of everybody *and* himself. I'm studying on it."

Interesting observation. "Do you say prayers, Helen?"

"I used to, not anymore. As soon as I start telling God I'm grateful for something, that something goes away. I mind my own business and hope God does too. That works better."

Matilda had adopted the same philosophy more than six years ago, and it had kept her alive… while she died inside.

"They're leaving," Helen said as farewells sounded from the landing below. "Must be married gents who have a missus to go to."

Matilda rose, because the day had been long, and Helen needed her rest. "Mr. Tresham lives across the corridor."

"Then he's off to see his fancy piece. Do you say prayers, Mrs. B?"

"I'm Mr. MacFarland. Matthew, and yes, I say prayers." Now Matilda did. For Ashton's safety, Helen's future, and a little bit—a quiet little bit at the end of the list—for her own well-being.

"You're getting better at the mister-ing," Helen said. "I'm thinking of not cutting my hair."

What to say? Golden braids would put Helen at greater risk of harm. "You'd have to give up your trousers."

"I'd have to give up a lot." Helen turned on her side to face the door. "Ladies wear breeches under their riding habits. Did you know that?"

Long ago, Matilda had owned three gorgeous riding habits and a darling bay mare named Adelaide.

"I have heard the like. Go to sleep, Helen. Tomorrow his lordship has the court levee, and we must be up and about early."

"You're thinking of piking off," Helen said. "Don't ask me to go with you. I told Sissy I'm not coming back to her room, not for anything. His nibs said I would make a top-of-the-trees goose girl, if I wanted to."

"His lordship would never lie to you." Hearty male laughter drifted up the stairs, somebody making a parting joke, probably about Ashton's obligations at court tomorrow. "Helen, the handbills are everywhere. Pippa has seen Samuels on Pastry Lane."

Helen yawned and cracked her jaw, managing to look both female and masculine at the same time.

"Good. If Samuels is on Pastry Lane, he ain't here, or swilling ale at the Goose, and his nibs won't have to put out his lights. It's the hen that leaves the heather who gets shot out of the sky."

How small Helen looked, tucked up in her cot. "Harboring an accused murderess puts his lordship in danger."

"You ain't no murderess. If you decided to kill somebody, you'd make a proper job of it and go about your business, nobody the wiser. If I did pray, I'd ask God to look after you and Marmaduke."

Being categorized with a rescued jackass was a nice comment on Matilda's reality. "What about his lordship?"

"He's doing fine on his own. You should marry him."

Matilda blew out the candle rather than argue that point. "Good night, Helen. Sweet dreams."

The girl snorted.

The last of the guests had called his farewells, and the stairway was silent. Matilda kissed Helen's forehead before the child could protest, pulled the covers up over skinny shoulders, and left Helen to her dreams.

* * *

All evening, Ashton laughed, talked, and kept the two footmen running up and down from the kitchen and the cellar, while he'd lost a bit at cards and won a bit at friendship.

And he missed Matilda. He couldn't shake the sense that he'd turn around and she'd be gone, never to be seen again.

Ashton's guests tarried forever on the landing, wishing him and one another good night. The Duke of Murdoch's younger brother, Lord Colin, had contributed several bottles of exquisite whisky. Jonathan Tresham, the ducal heir across the corridor, had brought French chocolates.

Hazelton's countess had contributed flowers, about which Ashton would tease his lordship mercilessly on the way to tomorrow's blasted levee. Hazelton had taken half the evening before he'd relaxed and simply played cards, rather than supervise Ashton's every comment and congeniality. His lordship had lost the most of anybody, though he could easily afford it.

A quiet step sounded on the stairs above.

"If you're not coming down to join me, Mr. MacFarland, then expect me to accompany you wherever you're going."

Matilda's tread paused, then resumed. "You'd come with me to the jakes?"

"This time of night, there's safety in numbers, even at my august address. Care to join me for a nightcap?"

She stopped one step above him, so they were almost eye to eye. Ashton would content himself with a shared nightcap, if that's all Matilda offered him. He'd sit up all night holding her hand, if need be, just to make sure she didn't hare away with nothing but Cherbourne's altered finery on her back.

"Your evening sounded convivial," she said.

"Come," he replied, gesturing to the open door. "I'll tell you all about it. The Duke of Murdoch is shy, but his brother Lord Colin is a rascal. Our neighbor Mr. Tresham is lonely, and Hazelton's cousin—Sir Archer Portmaine—has an abacus for a brain when it comes to the cards. The damned man could be a professional card sharp if he ever chose to give up investigating."

Matilda came down the last step. "He investigates scandals?"

"He prevents them," Ashton said, tucking his hands behind his back, lest he be caught brushing his thumb over his secretary's lips. In men's attire, without skirts swishing or a bonnet to hide her expression, the fatigue dragging on Matilda from within was more apparent. "Will you sleep with me tonight?"

"*Sleep* with you?"

"That too."

She walked past him into the apartment's antechamber. "What of the footmen? Won't they be cleaning up?"

"I sent them to bed. The mess will be here in the morning." The mess was modest. A few dirty glasses, two empty decanters, a deck of cards stacked in the center of the reading table.

Matilda worked her way around the room, blowing out candles so the smoke of beeswax joined the fading odor of good tobacco.

"I will share your bed tonight, but Helen is likely to be up at first light. She's more excited about your attendance at the levee than you are."

"Will you come away with me to Scotland?" Ashton asked as the room became shrouded in shadows.

Matilda held a single taper, the flame turning her features spectral. "You hop from a night in your bed to a flight over the Border?"

"If I asked you to marry me, you'd laugh," Ashton said, leading her by the wrist into the bedroom, "or worse, favor me with your pitying expression. I figured I'd get you to Scotland first, and then enchant you with my manly charms."

She closed and locked the door. "You've already enchanted me with your charms, but there's a warrant for my arrest being shouted from every street corner. If you assist me to flee, you're an accessory after the fact."

He was tempted to kidnap her. Once over the Border, Matilda might be calm enough to see the wisdom of marrying him. As his Scottish countess, she'd be safer than Mrs. Bryce, late of Pastry Lane, had ever been.

"Helen is taking down the handbills as fast as Samuels puts them up," Ashton said. "The Season will soon start in earnest, and you'll be able to travel north with me. Please assure me you'll think about it."

Matilda took his cuff in her hands and undid the sleeve button. "I'll think about it." She extended her wrist, and in an odd exchange of courtesies, they valeted each other. While Ashton made use of the toothpowder, Matilda dispensed with her wig and tended to her hair.

Ashton was tall enough to see her over the privacy screen, though she doubtless thought herself unobserved. Sitting at his vanity, Matilda hunched forward, her face in her hands, her hair spilling about her.

Her posture radiated defeat and sorrow, and that ripped at him with more force than any taunt he'd endured as a bastard Scot coming of age in a world ruled by legitimate English sons.

"Your turn," he said, coming around the privacy screen. "Do we leave the window open?"

"The fresh air helps me sleep. I feel safer with a window open."

No woman should need assurances of a means of escape even while she slept. Drexel and his greedy heir would be held accountable. Ashton had made quiet arrangements to meet with Archer Portmaine later in the week to start that process.

Matilda wore Ashton's dressing gown, and he'd kept his breeches on. They shed their last articles of clothing at the same time and smiled at each other across the bed. She was not a blushing girl, and he wasn't a callow swain.

Thank God. They climbed into Ashton's bed from opposite sides, meeting in the middle and entwining bodies as naturally as a couple ten years married.

"I truly do want to marry you," Ashton said, wrapping an arm around Matilda's shoulders. "I've always carried a restlessness inside. I attributed it to bastardy, because my father's name was a gift, not a birthright."

Matilda took his hand in hers. "You strike me as a determined man rather than restless. Your energies are expended to a purpose."

"The restlessness was for want of you, Matilda. The earldom is my responsibility, but you are my home. You don't need me to be titled, charming, witty, or tactful, and you don't care if I'm wealthy or laboring for my bread."

He knew this the way he knew the contour of her jaw or the rhythm of her breathing. The knowledge was complete, not like a language mastered in slow increments.

"I've kept company with many witty, charming titles," Matilda said, ruffling the hair on his chest. "My father was such a one, and I'm sure the third cousins in Cornwall who inherited his earldom are too. Where were those cousins, where was anybody, when Kitty and I were friendless and orphaned?"

Matilda hardly knew her sister, and yet, she'd risked her life to stay close to the child. "Kitty will be safe, and you will be safe. I promise you this."

Ashton could go into hiding with her, buy them new lives in the New World, seize the child from Drexel's grasp, and repudiate the title he'd never wanted in the first place.

Except... Matilda deserved to be his countess, not simply his common-law wife. Their children deserved legitimacy, and Drexel deserved the hard boot of justice applied to his titled backside.

Matilda rose over Ashton, straddling him. "I need you to be safe too, Ashton Fenwick. Helen needs you, your family needs you. Make love with me."

He wanted to assure her that she too could need him. She could rely on him, and trust him, with her life and with her heart, but Matilda kissed him to silence. She paused to blow out the candle on the bedside table, then set about stealing his heart.

Her weapon of choice was a patience so vast, time became a progression of caresses and sensations. Ashton lost his grasp of the arguments he needed to impress on her, lost track of his list of exhortations regarding her safety. He returned her kiss, became a reflection of her passion, and made her the reflection of his.

Beneath the ecstasy of being loved with such abandon lurked a terror: Matilda could surrender to passion like this only because she'd surrendered equally to despair. Perhaps not tomorrow, perhaps not even this year, but one day, she'd quietly disappear, or worse, turn herself in to the authorities rather than allow any criminal taint to touch those she cared for.

He could not bear to indulge her in such nobility of character.

When Matilda had shuddered through a silent completion, Ashton held her, memorizing her features with his fingertips. Her breathing slowed, her skin cooled, and she kissed his chin. A thank-you, perhaps, or a good-night.

Ashton shifted so Matilda lay beneath him. He slipped back inside her in one smooth thrust.

"Again, Ashton?"

"And again." He loved her gently and relentlessly, until "Stay with me" and "I love you" became a unified cry of silent determination in the darkness.

Ashton felt Matilda trying to hold off her satisfaction, but in this, he could not allow her will to prevail. She bested him nonetheless.

When, at the last instant, he would have withdrawn and spilled his seed on her belly, she wrapped her legs around him and kept their bodies joined. Leaving would have made all the sense in the world, and yet she bid him to stay.

He pondered that gift late into the night and was still cheered by it when morning came and Matilda remained in his arms.

* * *

Hazelton paused, half in and half out of Ashton's town coach. "By the infernal imp, you're wearing your damned skirt."

While Hazelton was attired in the old-fashioned splendor of court attire.

"Get in, or leave your backside waving in the wind, for all I care," Ashton responded. "Perhaps you're the lone soul of good breeding who's neglected to read Sir Walter Scott. Kilts are dashing, and I'm told His Majesty looks marvelous in tartan wool."

Hazelton took the backward-facing seat, and Ashton thumped the coach ceiling twice with a gloved fist.

"George has doubtless been told the same lie," Hazelton said as the coach moved off. "Pleasant gathering over cards last night. Will you make it a regular event?"

"Possibly." If Ashton could put Matilda's situation to rights. "Can you get Hannibal Shearing admitted to your fancy club?"

Hazelton rested his hands on a smooth-grained walking stick carved to resemble the head of a dragon. "If I can get you admitted, I can get Beelzebub himself an invitation. Why?"

"Shearing pines for a barony to appease his lady wife, and I expect he'll again be disappointed. He's a decent chap, and I know how it feels to be excluded by people who are no better than they should be."

Hazelton pretended to study streets he'd been frequenting for years. "You are intent on causing trouble. Your marital prospects are already the subject of bets on the book at White's."

"Bet on me being married by George's next birthday." August was months away, time enough to address Matilda's situation and court her properly.

The coach slowed, traffic being a predictable nuisance. "Do you recall asking me to research a scandal involving somebody named Althorpe?"

Well, damn. "I should have saved you the trouble. No need to spade that turf now."

"I had extensive notes regarding the alleged murder of an earl's heir," Hazelton said. "A nasty situation, though the suspect was never brought to justice."

"Drop it, Hazelton. We can agree justice was never served."

The distance they had to travel was not far and would in fact have been covered just as quickly on foot. Today, however, Ashton wanted to make an entrance worthy of George himself, or he would have sprung from the coach rather than continue the discussion.

"Fenwick, a murder warrant doesn't expire just because you've fallen in love. Don't look so horrified. Maggie put the relevant facts together. Even knowing you, I would never have concluded that you've lost your heart to a missing heiress-turned-felon."

"That's Kilkenney to you, and if you accuse my lady of murder ever again, I will see that your wee lad comes into his title much too soon."

"I have questions about the case," Hazelton said. "Archer Portmaine does too."

Was this how Matilda felt when the thief-takers dogged her footsteps? "You'll not be getting answers from me."

"Was a coroner's examination done of the body? In every case where murder is suspected, the magistrate must have the deceased examined by a competent medical practitioner, else every wealthy woman whose husband died of apoplexy would find herself accused of foul play."

Ashton hadn't known a medical examination was required, though it made sense. "If some meddling buffoon hadn't obligated me to attend the royal pantomime today, I might be pursuing that very line of inquiry instead of flaunting my knees for the delectation of my less-stylish English cousins. But here I sit, wasting a fine morning, when I should be righting a grievous wrong against an innocent woman."

The coach lurched forward, nearly tossing Hazelton from the bench. He switched seats so he and Ashton were side by side.

"For God's sake, Kilkenney, I want to help. If you'd been less cryptic, less stubborn, less impossible—"

Hazelton so seldom lost his composure that Ashton was intrigued—also touched. "Did your countess put you up to this?"

"My count—you think Maggie...? You daft barbarian, *I am in your debt*. You guarded my interests at Blessings for years and were the sole comfort and confidante of my entirely blameless sister when polite society turned its back on her. Now you... I don't want to help, I *need* to."

"You should shout more often," Ashton said. "Puts the roses in your cheeks. Be kind to Shearing, will you? He's poured more money into the royal pockets than is decent. We'll talk about Matilda's situation, when a coachy, two footmen, and two grooms aren't a whisper away, aye?"

"Archer Portmaine should be a part of that conversation," Hazelton said *quietly*. "He's damned canny and has more charm than a mortal chambermaid can resist."

"And you say the man's a cousin. Hard to credit, such a divergence of traits in close relations."

Hazelton let the remark pass, because they were nearing their destination. Ashton had been to court twice previously and thus wouldn't be required to literally kiss the royal ring, though the day would be tedious as hell nonetheless.

Within five minutes of their arrival, Hazelton was pulled away, and though the Season had barely begun, the room was packed with the well-to-do and well titled—also the heavily scented. After an interminable while of pretending to recall names and titles, Ashton spotted Hannibal Shearing pressed into a corner, where the king's henchmen would doubtless see that he remained.

"Kilkenney, let's have a look at you," drawled a voice that embodied command, amusement, and genuine curiosity.

Ashton turned to behold the monarch in all his corpulent majesty. The requisite obsequies were observed—the deep bow being something of an adventure in a kilt—and the crowd gave the royal person enough room that Ashton could present his finery for inspection.

"Is that badger fur adorning your sporran?" George asked. "Very fierce fellow, the badger. Tenacious too. Rather like our fine English journalists when scandal's in the air. They tend to unfortunate teeth too, as it happens. How goes it in the Borders, Kilkenney?"

Where George's extravagances were concerned, scandal was always in the air.

"At the risk of offending my betters," Ashton said, unbuckling his sporran, "the Borders are among your most beautiful holdings, sir, and we're faring well. Keep the sporran, from one fierce, tenacious fellow to another."

The damned thing weighed a ton, and the tassels tickled Ashton's knees. George looked momentarily perplexed, then touchingly pleased.

"Thank you, Kilkenney." He leaned closer. "Don't suppose I can talk you into marrying Hannibal Shearing's daughter? Damned plaguey fellow haunts me for a mention on the honors list. You and he are nearly neighbors, aren't you?"

Tenacity was apparently contagious, unlike a grasp of British geography. "His daughters are all spoken for, sir, though he's much respected in the north, and I'm sure Shearing would reciprocate any kindness generously."

"Heaven preserve us, here he comes. Kilkenney, your servant."

The royal back turned, and Ashton's job became to intercept Shearing as he elbowed, jostled, and pushed his way through the crowd.

"Not today," Ashton said quietly. "And you won't get anywhere by breaching protocol."

"But that's the thing, Kilkenney," Shearing retorted. "I've observed protocol, I've poured a fortune into his damned monstrosity by the sea, and the equally inexcusable—"

Ashton clapped Shearing on the shoulder, hard. "I understand your frustration, but now is not the time. Have you met the Earl of Hazelton? He's lurking about here somewhere and has a fine holding in Cumberland. You're nearly neighbors."

Ashton cajoled, gossiped, and all but pushed Shearing in the direction of the corner from whence he'd sprung, which afforded a fine view of the sovereign, chatting affably with the wealthy and powerful and, all the while, stroking the fur of a dead badger.

George was still holding the sporran when he bid his guests farewell. His Majesty looked for all the world like a fellow who'd been given a toy he'd longed for since boyhood, while all Ashton wanted was a wee dram or three and the chance to turn Hazelton and his cousin loose on the accusations made against Matilda.

* * *

"You're doing a bunk," Helen said, stepping directly in front of Matilda. One moment, Matilda had been striding down the alley trying to look like a man with a purpose—she had the finest example of one of those—the next, Helen had dropped in front of her from the hay mow above the mews.

"You should at least take that satchel," the child went on, falling in step beside her. "Put your coin in your smalls, but carry the satchel like you're about your normal business. Gives you something to do with your hands, so you don't look twitchy. You could put some rocks in it and use it for a cudgel."

"I'm not leaving." After last night, Matilda couldn't leave. Her body had known it, her heart had known it, and now her mind was realizing it too. She and Ashton might have conceived a child, and there could be no greater proof that she trusted him.

And he trusted her, for Ashton Fenwick would never allow a child of his to grow up without a father's love and protection.

Helen skipped along beside her. "If you're not leaving, *Mr. Mac*, then why are you in this alley, without his lordship, without a footman, or even old Bedbug to keep a look out?"

"You should not be so disrespectful of his lordship's valet."

"Bedbug should not be so disrespectful of me. If you're not running off, what are you about?"

Helen's cautions brought to mind Ashton's last warning: *Wait for me, and we'll talk.* In his formal clan attire, he'd been not merely the earl, but the Border lord, ready to defend the realm in lands beyond the monarch's reach.

They arrived at the end of the alley and had to pause to find a gap in traffic to cross the wider street.

"Pippa sent a note," Matilda said. "She asked urgently for me to come to her, and she would not have imposed without good reason. I'll make a quick visit and pick up the copy of my marriage lines and baptismal lines, as well as the deed to the house, because my name appears on each. I also want the bundle I keep with those documents at the bottom of my wardrobe."

"I could have fetched all of that," Helen said. "Whyn't you send me? D is for daft, dimwitted, and deceptive. His nibs taught me that last one."

Matilda took Helen by the hand and started across the street. "I'm not deceiving anybody. That evidence could be useful to his lordship, and I should not have left it behind. I'm also worried about Pippa. Her note sounded urgent."

"Himself will tear a strip off us both for being so rotten damned stupid as to go jaunting about in broad daylight without him. Who brought you the note?"

Helen was dragging on Matilda's hand, as children will when they're being led somewhere against their will.

"One of the footmen brought it up."

"And who brought it to him?" Helen pressed. "Pippa knows damned good and well where the Albany is, and where we bide there."

"For all I know Pippa gave him the..." Matilda fell silent as they reached the next alley.

If Pippa had brought the note, she could just as easily have come up to the apartment and shared her news in person. Had Pippa asked her beau to deliver the note? He too would have delivered the note in person rather than hand it off to a footman unknown to him.

"She's alone in that house," Matilda said, "and I know what that feels like. Pippa has no one to turn to, she's been loyal to me, and I'll be back to the Albany with no one the wiser. I also miss Solomon."

"Jesus in the Middle Temple, I coulda brought you that damned cat. You can't always be looking after every creature what's too stupid to look out for itself. You have his lordship to do some looking out, and he has you. My pa always said the Quality is dicked in the nob, and Pippa agreed. Said money and book learning curdles the common sense."

Matilda took the turn that led down to the alley behind her house, though instead of a sense of homecoming, the scraggly trees reaching for the meager sun struck her as pathetic… and possibly sinister. Compared to the lush greenery of the parks, or the tidy repose of a Mayfair garden, Pastry Lane was downtrodden and messy.

Fit for tomcats and urchins. She'd been right to hide here, and right to leave.

"Pippa could do with more book learning," Matilda said. "Perhaps in time, she can…" A shivery feeling slithered through her insides. "Helen, turn around and run as if you don't want to accompany me. Do it now."

"Why?"

"Because I'm almost certain Pippa can't spell the word 'immediately' correctly."

Helen wrested free of Matilda's grasp. "I'm not coming with you! You can't make me, and I'm tired of doing what you say."

Matilda's plan was to chase the child back up the alley, all the way to the Albany, but a man in plain brown leaped over her own garden wall and clamped a hand around her arm.

"Lady Matilda Derrick, good day. Fetching ensemble, and you had me fooled for a bit. Jonas Samuels, at your service. You needn't worry about the little pickpocket. I promised her sister I'd not touch her, and I always keep my word."

CHAPTER FOURTEEN

"That is a jackass," Hazelton said as he and Ashton emerged into the early afternoon sunshine. "I wash my hands of you. Your pet jackass and its equally disreputable groom are arguing with your coachman on the very steps of the royal establishment. Have you any idea—?"

"Hector!" Ashton called, breaking into a run. "What's wrong?"

Both braids had tumbled free of Helen's cap, and her cheeks were streaked with tears.

"He has Mrs. B! The damned stinking rat plucked her from the alley, and this bloody goddamned bloated excuse for a farting disgrace of a coachman wouldn't fetch you."

"I'm sorry, my lord," the coachman began. "The child has no place—"

"She has every place. Helen, who has Matilda?"

"S-Samuels. He took her to that lawyer's office. I followed him, but I couldn't get inside, so I ran back to the Albany, asked Mr. Tresham's groom how to get to the levee, and grabbed Duke. She could be at Newgate by now, thanks to this ignorant, puking—"

Ashton put a gentle, firm hand over the child's mouth and snatched her up in his arms, lest she kick John Coachman's shins—or worse—clear to Scotland.

"A thief-taker has to take a suspect before the magistrate," Hazelton said. "Nobody goes straight to Newgate. If Samuels took her to the solicitor's office, he's under orders not to create a scandal."

"In which case, Matilda could simply disappear forever, nobody the wiser," Ashton said, depositing Helen into the coach. "We're for Basingstoke's law office, John Coachman, as fast as you can get us there. Have a groom lead Marmaduke back to my stable."

Hazelton piled into the coach and produced a handkerchief for Helen,

Ashton's being in his sporran.

"Mrs. B got a note from Pippa, but it's my fault," Helen said. "I heard Samuels tell Mrs. B that Sissy tipped him off, which is why he let me go. I don't think he knows I followed him."

"He might not," Hazelton said. "Particularly if the suspected murderer was struggling to escape."

"Don't call her that!" Ashton and Helen shouted in unison.

"You did the best you could, Helen, better than I might have done," Ashton said. "Why was Matilda on the street at all? She knows better."

Helen finished wiping her cheeks with Hazelton's fine linen, then passed the earl back his handkerchief.

"Keep it, child."

She peered at him. "It's not your lucky piece?"

"You are our lucky piece," Ashton said. "I've never met a girl with such pluck and determination. About Matilda?"

"That lying, crawling, worthless rotter sent her a note that Pippa was in trouble, but pretended it was from Pippa. You know how Mrs. B is, and then there's Samuels, like a snake from under a rock snatching her in my alley. I'll be having words with Sissy if she really did tip him off."

Ashton tucked Helen's braids back under her cap. "Your sister might not have had much say. Samuels probably offered her a choice between being arrested or peaching on Matilda."

Helen glowered out the window, blinking furiously. "Not much of a choice is right. I don't want to be a boy, but I don't want to be a girl much neither."

"You don't have to decide today," Ashton said. "Today you're the most loyal factotum an earl ever hired and the best friend Lady Matilda could wish for."

"Who's she?"

"I knew it," Hazelton muttered.

"Lady Matilda Derrick, known to you as Mrs. Bryce."

The coach slowed, and abruptly, the rage Ashton had been trying to ignore rose like an incoming tide. Drexel's four in hand sat before the solicitor's offices, a coachman and two footmen at their posts.

"Hazelton, don't let me kill anybody."

"Kill Samuels," Helen said. "Kill him a lot."

"Helen will keep you sensible," Hazelton rejoined. "As will Lady Matilda. My own feeble efforts to restrain your temper would pale compared to their good offices."

"Don't he talk grand," Helen said, hopping out of the coach before either Ashton or Hazelton. She opened the door to the solicitor's establishment before one of Ashton's footmen could reach it. "I'm his lordship's general factotum. Who are you?" she asked the footman.

"Helen, you'll stay here," Ashton said. "I need somebody I can trust to stand lookout."

Helen stuck her tongue out at the footman. "You heard his lordship. I'm the lookout."

She clambered to the top of the coach without another word and glowered in the direction of Drexel's conveyance.

"Thieves tend to post lookouts," Hazelton said. "Have you a plan for rescuing your damsel, or have you involved me in an impromptu kidnapping of a suspected felon, by daylight, while men of the law look on and take notes as you wrest the prisoner from the custody of the authorities?"

Valid point. No self-respecting Scotsman went raiding without a plan.

"You two," Ashton said to the footmen, "get around back and detain any who seek to leave through the alley. You and you," he said to his grooms, "stop anybody coming out the front door. No fisticuffs, but no exceptions either."

"That's a start," Hazelton said.

"If you have any suggestions, Hazelton, now is the time to make them."

"Kill Samuels a lot?"

"He's simply a henchman. Drexel is the puppeteer, and Basingstoke the Elder dances to his tune. John Coachman, move up so you're blocking the other coach where it stands."

"I'll have to back in from the corner, my lord, but our boys can do it handily, and they'll stand until Domesday if I tell 'em to."

"We won't be long."

"Your plan?" Hazelton asked again, eyeing the gray stone façade. Pots of red salvia adorned the front stoop, a brilliant contrast to the somber exterior. Once upon a time, this had been a fine town house, two small balconies fronting the street one floor up.

"I wish I could blow the place to kingdom come." A Scotsman's honest sentiment, a bastard's frustrated longing. Matilda needed Ashton to be a reaver prepared to enforce some Border justice.

"We'll speak sweet reason to another peer of the realm," Ashton said, "and threaten the hell out of him if reason doesn't prevail."

"Simple," Hazelton said. "I like it. Let's hope it works."

* * *

Drexel had aged in six years. His hair was thinner, his belly rounder, his jowls saggier than Matilda recalled.

This was the man who'd figured in her nightmares? This was the fiend who'd plotted to hand her over to the hangman? She'd never mistake him for harmless, though she was finished with mistaking herself for helpless.

"The situation is most unusual," Myron Basingstoke was saying. "Most, most unusual. Samuels, you've done your bit. Why are you tarrying among your betters?"

Samuels was the man who'd been following Matilda for the past two weeks.

As Ashton had said, he was attired to blend in. Medium height, medium build, tidy brown clothes without distinguishing details. Brown hair neither short nor long. The single feature Matilda focused on was the coldness in his eyes.

"I want my fee," Samuels said.

"You'll get no fee until she's been convicted," Drexel spluttered. "For God's sake, I shouldn't have to tell you the terms of your trade."

Drexel stood behind Basingstoke's desk, while Matilda occupied a chair by the bow window. She'd have to elude three men to get to the door, but neither Drexel nor his attorney concerned her.

Samuels, who lounged by the door without an apparent care in the world, concerned her very much.

"Your terms were the usual, guv," Samuels said. "Reward upon conviction. Mr. Stephen Derrick promised me ten pounds' payment upon apprehension of the suspect. I've done the apprehending, now somebody had better do the paying."

"Stephen offered you ten pounds to kill me," Matilda said.

All three men gawped at her as if a potted palm had spoken.

"Madam, you will remain silent," Drexel snapped. "You've caused enough trouble as it is, gallivanting about in that ridiculous getup, leading your family a dance, and involving the likes of a thief-taker."

"You will address me as your ladyship, he's not my thief-taker, and I'm dressed as you are," Matilda retorted as a racket came from the street below. A second coach had pulled up behind Drexel's four-in-hand, perhaps another wealthy—

She knew that team of chestnuts, and she knew very, very well the child and the kilted man who emerged from the coach. Matilda rose. She wanted to open the window and shout out her location, but the best she could do was try to catch Ashton's attention.

"You presume to judge me," she said, sweeping an arm in Drexel's direction. "You who did nothing to provide the authorities the truth and instead suborned Stephen's perjury. If that's not a felony, it should be."

Basingstoke glanced uneasily at his client. "Perhaps it's time we paid Samuels, my lord. The matter under discussion is delicate."

"I was delicate six years ago," Matilda retorted. "I'm considerably tougher now, and more resourceful, thank you."

"You will be silent," Drexel snapped. "My brother is spinning in his grave at all the trouble you've caused. Had you remained out of sight for another year, I might have been able to help you."

"Don't believe him, missus," Samuels said. "Man's going to get you killed, he should at least be honest about it."

"I am being honest," Drexel bellowed. "I had no intention of pursuing that damned woman. The less seen of her the better."

"About my money?" Samuels said.

"Basingstoke." Drexel waved a hand in Samuels' direction. "Get rid of him." Basingstoke withdrew a form book from his desk drawer and uncapped an ink bottle.

"None of that," Samuels said. "Cash, gentlemen, just like on all those lovely flyers Mr. Derrick had me put up."

"I will kill Stephen," Drexel muttered.

"*Him*, I'd do for ten bob," Samuels said, "me having a civic nature and all. Missus, best of luck. Plead your belly. Pretty as you are, transportation is the worst you'll face."

He pocketed coins Basingstoke had set out on the desk and departed with a tip of his hat.

"Now that the closest thing to a gentleman has left the room," Matilda said, turning her back on both men, the better to spy out the window, "I can speak freely. You had best see me hanged, Drexel, because if you don't, I will see you held accountable for suborning perjury, stealing from me, stealing from Kitty, encouraging your disgrace of a brother to drink himself to death, and your idiot nephew to molest me. I will, as publicly as possible, make it apparent that I sought the advice of midwives, physicians, and even a madam in an effort to find a solution to Althorpe's impotence, and if that's not enough—"

Helen waved from the top of Ashton's coach, which now sat directly below the window and in front of Drexel's vehicle.

"If that's not enough," said a soft male voice, "I'll kill ye where ye stand."

Ashton Fenwick stood in the doorway in all his Highland finery, save for the fancy sporran. Another sizeable, dark-haired gentleman in court attire stood with him.

"Basingstoke," Drexel said, "what manner of establishment are you running that strangers can interrupt confidential discussions unannounced?"

"My Lord Hazelton." Basingstoke rose and bowed. "If you would introduce us to your companion?"

"My lady," Ashton said, "you're well?"

"I'm furious," Matilda replied, blowing him a kiss. "I rather liked your first idea better than this small talk. In other regards, I'm fine." Matilda was also relieved—vastly, enormously relieved—and pleased. She'd spoken up for herself, and she'd meant every word.

Let the whole matter come to trial, *let it be over with*. Drexel, Stephen, and the fear they'd traded on, had ruined enough of her life. She had the resolve to fight them now, and she had an ally who'd never desert her.

"Ashton, Earl of Kilkenney," Hazelton said, "may I make known to you Myron Basingstoke, whose privilege it is to own this establishment. He used to be honest. I can't vouch for his principles now."

"I can," Ashton said, "if such as *that* is Basingstoke's favored client." *That* being Drexel, whose complexion was more choleric by the moment. "The best we can say about Mr. Myron Basingstoke is that he's incompetent and lazy, has no respect for the law and even less respect for the ladies. He might be a solicitor, but he's no sort of gentleman, and I'm not much impressed with his intellect either. Because a lady is present, I'll not favor you with my opinion of Lord Drexel."

"Oh, please," Matilda said. "Favor us."

Ashton bowed, the gesture painfully courteous, though a rage burned in his eyes that took Matilda aback. He wasn't merely angry, he was furious, and holding on to his temper by a thin skein of decency.

"Who the hell are you?" Drexel spat, "and what gives you the right to insult people who know a damned sight more about Matilda Derrick's sordid past than you?"

"I am *her ladyship's* intended, if she'll have me, and you are, to quote another female I esteem, a lying, crawling, worthless rotter. Sit down, and I'll enumerate the reasons why you and your weasel of a nephew are going to jail."

Drexel apparently wasn't used to being addressed like a sluggardly boot boy. He took a chair, more falling into it than sitting.

Lord Hazelton locked the door.

A woman was safer when she could bolt at the first opportunity, and that meant Matilda stayed right where she was: on her feet.

* * *

Too many times, Ashton had responded with his fists to taunts about his legitimacy. He was a damned fine pugilist, but had perceived even as a young man that violence was as dangerous for those who relied on it as for those upon whom it was inflicted. Bloodshed could become a drug, as intoxicating as opium, and as readily available.

Matilda watched him with a steady, trusting gaze, and that alone kept his fists at his sides.

Time to ply sweet reason, then. "Drexel, you will explain how a murder warrant came to be issued for your sister-in-law."

"She killed my brother, that's how."

Hazelton took the chair next to Drexel's. "Saw it with your own eyes, did you?"

"Of course not. I was in the library across the corridor from the family parlor. My nephew is the one who swore out an affidavit."

Ashton propped an elbow on Basingstoke's mantel. "Do tell."

"Stephen was in the game room, which shares an interior door with the library. He heard Mrs. Derrick—"

"Lady Matilda," Matilda said with ominous sweetness.

"Matil—Lady Matilda, shouting at my brother, threatening him, vowing to kill him. Stephen burst through the door, fearing for his father's life, and found her ladyship abusing poor Althorpe terribly with a wrought-iron poker. Before Stephen could wrest the murder weapon from her, his father lay on the floor, bludgeoned to death."

Now for the interesting part.

"So you summoned the magistrate," Hazelton said, "because all of the evidence supported Stephen's version of events?"

Drexel jerked down his waistcoat. "It most certainly did."

Matilda had turned her back to the room and waved, probably to Helen.

"What time of the evening was this?" Ashton asked.

"After supper, about ten," Drexel said, "and a horrible end to the day, I must say."

For Matilda. "Ten o'clock is a busy time in most fashionable households. The staff would have been right down the corridor, clearing the dinner table. The footmen would have been filling the lamps, trimming wicks, replenishing coal buckets. The chambermaids would have ensured fires were lit in the bedrooms, and at any moment, somebody might have rung for a final pot of tea, meaning the kitchen help was still at their labors. Am I right?"

"You're right," Matilda said over her shoulder.

"How many servants did you have the magistrate speak to?" Ashton asked. "Such a great, uncivilized row had to have been overheard by somebody besides the men who benefitted enormously by accusing her ladyship of a crime she didn't commit."

Drexel's brows twitched. He opened his mouth. He closed it.

"You failed to make any other witnesses available to the authorities," Ashton said. "Well, no matter. I'm sure the blood all over the carpet spoke for itself. Perhaps there was even blood on her ladyship's hems."

"There was not a drop of blood," Matilda reported with ferocious good cheer.

"So," Ashton said, "Mr. Stephen Derrick alleges that Lady Matilda whacked poor Althorpe repeatedly with a cast-iron poker, in a towering rage, and yet… no blood. No servants recalling her ladyship shouting threats. None."

"It's possible," Hazelton said. "In theory."

The lawyer squirmed in his comfortable chair.

"Very well, let's deal in theories," Ashton said. "Lady Matilda is unhappy in her marriage, and because she's an utter idiot, as any who know her will testify, she chooses to dash out her husband's brains while a house full of servants is bustling about, the man's son is in the next room, and his titled brother right across the corridor. Makes perfect sense."

"She chose her moment with the lack of wisdom common to her gender," Drexel said, shooting to his feet. "She advanced on him from behind, and he was all unsuspecting. Althorpe had enjoyed a few glasses of wine, as a man will, and Lady Matilda waited to catch him alone when his powers of discernment were not at their best."

Hazelton put a hand on Drexel's shoulder. "Until Kilkenney gives you leave to rise, you will sit."

Drexel sat.

"That balderdash simply won't serve, your lordship," Ashton said. "Was Althorpe all unsuspecting of the woman supposedly shouting threats of murder at him? He typically turned his back on irate women who promised to do him violence?"

"He was in his cups, I tell you, and she crept up behind him with malice aforethought and murder in her heart."

"Yes, yes," Ashton said, twirling his wrist, "and bludgeoned your paragon of a brother to his final reward with repeated, violent blows to the head that resulted in no blood being spilled at all. What did the medical examiner have to say about the cause of death?"

"He agreed with me—I mean, he found that Althorpe had been bludgeoned to death, and a charge of murder was laid."

Hazelton sighed gustily.

"He found Althorpe's skull had suffered one blow, right about here," Ashton said, pointing to his own temple. "Meaning that if that one blow had been rendered with a poker, then Althorpe would have seen it coming. Lady Matilda, what were you wearing the night your husband died?"

Matilda remained with her back to the room, gaze on the street below. She might have been waiting for her coach to be brought around for a trip to the milliner's, so calm was she.

"I wore a new dinner gown of embroidered blue silk with six gathered flounces that exposed the ruffled yellow underskirt. Also two trimmed petticoats of lighter blue, both ruffled at the hem, a chemise, and the usual underlinen. I was also wearing a paisley shawl, because the room was drafty and the fire less than robust. The money I got for that ensemble fed me for a considerable time, and I still have the pawnbroker's ticket for it."

Ashton propped his chin on his hand. "Now that is a puzzle. How does a woman wearing two ruffled petticoats, a ruffled underskirt, a flounced overskirt, and a shawl move silently? Maybe her shouting hid the susurration of her clothing, but no... that won't wash either, will it?"

Drexel hunched forward. "What do you want, Kilkenney?"

"Oh, to kill you, I suppose. Lady Matilda?"

Matilda breathed a soft, ladylike sigh, then shook her head.

"Ah, well, then, no Border justice for your lordship, but your nephew may not be so lucky. The medical examiner's report said your brother died of a broken neck, didn't it?"

Basingstoke cleared his throat.

"Unburden yourself," Hazelton suggested. "You used to be a decent solicitor."

"There was no medical examination," Basingstoke murmured. "An oversight, I'm sure."

"Astonishing," Ashton said, "the oversights that follow when bribery is an option. No matter. We can exhume the remains, have a wee look, and get this poker-bashing nonsense straightened out. Do you contend that Lady Matilda snapped the neck of a man who outweighed her by five stone?"

Matilda opened the window, as if all this belated honesty had turned the air foul.

"I do not."

"I have a contention," Ashton said, shoving away from the mantel. "I contend that your brother was a miserable sod who couldn't behave decently toward his own wife, and his son was even worse. I contend that you have suborned perjury to get your filthy hands on not one but two sizeable inheritances, and—this contending business has grown on me—I further contend that Stephen Derrick has the strength, determination, and stupidity to have killed his own father. He did so in a manner that allowed him to blame his patricide on an innocent young woman and grow rich on his own lies."

"That's very good," Hazelton said, rising. "Has the advantage of fitting the physical evidence, and lord knows Stephen had motive. We can find all manner of witnesses to testify that Stephen resented his father, wished the old man into an early grave. Shouldn't be much trouble at all."

"You wouldn't dare," Drexel retorted.

"He would," Matilda said, "except I won't allow him to. Stephen did not kill his father, unless endless disappointment is a cause of death."

"All I want," Ashton replied, "is for a warrant to issue for Stephen's arrest. Let him take flight and manage as you have, without a friend in the world, no rest, no safety, nowhere to turn. Might give him some manners—or kill him."

"He's my heir, damn it," Drexel said. "My only legitimate heir. I am a peer of the realm, and I forbid you to have him arrested."

Ashton leaned a hip on Basingstoke's desk. "I'm a peer of the realm too. I've learned not to let it bother me. Mr. Damon Basingstoke, along with a solicitor of Hazelton's choosing, will review Lady Kitty's and Lady Maitland's finances. If so much as a penny has gone astray, you will provide reparation, with interest."

"Reasonable interest," Hazelton said. "Say, ten percent per annum."

Every last groat Drexel had wasn't nearly enough for all the misery he'd caused Matilda.

"Where is Stephen?" Ashton asked.

"I have no idea," Drexel said. "He keeps bachelor quarters and comes around when he wants money. He has a fancy piece by the name of Marceline in Knightsbridge somewhere. You can make all the allegations you want against my handling of complicated financial affairs, Kilkenney, but unless you can convince Stephen to recant his sworn testimony, you are harboring an accused murderess. She'll be taken into custody, there to await trial."

Ashton aimed his next words at the solicitor. "If Stephen recants, he'll be admitting perjury, and what I know of his character suggests honesty is beyond him. I expect him to pike off with as much money and wherewithal as possible, and I will have charges brought against him."

Basingstoke rose. He was nowhere near as tall as Damon, but then, the younger solicitor was likely not his son.

"His lordship makes a significant point, Kilkenney. The murder warrant has not been quashed, and any thief-taker would be within his rights to haul her ladyship before the nearest magistrate. I proffer that Mr. Stephen Derrick might be willing to modify his testimony without entirely recanting it, if your presuming notions of financial accountability can be set aside."

Hazelton extended his walking stick across Basingstoke's left shoulder and exerted pressure until the solicitor resumed his seat.

"You almost had me convinced," Ashton said, "that Drexel had bullied or blackmailed you too, but now your failure to properly oversee Lady Kitty's funds must come to light. Ah, well. Your titled clients will surely forgive a few thousand missing pounds, won't they?"

Basingstoke glared at Ashton like a chastised dog who dared not rise. "Her ladyship can still be arrested, and I will advise my clients that due deliberation will be required before any revision of testimony can possibly—"

"You can't have her arrested," Ashton said, pointing to the open window Matilda had slipped through moments before. "She did a bunk, and you will have to kill me to find her. Hazelton, we have a perjurer to catch, by any means necessary."

"Good day," Hazelton said, bowing slightly. "I'd pack a few bags if I were you two. A lot of bags, with as much haste as you're capable of."

Ashton got Hazelton by the arm and steered him to the door. "No more helpful advice, your lordship. They're on their own, as Lady Matilda was for six years."

As she might be again, that very minute.

CHAPTER FIFTEEN

"Here they come," Helen said through the speaking slot between the coach's interior and the bench. "His nibs and Lord Hazelnuts."

Not Drexel, not that toadying little solicitor, not Samuels. Now that the moment of confrontation had passed, a suffocating dread had taken possession of Matilda's body and her wits. A choking sensation wrapped about her neck, and weakness pervaded her limbs. She had clambered down from the coach roof intent only on eluding Drexel, then found herself without the resolve to do more than scramble into the coach and shut the door.

Ashton joined her inside.

"I'm about to be sick, my lord." The further rocking of the coach as Hazelton took the opposite seat nearly proved Matilda's prediction true.

"So am I," Ashton said, "but ladies first. Try putting your head down and breathing slowly." He opened a small cabinet in the side of the coach, tipped a flask onto a serviette, and laid the wet cloth on Matilda's nape.

"Get me away from this place, Ashton, please."

He thumped the roof once. "At the walk, John Coachman."

The cold cloth helped, the knowledge that Ashton was taking her to safety helped more. "I am upset."

"I'm in a murdering rage," Ashton said, refolding the cloth and laying it gently over the back of her neck. "What that man and his nephew did to you is inexcusable, my lady. I knew that when you told me your history, but to see Drexel puffing and posturing like a crow in the gutter, not a repentant bone in his body…. Hazelton, any debt you owe me has been repaid. But for your presence as a credible witness, I would have pitched the pair of them to the cobbles headfirst."

"I would have wished them a hard landing," Hazelton said. "Basingstoke will be on the first packet for Calais, Drexel right behind him."

Matilda tried to straighten, but Ashton instead urged her to curl up on the bench, her head in his lap. A sensible arrangement under the circumstances.

"Can you estimate the value of your inheritance, my lady?" Lord Hazelton asked.

Matilda named a figure, one her father had muttered over morning coffee in the middle of the marriage negotiations.

"Sweet Jesus come to Mayfair," Ashton muttered. "You might be worth more than I am."

"Does that bother you?"

He stroked her hair from her brow. "Just shows my unassailable good taste in countesses."

"Kitty's portion isn't as great," Matilda said. "It's substantial, though, or it should be."

"About wee Lady Kitty…"

"Kidnapping is a felony," Hazelton said in oh-by-the-by tones.

"Separating two sisters needlessly for six years is an abomination," Ashton retorted, "especially when they have no other family worth the name. We'll fetch Lady Kitty for a visit with her sister and send a note around to Drexel thanking him for the suggestion. If a Border lord can't reave one child from the clutches of an avaricious Englishman, then he's no' worth his tartan."

"A Border lord are you now?" Hazelton asked.

"That's the Scottish term for an earl where I come from," Ashton said. "Lady Kitty isn't the problem."

Matilda was having trouble following the conversation, so she made herself sit up. "Is Kitty in danger?"

"Probably not from Drexel." Ashton lifted the cloth from Matilda's neck. "But Drexel professed ignorance of Stephen's whereabouts, and it's Stephen who's been backed into the tightest corner."

"Explain yourself, please," Matilda said. "My mind has all but stopped working." Her hand functioned well enough to lace her fingers with Ashton's, which had the odd effect of settling her belly.

"You decamped before we concluded our discussion," Hazelton said. "A nimble exit, I might add. As matters stand now, there is a valid warrant extant for your arrest. To have the warrant quashed, Stephen must recant his testimony."

"He's had six years to set the matter straight," Ashton said, "and in all that time, he's failed to do so. Going back on his word now will be impossible without raising the specter of perjury. The solicitor implied that Stephen might modify his affidavit without exonerating you per se, but you're still facing a trial."

"I have been through more than enough trials courtesy of Stephen Derrick."

"We can agree on that," Hazelton said, "but the chances of getting the present magistrate to quash a warrant bribed out of a predecessor six years ago are poor."

"I'm right back where I was six years ago." Except for losing her heart to Ashton, which very nearly made the entire ordeal worth the trouble.

"You will never be back where you were six years ago," Ashton retorted, "but I'm thinking you should pay a call on Hazelton's countess."

Hazelton's smile was bashful and oddly charming. "I thought you'd never ask, Kilkenney."

"I don't know the Countess of Hazelton," Matilda said. "I do know I want a bath and a nap." That nap would preferably be in a bed shared with Ashton.

"If we're to see your good reputation restored," Ashton said, "then I can't be stowing you in my dressing room at the Albany, can I, lass?"

"My good reputation…?" The weakness assailed Matilda again, because Ashton had named the prize she dared not wish for. The realization that Drexel had stolen this from her—this too—lodged like a fist in her throat.

"All I wanted," Matilda said, "*all I want* is to be safe and with you. If I can visit with Kitty, that's more than I dreamed was possible. My fortune, my good name… Those are trappings, and I don't need them."

How she longed for exoneration, though, for vindication of her decision to flee in the first place. She wanted assurance that she'd been wise, not foolish; resourceful, rather than imprudent.

And hang the title she'd prided herself on all for all of her life.

"Then humor me," Ashton said. "I need to see justice done, and now that we've confronted Drexel, we're closer to that goal, not farther away."

"He nearly had me," Matilda said. "He very nearly had me, Ashton. I'm still wanted for murder."

Ashton kissed her knuckles, and abruptly, Matilda's vision went dim at the edges and breath came short. She might even now have been locked in a cell at Bow Street.

"Hazelton's papa-in-law is a duke," Ashton said. "You'll be safe under Hazelton's roof, and I would pit his countess against any regiment of foot you'd care to name. Hazelton and I can round up Stephen and come to terms with him."

"You will be safe, my lady," Hazelton added. "Though you'll be pampered within an inch of your sanity."

"Pampering sounds… agreeable." Safety sounded too good to be true. "What have you planned for Stephen?"

The men exchanged some sort of look. If Matilda had had brothers, she might have been able to decipher it.

"What would you like us to plan for him?" Ashton asked as the coach swayed around a corner. They'd passed from the busyness at the center of London to quieter, broader streets. Mayfair, most likely, where Matilda had been by turns happy and miserable.

"Stephen has at least one child that I know of," she said, "an illegitimate daughter. If anything happens to Stephen, the child has a bleak future." The concept of justice as opposed to revenge was difficult to grasp. Revenge simply made more victims, while justice put matters right—or as right as they could be.

What did justice require where Stephen was concerned?

Ashton tapped the coach roof twice, and the horses swung into a trot. "As it happens, Stephen has two daughters, according to Hazleton. If their situation weren't a consideration, if you weren't forever trying to look after everybody but yourself, what fate would you wish on Stephen?"

"Not death," Matilda said. "When I first bolted, I imagined all manner of revenge upon Stephen. Dashing his brains out, seeing him hauled away in chains, accepting his groveling apology... My imagination sustained me until the struggle to survive took precedence."

"And now?" Hazelton asked.

"The whole time I've been a fugitive from the law, I've protected a corner of my dignity with the knowledge that I'm innocent. I might die a convicted murderess, but between myself and my God, I knew I was innocent. I never raised a hand to my husband, never wished him dead. What would it be like to be a fugitive from the law and know that you deserve to be caught? That you are guilty as charged and yet unpunished for the wrongs you've done?"

"You assume Stephen has a conscience," Ashton said.

"No. I assume he has an entirely selfish desire to live, and threatening that desire will be as much justice as I'm capable of. Scare the hell out of him, Ashton. Scare him so badly, he'll never be a threat to another woman."

"My countess would approve," Hazelton said. "She'd approve wholeheartedly."

"I approve," Ashton said. "But first we need to make a few plans."

* * *

Lady Hazelton had taken one look at Matilda's masculine attire and pronounced Ashton's beloved two adventures shy of daft. The countess had then whisked Matilda above stairs for a bath, a pot of chocolate, and a plate of raspberry scones.

Ashton sent his coach home, assisted Hazelton to change out of his court finery, and proceeded to wear a hole in the carpet of Hazelton's study.

"Should I have Archer Portmaine join us?" Hazelton asked from behind a massive, cluttered desk. "He's a fine one for locating people who don't wish to be found."

"Have Portmaine nose around Bow Street and chat with Drexel's staff," Ashton said, examining the signature on a sketch of the Portmaine family seat. "I made a lot of stirring declarations in Basingstoke's office, but it could well be the servants were bribed to conform their stories to Stephen's, or they've all been turned off."

The Blessings estate sat amid the Cumbrian hills, and the artist—Hazelton's sister Avis—had done justice to the subject. The bucolic image made Ashton miss the sprawling monstrosity at the seat of his own earldom. He was accustomed to missing his family, but when had he come to see Fenwick Manor as his refuge and his home rather than as his brother's house?

"I doubt Drexel would turn off staff en masse following a scandal," Hazelton said. "That's the surest way to spread talk at all levels. If there's a single chambermaid who recalls the night of Althorpe's death, Archer can find her and charm her honest recollections from her."

"What are the chances of having Althorpe's remains exhumed?" And how long could one woman soak in a bathtub?

"Exhumations are rare," Hazelton said, tidying a stack of correspondence piled on one corner of the desk. "Althorpe was an earl's heir, much time has passed, and if Drexel had a shred of common sense, he'd have found some poor fool who died of bludgeoning and switched the bodies prior to burial."

Ashton subsided onto a worn sofa, one upon which Hazelton had doubtless taken many a nap. "One fears for your dreams, Hazelton. Why is a nice earl like you offering conjectures like that?"

"Because one is honest with one's friends. I've seen worse machinations undertaken in the interests of stealing a fortune. Drexel is greedy. He's not stupid."

"He's evil, and that nephew of his worse. Would your countess do me an injury if I interrupted a lady at her bath?"

"Several. Maggie's father is a duke, and in all but name, Moreland's duchess is her mama. Tangle with my wife at your peril, and expect no sympathy from me."

Ashton toed off his boots and stretched out. "This sofa is too short by half. Am I getting you in trouble with your in-laws by bringing scandal to your doorstep?"

Hazelton propped his feet on a corner of his desk. "You'll make them envious. My father-in-law is the Duke of Meddling. He's married off all of his children, and his four nieces are steadfastly adhering to spinsterhood. Moreland's interfering can thus take an unpredictable turn. You and he would get along famously."

"Your countess and mine must be getting along famously. What can be taking them so long?"

"Lady Matilda isn't your countess yet, Kilkenney."

"A detail. Drexel has preyed on her for too long, and as my countess—" Ashton paused to yawn and was saved from further blustering by a knock on the door.

"Am I interrupting?"

Matilda stood in the doorway, but not any version of her Ashton had beheld before.

Hazelton was on his feet. "Your ladyship's appearance spares me from tying yonder kilted lout to the piano. I'll see about getting some decent sustenance up here and have a word with my countess. My lady."

He sketched a bow at Matilda, sent Ashton a glower, and marched off.

Ashton closed the door and fastened the lock. "Sweet Jesus at the fashionable hour. Look at you."

Gone were the brassy highlights in Matilda's hair, replaced by golden tresses styled half up and half tumbling over her shoulder. She wore a blue day dress with minute green and purple embroidery about the collar, hems, and cuffs, and completed the ensemble with a green paisley shawl.

"You wear colors beautifully." She wore them magnificently, the blue bringing out the beauty of her eyes and the roses in her cheeks.

"You thought me beautiful when I wore brown homespun."

Ashton would like to see her wearing nothing at all, but in a lady's attire, Matilda was stunning. He took her hand and kissed her knuckles. "And you saw me when I badly needed to be put into my kilt. I've missed you."

"I left you not two hours ago, and I'm the same person, Ashton Fenwick."

"No, you're not," he said, leading her to the sofa. "You glow. I daresay had Hazelton and I not come along, you'd have dealt handily with Drexel. Hazelton and I were discussing next steps."

Marriage figured prominently on Ashton's list, but so did kissing his prospective countess. He set about addressing that item as soon as Matilda took the place beside him on the sofa.

"I liked wearing breeches," she muttered against Ashton's mouth.

"I like you wearing that scent. What is it?"

"French soap," she said, straddling his lap. "Millefleurs, maybe. Skirts do have a few advantages."

The scent she was wearing should have been named Loss of Reason, because Ashton could think of only one advantage to skirts at the moment: He could stroke Matilda's bare legs when she was wearing skirts, without anybody having to remove a single article of clothing.

"No stockings, my lady? You shock me."

"This dress belongs to Lady Hazelton's youngest sister, but we couldn't find stockings that—yes, please."

Ashton left off caressing Matilda's calves long enough to undo the bow at the front of her bodice. Two more bows were secreted beneath that, for she wore an extra chemise rather than stays, but diligence and manual dexterity soon saw her breasts freed.

"I feel a bit mad," Matilda said, scooting closer. "I could be behind bars now, on my way to the gallows."

"Don't say such things. Don't even think—"

She kissed him, and he could taste the frenzy in her, part triumph—they'd bested Drexel for now—and part terror.

What if Helen hadn't found him? What if Samuels had taken Matilda straight to the magistrate? What if Stephen had chanced upon her?

"If Drexel can bribe a magistrate, he can bribe a judge." Matilda knelt up and got hold of Ashton beneath his kilt. "I'll not go peacefully."

Despite the growing haze of desire, Matilda had raised a terrible specter. The whole criminal justice system, from the thief-takers, to the magistrates, to the wardens, to the judges, was subject to bribery and coercion, and Drexel had a six-year start on Matilda in that race.

"You'll not go at all, as long as I'm alive," Ashton said. "I'd have you away to Scotland before—"

Matilda had settled over him, joining them in a slow, exquisite descent. Despite her finery, and her expensive fragrance, she was still his Matilda, still the woman he'd sacrifice everything to spend the rest of his life with.

"This," she whispered. "I want this, for all my days and nights, with you."

Matilda was a fast learner. Though Ashton hadn't made love with her often, she'd already figured out that she could torment him with pleasure, turning mutual arousal into a game of endurance. As they made love, everything else— worries and plans, past and future—fell away. Ashton feasted on the taste and feel of her, on the soft sighs and welling pleasure.

This was what he'd been searching for, this sense of union with a woman who knew herself well and valued herself highly. He shifted the angle of his hips, and on the next thrust, Matilda surrendered to completion. For long moments, he held her, denying himself satisfaction.

"You'll withdraw?" Matilda panted.

"I should. We're not yet married." Not even under Scottish law.

"I'll bear your children gladly, Ashton. Surely you know that."

He'd hoped, though her words bore a lurking rejection, despite their bodies being joined. "The protection of my name and title should be yours, Matilda. I want to give them to you, and I thought you'd welcome them."

Her sigh bore nothing of contentment. After another moment, she drew away, leaving Ashton with an ache both physical and emotional—a bad ache.

"I cannot marry you while I'm wanted for murder," Matilda said, settling beside him. "I'm sorry, but I've been clear on this. Marriage in England must be publicly documented to be valid. I expected you to understand."

Ashton understood that Matilda had rejected his marriage proposal, also that he'd made a bad job of presenting it. Thwarted desire and a tearing need to get to the bottom of Matilda's stubbornness created an exquisite mixture of misery.

"You will explain yourself," he managed. "Please. I will listen to you, and then you will hear me out as well."

Matilda rustled across the room and unlocked the door. She even moved differently in that pretty dress, and yet, she was still his Matilda.

Or was she?

* * *

"What's all this?" Stephen gestured to the three trunks open in the center of his uncle's library. One held a few books, but was mostly full of silver—pen trays, ink bottles, candlesticks, all piled inside without benefit of straw to prevent damage. Another held several valuable paintings. The third was packed with snuff boxes and pipes.

"I'm going abroad," Drexel said. "For an extended period. Basingstoke's office will see to your quarterly allowance."

Stephen took a closer look into the nearest trunk, though the idea of sending his lordship to the Continent was singularly cheering.

"These are my snuff boxes!"

Drexel folded up an exquisitely clever card table that had to be at least two hundred years old and tucked it in with the paintings.

"You purchased those snuff boxes with advances over and above your quarterly allowances, ergo, they are not yours. They are my security for the debt you owe from the funds you'll eventually inherit from your father."

The previous night's excesses had left Stephen somewhat blue-deviled, but his instincts told him something was very wrong, and his instincts had never failed him.

"I can't inherit from dear Papa until Step-mama has been brought to justice, and her portion of his estate either given to me or divided between you and me. The worst case as you've explained it will be that the brat inherits Step-mama's fortune, and then we get the use of it for another ten years at least. What is this about, Uncle?"

Drexel stuffed another pair of silver candlesticks into an open trunk. "Your step-mother, God rot the woman, was picked up by your thief-taker earlier today. Fortunately, he brought her to Basingstoke's office, though word of her apprehension will be all over town by sundown. She slipped away this time, but thief-takers are like hounds on a bitch. They'll find her again."

Stephen poured himself a drink, though lately, even the drink didn't do much to clear his head.

"Finding Matilda is good. Now we can get on with her trial—assuming she doesn't have a tragic accident while incarcerated—and then Chancery will have to turn loose of her funds."

"Stephen, I vow your mother must have strayed, for no one of the Derrick blood could be as stupid as you are. When a felony conviction is handed down, the criminal's personal goods are subject to forfeiture to the crown."

"The juries don't do that anymore," Stephen said, tossing back two fingers of brandy. "They all say the bugger's got no goods, and—"

"Greedy as you are," Drexel went on, collecting a marble pen tray from the reading table, "our sovereign's ability to spend money makes your expenses look like the puling efforts that have characterized all of your exertions. Thank God the French flu hasn't robbed you of the ability to procreate, or the earldom would be doomed."

Talk of venereal disease unsettled Stephen's belly. He should not have had three cups of coffee upon rising, but how else was a fellow to wash the foul taste from his mouth?

"What's Fat George got to do with our money?"

"Fat George will never allow a jury to state that Lady Matilda Derrick has no goods. He'll intercede, if for no other reason than to see Lady Kitty made a ward of the crown upon my departure from the realm. Matilda's fortune will fall into George's hands as well if she's convicted, and he might go so far as to tie up your portion of Althorpe's estate too."

Uncle spoke with entirely too much conviction, and much too quickly for such an early hour.

"That won't wash," Stephen said, setting his empty glass down with a bang. "It's my money, Papa left it to me, and I need it."

"You will still have an allowance from the Drexel earldom," Uncle said, hefting the family Bible, then setting it back down. "Damned thing is too heavy, and you might get a fair bit of coin for it. I've left instructions that your allowance is to be paid quarterly, out of the rents. Myron Basingstoke will know how to reach me, assuming he doesn't take a repairing lease himself."

This whole conversation wasn't making any sense. "You're leaving?"

"You might consider a tour of Italy," Drexel said, surveying a library that looked as if pirates had come a-plundering. "Your lies to the magistrate are what's set this whole business in motion. If you'd been truthful, Matilda would never have turned up missing, and I wouldn't have been tempted to—"

"I did not lie, sir." Stephen's memory on this point was clear. "I related events to the magistrate in the exact sequence you suggested. Matilda was unhappy with Papa, they argued loudly, and she was standing over him with an iron poker in her hand. What else was I to think but that she'd killed him?"

Though Papa's neck had been at a strange angle. Stephen had stayed drunk for most of a month, trying to forget the sight of Papa dead before the hearth, his head flopped in that odd way. Matilda's violence with the poker might not have broken Papa's neck, but the fall she'd caused had, and that was nearly the same thing.

Uncle snatched up a porcelain figurine of Aphrodite and stashed her among the snuff boxes.

"Thinking is not your greatest strength, Stephen. Try to attend those wiser than you when they offer to guide you. I wish you the best, provided you sire at least three legitimate male offspring. Basingstoke can suggest a good barrister when the need arises."

Uncle really was not making much sense. "For marriage settlement negotiations?"

"Right, marriage settlements." Drexel strode across the room to retrieve a pink marble figure of Hermes. Uncle tried to wedge the messenger of the gods alongside Aphrodite. Stephen heard a cracking sound, and Uncle set Hermes—minus a winged foot—on the table near the Bible.

"Stephen, do you understand the tempest that's brewing?"

Stephen fished about in the trunk, because Hermes would mend fairly well—a few cracks made the replicas look more authentic—if that foot could be retrieved.

"I understand that you are disappearing to the Continent," Stephen said. "Perhaps taking the waters at some German spa, or maybe looking for a young wife. Got it."

He held up the foot and wing, a funny little bit of chipped stone.

"A fine story. Pay attention, boy, because there isn't time for me to write this down, not that I'd be that stupid. Matilda has apparently attached the affections of the Earl of Kilkenney, a Scot of no little consequence."

Stephen fit the foot to the damaged statue. "Never heard of 'im, and I know everybody."

"Do you recall the Earl of Hazelton?"

"He's the fellow who went from snitching and snooping to marrying old Moreland's red-haired gal. Can't say as I care for him." Stephen set aside the statue and put the winged foot in his pocket. "What's Hazelton to do with anything?"

"Kilkenney and Hazelton are apparently allied in defense of Matilda. The situation has grown complicated."

The coach came clip-clopping around the corner, the grays put to. They were Uncle's fastest team, and the door panel had been flipped so no crest showed.

"You're truly leaving?" Upon reflection, Stephen didn't like that idea. He didn't like his uncle either, but the old fellow was generous enough, not too much of a bother, and he dealt with all the unpleasantness that accompanied the earldom.

"Stephen, for God's sake, pay attention. Matilda has powerful friends now, and you thwart them at your peril. Recant your sworn statement to the magistrate. Blame drink, upset, fatigue, youthful exaggeration, anything, but recant that confession."

"Then she gets her money."

"And you get yours, you fool! Now that Matilda has turned up, your father's estate can be settled. If she goes to trial, we lose control of her fortune anyway, and you could be revealed for a liar."

"You persist in using a very ugly word, Uncle."

"And you persist in being an imbecile," Uncle said, moving toward the door. "Recant your statement, marry some fertile young lady, and try not to bankrupt my estates."

"Safe journey, sir."

Uncle directed various footmen to pack up this and that, then left orders for the trunks to be sent to some ship in Portsmouth. Stephen sat in the well padded chair Uncle had occupied on the occasion of so many lectures and remonstrations.

Godspeed, old man. So Uncle had dipped his fingers into Matilda's coffers and helped himself to some of Lady Kitty's funds. No matter. Women ought not to have more than pin money in the first place.

Stephen took out a sheet of foolscap, whittled a point onto a pencil, and drew himself a diagram.

If Matilda was convicted, the crown got her money, Lady Kitty's money, and possibly Stephen's money, at least for a period of years, while Stephen eked by on a quarterly pittance.

Bother that.

If Matilda was either acquitted, or Stephen modified his recollections, then Stephen got his money. She got her inheritance, and her Scot would likely be put in charge of Kitty's funds. Not a good outcome, but not tragic.

If Matilda simply disappeared again... the arrangements put in place by Chancery remained as they were, with all that lovely money still managed by the Drexel earldom. Twenty years from now, Chancery might realize Matilda should be declared dead, but they would be a very lucrative and enjoyable twenty years.

A power of attorney from Uncle would be easy to forge—Stephen had any number of examples of Drexel's signature—and another disappearance for dear Step-mama would be the work of a moment.

The best possible outcome, considering the woman had done murder or the next thing to it. A pity Uncle hadn't been clever enough to see that.

CHAPTER SIXTEEN

Matilda remained by the unlocked door, hating her in-laws all over again. "I would marry you if I could, Ashton."

He rose from the sofa, his hair in disarray, his cravat slightly askew. He looked anything but well pleasured, and his restraint had been for her sake.

"I was given to understand that your first husband is dead," he said. "If that's the case, you are of age, of sound mind, and free to marry where you please."

Matilda wanted to throw herself into his arms, but passion still hummed in places low and lovely. Ashton would oblige her—again—and they'd still need to have this argument.

"A marriage for an earl and an earl's daughter is a public undertaking," Matilda said. "Even if we marry by special license, you'll have to procure that license. Drexel was clever enough to set thief-takers on me. He'll be clever enough to set spies watching at Doctors' Commons."

Ashton brushed her hair back from her shoulder. Without touching her skin, he yet made her shiver. "I can have Damon Basingstoke certify our eligibility to marry and procure the license. Nobody needs to know we're still in London."

Matilda took his hand and led him back to the sofa. "You have learned how to stand alone and be seen as someone other than the Earl of Kilkenney's charming by-blow."

He settled beside her, but with the air of a cat waiting for an opportunity to leap away. "I'm not feeling very charming now, Matilda mine."

And yet, charm her, he did. With his passion and with his protectiveness.

"You fought to be seen for yourself, Ashton. I fought to remain hidden, and hiding well has kept me alive. Think like a criminal. If you wanted to snatch Lady Matilda for a reward ten times the annual salary of most chambermaids, what lengths would you go to?"

His sigh was masculine and impatient, but not defeated. "I'd hang about Doctors' Commons or the archbishop's palace. I'd watch Mr. Damon Basingstoke, whose office is conveniently located under the very roof where you were last seen. I'd bribe the clerk in the archbishop's office to tell me who had applied for a special license, and I'd watch carefully to see where all those licenses were delivered."

Matilda took his hand. "You would also nose about, asking questions regarding the two fine coaches clogging the lane before Basingstoke's offices earlier today. Two crested coaches, one of which bore a man in a kilt and a second man in court finery. Somebody might identify the crest on your coach. Somebody else might have seen that same kilted man at the Albany."

"Shite."

"You'd set people to watching the Albany, and eventually, a casual remark would connect the Earl of Kilkenney with the Earl of Hazelton, so Hazelton's house will be watched as well. The countess might be kidnapped and held hostage to secure my cooperation. Kitty might become a pawn. Helen has already been used by her scheming sister."

Silence wrapped like a shroud over the hopes Matilda had begun to cherish. Ashton wasn't arguing with her, because there were no arguments to offer.

"You're saying we were better off as plain Mr. Fenwick and Mrs. Bryce?" he asked. "We were safer."

"*You* were miserable."

"We can run," Matilda said. "Not to Scotland, because I'll be too easy to find, but somewhere far away, somewhere beyond the reach of the crown. I'll be your wife in all but name, and nobody will be the wiser. We can be safe and happy."

Ashton slipped his hand free of her grasp. "You don't believe that. You had six years to be safe and happy, and you were neither. You looked over your shoulder every day, made no friends, had the smallest life you could squeeze yourself into. The only people you allowed near were worse off than yourself. Will you turn your back on wee Kitty now, and on me as well?"

Matilda rose, though she didn't dare approach the desk or the sideboard. She'd break something valuable, make a stain on the carpet, and ruin good furniture in a display of heartbreak that only looked like temper.

"I want to live, Ashton. I want you to live. Kitty's life isn't in danger, and right now, neither is yours. If I tarry here too long, if I can't find safety again, that could change. Drexel has a care for appearances, and he's shrewd. Stephen cares for only himself, and we've already underestimated him once."

Ashton rose.

Matilda braced herself to be shouted at, held tightly, or possibly both at once. Instead, he regarded her steadily from across the room.

"You are not wrong, my lady. Your fear has kept you alive, and for that I'm grateful. Your fear will also keep us apart. I am the Earl of Kilkenney, whether I want to be or not. I know well the stigma an earl's bastard bears, and a loving father does not impose that burden on his own children. Add to that, my family will lose the earldom if I can't produce a legitimate heir, and you see that the scheme you propose for us—an unsanctioned union in some far-off land— only shifts our peril onto our children."

Matilda sagged against the battered desk. "I can't be your lawfully wedded wife until we are in that far-off land, Ashton. Even then…"

"By then," he said, "it might be too late. We've already risked conception, Matilda, and my firstborn child will not be illegitimate if I can help it."

Now Matilda had no arguments. She'd been brought up in the lap of privileged respectability, and while the privilege had been a mixed blessing—privileged young women were too often ignorant young women—the respectability had also saved her life.

Her upbringing had allowed her to become a respectable widow, a respectable neighbor. She'd fit right in at Sunday services, and she'd been able to read and write in several languages. Her children deserved at least that much of a start in life.

"I want to bear your legitimate heirs, Ashton. I don't see a way to do that while remaining in plain sight."

"I want you to be safe, and if we run, that will never be the case."

She reached for him, and he came to her. "So now what?"

"Promise me you'll not leave without telling me."

Life had made Ashton wise. He'd not asked her to promise she'd stay. "I'll not leave without saying good-bye."

By the time the Earl of Hazelton returned with his countess, Matilda had taken the opposite end of the sofa from Ashton, and Hazelton's cat sat between them, tail switching back and forth, like an impatient feline chaperone.

* * *

On Hazelton's advice, Ashton did his best to impersonate an earl searching for a prospective countess. He waltzed by evening, he hacked out at dawn, he played cards, he even flirted.

And he worried.

One week after parting from Matilda, he was ready to snatch up his claymore and go after Stephen Derrick, to the point that even Helen's company in the spacious rooms of the Albany annoyed him.

"You want to visit her ladyship?" Helen asked without looking up from her book.

"Of course I want to visit her. I want to marry her, I want to spend the rest of my life with her. What are you reading?"

The girl set the book aside. Breakables she handled with cavalier disregard, but books she touched reverently.

"I'm not reading anything. If you want to pay her a call, you hop on your horse and ride up the street. You were calling on Hazelton before, and you can call on him now."

How could a room with twenty-foot ceilings feel cramped? How could gorgeous carpets, gleaming gilt, and precisely draped velvet feel oppressive?

"I'm to avoid anything that reinforces my connection with Hazelton. His investigations are progressing, and I must be patient."

"Patient? You? And you let old Hazelnuts order you about like that?"

Not exactly. Ashton had conducted a few investigations of his own, late at night, when Stephen Derrick was three sheets to the wind and enjoying the free food and drink available at Mayfair's best gatherings. A few quiet questions revealed that Derrick was disliked, but as an earl's heir he was welcomed by every hostess.

He had two illegitimate daughters about whom he cared not at all, a mistress who led him about by his nose, and enough bills overdue on Bond Street to impress even King George. Ashton's English tenants, on their most charitable day, would have torn the roof from Stephen's head and charged him for their labor.

And Stephen was next in line for an earldom full of English tenants.

"If you want to see her ladyship," Helen said, "you tag along with the tom-turd-man of an evening, and nobody will come near you. Slip through the garden, climb up the trellis to her balcony, and there you are. Stay upwind of the night-soil man, and you won't even stink much."

"The things you know, child."

"Stink will keep you safe. Illness can keep you safe," Helen said. "You ever get into a bad situation in the wrong sort of crowd in the wrong sort of place, you just gag like you're about to flash the hash, and they'll back off three paces without even realizing they've done it. Do you think those curtains would hold my weight?"

Flash the hash was likely a genteel reference—by Helen's standards—for casting up one's account.

"You are not to climb the curtains." Though she climbed the doorjambs, as nimbly as an organ grinder's monkey scaled a lamppost.

"You're climbing the walls, guv. Go see her."

A tap sounded on the door, two short knocks, a pause, then three more. Hazelton had at long last come to call, or at least sent an emissary.

"I'll get the door," Ashton said. "You go back to deciphering French."

"That's damned Frenchy?" Helen said, picking up her book. "No wonder it didn't half make sense. You mighta warned a girl."

"I might have, but as soon as you've conquered English, French is the next logical step." And she'd be on to Latin and German by Michaelmas.

Two men waited outside Ashton's door, one familiar from the evening of card playing, the other the Earl of Hazelton in footman's attire.

"Hazelton, good day. You took your sweet, damned time paying a call. Sir Archer, welcome."

Archer Portmaine was Hazelton's cousin and, in the family tradition, an investigator at large. He was tall, blond, and attired with the exquisite understatement of a gentleman of means. His gloves were the exact buff shade of his breeches—probably cut from the same hide—and his cravat pin sported a ruby.

A touch of sartorial daring, for the hour was barely past noon.

"We've been busy," Hazelton said, waiting for Portmaine to precede him into Ashton's parlor. "I bring you felicitations from Lady Matilda."

"She's well?"

"If you can call the ladylike version of a caged bear well," Hazelton replied, "she's thriving. Helen, greetings."

"That is a girl," Portmaine said. "A lovely little girl, for all she looks like she's about to skewer me."

"Don't talk about me like I'm deaf," Helen said, taking a perch on the windowsill. "I'm his lordship's general factotum."

"She's also my resident bad influence," Ashton said, "so tread carefully, but speak honestly. Helen has my trust."

Helen abruptly found her fingernails—her clean fingernails—fascinating.

"Do you have her trust, though?" Portmaine asked. "Of sorry necessity, the ladies learn greater caution than we gentlemen do."

That earned Portmaine a grin from Helen, but no reply. She returned to her window seat, opened *Candide,* and resumed puzzling over the French—or pretending to.

"Here's what we know," Portmaine said, flipping out his tails and subsiding onto a blue velvet sofa. Footman-fashion, Hazelton remained standing by the door. "The Earl of Drexel has taken ship from Portsmouth, bound for Rome. He filled three large trunks with valuables and left instructions with Myron Basingstoke to pay only Stephen's quarterly allowance. The bank draft Drexel took with him all but beggared the earldom's immediate resources."

"Damn and bugger," Ashton muttered, crossing to the sideboard. "Drexel's the one who's been stealing from Matilda. He's the one who could have prevented Stephen's lies from being believed, and our best crack at getting Stephen to change his testimony. Would you gentlemen care for a drink? I certainly want one."

"Such fine manners he has," Helen muttered from the window. "Doesn't offer me no drink."

"Nip down to the kitchen and have some ale," Ashton said.

Helen glowered at him and went back to her farce.

"A tot of brandy would be appreciated," Portmaine said. "A pity a footman never drinks on the job."

Hazelton studied the ceiling.

"You should be glad Drexel has decamped," Portmaine said. "As of this morning, Stephen Derrick has moved back into his uncle's town house, which makes him much easier to watch. The staff at Drexel House is less than respectful of their employer's privacy when enough coin is offered. The maids in particular have no use for Stephen, and the governess positively loathes him."

"*I* have no use for Stephen," Ashton retorted. "He's a lecher, a liar, and a thief."

"He's worse than that," Portmaine said, accepting a glass of Ashton's best brandy. "Samuels confirmed that Stephen wants Matilda to disappear, very quietly, so Chancery will lumber along, leaving the financial matters just as they are for years to come."

The glass in Ashton's hand slipped to the floor and shattered. "Matilda was right, then. She's safest if she runs, unless I kill Derrick as quietly as he would like to do away with her."

Helen shot a worried gaze at him. Sir Archer took a deliberate sip of his brandy.

"You are not a murderer," Hazelton said, "though I grant you, Stephen is a blight in breeches. If you've a plan for making him repent of his sins—and recant his lies—we are at your service, for his sworn recounting of events the night of the murder is the sole evidence against Lady Matilda. The servants were not interviewed by the magistrate. When Sir Archer spoke to them yesterday, they claimed not to recall anything that would corroborate Stephen's version of events."

Helen hopped off the window seat and used the broom and dustpan from the hearth to start sweeping together the shattered glass.

Ashton picked her up, the implements still in her hands. "Footmen clean up spills, child. I wouldn't want you to cut yourself."

"Got you," Sir Archer said, smirking at his cousin, "and got me, because Kilkenney's right."

"Do a thorough job," Helen said, "and then you should scrub the spill up, or it'll bring the ants. Waste of good brandy, though. Somebody should get a proper switching."

Ashton set her down. "Stephen should be…"

"What?" Helen stuffed her braids into her cap as Hazelton swept up the mess.

"Switched," Ashton said quietly. "Stephen holds two advantages over us, one being his sworn testimony. The other is Lady Kitty. As it happens, I have a plan for how her little ladyship can be wrested safely from the Derrick household. Helen, how fast can you run in a dress?"

"Damn fast. I can also climb trees, swim, and scream bloody murder. Won't even cost you too many cobblers either."

* * *

"Pippa is a natural," Sir Archer murmured, twirling his walking stick. "I could use her. She has the knack of being smarter than she looks."

Hazelton walked along at Portmaine's side, while across a grassy swath of Hyde Park, Pippa and Helen played catch. Helen was attired as the child of a well-to-do family and Pippa as her governess. The day was beautiful, and the game was on.

"Helen is the one you want to recruit," Hazelton said. "She's devilish observant, nimble, and has a healthy sense of self—"

"So that's Lady Kitty?"

Right on schedule, another small girl and her governess came trundling down the path from the direction of Park Lane.

"Lady Kitty," Hazelton said, "and your recently acquired best friend, Miss Reynolds. I assume you offered her a Banbury tale?" Lady Matilda had drawn a sketch of the child, and the resemblance between sisters was marked, even given the difference in their ages.

"Cousin, you shame your upbringing," Portmaine replied. "I told Miss Reynolds the God's honest truth. I might well be in the market for a governess, though I haven't raised the notion with my lady wife."

"Coward." Hazelton took out his handkerchief and pretended to mop his brow, the signal that Lady Kitty had arrived rather than some other girl.

Pippa and Helen switched to kicking the ball, their acknowledgment of Hazelton's message.

"You miss the game," Sir Archer said. "You were too bloody good at it not to miss it sorely. If Kilkenney hadn't come up with this scheme, you would have proposed it by sundown, or something even more clever."

"More clever than kidnapping an earl's daughter from the park in broad daylight?"

"The occasional felony adds a bit of spice to the—Good God, that girl can kick."

Helen's ball went sailing off toward a hedge. Retrieving the ball took Helen right past Lady Kitty, who was occupied with tossing a ball to her governess.

"Recall Helen's prowess with a kick if she's ever aiming for your privities."

"Saints defend me if that child takes me into dislike. What's stopping you from accepting the occasional case? You're quite the earl now. You wouldn't have to do it for money."

If Helen had been playing at footman, she'd never have stood by and watched another clean up a spilled drink. She became the role she'd rehearsed, in this case, a genteel girl lonely for the company of another genteel girl. She and Lady Kitty were soon kicking the ball back and forth between themselves, while the two governesses settled onto the same bench to supervise and socialize.

"Earls don't sneak about," Hazelton said, "peering through the hedges and listening at keyholes."

"You sound so wistful, and you did far more than peer and listen. Have a word with your countess, promise her you won't do anything dangerous, and then keep your word. More or less."

Maggie had all but told Hazelton to find a hobby, for being an earl was downright boring compared to investigations.

"My countess has no objection to the occasional case. She would assist me to the extent she could. One hesitates to court the disfavor of my father-in-law."

"Moreland? You're daft. His Grace would be envious if he learned you'd resumed your investigative activities."

Helen was playing Lady Kitty like a fish on a line, kicking the ball seemingly in all directions, but ending up ever nearer to the hedge behind which Maggie waited with a puppy in a basket. The puppy had been Kilkenney's suggestion, immediately seconded by Helen. Archer would rush to the aid of the soon-to-be-distraught governess and offer her a goodly sum to look after Lady Kitty in a different household without giving notice.

Or screaming.

With any luck, Lady Kitty would have no idea she'd been kidnapped.

"If I took an interest in investigating again," Hazelton said, "the Duke of Moreland would not merely be envious, he'd meddle. His Grace's ability to meddle is excelled only by his duchess's ability to do the same, smiling graciously all the while. And there they go."

The girls made a third foray behind the hedge, nominally searching for a well-kicked ball, but mostly laughing and chasing each other. The governesses continued to chat happily on their bench, and the satisfaction of a well-laid plan coming together coursed through Hazelton like new wine on a crisp autumn day.

Five minutes passed before Miss Reynolds left off speaking to rise and call for Lady Kitty.

"That is your cue to be charming," Hazelton said, "and my cue to leave."

Damn it.

"Take one case," Sir Archer said, propping his stick on his shoulder. "Take just one case, then tell me again you don't miss it."

Hazelton watched him stride off, a gentleman determined to be of assistance to an increasingly distraught pair of governesses.

Lady Kitty's safety mattered, but having spent the last day conceiving and executing the plan to keep her so had been the closest thing to excitement Hazelton had had since… well, since courting Maggie Windham.

* * *

Without Helen's company, Ashton's rooms at the Albany became a prison.

He sent a clucking, fussing Cherbourne off to visit relatives, and the two footmen spent most of the day lounging about in the kitchen, waiting for Ashton to concoct errands for them.

He'd taken Helen's suggestion and paid a late-night call on Matilda. Her ladyship was as impatient as Ashton, and worse, she was anxious to take flight.

The time had come to confront Stephen Derrick—or to make him disappear.

A knock sounded on the door, but not in the right sequence to herald a call from Hazelton. Ashton opened the door the width of two inches and beheld Hannibal Shearing.

Sweet Jesus in the garden, not this again.

Ashton unfastened the chain. "Shearing, how do you do?"

"You'll not let me in? Have I become that much of an outcast? I expected you, of all people, to give a fellow a fair hearing, Kilkenney."

Ashton did know how easily a fair hearing was denied on the basis of class, standing, or family associations.

"I was about to go out and haven't much time for socializing."

"And Fat George hasn't much time for me," Shearing said, pushing past Ashton. "You said you'd do what you could for me. If it's a matter of money, then say so. I've pots of the damned stuff."

Shearing offered an insult, and Ashton would have tossed him back over the threshold for giving offense, but for the despair in the older man's eyes.

"You want your barony so badly that you'd insult me for it?"

"Personally, I don't give a single hearty goddam,"—Shearing thumped his walking stick once against the floor—"for a title, but my missus has asked only one thing of me. The old girl has stood by me, for richer and for poorer, and she suffered far too many years when poor was putting it nicely. She raised our daughters to be ladies, despite the snubs and the talk. You think titled men put their noses in the air? You should see the cruelty their wives and daughters are capable of, but my wife endured it all without complaint."

Shearing's Yorkshire accent had become thicker as his lament went on, until he sounded not like a wealthy gentleman of means, but like a mine foreman weeping for his beloved.

"Is your wife ill, Shearing?"

Shearing examined the Gainsborough portrait above the mantel. A smiling, rosy young family, such as a wealthy bachelor might see in his future.

"I doubt she'll last until Christmas, though we've a grandchild on the way, and that's put some heart back in her."

What mattered damned money, or a damned title, when the woman you loved was leaving you forever?

Shearing produced a handkerchief and wiped his eyes. "I'll be going. I mean you no insult, Kilkenney, but there's nothing I'd not do to secure my wife's happiness. I'd give George my whole fortune, crawl down Park Lane, or swear an oath never to touch another drop of drink, if I could grant my lady this boon."

I know how you feel. "I have pled your case to George, and I will do so again. May I offer you a drink, Shearing?"

"I'll stop 'round the Goose and have a good old pint of ale," Shearing said. "They rob me blind there, but I'm happy to do my bit by a hardworking publican. For too many, his is the only reliable comfort, aye?"

Shearing left, closing the door softly.

Ashton was still standing behind the closed door, trying to ignore a dawning sense of hope, when another knock sounded on the door. Two short taps, a pause, and three more.

"For God's sake," came a low voice, "let me in, Kilkenney. I bring news." Hazelton himself, and in a foul humor.

"What news?" Ashton asked, opening the door and standing aside.

Hazelton charged past him, straight into the sitting room. "Stephen has Lady Matilda, snatched her right off my back terrace with an entire press-gang of toughs. The ladies were having tea outside, Maggie was summoned to the nursery, and in the next instant, Lady Matilda was seized. The equally bad news is that we can't find Helen."

CHAPTER SEVENTEEN

After much wandering about the city, possibly in the interests of avoiding pursuit, the coach finally meandered into familiar territory. Matilda knew Knightsbridge, having walked its streets many times. If she was being taken to Knightsbridge, there was good news—Bow Street lay to the north and east—and bad news.

Ashton would never think to look for her here.

"Don't attempt to escape," the larger of her captors said. "The warrant says you're a murderess, and if you're shot while fleeing arrest, nobody will care. And you would be shot dead."

He chucked her on the chin with the barrel of a big, ugly pistol. Samuels was an angel compared to this thug. Whereas Samuels' attire had been nondescript, Matilda's captor was a rogue dressed to mock his betters.

His clothes were the battered castoffs of some fine gentleman, for all that his cravat was perfectly tied and he wore gold at his cuffs. His incisors were gold as well.

"We could have some fun with her first," the second man said. He was small and dirty, though he had all of his teeth and displayed them in a rodent's smile.

"No time," the leader replied. "Sooner we dump her off, sooner we get paid. I do fancy a lively murderess from time to time. They have a lot of fight in 'em."

"I have plenty of fight, but I'm not a murderess." Neither was Matilda a countess, though she could have been, in which case these men might have been unwilling to kidnap her at any price.

"Word to the wise," the leader said, "save your fight for the man who means to kill you. He's stupid as shite, and it's him you hate. This,"—he waved his pistol—"is just business."

Helen might understand that definition of business. Matilda understood only that she'd fallen into Stephen's hands and had thus put herself and Ashton at risk.

Kitty was safe, though. Ashton had seen to that. The girl had been taken to Sir Archer Portmaine's, along with her governess, and was enjoying life in a house where servants smiled, and she was allowed out of the nursery whenever she pleased.

Matilda had not enjoyed life since the day she'd met Althorpe Derrick.

"Wouldn't take but a minute to toss up her skirts," the smaller man said, "and such fine skirts they be too. Marceline'll—"

The leader leveled the gun at his cohort. "How many times do I have to tell you? No names when we're on a job."

He sighted down the pistol barrel, gold teeth winking in a cold grin.

"You're bluffing," Matilda snapped. "If you fire that gun in the middle of a respectable neighborhood, you'll attract notice, particularly when I start screaming. You'll also use up one of only two bullets and increase the odds that I'll escape when the horses bolt because of your need to bully all before you."

The pistol barrel swung back in her direction. "So you're not a murderess, else you'd never have defended my dimwitted friend. Derrick doubtless takes offense at your brains more than at any crimes you might have committed. You'll want to recall that when you're reunited with your step-son."

He implied that Matilda should make it a point to act stupid if she encountered Stephen again. *That* was good advice.

"You're free enough with Stephen's name."

"All I want from that one is coin. From my men, I expect obedience."

Althorpe had wanted obedience. "Wouldn't loyalty stand you in better stead?"

"Quite the philosopher, you are. A pity we haven't the time to get better acquainted."

The coach—a clean conveyance, despite some age—rattled around a corner into an alley and then took a few more turns before coming to a halt. The leader got out, then trained his pistol on the coach door, while the second man shoved Matilda down the steps.

A woman stood by a sagging garden gate. "You took your sweet time. Himself has been cooling his heels half the day, wearing a hole in my patience. So this is her?"

She was a pretty brunette of about twenty, though her eyes were ancient and pitiless, and her dress was less than pristine about the hems.

"No damned talk in the open air," the leader snarled. "I'm surrounded by incompetents."

He hustled Matilda through a weedy patch of dirt into the kitchen of a house very much like the one she owned in Pastry Lane. Genteel, but not for much longer.

The man with the gun jerked his head when they got inside, and the smaller man locked the back door.

"You watch her," the leader said, passing the woman the pistol. "She gets away, it's on you. I have business to transact with Mr. Derrick. You," he snapped at his lieutenant, "mind the stairs."

The men clomped up the steps, while Matilda considered the windows. "You're Marceline?"

"You wasn't to know that," the woman said, "but Ducky's got a big mouth. Might as well have a seat. Stephen swears you killed his pa, though he doesn't seem to mind his pa being dead."

"And now Stephen means to kill me," Matilda said. The words made her sick, also furious in a whole new and reckless way.

Why hadn't she married Ashton when she'd had the chance? She could have been across the Border by now—with him.

"He says he only wants you to go away." Marceline slid into a chair at a small wooden table. "A smart woman doesn't put too much stock in what Stephen says, though."

The window over the dry sink was locked tight, and cobwebs suggested it hadn't been opened for ages. The window in the back door was too small to wiggle through, and that left only the stairs as an exit.

"Has Stephen promised to marry you?"

"He has… when he's drunk. He's drunk a lot."

If Marceline hadn't been holding that loaded pistol in a competent grip, Matilda might have felt sorry for her.

"Did he tell you he has two children already?"

"*Two?*"

"The oldest is six, and the younger closer to four." Ashton had shared those details. "Both girls. He never sees them and makes no provision for their care. That job fell to Drexel, who has left Stephen only an allowance and a lot of debts."

If anything, Marceline's grip on the gun steadied. "What do you mean, Drexel left him an allowance? Stephen gets the title, the whole lot, and Drexel ain't dead yet. I can read the papers, and they make news of it when an earl dies."

"Marceline!"

Matilda would have known that bellow anywhere. Stephen was in a pet, and not entirely sober.

"Marceline, bring her up here!"

"He wants me dead," Matilda spoke quickly and quietly. "He wants me very discreetly dead, so Chancery won't notice and Stephen can continue to steal from my fortune and my younger sister's fortune. If you know Stephen is responsible for my death, then you're a liability to him."

Marceline rose, and for a moment, doubt showed in her eyes.

"We can leave out the back," Matilda said. "I'll see you're kept safe, and Stephen will pay for his crimes."

"Can't have that, can I?" Marceline said, gesturing with the gun. "I love him, you see, and in his way, he's good to me. He comes to me when he has nowhere else to turn, because he knows I'll do right by him. Nobody ever has, but that's not your concern. Up you go, missus."

Stephen had been born with every privilege, spoiled endlessly, and indulged even in criminal wrongdoing.

"You are deluded," Matilda said, "and you will address me as *my lady*."

Marceline's smile was pitying. "Oh, aye, then. My lady, if it would please you to go up them steps, I'll kindly refrain from blowing a hole in your guts."

"Marceline!"

"Coming!" She waved the gun at Matilda. "Up you go, and no tricks. He doesn't want you dead, he only wants you far, far away for a very long time."

Matilda started up the steps, feeling as if she were ascending the stairs to the gallows.

My life cannot end this way, not now, not when I've found a man worth loving, a life worth fighting for.

"Parlor's on the right," Marceline said when they reached the top of the steps, "and it's half day, so don't be thinking some footman will rescue you. You're done for, *my lady*."

"Then so are you. Stephen can't have any witnesses, Marceline. He'll repay your love with a grave."

Marceline jabbed the pistol at Matilda's back. "Move."

Matilda moved at a pace suited to a lady in no hurry at all. When she entered Marceline's parlor, Stephen remained sitting on a red velvet sofa.

"Step-mama, what a lot of trouble you have put me to."

The adolescent bully had evolved into a worse article, all the more repugnant for being handsome.

"Stephen, how nauseating to see you again."

He sprawled on the sofa, one button on the left side of his falls undone, a glass of red wine in his hand. His blond hair hung lankly, and he'd clearly slept in his clothes.

"It's marvelous to see you," he said, pushing to his feet and spilling a few drops of wine on the carpet. "I wanted to be sure Tyburn had the right woman, though you have a bit of age on you now. Perhaps a guilty conscience has robbed you of your slumbers these past six years, hmm?"

The stink of dissipation clung to him, and yet, his word alone could see Matilda hanged.

"My conscience is clear, Stephen. What about yours? Pushing strong drink on your father night after night, knowing the more he drank, the more difficulty he'd have siring other children? Did Drexel put you up to that?"

"Drexel was my example," Stephen said. "And now he's kindly taken himself off to the Continent and left me the freedom to deal with you. Marceline, get over here with that gun. If she moves, aim for the heart, and don't miss."

* * *

"Find Helen," Ashton said, "and you'll find Matilda. How long have they been missing?"

"Not thirty minutes. I sent word to Portmaine, who'll have half the street urchins and pickpockets looking for her already."

Fear and rage were battling for possession of Ashton's wits, along with guilt. This was his fault. If he'd listened to Matilda, if he'd only listened...

"Start with Stephen's mistress," Ashton said. "He'll expect her to abet his schemes, and she's no farther away than Knightsbridge."

"Good point," Hazelton panted. "While you do what?"

"Can your father-in-law get me in to see George without an appointment?"

Hazelton was bent over, hands braced on his thighs. "You want me to involve the *Duke of Moreland* in a kidnapping and murder?"

Ashton grabbed Hazelton by the cravat and hauled him upright. "I want you to help me save the life of the only woman I'll ever love. Tell Moreland I need to see George so I can propose a solution to the problem of Hannibal Shearing. A solution that will cost George nothing. If Moreland can't help me, I'll go to the Duke of Murdoch, to anybody with the standing to get me in to see the king."

One of the oldest privileges of a peer was the right to advise the sovereign, and by God, Ashton had some urgent advice for the king.

"You are mad," Hazelton said. "What does King George have to do with—?"

"Get me the hell in to see the king now, ye gobshite dung-heap of a ditherin' Englishmon!"

Half the lodgers at the Albany had probably heard Ashton's broad Scots bellowing. He turned loose of Hazelton, who wore a curious hint of a smile.

"We have some time, *your lordship*," Hazelton said, striding toward the door. "A commotion in the middle of a decent neighborhood will bring hordes of curious Londoners on the instant, which is the last thing Stephen needs and the first turn Lady Matilda will serve him. He'll not kill her with his bare hands, lest she unman him. Moreland House is two streets over, and you can take my horse once we get the requisite note of introduction from His Grace."

"I owe you, Hazelton. I will always owe you."

"We're even, then."

Less than thirty minutes later, with a sealed missive in his hand, Ashton was one functionary shy of an audience with his sovereign.

"My lord, you do not have an appointment." The groom of the scheduling book or minister of the royal pocket watch—whatever the hell he was—was a small, balding man who had a habit of hopping his heels together at the end of his sentences. "If I allowed any importuning courtesy lord to barge in on the royal presence, my position wouldn't be worth—"

"Sir, I am the Earl of Kilkenney, Viscount Kinkenney, and Baron Mulder. I bring urgent communication for His Royal Majesty from Percival, Duke of Moreland, and Benjamin, Earl of Hazelton. If you value *your life*, you will show me in to see my king now. I'd barge into hell itself to accomplish my purpose."

Ashton had shouted and in a corridor so vast that his words echoed against marble, gilt, and glass.

The door behind the secretary opened, a footman in powdered wig and livery peering about.

"I'm here to see His Majesty," Ashton started again. "I bring—"

"We heard you the first time," caroled the royal drawl. "Come in, Kilkenney, and you had better not ask for that sporran back. It's become quite our favorite accessory."

Ashton scooted through the door before the secretary skewered him with a quill pen. "Your Majesty." He bowed as court protocol required, then thrust Moreland's missive under the royal nose. "Apologies for my attire, sir. The situation has arisen of a sudden."

George scanned the epistle, two footmen hovering at his back. "Moreland says you have a solution to the Hannibal Shearing problem, but he'd appreciate my gracious consideration of your own small contretemps. Moreland does not exert his favor where *small* contretemps are concerned, Kilkenney. You'd best tell us what this is about."

George settled on a sofa that looked too delicate for his weight, the footmen positioning themselves at either side.

"I need to quash an arrest warrant, as of yesterday, not when some solicitor gets around to drawing up the proper motion and some barrister argues it before a judge who might withhold a decision indefinitely."

"Have you been naughty, Kilkenney?" George asked, shaking a finger.

Sweet Jesus in a ball gown. "The woman I love was sorely mistreated six years ago, wrongly accused of her husband's death, and forced to flee for her life. Her in-laws sought to control her fortune and thus saw a warrant issued for her arrest. She's been living in hiding ever since, while they plunder her inheritance. The warrant is based on the affidavit of the very man who now stands to benefit most from my lady's ill fortune. All other available evidence exonerates her."

"Damsel in distress," George said, wrinkling his nose. "Those can be so very sticky, you know."

"She's innocent, sir. My life on it, and I'm prepared to add a barony into the bargain."

George waved a beringed hand. "Away with you, lads."

The footmen bowed and backed from the room.

"We don't trade clemency for coin, Kilkenney. Why not have the matter come to trial and allow justice to take its course?"

Ashton paced before the couch and to hell with protocol. "Because the same man who laid information against my lady has now abducted her. He did not take her to the proper authorities and has already tried to hire someone to kill her once."

"Who is this scoundrel?"

"Drexel's heir. His name is Stephen Derrick."

"He's a vain little peacock." George's tone suggested vanity was a worse offense than bearing false witness or conspiring to commit murder, though George himself was the biggest peacock in the realm. "Drexel was much the same as a young man. What have you in mind for Mr. Shearing?"

"I have a barony for him, sir. Beautiful little parcel of property situated right on the Border. He and I would be neighbors, in a manner of speaking."

George left off fluffing the lace at his cuffs. "How came you into this parcel?"

"I own it. About four generations back, a river shifted and put a portion of my earldom on the English side of the Border. The river has refused to shift back, and thus about one-eighth of my acreage lies in England. I propose to yield that property to the crown, to be disposed of however Your Majesty pleases."

"Don't suppose we could get two baronies from it?"

Thank God for a king more pragmatic than he was given credit for. "Those two baronies would have to share a single village, but it could be done. I'd further ask that Shearing's barony descend through heirs general, sir. He has only daughters."

"We like a man who considers the details, Kilkenney." George rang a bell sitting on the side table, and both footmen came through the door. "We need our desk and sealing wax. Kilkenney has served us well this day."

"There is one other matter, sir, though it's not as pressing."

"Imagine that, a matter that isn't pressing. Is this an example of Scottish humor?"

The footmen produced a beautiful oak lap desk, and George set it on the low table before the couch. The king wielded the pen with a competence at odds with his languid speech and fussy airs.

He set the paper aside and sat back. "What is the other matter, Kilkenney? I'm doubtless late to watch a tennis match or preside at an archery contest. Maybe the duck races were today, such is the lot of your sovereign."

Ashton endured a stab of fellow-feeling for his sovereign. George had been doomed to rule from the moment of his birth. Ashton had had nearly thirty years free of a title, and they had been good years.

Very good years, in hindsight, and perhaps Ashton's father had wanted that for him.

"Your warrant is quashed," George said, impressing the royal seal on what amounted to Matilda's pardon. "Now about that other matter?"

Ashton explained about the other matters—both of them. Then he took a decorous leave, waiting until he'd quit his sovereign's immediate presence to bolt through the royal residence at a dead run.

* * *

"I'll not commit murder!" Marceline retorted. "You said you wanted her to disappear. I thought you'd ship her to the Antipodes, quiet-like, not make a murderess of me."

"It's worse than that," Matilda said. "He'll make a murderess of you, then swear an affidavit as a witness claiming he tried to stop you, but you were jealous of me, or some such rot. Stephen will be overcome with grief at having to do his duty, despite his tender regard for you, and the magistrate will haul you away in chains. Stephen gets everything, including a reputation for honorable conduct, and you and I are dead."

Matilda spoke steadily, despite the likely accuracy of her prediction.

"Shut your mouth," Stephen shouted. "Shut your lying, murdering mouth. Marceline, you should kill her for her disrespect of me."

"Kill her yourself, if that's your plan now. I'm done with this." She set the gun on the mantel to Stephen's right and flounced out.

Behind Stephen, a movement at the window caught Matilda's eye. Ashton put a finger to his lips, and a knife blade slipped through the crack between the sash and the sill.

Thank God, and please keep Ashton safe. "Now what, Stephen?" Matilda said, inching toward the door. "You shoot me, and Marceline testifies against you. The Earl of Kilkenney has already set the lawyers on your uncle's ledger books, and embezzling is a serious crime. Will you add another blot to the family's already much-spattered escutcheon?"

"You were the blot on the escutcheon." Stephen retrieved the gun from the mantel. "What man in his right mind feels compelled to produce a spare when the heir is nearly of age, in roaring good health, and a sound breeder? Everything was fine until *you* showed up."

The window sash raised two inches, enough that Ashton could get a grip on it.

"How odd," Matilda murmured, half turning her back on Stephen and pretending to study a framed print. "I could say everything in my life was fine until you showed up. Your father wasn't evil, Stephen. He was difficult and struggling with demons you and Drexel kept well fed. Marceline's taste in art runs to Hogarth. Are you familiar with *A Rake's Progress?*"

"I bought her the damned thing. Stop moving about."

"I suspect you can't kill me," Matilda said. "I suspect somewhere, beneath the bully, the spoiled boy, the venal rake, and the thoroughgoing rotter, there's still a man who dreads to have murder on his conscience when he meets his Maker."

"You will have murder on your conscience."

For the first time, Matilda considered that *Stephen truly believed her to be guilty.* The notion was disquieting in the extreme.

"I did not kill your father, Stephen. He'd had far too much to drink. He overbalanced and struck his head on the hearthstones. If you search your memory, you'll recall the racket of the hearth set falling over, clattering loudly. I was putting the hearth stand to rights, thinking your father had simply succumbed to drink—as he so often did—when you rushed in, making vile accusations and embellishing to a criminal extent on what you saw."

The window sash scraped against the frame, and Matilda commenced a coughing fit.

"Stop that. Fetch yourself a glass of water, but stop coughing." Stephen's upper lip was beaded with sweat, though his hold on the gun remained steady.

And the window was open as far as it could go. Ashton might be able to squeeze through, but as he made the attempt, Stephen could easily shoot him.

Matilda crossed to the sideboard and fumbled about pouring herself a drink—her hands shook that badly.

"I never threatened your father's life," she said. "You made that up. You neglected to tell the magistrate that the hearth set was scattered about. You didn't mention your father's broken neck. You didn't mention that I'd never raised a hand to anybody in all the years you'd known me, never threatened to so much as sack the tweeny when she was tipsy before noon. You lied, Stephen, over and over, and turned a tragic accident into a murder. Damn you for that. Damn you, damn you for stealing six years from me, and damn you for trying to steal even more now."

Ashton had one leg through the window.

Stephen cocked the gun. "You killed my father, my only surviving parent. *You took him away from me*, you did. You smacked him with that poker—I saw the wound on his temple—and he overbalanced and broke his neck and thus his death is *your fault*."

Insight came, too late to do any good. Stephen might dimly suspect Matilda was innocent of murder, but he was equally convinced that Matilda had taken his father's affection from him. In Stephen's mind, Matilda—not his own debauches at university, not his sexual irresponsibility, not his profligate spending—had turned Althorpe away from his only son.

"If you don't put that gun down, Derrick," Ashton growled, "I will take away your life."

Matilda tossed the glass of water in Stephen's face just as his gun went off. A searing pain hit her chest, and the sound of Ashton's cursing followed her into a pain-filled haze of red.

CHAPTER EIGHTEEN

"Let me go, you bloody, thrice-damned, interfering, grub-shiting excuse for an earl, or I'll hoop yer barrel until yer countess won't recognize you."

Helen thrashed in Hazelton's arms, a small tempest of elbows, knees, teeth, and determination.

"You have to stay here," Hazelton said, giving her a shake. "Stay here quietly, or you'll bring the authorities down on us—"

A single pistol shot exploded across the afternoon quiet.

Hazelton's attention was diverted for one instant, during which Helen bolted for the back gate of Marceline's property.

"Damn it, child, don't you dare—"

She was over the back gate—didn't take the time to unlatch it—and heading for the open window Kilkenney had eased through moments earlier. Hazelton followed, admiration, terror, and an odd sense of exhilaration giving his tired feet wings.

"He's not hurt," Helen yelled over her shoulder, "but my lady's bleeding fierce. The rotter's still standing, but he won't be for long when I get through with him."

Hazelton got to the window in time to see Helen march up to Stephen Derrick and punch him twice—a left, then a right—in the privities, hard enough to express a lifetime of anxiety, fear, resentment, and anger.

Stephen stood for the space of a shuddering breath, then went down in a gagging heap on the faded carpet.

Hazelton wedged himself through the window, while Helen walked a circle around the fallen man.

"Wish I'd thought to do that," Ashton said, shoving the gun at Hazelton, handle first. "Well done, Helen. Matilda, love, can ye hear me?"

Lady Matilda sagged against a dusty sideboard, her posture similar to Stephen's, but her stillness unlike his writhing misery. Worse, her bodice and sleeve were spattered with blood, and a bright red stain bloomed at her shoulder.

"It stings," she said, straightening gingerly. "Good God, it stings awfully. Is Stephen dead?"

"Not yet." Kilkenney carried the lady to the sofa, glass crunching under his boots. "Helen will see to that, I'm sure. This isn't a bullet…"

He probed delicately at the greatest source of the bleeding and held up a bloody shard of glass. "You've been attacked by an exploding decanter. Thank God, you've not a bullet in you."

Stephen's breathing took on an odd rasp. "Don't let… her… hurt me again."

"You fired your gun at the woman I love," Kilkenney retorted, brushing more glass from Lady Matilda's sleeve and bodice, "and I witnessed your attempt at murder. A drubbing is merely the start of what you deserve."

"Didn't mean to fire," Stephen said. "You startled me. Damned gun had a hair trig—keep her away from me!"

He curled up tight while Helen stood over him, her fists clenched. "You set *Tyburn* on my lady, you rat-infested barge of pig manure. *Tyburn*, and that damned Ducky, who'd as soon kill a body as look at her."

"Who's Tyburn?" Kilkenney pressed a handkerchief to Lady Matilda's shoulder.

The name alone justified Helen's rage. "A very bad hat," Hazelton said. "A very, very bad hat. He owns magistrates, MPs, and half of London, along with a few bits of Paris. His word is a law beyond the law; nobody who crosses him lives to brag about it for long."

"Makes owning a lot of sheep and putting up with a few grouchy tenants seem like a lark." Kilkenney refolded his handkerchief and pressed it again to her ladyship's shoulder. His touch could not have been more gentle, though his hand shook a bit. "Don't get up, Derrick, or Helen will have to deal severely with you."

"She hasn't… already?"

"I haven't even started to deal with you," Helen said, cracking her knuckles. "Your kind set a lot of store by your almighty cods, because you want heirs and spares and such like. His lordship keeps a nice, sharp knife on his person at all times. I might borrow it."

"I have a spare blade," Hazelton said, because Stephen Derrick deserved a lifetime of dread for what he'd done. "Also a spare handkerchief."

He passed it to Kilkenney, who was on his knees before Lady Matilda.

"Am I interrupting?" Sir Archer Portmaine, looking entirely too composed, stood in the doorway. "Dear me, has somebody had an accident?"

"Somebody crossed Helen," Kilkenney said. "Where's Marceline?"

"Chattering like a magpie to one of my better-looking solicitors," Portmaine said. "Do we need a surgeon?"

Kilkenney put the clean handkerchief to her ladyship's shoulder. "Matilda, shall we summon a surgeon? The bleeding has slowed, though I'll not rest until each of these cuts has been tended to."

"Somebody needs to toss out the slops," Helen said, nudging Stephen with the toe of her boot. "Maybe we should tell Tyburn we have a job for him."

"Make her stop." Stephen sat up enough to put his head in his hands. "Make this demon child go back to whatever hell she emerged from."

"You'll see her in your nightmares," Kilkenney said, taking a seat on the sofa beside his lady. "What do we do with him, Matilda?"

Hazelton would not have thought to defer to the lady, but then, he wasn't in love with her, while Kilkenney was hopelessly smitten.

"After six years of being hounded and frightened and hunted," Lady Matilda said, "you'd think I'd know how to answer that question. Stephen told Marceline to shoot me, as casually as he'd order a pot of tea."

"I only suggested she should shoot you," Stephen said. "Marceline never does what she's told."

"And I thank God for your mistress's obstinate nature," Kilkenney retorted, rising from the sofa. "When I think how close Matilda came to—"

"I can hit him again," Helen offered.

"I need time to think," Lady Matilda said, "but I killed no one. If you'd taken five minutes to consider the evidence, Stephen, you'd see that. I also need to get out of this dress. Lord Hazelton, may we prevail on your hospitality?"

"I'll take Mr. Derrick," Sir Archer said, letting out a short whistle. "He and I will have a nice chat about English criminal law, Newgate, and hanging offenses. He'll look marvelous in chains."

Two large, muscular men appeared from the corridor, each one taking Stephen by an arm.

"Watch out for the girl," Stephen said. "She's faster and meaner than she looks."

"And don't you forget it!" Helen delivered a kick to Stephen's retreating backside. She stood with her hands on her hips, looking for all the world like a half-pint, trousered governess whose last nerve had been plucked.

Sir Archer followed the prisoner out, and an odd sense of what the French called *déjà vu* assailed Hazelton. He and his cousin had completed many an investigation together by bringing a miscreant to justice. It felt good to see Derrick hauled away to face the consequences of his mischief—it felt too damned good.

"My countess will be worried sick," Hazelton said, "and I'm sure Lady Matilda could use a medicinal tot and a hot bath."

"I could use a tot," Helen said. "I'm not so keen on that bath part."

Kilkenney kissed his lady's cheek. "Matilda, shall I carry you?"

Helen snorted unconvincingly, if such a thing were possible.

"Come along," Hazelton said, swinging the girl onto his back. "They'll be an eternity tossing rose petals at one another. They've had a close call and are due a moment of privacy."

"I'm due some food," Helen said. "I'm famished, in fact. Food, famish, and fact all begin with *f.* So does Frenchy, and fornica—"

"Enough showing off," Hazelton said, taking the steps down to the kitchen. "All's well enough for now, and her ladyship is safe. You are to be commended for your role in that happy outcome, and I'm sure her ladyship will be very impressed when she learns you followed her carriage over half of London."

"Three-quarters at least," Helen said, the pugnacity leaving her tone. "Hazelnuts?"

"If you tell anybody I allow you to call me that, I'll send you straight to a French finishing school where you'll bathe twice a day."

"I might like bathing, if I had a real bathtub to wash in instead of the laundry tubs." She took an unsteady breath as Hazelton unlocked the back door and crossed the garden. "I was scared."

Ah. "So was I, child. I was terrified. I'm still not entirely myself."

"Lady Matilda was scared *all the t-time,* for *y-years*." A shudder racked the small body affixed to Hazelton's back.

"Lady Matilda is safe now, Helen, and if I know Ashton, Earl of Kilkenney— and I do, quite well—you are safe too. I promise you, child, you are safe. You are well and truly safe."

The fierce little mite dissolved into open weeping, and as Hazelton set her on the garden wall and patted her back, he realized that if he and Maggie were blessed with another child, he was hoping—very much hoping—that they'd be blessed with a daughter.

* * *

Matilda was clean, at least physically. Washing the fear and anger from her soul would take more than hot water and expensive soap. Only love could do that, and time.

"I can wash your hair, if you like," Ashton said.

Never had a lady had a more unconventional or devoted attendant at her bath.

"I washed it just this morning, but I've soaked long enough." Matilda braced a hand on the side of the tub, and Ashton drew her to standing with her uninjured arm. Only the one cut on her shoulder would be troublesome, though the bleeding had ruined a pretty dress.

"Stay there. I'll fetch you a towel."

"Ashton, I'm not about to indulge in strong hysterics." Weak hysterics remained a possibility.

"I am," he retorted, draping a towel about Matilda's shoulders and hugging her close. "Stephen aimed a loaded gun at you. That… I need Helen to teach me more curses. The girl's a prodigy, in some regards."

"And a terror in others," Matilda said. "You need to stop worrying so."

"I need you."

He kissed her, and the sense of his words sank in. He needed *to make love with* her. "I need you too, and I'm sure the countess left orders we were not to be disturbed for any reason."

Ashton dried Matilda off nonetheless, gently patting at the cuts on her chest and arm, then going limb by limb. They were in the bedroom she'd been assigned more than a week ago, a peaceful yellow, blue, and cream chamber that overlooked the back gardens.

"Are you sure you wouldn't like something to eat?" Ashton asked. "I can ring—"

"Make love with me, Ashton. I need you now too."

"I need you forever."

Their lovemaking explored new depths of tenderness, new horizons of trust. Matilda unabashedly clung, Ashton clung right back. She held nothing back, not tears, not passion, not joy, and certainly—most certainly—not pleasure.

And neither did he.

They lay amid the lavender-scented sheets and fluffy pillows, skin cooling, hearts calming. Sleep tugged at Matilda, as did peace.

"I do love ye," Ashton whispered. "I lost years off my life when Hazelton said you'd been taken."

"I lost years off my life too. I don't want to waste to any more years, Ashton. A special license will do nicely, and we must invite Hazelton's duke."

The Duke of Moreland had apparently smoothed the way for Ashton to see the king, and a lovely royal decree quashing all bothersome warrants sat across the room on the vanity.

"We must invite George himself," Ashton said. "If we're lucky he'll send regrets. We can put haggis on the menu for the wedding breakfast. That might put him off."

Matilda found the energy to situate herself over her lover, soon to be her husband. "You make such a lovely pillow, my lord."

"You make an equally lovely blanket, my lady. What shall we do about Stephen?"

Matilda wished Ashton wouldn't ask her. Let those whose perspective wasn't as bitter decide what to do about Stephen, for his intentions had been vile.

"I hesitate to turn him over to the authorities. I'm not sure why."

"Because all you've been through has made you more compassionate, not less," Ashton said. "All you've been through gives me nightmares. Stephen deserves to suffer, at the very least. I leave it to you whether he deserves to die."

Matilda rested her cheek over Ashton's heart. "I like the smell of you. You smell clean, but not too fussy."

He stroked her hair away from her brow. "Not too much like an earl?"

Stephen had reeked of cheap perfume, tobacco, stale breath, sweat… if that was the scent of a wealthy gentleman, Matilda wanted no part of it.

"Stephen looks like a man, but he's still thinking and acting like a spoiled fourteen-year-old. That's how old he was when his father decided to remarry, and in Stephen's mind, I stole his father. I think Stephen convinced himself I was responsible for Althorpe's death, even if only indirectly. I'd like to give Stephen his father back."

"In what sense?"

"The best punishment for Stephen is to grow up," Matilda said, feeling for words. "He will become the next Earl of Drexel, but he's been abandoned by his uncle, with scandal looming, personal debts mounting, the earldom in failing financial health. Drexel was old-fashioned, insisting land rents were the only respectable source of income. That path is doomed—my own father said as much—and Stephen will have to sort through all of that if he wants to be the earl."

Ashton rolled them so Matilda was beneath him. "You're sentencing him to an earldom?"

"You have Marceline's sworn statement. You can press charges for kidnapping, conspiracy to commit murder… I like it when you look so fierce."

Liked how Ashton's dark hair needed a trim, liked the strength and passion in him.

Matilda liked his passion very much.

"I stepped into an earldom that was running like a top," Ashton said, "and my brother made sure I knew what I was about. Ewan spent months tramping the tenant farms with me, going over the books, introducing me to the neighbors all over the shire, and explaining strategy and scheduling to me. I'm relying on him now to mind the earldom's affairs in my absence."

Matilda lifted her hips in an experimental greeting and found that Ashton was working on a greeting of his own. What a profound pleasure to be in a bed with a man who enjoyed a healthy sense of desire and let his lady know it.

"The Drexel earldom is in a bad way," she said. "The steward is older than the monarchy, the family seat is crumbling, even the town house was starting to leak in the attics six years ago. Drexel probably relied on embezzling to make ends meet."

"While Stephen will have to repay the funds stolen." Ashton kissed her cheek, then her nose. "You're consigning him to years of penury and disgrace. I suppose that's fitting."

"You like this idea? Stephen has to put right what he and his uncle put wrong?"

Ashton hitched closer, his arousal nudging at her sex. "I like *this* idea. I never asked you if you want a large family, Lady Matilda."

"I do. For years, I was an only—oh, that's lovely, Ashton."

He'd got a hand under her backside, and the resulting angle, as well as the snugness… Matilda gave up on coherent speech for the next twenty minutes, and conjectured that she and Ashton would have a *very* large family.

"I might have to climb back into that tub just to cool off," Matilda said, when she could form sentences again. "Will you always be this passionate?"

"Lass, I'm exercising considerable restraint."

She hit him with a pillow, then cuddled against his side. "I thought children would be denied to me, but I do want them. Helen made me realize that. She's a good girl, but she hasn't had the right guidance. It's not too late for her, though. I hope you won't mind including Helen in our household?"

Ashton curled an arm around Matilda's shoulders. "I wouldna turn my back on the best general factotum an earl ever had, but there's something I haven't had time to tell you."

"If we stay in this bed much longer, Helen will be climbing in the window. What haven't you told me?"

"I gave up my English land so Shearing could have his barony, and I'm confident he'll put that situation to rights faster than I ever could. He'll also be a fine neighbor."

Matilda's kissed Ashton's chin, which was a bit bristly. "Stop stalling."

"I asked George for a wee boon, while I was imposing on the royal favor. George had a daughter once, you know, and he lost both her and his grandchild. He's keen to look after children, given a chance."

"Ashton Fenwick…"

"By virtue of royal meddling, I will soon become Helen's guardian. She needs to know she's loved, and I do love the girl, when I'm not tempted to toss her into the sea."

Matilda searched through the feelings struggling for names and found… relief, approval, and joy.

"I'd love you even if you hadn't asked George to see to the legalities, Ashton. That was a beautiful gesture, though Helen will tell you she doesn't need a guardian and never asked for one."

Ashton was quiet, and Matilda waited, because apparently the conversation wasn't over.

"I asked to be made Lady Kitty's guardian too. Drexel has doubtless pilfered from her inheritance, but we'll take good care of her."

The tears caught Matilda unaware, an ambush of more joy, and more relief, also more love. She hadn't thought to ask this of her prospective husband, hadn't even figured out how to reintroduce herself into her younger sister's life, though she was determined that Kitty would never be taken from her again.

"Thank you," Matilda said, wrapping herself around Ashton. "Thank you so much, Ashton. Kitty and Helen have already started on a friendship, and that's... that's... Oh, I do love you. I do love you so very, very much."

"Did I tell you we have three bonnie wee nieces? We'll be awash in young beauties in about ten years, and I'll have to beat the lads off with my claymore."

"You're looking forward to that."

"I look forward to whatever life brings, as long as you're at my side."

As it happened, life brought the Earl and Countess of Kilkenney two fine, strapping sons, a pair of daughters, and then more sons. Those children grew up with no less than five cousins, and when the young ladies came of age, the lads did indeed take notice and paid their addresses in impressive numbers.

The earl never once threatened any of the adoring swains with his claymore. He didn't have to when his countess explained to every potential suitor that she'd once been accused of murder, and only a royal decree—and a handsome earl—had seen her perilous fate exchanged for true love and a happily ever after.

To my dear readers,

I first met Ashton Fenwick in **Hadrian: Lord of Hope**, and for years, I'd been wondering, "What's with that earldom on the last page, Fenwick? Tell me what's going on with that earldom, or I'll…" Well, all I could do was wonder. Now we *know* what's going on with that earldom, and I hope you'll agree the tale was worth the wait.

You won't have to wait nearly as long to learn more about the Duke of Murdoch, whom Ashton invited to his card party. We first met Hamish MacHugh in **The Captive**, and Hamish too is struggling under the dubious honor of an unwanted title. **The Trouble With Dukes** comes out on December 20, 2016, and begins my **Windham Brides** series. These are the stories for the Windham cousins, who are determined to remain happily contented spinsters… or so they claim.

I've included an excerpt from **The Trouble With Dukes** below, but if December is too long to wait for your next Grace Burrowes happily-ever-after, you'll be pleased to know that in October, I'm releasing a pair of Yuletide Regency novellas, **The Virtues of Christmas**. Henrietta Whitlow and Michael Brenner find true love under the mistletoe in *Respect for Christmas,* and advice columnist Patience Friendly and her publisher Dougal MacHugh unwrap an unexpected attraction in *Patience for Christmas.* Read an excerpt **or order your copy at http://graceburrowes.com/books/virtues.php.** This duet will be available on my website store by October 15, and on retail platforms October 25.

To stay up to date with all of my releases, signings, special events, and sales, **please sign up for my newsletter at http://graceburrowes.com/contact. php.** I also have a **newsletter just for writers**, and I'm recently home from my first *Scotland With Grace* tour. That trip included readers, writers, and lots of just plain nice folks. Learn more about the 2017 **Scotland With Grace** tour here: **http://graceburrowes.com/retreat.php.**

As always, happy reading!
Grace Burrowes

Follow me on Twitter: @graceburrowes
Connect with me on Facebook:
Facebook.com/Grace-Burrowes-115039058572197/

THE TROUBLE WITH DUKES

"My dear, you do not appear glad to see me," Fletcher Pilkington purred. *Sir* Fletcher, rather.

Megan Windham ran her finger along the page she'd been staring at, as if the maunderings of Mr. Coleridge required every iota of her attention. Then she pushed her spectacles halfway down her nose, the better to blink stupidly at her tormentor.

"Why, Sir Fletcher, I did not notice you." Megan had smelled him, though. Attar of roses was not a subtle fragrance when applied in the quantities Sir Fletcher favored. "Good day, and how are you?"

She smiled agreeably. Better for Sir Fletcher to underestimate her, and better for her not to provoke him.

"I forget how blind you are," he said, plucking Megan's eyeglasses from her nose. "Perhaps if you read less, your vision would improve, hmm?"

Old fear lanced through Megan, an artifact from childhood instances of having her spectacles taken, sometimes held out of her reach, sometimes hidden. On one occasion, they'd been purposely bent by a bully in the church yard.

The bully was now a prosperous vicar, while Megan's eyesight was no better than it had been in her childhood.

"My vision is adequate, under most circumstances. Today, I'm looking for a gift." In fact, Megan was hiding from the madhouse that home had become in anticipation of the annual Windham ball. Mama and Aunt Esther were nigh crazed with determination to make this year's affair the talk of the season, while all Megan wanted was peace and quiet.

"A gift for me?" Sir Fletcher mused. "Poetry isn't to my taste, my dear, unless you're considering translations of Sappho and Catullus."

Naughty poems, in other words. Very naughty poems.

Megan blinked at him uncertainly, as if anything classical was beyond her comprehension. A first year Latin scholar could grasp the fundamental thrust, as it were, of Catullus's more vulgar offerings, and Megan's skill with Latin went well beyond the basics.

"I doubt Uncle Percy would enjoy such verse." Uncle Percy was a duke and he took family affairs seriously. Mentioning His Grace might remind Sir Fletcher that Megan had allies.

Though even Uncle Percy couldn't get her out of the contretemps she'd muddled into with Sir Fletcher.

"I wonder how soon Uncle Percy is prepared to welcome me into the family," Sir Fletcher said, holding Megan's spectacles up to the nearby window.

Don't drop them. Don't drop them. Please do not drop my eyeglasses. She had an inferior pair in her reticule, but the explanations, pitying looks, and worst of all, Papa's concerned silence, would be torture.

Sir Fletcher peered through the spectacles, which were tinted a smoky blue. "Good God, how do you see? Our children will be cross-eyed and afflicted with a permanent squint."

Megan dreaded the prospect of bearing Sir Fletcher's offspring. "Might I have those back, Sir Fletcher? As you've noted, my eyes are weak, and I do benefit from having my spectacles."

Sir Fletcher was a beautiful man—to appearances. When he'd claimed Megan's waltz at a regimental ball several years ago, she'd been dazzled by his flattery, bold innuendo, and bolder advances. In other words, she'd been blinded. Golden hair, blue eyes, and a gleaming smile had hidden an avaricious, unscrupulous heart.

He held her glasses a few inches higher. To a casual observer, he was examining an interesting pair of spectacles, perhaps in anticipation of considerately polishing them with his handkerchief.

"You'll benefit from having my ring on your finger," he said, squinting through one lens. "When can I speak with your father, or should I go straight to Moreland, because he's the head of your family?"

That Sir Fletcher would raise this topic at all was unnerving. That he'd bring it up at Hatchards, where duchesses crossed paths with milliners, was terrifying. Other patrons milled among the shelves, and the door bell tinkled constantly, like a miniature death knell for Megan's freedom.

"You mustn't speak with Papa yet," Megan said. "Charlotte hasn't received an offer and the season is only getting started. I'll not allow your haste to interfere with the respect I owe my sisters." Elizabeth was on the road to spinsterhood—no help there—and Anwen, being the youngest, would normally be the last to wed.

Sir Fletcher switched lenses, peering through the other one, but shooting Megan a glance that revealed the bratty boy lurking inside the Bond Street tailoring.

"You have three unmarried sisters, the eldest of whom is an antidote and an artifact. Don't think you'll put me off until the last one is trotting up the aisle at St. George's, madam. I have debts that your settlements will resolve handily."

How Megan loathed him, and how she loathed herself for the ignorance and naivety that had put Sir Fletcher in a position to make these threats.

"My portion is intended to safeguard my future if anything should happen to my spouse," Megan said, even as she ached to reach for her glasses. A tussle among the bookshelves would draw notice from the other patrons, but Megan felt naked without her glasses, naked and desperate.

Because her vision was impaired without the spectacles, she detected only a twitch of movement, and something blue falling from Sir Fletcher's hand. He murmured a feigned regret as Megan's best pair of glasses plummeted toward the floor.

A large hand shot out and closed firmly around the glasses in mid-fall.

Megan had been so fixed on Sir Fletcher that she hadn't noticed a very substantial man who'd emerged from the bookshelves to stand immediately behind and to the left of Sir Fletcher. Tall boots polished to a high shine drew the eye to exquisite tailoring over thickly muscled thighs. Next came lean flanks, a narrow waist, a blue plaid waistcoat, a silver watch chain, and a black riding jacket fitted lovingly across broad shoulders. She couldn't discern details, which only made the whole more formidable.

Solemn eyes the azure hue of a winter sky, and dark auburn hair completed a picture both handsome and forbidding.

Megan had never seen this man before, but when he held out her glasses, she took them gratefully.

"My most sincere thanks," she said. "Without these, I am nearly blind at most distances. Won't you introduce yourself, sir?" She was being bold, but Sir Fletcher had gone quiet, suggesting this gentleman had impressed even Sir Fletcher.

Or better still, intimidated him.

"My dear lady," Sir Fletcher said, "we've no need to ignore the dictates of decorum, for I can introduce you to a fellow officer from my Peninsular days. Miss Megan Windham, may I make known to you Colonel Hamish MacHugh, late of his majesty's army. Colonel MacHugh, Miss Megan."

MacHugh enveloped Megan's hand in his own and bowed smartly. His grasp was warm and firm without being presuming, but gracious days, his hands were callused.

"Sir, a pleasure," Megan said, aiming a smile at the colonel. She did not want this stranger to leave her alone with Sir Fletcher one instant sooner than necessary.

"The pleasure is mine, Miss Windham."

Ah, well then. He was unequivocally Scottish. Hence the plaid waistcoat, the blue eyes. Mama always said the Scots had the loveliest eyes.

Megan's grandpapa had been a duke, and social niceties flowed through her veins along with Windham aristocratic blood.

"Are you visiting from the north?" she asked.

"Aye. I mean, yes, with my sisters."

Sir Fletcher watched this exchange as if he were a spectator at a tennis match and had money riding on the outcome.

"Are your sisters out yet?" Megan asked, lest the conversation lapse.

"Until all hours," Colonel MacHugh said, his brow furrowing. "Balls, routs, musicales. Takes more stamina to endure a London season than to march across Spain."

Megan had cousins who'd served in Spain and another cousin who'd died in Portugal. Veterans made light of the hardships they'd seen, though she wasn't sure Colonel MacHugh had spoken in jest.

"MacHugh," Sir Fletcher broke in, "Miss Windham is the granddaughter and niece of dukes."

Colonel MacHugh was apparently as bewildered as Megan at this observation. He extracted Megan's spectacles from her hand, unfolded the ear pieces, and positioned the glasses on her nose.

While she marveled at such familiarity from a stranger, Colonel MacHugh guided the frames around her ears so her glasses were once again perched where they belonged. His touch could not have been more gentle, and he'd ensured Sir Fletcher couldn't snatch the glasses from Megan's grasp.

"My thanks," Megan said.

"Tell her," MacHugh muttered, tucking his hands behind his back. "I'll not have it said I dissembled before a lady, Pilkington."

The bane of Megan's existence was *Sir Fletcher*, but this Scot either did not know or did not care to use proper address.

Sir Fletcher wrinkled his nose. "Miss Megan, I misspoke earlier when I introduced this fellow as Colonel Hamish MacHugh, but you'll forgive my mistake. The gentleman before you, if last week's gossip is to be believed, is none other than the Duke of Murdoch."

Colonel MacHugh—His Grace—stood very tall, as if he anticipated the cut direct or perhaps a firing squad. With her glasses on, Megan could see that his blue eyes held a bleakness, and his expression was not merely formidable, but forbidding.

He'd rescued Megan's spectacles from certain ruin beneath Sir Fletcher's boot heel, so Megan sank into a respectful curtsy.

Because it mattered to her not at all that polite society had dubbed this dear, serious man the Duke of Murder.

Order your copy of *The Trouble with Dukes* at http://graceburrowes. com/books/trouble.php

Made in the USA
Columbia, SC
12 August 2019